The Daffodil Library

Charles Mosley

To John

Happy Birthday

ISBN: 9780957297746
Published in the UK by Hopcyn Press
42 Russell Road
London
W14 8HT

www.hopcynpress.com

Printed & bound in the UK by Berforts

Charles Mosley was born in London and educated at Eton and King's College, Cambridge. He has been Editor-in-Chief of *Burke's* and *Debrett's*, London Editor of *The Encyclopaedia Britannica*, and his other published works include *Lichfield in Retrospect* (1988), *American Presidential Families* (1994), *Debrett's Guide to Entertaining* (1996), *Blood Royal* (2002), *The Art of Oratory* (2007) and *Charles Dickens: A Celebration* (2012). He has contributed articles to *The Guardian, The Irish Times, The Spectator* and *The Times* and is a frequent broadcaster on television and radio.

CHARACTERS

Forenames

Angelo: see Devene, Angelo
April: see Breakspear-Pole, Chrissie
Arlene: see Strepsky, Arlene
Barb(ara): see Barnes, Lady
Ben: see Lee, Ben
Bern/Bernie: see Stevens, W. Berndorf
Charlotte: see Elver, Charlotte
Chrissie; see Breakspear-Pole, Chrissie
Clive: see Lane, Clive
'Crow'/'Crowy'; see Crowthorne, Earl of
Debbie: secretary
Dickie: barman
Ed(gar)/Edwin: see Go(o)dwin, Ed(gar)
Estelle: Jeff's great-aunt
Felix: civil servant
Frankie: see Evans, Frankie
Gary: security guard
Gav(in): see Doresett, Gav(in)
Jeff: see Calhoun, Jeff(erson) P.
Jimmy: barman
Joe: see Bramcusi, Joe
Jules: see Miller, Jules
Karola: see Wyczowski/-a, Karola
Laura: see Deller, Laura
Leo: see Horne, Leo
Mandy: Angelo Devene's daughter
Mark: see Barnes, Lord
Mel(usine): see Ahmadi, Olfert
Micky: see Frost, Micky
Nick: see Kerr-Tait, Nicholas/Nick
Pierre: male prostitute
Piers: see Boadiam, Piers
Sam: see Knighton, Sir Sam(uel)
Si: see Mecklenburger, Si(las)
Tod: see Snaith, Tod(morden) C.
Tucky: kitten
Verna: Angelo Devene's wife

Surnames

Ahmadi, Olfert: prostitute trading as Mel
Barnes, Lady: Lord Barnes's wife
Barnes, Lord: political fundraiser
Boadiam, Piers: journalist
Bramcusi, Joe: US media mogul
Breakspear-Pole, Chrissie: prostitute
    trading as April
Calhoun, Jeff(erson) P.: journalist
Cotesworth IV, Brewster: Ambassador
Crowthorne, Earl of: ecumenical peer
Deller, Am(ethyst): Vic & Laura's
    daughter
Deller, Lapislazuli: Vic & Laura's daughter
Deller, Laura: procureuse
Deller, Vic(tor): UK media mogul
Devene, Angelo: thug
Doresett, Gav(in): fact-checker
Elver, Charlotte: PA
Evans, Frankie: thug
Farrer, Sir Michael: scientist
Field, Dame Fern: designer
Frost, Micky: thug
Godwin, Ed(gar), aka Ed Goodwin/Edwin
    Godber: public affairs consultant
Horne, Leo: lawyer
Kerr-Tait, Nicholas/Nick: whip
Knighton, Sir Sam(uel): politician
Lane, Clive: slaughterhouse foreman
Lee, Ben: political adviser
Lynton, Chazza: former Prime Minister
Macnamara, David: press baron
Matheson, Mary: Prime Minister
Matheson, William: Prime Minister's
    husband
Mecklenburger, Si(las): diplomat
Miller, Jules: security guard
Porter, Sir Pip: pop singer
Psalt, Sammi: journalist
Russell, Bernard: club secretary
Sanders, Robbie: slaughterhouse manager
Snaith, Beth: Tod Snaith's widow
Snaith, Tod(morden): dead journalist
Stevens, W. Berndorf: magazine editor
Strepsky, Arlene: magazine publisher
Washington, Wilmur: US President
Wyczowski/-a, Karola: cleaner

ONE

Guinevere's lies up in the East Seventies. Its name tells you the era it opened. Camelot. Time with both the restaurant and the Court of the Kennedys has peeled repute's smooth mask from reality's blemished features. Guin's cuisine – Italo-American – now comes steeply price-hiked from that January of 1961 when JFK re-founded Camelot on Washington's Pennsylvania Avenue, an ocean away from Cadbury or Tintagel.

The Guinevere décor is French provincial, Biedermeier touches. Cutesy. Even seductive, though never quite arresting enough to make *Nest*, the late-Nineties/early-Noughties interiors quarterly so hip it hurt.

The margaritas are what justify a visit. They're that toothsome they're wicked. Malign wicked too, not just the cool kind. Some customers the old days ended pedestrians' lives after one too many. Shooting a red light looked like another neon Coke ad. Or jumping the sidewalk entranced by Beverley Sills in *Opera Hour Aria* on KLCHBC.

Guin's is a two-clientele place. Evenings, the brokerage crowd unwind there. Lunchtime, it's more magazine and newspaper people drop by. Executive editors, editors-at-large, special projects editors, development editors, senior writers, staff writers, editorial assistants, copy chiefs. Now and then an author guest, dazed as a Trobriand Islander at an anthropologists' conference by how many leeches his simple existence supports.

The Guin's lunchtime leeches discuss trends, concepts, angles, treatments, circulations, readership profiles and serializations, hint at print runs, deprecate rumors of princely fees. They dissect reputations. Who's one to watch. Who's hot. Who's peaked. Who's dead. Who's been so dead so long he might pull off a come-back.

Personalized human mortality, brain-stem cessation in someone you know, that doesn't much feature. Today was the exception.

'Arlene, what *exactly* did Tod die of?'

Arlene shrugged.

It was *Hence* magazine's editor, W. Berndorf ('Bernie') Stevens, put the question. Tod had been their London correspondent till two weeks ago. Stevens was lunching with Arlene Strepsky, the *Hence* publisher and StrepMag Inc. Life President; her attorney, Leo Horne; and Joe Bramcusi, CEO of the media conglomerate Vere, Bramcusi. Joe sat on *Hence*'s Editorial Advisory Board.

They had Arlene's usual table. It's the one behind the maître d'. From it you can glimpse everyone he lets in. Also those he doesn't, which is the real fun. Leo mostly just ate, keeping his head down and saying little. Joe on arriving had made for the men's room, citing heartburn.

Citing; pleading was for losers.

Stevens wasn't giving up on Tod. He speared half a pan-seared bell pepper, lifted it toward his bridge work. It was almost there when he said, 'We ran him thru a medical before he went. He was in terrific health for a man his age. We'd never have gotten him affordable insurance else.'

Arlene gestured for the waiter to freshen her glass from the split of water, a hi-calcium brand desirable just now as foil to osteoporosis, the hottest social affliction to hit town since disco fever.

'It got called Sudden Adult Death Syndrome', said Arlene. 'I don't know what that means and I'm in the word business.' She wasn't often so frank.

'Sudden?' Leo looked up from his linguini. 'How sudden?'

Arlene shrugged again. 'An embolism? An aneurism? A myocardial infarction could hit anybody? The British handled the paper work. I can get Si Mecklenburger at our Embassy to rush me a report – God, I pushed his appointment hard enough – but why call in favors for something that's so much...?'

She let her sentence die.

'A wrap?', mouthed Stevens. Leo too. Not quite simultaneously. Leo had to swallow first.

If Arlene saw it she didn't say. Or not directly. 'Look, Tod passed on.' She held her fork like a trident, a defensive weapon. 'In harness. I don't even like to kill a story. I sure as hell don't like my newsmen to kill themselves.'

'Suicide?' Stevens put down his own fork, the ruddy flesh of the vegetable still impaled on the tines. He placed his finger tips together and leaned forward. He looked very serious.

Arlene shrugged a third time. This signalled retreat. She rallied. 'Less he drank himself to death.'

'You have to be kidding me.' Stevens leant back in his chair, peering over the tops of his integrated all-focals. The staffer handled the men's style section swore blind the half-moon look was both smart and made a statement at senior executive level. 'We operate a dry code', he said. 'In-house and out-of-town.'

'Oh sure. But foreign postings are way under *Hence* jurisdiction's radar. Maybe Tod honored the code. Didn't save him. Anyhow, foul play is out. And no spice means no mention even in *Newslets*.'

'*Newslets*' was three columns of single-para. gobbets, buried deep on an inside page.

Arlene paused, sipped more water and rolled it round her mouth before swallowing: 'Some of what just got said could make me look uncaring. Means it doesn't go beyond this table. Enough of Tod. I want his replacement fixed by this evening.'

With a gun at his head, Stevens plumped for the choice had been jelling inside of him almost a week. 'There's Cal.'

'Remind me.'

'Calhoun, Jefferson P. My most promising associate editor.'

'Yes?'

'He's done a few TJs. More than a few. He's good with people...'

TJs were tearjerker pieces, a term for in-house use only. Interviews with knocked-up fiancées, eight months gone and now on welfare, of budding football heroes cut down in drive-by shootings. Or with widowed moms of high school twirlers OD'd their first upgrade from Ritalin, a kid product, to a serious recreational line.

'...We toyed with running him for this year's Greeley. Stepping stone to maybe a Pulitzer. We didn't feel he was ready.'

'Ready? How long's he been with us?'

'Four, five years. Came straight from college.'

'I know who you mean. Medium to tall, around a hundred fifty, dark hair, slim?'

'That's the guy. When I say "ready" I mean not for this year's judges. Wrong ethnic mix.'

'The judges or him?'

'Same thing in the end. Him, them. Him more.'

'Wasp huh?'

Stevens took his time before answering. 'I don't know where he says his prayers, or who to. Could be he doesn't do prayer period. But he's from the South, and straining on the leash to make good. Learns fast too. An older man…'

'Or woman' said Leo, not looking up from his plate, but gulping out of sync at a wodge of linguini. A pine kernel went down the wrong way. He spluttered.

'*Or* personage of another genderal persuasion…' Stevens nodded at Leo, whose back Arlene now hit twice, very hard, '…might make more of a surficial splash. But Mister Jefferson P. Calhoun's energy levels rate high.'

Arlene paused in her hitting of Leo. 'His looks too… if it's the guy I think.'

'Now Arlene, you know a man's face never pushed me either way.'

'Not you.' She resumed her hitting. 'The British. His job's to report on the OMG! people, their boffing, feuds, social triumphs and defeats, plus Palace palaver and other royal in-fighting, not just the meat and potatoes, the politics. You know how frustrated society bitches get any place, there or here.'

'The old dogs too. Gay old dogs.'

'For Christ sake.' Leo had got his breath back. 'He coped here, he'll survive in England.'

'Only that type dog's hard to spot over there. Blueblood British talk cissy whatever their orientation.'

'Not now. Even the aristocrats are gotten halfway Cockney-fied lately.'

'Tell that to Gav back at the office.'

'Not him, I agree. He's a period piece. Pure cut-glass voice as ever.'

'Calhoun better develop a quick ear for any tricksy nuances.'

'It was you said he learns fast.'

'That's enough, children.' And Arlene turned to Leo. She was buying his lunch so he owed her his two-bits-worth solo. He ate too much anyway. 'Leo, any wider implications?'

Leo wiped his lips. They were thin for an African-American. He rearranged the knife and fork on his empty plate, laying them neatly together so they bisected the circle in a diameter. He'd learned the importance of 'business' back at Huey Newton High, nonchalance affected when up against those godawful bullies the basketball squad.

'Bernie's subtext, Arlene, is that learning fast is important', he said. 'But so are reinforcements to London, England. You got a dead newsman there. OK, so he succumbed to Sudden Death Syndrome. Which may be a British health issue specialty, like their snaggle teeth. Want to know what I really think? They got too many body bags on their hands to unzip 'em all, take a good peek. But your new guy can look into Tod's death, if…', Leo glared at Stevens, '…he can combine crime investigator with social reportage.' Leo turned to Arlene. 'Can he even do social reportage? You need to get it right with a posting to England or your prestige could hurt. Kid isn't ready to write up that London doohickey you mentioned – Palace palaver? – can he cut it with a potential homicide? And if it's a *bona fide* slaying, can a college kid been with us four years outsmart the London cops which they'll be sore as hell an outsider shows they screwed up? *Hence* may not be the nation's biggest news magazine, but it's high-niche. Innovative where it matters, yet pro-motherhood too. OK, all that you're aware of. Here's something you might not be. Got it from a guy I know, back from Washington last night. Guy runs with the White House press corps. The President will quote from *Hence* even if no rival publication confirms it – something she will never do with any other title. No East Coast one, leastways.'

Bernie said, 'Albany loves us. Calls us the bloom on the Big Apple.'

Arlene stepped in. 'This is a strategy lunch. Where straight talk's the dish *du jour*.' She turned to Bernie. 'The Big Apple concentrate is exactly what spooks me. There's a whole bunch of Little People subscriber timber ripe for signing up out west of the Hudson. The boonies as well as Manhattan. I want you should go get 'em. Too, New York nowadays is gotten awful near semi-boonies compared with London, England, this century's global capital. Not that you hear me say it. Anyone heard me say it, they're very morgued.'

'Interesting you do say that', said Leo, reaching forward and spearing the other half of Stevens's bell pepper. 'OK with you, Bern?' Leo placed it on a buttered chunk of bread and bit into it. He swallowed and turned to Arlene. 'Back when Our Town was still the world hub it was also muggersville. Did Zero Tolerance spike the hub thing well as the muggers? There may be a connexion. London, England, the school kids are muscling in on the murder stats. It's

5

almost gotten to be a youth cult thing, British homicide. So maybe us sending a college boy to investigate would be a smart move after all.'

This pushed Stevens too far. 'When you're through trashing your own city, and wisecracks about my nominee for the London posting…'

'Enough already', said Arlene. 'Let's talk circulation. We turn a pretty dollar for now.' She pushed her plate and glass away. 'I could do with deeper market penetration off of the sophisto seaboard. That said, profit alone is not our *raison d'être. Hence* is a sacred trust.'

'Affirmative', said Leo. God, he thought, you can almost hear that bitty roof shape doodad over her *être*. It was a legend round the office how she honed her Berlitz accent on regular spring vacations in Paris, even to ordering aloud from the menu at *Le Grand Véfour*. 'The best kind of trust', he said, 'the kind the Sherman Act can't touch.'

Arlene laughed. She was not without all sense of humor. Unlike her magazine.

'Where's Joe?' said Leo, turning the conversation. Stevens was a horse's ass, but he wasn't going to let that bug him. He looked over his shoulder. 'Been gone a coon's age. Should we order for him?'

'He has the Erythroxylon Special', said Arlene.

'What? I don't see it. Where?' Leo studied the menu like it was a fresh Constitutional Amendment.

'Sourced in the Andes', said Stevens, taking off his glasses and putting them in his coat top pocket, then patting it. Leo wasn't the only one did 'business'. 'That's how it's special.'

'Joe brings his lunch', said Arlene.

To keep his mind clear and BMI *perfecto* Joe chewed coca leaves. It wouldn't do to let Leo in on this, even though they supply not just a pleasing high but calcium, fiber, iron, protein, and vitamins.

Joe now appeared. 'Glad you went ahead without me', he said. 'I'm just not that hungry. Fact, I sort of ate already.' A waiter arrived. Joe gave way. 'A Waldorf Salad then. But go easy on the Waldorf.'

TWO

The lorry was only a four-wheeler but custom-built on an unusually long base. The biggest you could run without over-frequent spot checks by police or vehicle inspectorate officials.

Inside was a refrigeration section up snug against the back of the driver's seat, loadable either through a side door or the main space. The latter was unrefrigerated and accessible directly from the rear doors. There was a third secret but confined compartment wedged between the other two.

The lorry, a white one, was unmarked. Its papers proclaimed it the property of Meadow-Sourced Meat Products, of Hereford, accessible at www.meadowmeat.com and leased to something called TransitCo, accessible nowhere at all.

Its current load was thirteen young women from Moldova and the Marmara Region of Turkey. They were on a clandestine passage to supposedly plum jobs in the British hotel and catering sector, exploiting the French ban on vehicle X-ray scans by the UK immigration agency OfIm.

In brute fact they were headed for a three-room brothel, lodged over a doner kebab takeaway in the St Paul's district of Bristol and soaked in Fern Field's High Society, that cheesiest of fragrances, to smother the smell of damp, the frowst and stray meaty whiffs.

Angelo Devene and Micky Frost took it in turns to drive. The other's job was to keep the cargo cowed and an eye out for any Albanian marauders after a slice of some very juicy action. A real risk, the Albs. It made Angelo's blood boil the way the authorities did nothing to protect English freebooters showing a bit of get-up and go in the good old Francis Drake tradition.

This consignment of Meadow-Sourced Meat Products had been quiet as lambs from Varna to Zagreb, and only a mite restless from Zagreb to Geneva, when the mild narcotic they'd been fed under the guise of travel sickness pills began to wear off.

Poop'n'pee stops every four hours, in maximum-isolation spots long known to Angelo from past trips, kept them reasonably well exercised. Dead of night was best. The air was cooler. And fear of the dark discouraged belly-aching.

It was the long, smooth crossing through France roused the cargo to insubordination. The ennui, perhaps. At that point Micky had wanted to get rough. Angelo had told him he mustn't mark them or they'd lose maybe up to twenty percent value. Chemical warfare wasn't on the cards either: they were out of fake travel sickness pills.

Angelo's past jobs from his time with the police had included both eavesdropping and DJ-ing on social nights. He'd got his audience to listen to just about any decibel dosage going.

On this occasion he'd tried boosting the speakers till they pummelled the brain like Bouji's on a Harry night. The din had drowned out the cargo's protests, for a time. Now they were over the Channel. A rough crossing had imposed further discipline via multiple pukes.

Yet the cargo was getting restless.

'Where our ID?'

'Where our job? Wait on table, you say. Four stars place, you say. Don' see no table. Don' see no star.'

The whinges were audible through the bulkhead. Angelo had fitted mikes back there to help the crew assess what went on. You could never know too much about a cargo brewing mutiny.

'You no take our ID off of us, you hear mister?'

'My cousin a-wait me at Birm'n'm. He no see me he grow mad. *Mighty* mad.'

Micky turned round in his seat and banged on the panel. 'Shut your slutty faces.'

'Micky, you're losing the argument.' Angelo assessed his partner like a driving instructor an L-plate novice geared up for the test. 'Least controlling prossies is one charge they can't make stick', he said, as if from a magistrate's bench.

Micky glowered.

Presently Angelo leaned forward, peered out of the windscreen and said, 'There's a lane leads down a hill to a nice little stream five miles up the road. Keep 'em from fretting any further till we make it. I'll take over soon as we do.'

'Just let me dish out a single black eye… Don't need more than the one, I swear. Would'n last more'n a fortnight. A blackie puts the fear of God in the fuckers and next month most look good as new.'

'No. Area Manager said we deliver damage goods once we lose the bonus.' Security dictated they call their immediate boss by rank only. 'For you the job satisfaction's enough. Me, I got a wife to clothe and three kids to put through school. '

Presently they pulled off the main road. The overgrown hedges slashed at the sides, once tilted a wing mirror. The stream had dried up in the weeks of Indian summer. Angelo could remember this time last year when it had been a torrent. Weird thing, world warming. He pulled the lorry to a halt, got clumsily down from the driving seat then stretched to loosen his limbs. It was five forty-five a.m. He rummaged in the tool box and took out an industrial size adjustable spanner. Time to seriously kick some babe ass.

'Everybody out.'

'Time too.'

'Height time.'

'High, not height.' Angelo hated foreigners mauling the English language.

'Hi.' Pause for breath. 'Time, OK?'

An intervention: 'Is our rights we wan'.'

'Our ID.'

Others joined in: 'Olfert here still pretty sick.'

'She sick. You hear, mister?'

They slowly debouched, shaking their hair, smoothing down ruffled garments, picking bits of straw and fluff from their legs, hobbling as a tight shoe chafed a heel. Soon they'd start preening themselves. Angelo was determined to nip any such self-reassertion in the bud.

'Line up, *ladies*.'

'Some us wan' go toilet.'

'Olfert still sick.'

What a name, thought Angelo. Where'd they get one like Olfat? Sounded like an oil you deep fried chips in. A saturate at that. When he'd told her to spell it out, she'd called it Persian. She had to be having him on. Persia was some old-time place. Didn't exist on his road map. Just another stupid migrant, then.

'Sick. You hear, mister?'

'Line up, please.' Angelo knew soon as he said it the polite-sarky tone was a mistake, way over their heads. At least the next bit wouldn't be.

'Not no "line please". No, no way. Not till you let her go an' sick up.'

9

'Not till you give back our rights.'

'Rights. Tha's right. She right. You tell us where you take us.'

'Our ID too. Big thing, ID.'

'And shut up too.' Angelo was beginning to seriously lose his cool. He swung the spanner with his right hand, thwacking it against his left, 'or you'll get this.'

Inured from childhood to beatings by their menfolk, the cargo sulkily shuffled into a semblance of order.

'OK, listen. We're in England now. Still some cops here not on the take, think they can get by on their pay. More fool them. Point is, one peep from now on, you wind up in a detention centre then get sent back to Moldy whatsit. Over. Over mouldy, says it all. Or Turkey. Too right, real turkey of a place.'

This was above their heads as well, but his tone was unmistakeable. They grumbled but most said nothing.

Only most. 'Birm'n'm. You say before how we go Birm'n'm. I think this not Birm'n'm.'

'No it's not.' Angelo's patience was exhausted. Time to turn the heat to max. 'There's been a change of plan. Cops, and believe me I really got a nose for this, could be on to us. We're goin' somewhere else.'

'Where this else?'

'You trick us with lie, maybe?'

'You lie, my Birm'n'm cousin pay you back. Pay you back good.'

Angelo had already decided which he was going to go for even before the last salvo of whinges. The tall dark one. She'd turned him down the night they'd assembled at the departure point. But since you couldn't force-fuck them ('rape' was such an ugly word) till they were shut away in Bristol and the training sessions to break their shreds of spirit had properly commenced, there'd been nothing he could do about it.

This here was his moment of payback. But he hadn't lost all sense of caution. It mustn't look like he was victimising her. The rest of them might work up a sense of fair play or feminine solidarity. What he had to do now was scare the bejasus out of the lot of them or it was bye-bye discipline.

'Waitresses my arse, see how you like this sort of gratuity. Micky!'

'Here.'

'Cover the right flank case they make a break for it.' Angelo began a counting game, pointing with his finger at each member of the cargo in turn. The game had been fixed in advance. 'Eeny meeny miny moe, catch a nigger by his…'

There was silence. Angelo had used the only Word of Power left in the West. The mere utterance of it can destroy the speaker.

'Hey, you can't say "nigger".' Micky, miffed ever since his powers of control had been mocked. 'It's abuse. Plus it's against the law.'

'What bloody law?'

'How should I know? Wasn't me used to make people toe it.'

'Like hell you didn't. Break it's more like.'

'Not this one. It's you doin' that.'

Micky's preachy tone made Angelo see real red, searing. 'Nigger, nigger, nigger moe. Nigger, nigger…', he said.

'Equal race law you diss it and we might as well live in a jungle. My nan's from Mandeville. We proud of our heritage. You fuckin' take it back.'

'…toe. Looks like you're elected to handle this particular order, darlin'.' Angelo turned and pointed at the tall dark one. She scowled, but stepped forward. Fine, give him a clear swipe at her. Angelo struck her violently three times with the spanner, once round the back of the head, twice on the neck. She started to fall to the ground the first blow. The other two were to make sure she didn't get up.

Three was just right. One the coop de grass thing, the other two to rub the rest of the cargo's noses in it.

'Jesus, what the fuck've you done?' Micky was appalled. But the effect on the survivors was magic. They huddled together, silent except for the odd stifled sob. Angelo prodded the tall dark one with his foot. She rolled over. Her name escaped him. The one they called Olfat threw up again, just warm spittle this time.

'Was thirteen.' Angelo turned to the rest of the cargo. He was still peeved, but sufficiently off the boil not to show it. 'An unlucky number. We're down to twelve, a dainty dozen. Let's try and keep it that way.' Now it was a doddle herding them back inside the lorry. He fastened and locked the rear doors.

'She's dead… it looks like.' Micky had been examining the body.

'You think I was trying to do, slap her wrist?' In truth, he hadn't at first intended much more.

11

'You said not to mark 'em. Jesus, you *said*.'

Angelo took a deep breath. The thing to do was trot out some stats, sound in control. 'One thirteenth – less 'n eight percent – wastage to keep the rest in line's good business thinking', he said. 'Besides, she was too tall. *And* snooty. Would've made the punters shy. Droopy dicks don't fill the till.'

'A blackie'd've done the trick.'

'No it wouldn't. Now lug her in the fridge.'

'Whuh?'

'This.' He poked the tall dark thing on the ground in front of him with his toe cap. 'We can't leave her here. Cops'd find her. Lug her in the fridge up the front.' He had a brainwave. 'Make good pet food once we get her to the plant. At least she'll be paying her fare after all that HGV fuel she cost us.'

Micky sniggered and said, 'The environment she got slaughtered in wasn't 'xactly stress-free.'

Angelo laughed. 'Your average dog can't taste the difference.'

Meadow-Sourced Meat Products had a subsidiary line in off-piste canned comestibles, doing pretty well at farmers' markets and over the net. Management paid Angelo and Micky a commission, no king's ransom but sure money in the bank, on any reasonably unmaggoty animal remains they brought in, not excluding road kill.

This here was road kill, come to think of it. True, mankind-sourced meat products would be something of a brand line extension. Have to negotiate private like with Clive the foreman. He'd been game for some pretty hairy things in the past.

'Should come to four dozen tins at least', said Angelo out loud. He remembered the horse meat scandal of a few years back. Could they really get away with it? How else d'you dump her? At least the meat plant had top-of-the-range processing equipment.

'Jesus she weighs a fuckin' ton', said Micky. 'Give me a hand, will you?'

'I'm busy strategising. Try and piss with your own prick for once.' Angelo reached for a spare can of petrol. He kept a separate stock on board, bought cheap in Romania at 74 octane-strength but still combustible, to take home and top up his lawnmower. He sloshed a score of dollops on the flattened yellow grass where in the growing dawn some flecks of blood showed, at first dark, now more vividly. As they turned to drive off he pressed the lorry's cigarette lighter in a few seconds, took it out and leaning from the cab window tossed it well clear.

The slope behind them hesitated a few seconds then went up in flames. They felt the sudden surge of heat in the cab. Micky turned to peer in the wing mirror. 'You crazy? Whole countryside'll burn down this drought.'

'Who cares? Bar some sandal-crazy green geeks with beards. And that's just their women.' Angelo loved such jokes.

'You care *any*thing about this planet we're on?'

'Gaia, Gaia, pants on fire. For your information, Micky, it was unleaded.'

'Very funny.' And a minute later, 'You did'n' have to torch a whole countryside.'

'Wrong. Time the fire brigade's stopped squirting, which'll be about next week with this breeze to fan the flames, cops'll find zilch. Reminds me, you clean the blood off the spanner like I told you?'

As he said this, a vision of the tall dark one lying on the grass made him want to vomit. A few seconds and it passed.

'Yuh', Micky was saying. 'Had to use the last the Dettol, though. They start pukin' again back there, have to let it ride. Stay all stinky.'

'From now on I guarantee they'll be good girls. Trust Uncle Angelo.'

THREE

Stevens made an appointment for Jeff Calhoun to get briefed by Gavin Doresett.

A bibulous veteran long put out to grass in fact-checking, Doresett was *Hence*'s resident Britisher, as which he got away with bucking the house dry code. Stevens found him too useful to enforce it. Doresett had been with *Hence* since before green cards were common currency, back when huddled masses, even Limeyland's cast-offs, were still free to scramble aboard the USS *USA*.

Stevens tackled the Doresett matter right after a couple of firings (his drama critic and a lifestyle guru whose platitudes hadn't proved feel-good enough to win syndication).

'Make Gav take you to the Patroon, Cal. He's a member there going back years. *Hence* picks up the tab.'

'I put together some topics to discuss.'

'Don't fire your asks straight off. Gav only gets real informative from the fifth dry Domecq on.' Stevens grew expansive. 'They call people like Gav walking encyclopaedias. He's more a sitting one. But he knows where to search. The wall behind him, mostly. Swivels in his chair and just plucks books off of the shelf. Could do it in his sleep.'

'Why use books at all when there's the net?'

'He says the net's like all nets. Big holes between thin threads.'

Stevens opened and shut several drawers in his desk, looking for something. He found it – a fresh pen. 'Gav studies the big hitters in Grand Canyon depth', he said. 'Art: the movies they take in, if they're opera buffs or balletomanes, collect chocolate box Monets or zaftig Renoir broads... Sociological, who they party with; ideological, how they vote.'

'What book tells you that much?'

'He's not just into books, though he guts every new biog, set of memoirs, letters, diaries. He OCR-ed all the documentary sources, spoke with a whole heap of people, met with others face-to-face, updates daily. So he put it all on electronic files, which in a couple seconds he can do searches, download... bingo.'

14

'Gav's problem is he's like all exiles...', Stevens added, speaking over his shoulder now as he rummaged in his attaché case. Another pen maybe; he shed them like a Malamute its fur. '...Views the old country too much like it's in aspic. But he knows the system there. He was classmates with that attorney their Prime Minister just went and named a lord, put him in the legislature.'

'So now the attorney gets to make the laws instead of plead them?'

'Nice, Cal. Very nice. Use it in a piece some time.'

Jeff determined to stop it bugging him how Stevens called him Cal. *Least he must mean Calhoun not some half-assed church-related handle like Calvin belongs to a preacher I never even subscribed to his take on God.* Jeff Calhoun's folks were Episcopalians. But they hadn't been able to hold their heads up in pride since Second Manassas, as they called the Battle of Bull Run re-run in the Calhoun home. Moderate ritualism might meet the family's worshipping needs. Optimism was Jeff's only sane emotional choice. He'd gotten extremely tired of cornpone obscurity, all the worse for being brought up by his crazy mother and widowed great aunt Estelle on 150-year old legends of dynastic luster.

Sure, he still wore round his neck the Confederate silver dollar Mama had given him when his Dad died. But that was more an in-the-sack accessory than an existential crutch. Heavy dates, it gave girls something to toy with, psyched them up for when he'd get business-like lower down, which he did once the silver dollar had cast its spell.

Jeff had done independent research on Doresett. At Julep State, though majoring in media studies, he'd taken history and British domestic politics as minors, suspecting white European males, even dead ones, could turn out more important than the faculty dared acknowledge.

He was now able to upgrade his superior factwise. Mustn't sound like a put-down, but would flag he'd done prior digging.

'More specifically, sir', he said, 'when Doresett was at college he roomed at a place they call The House. Cult name for this preppy men's dorm at Oxford U. Studied with their Prime Minister's Mister Fixit, guy arbitrages party fund-raising, his boss's aide in identifying contributors...'

'Lord Mark Barnes, yeah. He was just another attorney all the same.'

15

'…Barnes, that's a southside London neighborhood.' Dwell on your subject, do it big. 'His real name's Gray. Was before he got to be a lord. It's crazy how the British run that upper house of theirs. Like a Witness Protection Program, give a guy testifies against his *capo* a new ID.'

Stevens turned domestic. 'You planned your housing over in London?'

'Sir?'

'You could use Tod's place while you look round for a new apartment. There's maybe a couple months the rental to run.'

'Great.'

'One thing. You're not superstitious, are you?'

'Hell no. You telling me the place is like haunted?'

'It's nothing should spook you. Only Tod was found dead in bed there. You get much leisure from the big stories you could nose around whiles, see if you make anything out of it… Oh, and Cal?'

'Uh… yeah?'

'You'll never find a British shower can get the right hot-and-cold mix, still less strong pressure. So when you look for a new apartment, don't even try.'

FOUR

These days the Prime Minister couldn't see as much of Mark Barnes as their ancient friendship warranted. High office was the culprit. It eroded social ties and turned even blood ones into tactical pluses or minuses. The pluses (winsome toddler, supportive, photogenic spouse) to be exploited as evidence of a Premier's devotion to family values. The minuses (teenage tearaway offspring, marital partner with attitude, wayward sibling, gabby in-law) to be pushed far from the public gaze.

Barnes's target, money, made him of supreme importance nonetheless. Without money, politicians might have to go round wooing the electorate. Get their hands dirty by pressing the flesh. Even embark on constituency-level membership drives.

Which was how Barnes qualified for a desk in the ColLaborative Party headquarters building at 1 Confessor Street, a dark, narrow, medieval-stone-wall-lined lane just behind Westminster Abbey.

He also had a title. Not just a grandiloquent job one, but the solid sort, officially recorded in orotund letters patent, surmounted by a coronet, flecked about the shoulders with an ermine tippet and underpinned with a House of Lords seat in puckered crimson leather. Accessories with which to coax potential donors into disgorging to Party funds.

It wasn't high politics. But it formed a chassis for the elegant coachwork of policies, slogans and emotional appeals or high-minded calls to action erected on top, the bodywork that caught the eye and promised a high-performance ride.

Barnes's attitude to money-raising was ambivalent. In one way his new job was simply to encourage generosity in others. But in politics no quid got handed over without a compensatory quo. It bothered him. Not that anyone said so in outright terms. Indeed they smothered it in euphemism. Or rhyming ad-copy-esque jingles. 'Offers to our Coffers' was how Ben Lee, the ColLaborative National Liaison Coordinator, had christened in internal memos the latest funding campaign, the journalist in him elbowing aside the apparatchik so as to foster a team spirit.

Lee was close – exceptionally so, he liked you to understand – to the PM. And most of her inner circle would have rated him higher as influence-wielder than Barnes. True, the PM, on coming to power last year, had appointed Lee to mastermind a snap general election campaign. The snap element had been successfully engineered by the PM herself, however, albeit to draw a line under the break with her grubby predecessor, Chazza Lynton.

Lee almost immediately justified his six-figure salary. His was the concept of micro-managed candidate accountability that over the election period got talked about more than the contending policies. It involved forcing all would-be MPs under the Party's banner to appear on the hustings with a message on their campaign literature, transport vehicles and, among the more enthusiastic canvassers, even their backs, saying 'How's my campaigning? Txt msg 0800 111 111'.

It worked, delivering copious feedback in double quick time so the party machine could be fine-tuned instantly. Just as well, since despite the new PM's moderate proposals and winning public personality, her party's reasonably attractive candidates and an opposition caught off balance, the resulting majority had been paper thin.

Still, she had her mandate. Media kibitzers, more obsequious towards a recent member of their profession than to a long-serving party hack, showered Lee with plaudits, rising in shrillness the more tabloid-y the paper: 'savvy, sassy'; 'Downing Street-wise'; 'major player'; 'big beast-ability'; 'Love-Lee'. Barnes had shuddered. As far as he was concerned the Lee bull market was just that, bull.

The Barnes-PM friendship had social bottom. It dated from a time when, with a handful of regular fellow holiday-takers, the two of them had each year of an entire lustrum gone abroad for a few weeks' late summer relaxation. It was at a point in their careers when Barnes and the PM had been fledgling barristers, newly called, the PM a nobody, Barnes plain Gray, both struggling with pupillage, avid for their first briefs.

For many years now, their paths having diverged, the bond had subsided into reminiscence, taking concrete form at occasional dinners together, when they pored over curling photos snapped twenty years back beside a bright blue pool or blazing yellow beach. As of a few months ago, with first the PM's elevation to supreme office then her confirmation in it by the people, all this had changed. First Gray, then his new incarnation Barnes, had got dragged upwards in her wake.

FIVE

They had a saying about Doresett round the office. 'What he hasn't gotten as to what's worth having on who's worth knowing's nothing.' You tried saying it when you were loaded. Or stoned.

Doresett himself, old-fashioned, didn't get stoned. Loaded he could become.

'...I wrote a put-down piece on a club-owner. Not this kind of club.' Doresett held the floor. He and Jeff sat in the Patroon Coffee Room. 'A *boîte*', Doresett explained. 'The Dark Night, it was called. *Date* readers want value for their one pound twenty. Dumping on people's their test of value. Unfortunately for me, the club-owner turned out to be the *Date*'s new proprietor's in-law, his even newer wife's brother. How was I to know? She was new too. Too new. Deller had only just married her, a week before he got his hands on the *Date*. It was my diary editor's foul up. But he wasn't going to own it. So it was me they made walk the plank.'

Doresett rolled his eyes, then went on. 'Ben, Ben Lee, my diary editor, they suspended a few months – on full pay, mind – then offered him a regular column. Years later he went back to editing the whole shebang. Now he's moved over to practising politics instead of discussing it. I doubt he's up to the task. That text message election tactic was meretricious gimmickry. Meanwhile I was jobless. So I high-tailed it over here. Made it my business ever since to know not just all about anyone important but all I can dig out on their wives, husbands, mistresses, lovers – transient, transsexual or fixed.'

The Patroon Club's Coffee Room is where you take pre-dinner cocktails. You have your coffee in the Library and borrow the latest books from a desk in the Morning Room.

Doresett nodded, though Jeff hadn't spoken. 'Where was I?'

'The Deller guy's then new wife', Jeff said.

'...Tall ex-TV weather girl, overtopped Deller by a head ...been married twice before ...double divorcee by age twenty; taken up serial matrimony...' Doresett searched for a suitably lurid simile. '...the way a ripper hacks whores' heads off.' He again nodded, hugging his imagery. 'She certainly wanted blood over this. Deller'd do anything to please her. Or he would then. He's had two more wives since. I was the sacrificial lamb.'

'That's too bad.'

'Bad? My dear fellow, it was a disaster. Especially for a diarist.' Doresett looked properly at Jeff for the first time. 'You haven't done a stint as one yet?'

'No, sir. They took me on as an intern one summer before I graduated. Then on the payroll as a trainee when I left college. Some news-stand deliveries, production experience, costing exercises, classifieds, then straight to newsroom. I never did a diary assignment.'

*

Much later, with the imported Stilton in the Patroon's Long Room, where you dine, Jeff said '...Can you give me the "feel" of the top guys over in England? Tell me who truly counts behind the gilt costumes and stiff faces at the big state shindigs, or the glazed smiles of folks at charity bashes? I consulted basic source material – *YooHoo!*, *Right On*, *Chic*, all the other society magazines – but your direct experiences are worth a life-time subscription to the whole damn bunch.'

'Fair enough.' But Doresett said nothing else till they'd moved to the Library and he'd got his cigar going. Jeff had leaned forward to light it. He didn't do tobacco himself, but carried a lighter as a hit-on tool in the al fresco area outside singles bars. Chicks with Big C sticks between their lips were especially easy meat.

Doresett puffed long, then 'The first thing to remember about Britain – Britain, mind, not England as you fellows over here call it – is that it isn't really a free country, for all that it likes to boast it is and joins you chaps in invading other countries and forcing them to be free too. I blame the obsession with health. It's the enemy of liberty. That was inevitable once the state medical program took over people's physical well-being, ballooning into a behemoth... The other enemy's corruption. Excessive concern with good health in public, putrescence in private. If half what one reads about dear old Blighty is true, the scale of the baksheesh is epic. From the top too.'

'You visit the old country often?'

'Not once since I first came here – bar a sister's funeral three years ago.'

'I wondered all through Tod's leave-taking who'd replace him', Jeff said.

'It does astound me how this great publication we both work for has buried his death.'

'Yeah? They gave him pretty good coverage given that quake in LA the same week, hell, swallowed the two Toms, busted the sidewalk outside of Grauman's Chinese, swept away half the Malibu beach homes. Not that Tod didn't merit it. He was good to me my first six months, time he was back here on refresher leave. Polished up my writing, introduced me places. He was a fine human being. But they said that in the eulogy.'

'I don't mean the *nil nisi bonum* guff. I mean a man of his age dying at all.'

'So what'd he die of?'

'I suggest you make it your first subject of investigation.'

It was late. They were the last occupants of the enormous room. A club servant flicked a napkin at the coffee table. Another wheeled in a trolley with new ashtrays. Jeff half stood up. Portraits of Van Loudons, Van Rensselaers and a single Van Wyck Brooks lowered down on him.

'Thank you for dinner. I should be going. Still got a whole heap of packing.'

Doresett had by no means finished his near-stogie. He took it from his mouth and looked long at it. 'I shall stay. Don't let me keep you. One needs sleep at your age.'

*

Jeff came out of the subway near his apartment. Two blocks to go. It was a warm night, with skittish sallies by a wind that blew dust in spirals. He sauntered, pleasantly liquored but nowhere near a skinful.

At first he thought the faint prick above his left kidney was a bug bite.

'Got spare change?' The voice was a man's, British. Jeff half turned. The prick turned to pain. 'Stanley knife', the voice said, 'You turn round, I'll push it home, pull it sideways, slice you like salami.'

Jeff was alert now. He half turned his head.

'Eyes FRONT!' The voice rose. The knife twisted slightly. The pain grew. Jeff felt blood ooze warm inside his shirt.

'Take out your pocket book, drop it on the pavement. Oops, sidewalk.'

'You British?'

'You Yanks talk too much. Do it.' The voice twisted the knife in the other direction. More pain. Less sharp than before but the blood flow fuller.

Jeff felt at his coat, patting it all over as if unsure where he kept his valuables. He looked inside the left breast inside pocket, where he carried a small flip-top notebook to jot down quotes from interviews. He felt inside his left hip coat pocket. His hand found his cigarette lighter. He slid his right hand inside the right lapel of his coat, a tricky maneuver. He withdrew the pocket book.

'It's kind of fat', he said. 'I drop it, the money'll likely bust out all over, get blown away this breeze.'

'Hand it over. Careful... or you get your wrist slashed. Slowly now. Don't turn round.'

Jeff flicked his lighter with his left, held it against a sheet of the flip-top he'd torn free from the rest, meanwhile edging his pocket book round his other side to distract the mugger. Its fatness held the guy's attention.

A gust of wind caught the flame. The sheet flared up. Jeff dropped it and sprang forward. The brief blaze lit up the mugger's face. A youngish man, sensitive, hungry looking, but from low diet not avarice. The man stepped back, losing the initiative, too far from Jeff now to inflict damage. The weapon he called his Stanley knife was a pathetic utility tool, its small silver tongue the only clue to the harm it could do.

'You want a Bowie, son', said Jeff. 'That thing's no good less it's close quarters. A Bowie you can lunge with. Throw, even.'

'I've got your wallet.'

'Nothing but business cards in it. You keep 'em.' Jeff took his money clip from his pants back pocket and peeled off a twenty. 'Here', he said. 'You look like you could use a meal too. Pay me back when you find work. You got my cards, so you know where I live.'

SIX

Chequers, mellow in the Chilterns Michaelmas sun. Exclusive, too – authentically so, not some callow property tout's slick hyperbole. Ashlar pediments, their slim decorative features set eyebrow-wise in the brickwork above windows whose multiple panes now shimmered, now shone as waving russet leaves filtered the old gold early autumnal light. Black snouts of new-mounted CCTV cameras at wall corners and doorways, providing what interior decoration essayists call accents. The whole a symbol of England's rulers, once landed, now ex-lawyers or *ci-devant* media professionals promoted to the statesman caste and sustained in visible power by the brutish apparatus of security quite as much as constitutionally by the votes of the electorate.

The PM in residence for a long but never less than working weekend. Lunch for twelve – the immediate attendants at court (aides, media consultants, speech-writers, to the number of six). Also Sir Michael Farrer, a distinguished scientist, his detached life of the mind increasingly sullied by every day he spent in an advisory capacity to HMG's renewed stockpiling, not of anything so illicit as a bio-chemical weapons arsenal, but of blueprints for the infrastructure to one. The American Mission's Head of Chancery, Silas Mecklenburger, standing in for his Ambassador (the Honorable Brewster Cotesworth IV, a genial Philly Main Line plutocrat appointed after a timely contribution to President Washington's electoral chest, currently discussing quarter horse bloodstock up in Aberdeenshire with HM's wife). The ColLaborative Party National Liaison Coordinator, Ben Lee. And the recently minted Lord Barnes. The PM's husband had gone to knock his Nike Ignite round Ellesborough, the local course. He wasn't expected back till the evening.

It was not till after lunch that the PM addressed Barnes directly, to his surprise calling across, as the house party rose from the refectory table, long as the high sort in an Oxbridge college hall, 'Mark. I've ignored you. Huge pressure of work. My apologies. What about a game of Scrabble?'

'Scrabble, Prime Minister? We... *I* certainly haven't played it for years.'

A third party intervention: 'Everyone who uses words for serious ends should keep their hand in. Scrabble's a good tool there. One of the best.'

Lee had a habit, when he spoke to you, of putting his nut brown head next to yours and looking straight at your face. Not in the least obsequious. Intrusive, rather. Even knowing. It unnerved people.

'Are you a Scrabble-player too, Ben?' The PM sounded keen to know. Part of a professional politician's technique, Barnes supposed. He himself would never be able to simulate such personal interest, least of all to Lee.

'I'd relish taking you on any time, Prime Minister.' Lee sounded like he meant it.

'That'd be fun. Just now I'm booked with Lord Barnes, here... if you're still game, Mark?'

'Of course, Prime Minister.'

Lee pursed his lips. He turned aside, fiddled with his mobile, as if to distract attention from his brush-off at the PM's hands, then slid it back in his breast pocket. The brush-off had been exceptionally gently executed. Apart from the 'Lord Barnes'. A more ingratiating politician would in addressing Lee have referred to her Scrabble companion as 'Mark', enfolding Lee in the intimacy.

'I thought we might play out of doors', said the PM to Barnes. 'Catch what may be the last of this summer's sun.' They moved towards the door onto the Lloyd George Lawn, so named a few months back to commemorate the Chequers estate's first prime ministerial tenant. It was a cost-free way of pleasing the DeLiberatory Party, which was within a few seats of holding the balance of parliamentary power. The DeLiberatories proclaimed themselves heir to Lloyd George's non-socialist radical vision.

Lee's phone chirruped.

'Yes? Ben here... Why good afternoon, Your Holiness... And top o' the feast day to you too.'

Lee's voice carried well, quite well enough to be heard by most of the company. That he knew it, hence had deliberately broadcast the status of his caller, was apparent. The PM and Barnes exchanged glances.

'Ben knows everybody everywhere', said the PM. She spoke almost musingly.

'Even the Pope?'

'Ah, but is it? The Dalai Lama's "His Holiness" too, though the FCO Protocol Section won't let me call him that. Officially we accept Chinese hegemony over Tibet.'

'An *Irish* Dalai Lama? Lee did say "top o' the feast day".'

'Well obviously not. But haven't the Buddhists just found a new Lama, the former chap having embarked on the cycle of rebirth, or whatever his followers call it when you die? Luckily there's no Buddhist vote to speak of in Britain. I can admit to ignorance of their customs.'

They were crossing the grass by now. 'Whichever world figure it is', said the PM, her tone bone dry, 'Ben will have filled me in on the gist of their conversation by tea time.'

They reached their destination, a teak table and two teak chairs. RAF-uniformed attendants came forward to pull the chairs back. The PM gave thanks, asked them to put up a large sun umbrella and fetch her a sun hat, then waved them away.

She said, 'You know it was Ben, not our advertising people, who came up with that slogan we used in the trickier marginals? Especially where focus groups showed our personal fitness policy had less appeal than – in all modesty – I'm told I did as the new Party leader? "A vote for So-and-So is a vote for Matheson". Pushing me, as what Ben says the public thought of as the new cleaner-than-clean face at Number Ten, rather than the would-be local MP.'

True, thought Barnes. The PM's majority, small as it was, had in the flabbier parts of the country owed more to her person than her platform. Her rascally predecessor as PM, Chazza Lynton, had in the end become so despised by the nation that any alternative would have been welcomed. But Mary Matheson exuded integrity independently of this default position. Barnes felt a surge of affection towards her for the self-effacing 'in all modesty'. Much of her attraction for him was this lack of eagerness to grab credit for others' success, so unlike most politicians.

Behind them Lee finished his call, snapped his mobile shut and became affably statesmanlike, engaging Mecklenburger and Sir Michael in a discussion of multilateral moratoria on national debt default. Mecklenburger got so absorbed that at one point, in stepping back, he cannoned into the RAF attendant carrying the PM's sun hat, causing her to drop it. He apologised, picked it up, dusted it assiduously with his sleeve and handed it back to her.

Barnes and the PM were soon absorbed in manipulating the plastic tiles and wooden racks. They sat on the far south side of the Lloyd George Lawn. At some point in the mid-1980s, round about the time they'd started pulling in enough to rent Umbrian villas rather than Lot gîtes, they'd got bored with the conventional game and invented a more complex version.

Analogous to six-pack bezique over the staider two-pack kind, it used several sets of tiles, not the regulation one. This allowed phrases. Punctuation had to be mimed. The dumb crambo element honed the acting skills a budding advocate was wise to cultivate anyway.

With years of practice they'd become expert. Later, with his Bar work eating into his time, Barnes had indulged less and less. So too, he had assumed, his old friend. But shortly after the new PM's arrival at Number Ten it was revealed to the British public that their new leader was a Scrabble nut. It made an interesting change from unarmed combat, the last PM's passion. Or butterflies, that of the PM before.

The two Counter Terrorism Command Close Protection Officers in immediate attendance considered Scrabble wussy. For Gary, the older of the two, it was a question of history.

'Not like the bloke was here till the end of last year.'

Lynton, the former PM, had been ousted the previous December, two weeks before Christmas, his cavalier party fund-raising methods his downfall.

'What about him?'

'Used to do judo and stuff with his Chancellor.'

'What, that tubby number-cruncher in pin stripes waves a battered red box and puts taxes up?'

'Nah, the other Chancellor, I/C the Duchy of Lancaster. Fancy title for one of the Prime Minister's pet pals can't hold down a proper job. It was a treat to watch them. Hear them too, shouting "banzai" as they kicked to within an inch of each other's faces.'

'Two point 54 centimetres.'

'Eh? Oh, yeah. Metric.' Gary reverted to history: 'Shouting, they were. These two say next to nothing.' He added, very very softly, 'Which is bloody odd considering one of them's a woman.'

'She won't keep fit for long playing a stupid word game', said Jules. 'I thought health was supposed to be the big thing from now on. Didn't this one say her first day how she wanted her own side to set the tone, go in for plenty of physical jerks?'

'She did at that. But the road to Number Ten is like the road to Aitch-Ee-double-Ell. Paved with good intentions.'

'So you think this good health prescription the new lot bang on about won't last?'

'Think? Use your eyes. Those two haven't shifted off their backsides in three-quarters of an hour.'

'Why's she want a sun umbrella? It's early autumn in England, not mid-August in the Med.'

'Keep her peaches and cream complexion I expect. Sensible woman. Sun can be as big a killer as lack of exercise.'

The PM had used up all her seven tiles. They read: 'NO PEERS'.

Barnes stroked his chin, then put down 'NUN EVER'. He tilted his head interrogatively.

There was no obvious need to converse using Scrabble tiles rather than speech. The Counter-Terrorism Control CPOs stood well out of earshot the other side of the Lloyd George Lawn. Indeed the PM and Barnes were out of earshot of everybody on the entire Chequers estate provided they spoke in a low tone. However, the flood of leaks throughout her predecessor's last grisly weeks in office had made the PM decide, in the most sensitive matters, to avoid not just written memos and keyed emails, but as much colloquy as possible.

'Even out of doors?' Her elegant young Principal Private Secretary had queried on the tactic's first being mooted, barely able to keep the sneer from his Balliol-first-in-Greats drawl.

'Especially out of doors, Felix.' The PM was fast with her ripostes, a lot faster than her sober City-law-firm-partner charcoal suit and pony-tail hair suggested. 'The Americans' satellites can pick up a *pet' jésuite* from 200 miles up, their drones from 65.'

The PPS, a priss-pot for all his high educational attainments, had pursed his lips. 'That may well be, Prime Minister', he'd said, conveying a bare hint of distaste, 'in audiometric terms. All the same, they can't read even automobile registration plates, let alone text on a smaller scale.'

'Can't they, Felix? NASA's Mars Reconnaissance Orbiter can spot objects as little as a foot wide 150 miles below. Yet NASA's budget is puny compared to the US National Security and Military's. So I've no doubt American spy satellites are more powerful than their space probes.'

'Well of course I don't have your level of security clearance, Prime Minister. You see reports of the latest advances in monitoring equipment that I don't qualify for.'

'Actually, Felix, I read about the Mars probe in a popular science magazine. *New Tron.* I recommend it. We should all keep abreast of technological developments. Two of the most eminent of my predecessors as Prime Minister were Fellows of the Royal Society. It's my belief it was their scientific training made them so effective politically. Objectivity is an invaluable qualification in a statesman, if rarely present.'

Her Principal Private Secretary had known better than to make any reply. He had inclined his head in a gesture of agreement, however.

The PM had gone on, 'May I tell you a story? When William and I visited the White House last month, the President herself (for Wilmur Washington is the soul of courtesy) showed us to our room. She quipped to him how *she hoped my snoring wouldn't disturb William's night's rest.*'

'I don't quite get your drift, Prime Minister…'

'How had President Washington, who I'd never met in the flesh till then, heard I snored? Who'd told her? Hardly my own husband. And I don't imagine they monitored my sleep patterns when I was an obscure young graduate over there on a Fulbright thirty years ago. I didn't even know of the snoring myself till William confirmed it… Bless him, he's never reproached me with it once.'

'I can only suppose one of the night staff, Prime Minister…'

'Nonsense, Felix. I'm being eavesdropped upon. It's my belief it's from the sky.'

'The security people carry out regular sweeps, Prime Minister. I…'

'That is fine for building-based spy systems. Walls. Ceilings even. What of the sky?'

She had not mentioned that on taking over as PM she had been shown a file by the JIC disclosing that Langley had damning proof of her predecessor Lyntons's trading honours for party funding and thereby, in exchange for its silence, wrung British support for the Administration's Seleukistan incursion. She had when out of doors become noticeably keen on sun umbrellas ever since. Employing heavy duty canvas reinforced with a lead-based coating, high-concentrate yet relatively light-weight (an invention by one of Sir Michael Farrer's team), they hid one from more than tumour-toting sun rays.

The PPS might nurse his doubts, but the PM had taken increasingly to Scrabble. A great pursuit in PR terms, her image-manipulators conceded. Popular yet brainy, but in a pub quiz kind of way, without any damningly elitist overtones such as the bridge mania that had dished Asquith. The image people warned the PM to cultivate an enthusiasm for something fluffy and dumbed-down too. Being a woman, she needn't be expected to know much about footie. But being childless and well into her forties, she and her husband lacked that other surefire prop, offspring. Get a dog, the image people advised. A mainstream breed like a springer, mind, not an It Girl's accessory toy. She'd be in danger of seeming cerebral, cold, perhaps uncaring, if she remained both child- and pet-less.

*

The PM put down plastic tiles that spelled 'NOT 4 NOW'. She meant less a taste for dogs than a halt to new peerages. The Indian Summer sun had stoked the Chequers grounds to light grill conditions. Tiny drops of salt liquid crept from Barnes's fingers to the tiles as he played with them, rearranging them, hoping for inspiration by the very act of fiddling.

'SO HOW DO I RAISE FUNDS' from Barnes, interrogative this time via a cocked eyebrow.

'SCANDAL'. And the PM said out loud, 'Which gives me 50 for getting rid of all my letters.' Her voice carried well enough now. It was important that they appeared to be playing a normal game. The sun dimmed.

Five long minutes later the PM put down 'HOW U GET FUNDS IS UP 2 U'. She had not waited for Barnes to take his turn. Then, quite swiftly, 'PROVIDED U DON'T PROMISE PEERGES'. The PM had no 'A'.

'I've got nothing else but a fistful of Qs and Ks and even an X', said Barnes.

It was a preposterous defence since for communication purposes they picked their tiles with deliberation, looking at them beforehand.

The PM's face grew stern. 'WE NEED MONEY' she put down. 'OR PARTY IS BUST'

Barnes put down 'OH' before the PM could continue.

'Is that all you can say?' said the PM. She sounded almost testy.

'It's the only word I can make with the letters in hand.'

'Baker, Uniform, Sierra, Tango', said the PM. She expressed herself more frankly than was advisable considering the SnoopSat 200 miles up was operated by a fellow NATO member, subscribing to the same NATO set of Able Baker Charlie letter-of-the-alphabet-identification aids she had just used.

'And I don't use the word lightly', she said. 'I think we'd better leave it there for now. I must dash.' They both rose from the table. 'There's a slight possibility a war will break out late this afternoon', she said. 'I can't mention its exact location, obviously. Not very near here, though.'

'The Middle East?'

'Don't probe, Mark!' The PM used the fierce voice she sometimes assumed in the Commons when swatting an inept Opposition spokesman. Her 'Indira Gandhi Growl', the *Date*'s political correspondent had once called it, the tag sticking. Barnes stood still, abashed.

She softened. She said, 'See that porch over there?' She pointed at the Chequers front entrance. 'It's where my predecessor gave the OK to sink the *Belgrano* during the Falklands business. I refuse to be commemorated in the same sort of way.' She reflected, then said, 'The war will be somewhere west of Eden. That much I can tell you.' She smiled forgiveness.

West of Eden, thought Barnes. Well Eden was in the Tigris-Euphrates delta. So it *is* the Middle East. And she wouldn't have bitten my head off if I hadn't guessed right. He texted a single 'B' (buy msg) to his first intermediary to pass to his second intermediary to pass to a nominally independent broker, heading it with 'O' for oil, their private code. If only war hadn't broken out by the time commodity trades started next morning. Barnes prayed for peace. Just a few more hours, he added in a codicil.

SEVEN

There were times Mark Barnes, *né* Gray, regretted his ennoblement. Not as a fact. It delighted him every time he opened his post, each envelope proclaiming it, though often blunderingly over detail. It was the wording of his new persona that was the problem. Theoretically he should on taking a peerage have become better known. In practice something perilously like the reverse had occurred.

He had chosen Barnes as his peerage title through having long lived in Barnes the place, only later migrating to Westminster. He dearly loved Barnes's pond, the Thames one side, on the other reservoirs, rich in wild birds. Moreover in Barnes a 'village atmosphere' really existed. Other parts of London laid claim to one on the strength of a pub with a dozen opinionated regulars, an overpriced deli and the absence of any nearby sink estate.

But he had overdone it. "Lord Barnes" was too stark a change. A hybrid, Lord Gray of Barnes, say, would have been more recognisable. Alliterative elements cropped up too. His wife Barbara, Barb to their friends, had been especially acid: 'I cannot, I simply cannot, go around being known as "Barb Barnes". You try saying it, Mark darling. The title sounds like a stuttering sheep.'

But her mouth had turned upwards in a soft hint of smirk as she'd uttered the word 'title'. Barnes had gone ahead with his original choice, serene in the knowledge that, though plaintive externally, his wife was purring within, a cat gorged on cream from a pedigree herd.

There were even existential problems. On perhaps a dozen occasions, over a few months, old friends he'd rung up had had to be reminded just who this Lord Barnes person was. Mere acquaintances were still more at sea.

One of the first meetings Barnes had set up after being introduced to the House of Lords was with the media magnate Victor Deller, a one-time client of his from his earliest years at the Bar.

Deller owned several papers, news-purveyors and opinion-pedlars alike, as well as a social media outlet, Yammer, and a TV station, 3.414, or Pi. He was feared by all politicians, fawned on by most, vilified by a few. With good reason. He was better at swaying the mob than they were.

31

Few non-politicians would have recognised him in the street. His own news outlets never ran pictures of him. His rivals didn't much either, acting on the Fleet Street dog-don't-eat-dog principle. A strong one, pit bull intensity. Press barons' solidarity, thought Barnes, far more robust than the old print unions' ever was, and its practices much more Spanish.

The two men were due to have a drink in Barnes's new works canteen, otherwise the House of Lords Strangers' Bar. Deller claimed never to have seen it. This was unlikely given his long-standing eminence. Had Barnes been less distracted by misgivings over his choice of title, he might have realised with utter clarity how disingenuous Deller's pleading such ignorance really was. Instead he was gratified. The greatest business advantage to ennoblement was how readily even nodding acquaintances were to come and see him in his new place of work, and for as little as a drink. No one could resist an office block called the Palace of Westminster.

Barnes had rung ahead to the Strangers' Bar to book an attendant for his sole use. He had not mentioned his guest's identity. When he got there, Dickie the head barman greeted him in person. Barnes chatted a bit with Dickie, officer to batman stuff. In doing so he happened to mention his guest's name. Dickie looked away and ejected some saliva into the tray he kept for slops.

Barnes couldn't believe his eyes. 'Did you just spit?'

'Catarrh. I'm trying to shake a cold."

'I'm less concerned with your health than with the public's.'

'Left overs. Don't worry. I'm not going to serve it to your lordships.'

'But you *spat*.'

'There's several kinds. The spit contemptuous. The spit disgusted. The spit infectious. The spit provocative – to entice an opponent to violence. Mine was the spit emphatic. Ram home a point.'

'And your point?'

'Since you ask, I don't think much of your guest.'

'That's none of my concern.'

'It should be. He's a destroyer.'

'A what?'

'A destroyer. You're new here, Lord B. It may not be the snake pit the Commons is, though since so many of the regulars here are ex-snakes in ermine camouflage, the difference is minimal, but…'

'What do you know about "Another Place"?'

Dickie sprang a land mine. 'I used to be one myself.'

'You?'

'A Commons man.'

'An MP?'

'One-termer. Lost my seat ten years ago. Not least because I crossed one of Deller's rags, became its whipping-boy. I was too old to find another constituency. Or that's what young Master Charles Lynton decreed. So I got a job here. Not the first ex-MP to wind up in the Lords. Just the first to do it pulling pints.'

'I've a good mind to report you to the Serjeant-at-Arms for disrespect.'

'The trouble with respect, "your lordship",' – you could hear the twin inverted commas, rattling either side of 'your lordship' like gale-buffeted shutters on a rotten casement – 'it has to be earned. Now you may be an honest lifer, but you've only been here ten minutes. You come back in six months' time and swear to me you haven't fallen in with the ways of the shower of expenses-fiddling, influence-flogging shites in this here House of Frauds and I'll extend you all the respect you like. But even if your record is immaculate now, it won't be once you mix with the likes of Deller.'

EIGHT

On the airplane it had at first been way too hot. Now, as they approached the eastern rim of the Atlantic, a coolness spread. The sweat Jeff had worked up in the first hours of the flight had dried on him. He'd developed a slight sore throat, might well be starting a cold in the head. A fine time to catch one of those damn things when you had to settle in a strange city, find another apartment, make new contacts, revive your predecessor's old ones.

He felt in his breast pocket for a comb to settle his hair, mussed by the compulsory ventilation, itself prime suspect in triggering his cold. It wasn't there. He dug in the side sheath of the attaché case beneath his feet. It wasn't there either. He pricked his finger on a corner of the business card the passenger next to him had handed over a few hours before.

Card exchange, the ritual of a thousand encounters. Ordinary stuff. Less so the guy. Almost alone of those riding in Chief Executive Class, he'd eschewed smart casual. Jeff had thought at first he might be a preacher, his front had so many buttons up and down it.

'Edgar Godwin.' The guy had squirmed in his seat, offering a hand, his movements constrained more by his clothing than the limited space. 'And you?'

Jeff had given him his own card.

'A journo, eh?'

'Hope you got nothing against us.'

'No, no. Salt of the earth. Valiant for truth. Only Fourth Estate, but in my opinion worth the senior three put together.'

'Mighty glad to hear it. Some folks think we're intrusive.'

'Not me. Not me. And with *Hence* too, eh? Isn't that grand?'

'You read it?'

'*Hence*? A bit solemn and overwritten for an old *Scrutineer* subscriber like me. I gather the White House rates you high, however. Whether it's healthy to be so much loved by the powers that be is another matter.'

'I doubt we're loved by the powers that be among any Administration officials I ever met with. Just what'd you hear about our White House rep?'

'Your Mzzzzz. President Wilmur Washington will cite a *Hence* magazine story when no other periodical publication has corroborated it.'

'She will? I'll be damned.'

'And what are you coming to Britain for?'

'They named me *Hence*'s London correspondent.'

'Isn't that grand?'

The 'grand' had begun to grate. 'And what's your field of endeavor?' Jeff had said. The card proclaimed Edgar Godwin a public affairs consultant. Might mean anything.

'"Field of endeavour", eh? I can tell I'm talking to a literary gent.'

This had grated period. Jeff hadn't shed his manners. 'Mr Godwin, you got my card. Call me anytime.' And Jeff had turned on Godwin as much of his back as he could manage and settled himself for some deep rest.

He'd just been drifting off when Godwin had dug him in the ribs. 'Are you lying on my sleep mask? No? Damn. I must have dropped it.'

'Have a nice night anyway.'

'Quite a wag, aren't you? You can't go bye-byes yet. We're only an hour aloft. As I can't find my sleep mask I might as well make a night of it. How about a drinkie-poo? My treat.'

Jeff hadn't really been ready for sleep. Or a drink. But he'd accepted on the principle that any contact had potential.

Appeased and plastic ice-filled cup in hand, Godwin had loosened up. 'I consult for a number of people. Can't give you their names. It'd breach client confidentiality. But I'd like you to meet one of the biggest. Lord Barnes. You may not have heard of him, unless as Mark Gray.'

Jeff had sat up. 'I heard of him alright.'

'Splendid. He, with a little help from my good self, is trying to enlist the support of the more public-spirited of our expats in the States. Fund-raising, voter registration and so on. That's what I was up to in New York. A feature on Mark Barnes and what he does in your magazine would go a long way to get the message across to them. They tend to get a bit too stuck in to life across the herring pond, forget their obligations to the mother country in the scramble to amass a fortune.'

'I can't promise anything.'

'Mark actually likes the press. It helps that he started out a lawyer. Used to earn a bit on the side legalling newspapers, so he's almost one of you lot.'

A hostess had passed, enquiring of the passengers in each aisle as to their needs, comfort, general well-being. As Jeff's idle glance had followed her retreating figure it had been caught and held by the real thing. No Franklin Mint-y flight attendant statuette in spray-painted chinaware but an altogether more classily upholstered article, a premier piece of luxury goods, seated two down across the gangway.

The luscious creature had glanced up and turned her head. Their eyes had locked. It had felt like she was the one holding his stare, not him hers. Presently she'd dropped her gaze to her book, Diana von Principessa's *Castle Dominance* in the semi-gloss sable airport-bookstall paper-back edition that stood out, almost priapically, from the other volumes in the Female Interest section on account of its author's name, the title and the excitingly discreet jacket design, a masterpiece of seductive packaging by the publishers, Vere, Bramcusi. She'd looked away, up to the directional light over her head, had killed it and had fitted a sleep mask over her generous eye sockets.

Jeff had felt let down, blackballed for the Mile High Club.

NINE

Barnes and Deller sat themselves at a reserved table in the Lords bar. 'What's the house champagne like?' said Deller.

'Non-existent', said Barnes. 'The old wine committee got closed down some years ago. Beverage procurement's outsourced these days.'

'As are the inmates.' Barnes looked puzzled. Deller, gesturing around at the historic walls, explained. 'Outsourced appointees. Not sons inheriting membership here from dads, as in the old days.'

Deller's mentioning Lords candidates gave Barnes his cue. He ordered their drinks, straightened his tie, checked his watch, smoothed his hair, gave his lips a swift lick, then plunged straight in. 'I might as well admit it, Victor (I may call you Victor, mayn't I?), I'm worried. More than. At my wits' end. I'm Party Treasurer, with a peerage to impress my "prospects". So far so good. But the PM is tasking me to raise money for the Party. There's a huge amount needs raising. What can I offer as inducement? Not influence over policy, perish the thought. But honours are so out just now.'

'"So" out?' Deller gave the "So" a thumping great Edith Evans emphasis.

'The big ones, the "for political services" sort. Too risky. The lesser kind, some letters after your name, that's different. The people they go to are harmless nobodies – suburban lollipop ladies, municipal swimming bath attendants…'

'There are the pop knights.'

'Yes, dubbed for services to the hearing-aid industry…' Barnes now had the bit between his teeth. '…Or sports heroes recycled as administrators once their wind has gone, superannuated showbusiness legends recast as charity boosters. But after Chazza Lynton nearly got caught red-handed making lords of every Tom, Dick and Harry who'd bung him a seven-figure cheque (and in one case I know it was a low five-figure one), there's this new bill limits donations by an individual to a hundred thousand. On top of which, the new scrutiny panel's come over preternaturally obstructive.'

'Forgive me,' and Deller swept his eyes coldly over the other drinkers, 'but should you be saying all this in a crowded room? This one, of all rooms?'

Barnes brushed the objection aside. 'The background noise frustrates any listening devices. If they exist. Elsewhere we play it safe with a wink and a nod. When I discussed all this with the PM down at Chequers, d'you know how we communicated?'

Deller shrugged. But not quite indifferently. Barnes's dropping the letters 'PM' into the conversation had won his attention.

'Guess', said Barnes.

'I hate quizzes.' Deller frowned, then relaxed. 'Though they do increase the circulation in bank holiday issues.'

Barnes pressed his advantage. 'Go on', he said. 'Guess.'

Deller pursed his lips before opening them. 'Deaf and dumb sign language?'

'I don't speak it… mime it, rather. Nor does she.'

'Morse code? Semaphore?'

Barnes grew indignant. 'An arm-waving Prime Minister would lose all face.'

'I give up.'

'Scrabble.'

Deller shifted in his seat. 'The genteel parlour game? Well, well.'

'That way we could break up the words the moment they'd been grasped by the other player. Nothing on the record. Nor a single sound any listening device could pick up.'

'Is she that insecure, after less than a year in office?'

'Well, she hasn't during the last six months had a single major leak. Bar those we've launched ourselves. Not bad in today's world, eh?' Barnes sat back in his chair.

The two men sipped their drinks almost simultaneously. 'Very impressive', said Deller. 'I've misjudged her.'

'Getting back to my fund problem, in the old days dangling a prospective "Sir" or "Lord" in front of their names got the deep pocketed chaps salivating.' Barnes's residual awe of Deller made him over-idiomatic. 'Without those big carrots, I'm impotent. I've got no stick, you see.'

'Hmmm.' Deller ran his finger round the rim of his glass, less testing for dust than as an aid to thought. 'Can you make it clear so-

and-so'll come in for a deferred honour several years away, when the fuss has died down? Pay now; lord it later.'

Barnes groaned. 'Hopeless. So many of the really big potential givers are into their last ten years of activity. You might as well offer them fast-track entry to the After Life.'

'Religions do.'

'I'm a temporal inmate here, not a spiritual peer.'

Just then a man in his sixties, clean-shaven but wearing a prelate's purple blouse and several gilt gewgaws round his neck, looked up from his table the other side of the room, caught the eye of an attendant and ordered two gin and tonics. He spoke in an authoritative voice, one trained to hector as if by long years in the pulpit. It carried to where Deller and Barnes sat. Deller nudged Barnes. 'At-thay un-way of-way em-thay?'

Barnes recalled just enough Pig Latin to respond. 'You'd think so to look at him.' Himself he'd had enough of idiolects for now and continued *en clair*, but *sotto voce* to be on the safe side. 'That's Lord Crowthorne, the we-must-all-love-one-another multi-faith evangelist. Surely you know him? The man the tabloids call "His Holiness".'

'I recognise him now', said Deller. 'It's a vivid appearance, a lot more striking in the flesh than photos. Those glossy mags of mine don't do him justice, let alone the dailies. Shocking likenesses they've chosen recently, not excluding *Chic*.' Deller had spoken the last words mostly to himself. He scribbled a note with a thin gold pencil on a match-box size gold-backed memo pad. 'Mullins to axe the picture editor on…let me think, not just *Chic* but *YooHoo!* too', he muttered. 'That should send a sufficiently powerful message to the others, restore some professionalism…'

Deller put his notepad away. He raised his head: 'Tell me about him.'

'Crowthorne?'

Deller nodded.

'But surely you know him?'

'I've met him several times. So socially, yes. Which means superficially. I want your take. His fellow legislator's. I'm not going to quote you. But one wants to know any philanthropic donations one makes, to whatever the enterprise, get curated by chaps with penetrating judgement.'

It had come. The statement of terms.

'Crowthorne?', said Barnes, giving himself time to marshal his words. They had to be bold, frank, or Deller's purse might snap shut. 'Evangelist and between ourselves Grade A pain-in-the-arse', he continued. 'Dresses like a bishop, sanctimonious as a firebrand preacher, bores like a golf club major, vain as a beauty queen and beneath his genuine learning as silly as a pubescent girl. But then he's not actually a cleric in a single one of the various religions he claims to see good in. As you'll notice, he wears on that chain round his neck not just a cross, which alone is impertinent since he's a layman, but also an ankh, a crescent, a Star of David and a Yin-Yang device. He has some connexion with that Interfaith Institute near Reigate.'

'He's a hereditary peer, isn't he? Surely he and his kind got expelled back in '99?'

'He came back in at one of those Lords by-elections. A sitting peer drops off his perch and the replacement gets chosen by the dozen or so hereditaries belonging to the same party the candidate does. Not a huge constituency. As for Crowthorne personally, some people love him. I happen not to be one of them.'

Deller grunted. Then, 'Come on, Markie. You sound sour.'

Barnes remained despondent. 'I'm desperate. I only got put here so I could raise money.'

'Well your chum the PM can hardly take your title away again because you don't.'

'I know. But I hate to let an old friend down. We did pupillage together. Under Sir Idris ap Dafydd-Gruffudd, what's more.' Barnes enunciated the name with care, negotiating the double 'd's gingerly. It took time.

'Who?', said Deller. 'And why the lisp?'

'Welsh', said Barnes. 'Ferocious prosecutor. Became just about the toughest-sentencing judge. One day he got shot point blank in the face by one of the hardened criminals he'd gaoled twenty years earlier.'

'Ah yes. A very pretty little story, that. My *Date* gave him a full-page obituary, a feature and a straight news coverage piece several column-inches thick.' Deller chuckled. 'The *Era* wouldn't do more than half a page. Bad decision. We put on 25,000 in sales. They stood still.'

'He treated his pupils as skivvies.'

'So I recall my *Date* implying. In case you didn't keep it, I'll get Mullins to send you a presentation copy of the issue, beautifully bound. The PM too.'

A short silence. It was Deller broke it. 'Loans?'

'Still technically feasible – just – but politically too dangerous, particularly after the stink under Lynton.'

Crowthorne was joined by a younger-looking man. Deller glanced briefly in their direction then quickly back to Barnes, who thought, or almost thought, for he was not at all certain, that he saw Deller nod in Crowthorne's direction. Why, if so? Deller had implied he barely knew him, hadn't he?

'Any idea who Crowthorne's friend is?' said Deller, putting Barnes's thoughts into words.

'One of those lobbyists. Or researchers. Or advisers. This place swarms with them. The name'll come to me in a minute. Got it. Godwin.'

'Godwin. I see. You know, Crowthorne has been good enough to contribute some opinion pieces to my problem child, the *Date*. They're not bad.'

'No? Why problem child?'

'Makes a loss. Not thumping, but a steady drain. I can't close it down, any more than you can have a real problem child dealt with by euthanasia. It's too much of a trophy.'

They ordered more drinks. Presently Deller said 'Tell you what, old son...'

Barnes looked up. The spuriously matey 'old son' was ominous.

'Speaking as a former client of yours, I knew you'd go far. I didn't think you'd end up here, though. Nice place.' Deller looked around, as if seeing it for the first time. 'Wouldn't mind joining myself.'

'It's rather tricky to get into just at the moment.'

'So you've as good as said. Let's see. How much in all does your party outfit need a year? Twenty? Twenty-five? Something in that region, I imagine.'

Barnes knew the figures well. 'Party HQ running costs alone absorb eighteen million per annum', he said. 'It's a lot more in an election year. And we have elections all the bloody time. Local ones, Euro ones, devolved ones...'

'Here is what I would do...' Deller's voice had got very low, but icy clear. '*...in the event I was minded to help*. Consolidate up to

41

seventy-five percent of your major fund-raising efforts under one umbrella. Give pledges for advances by a third party or parties, probably the latter, in other words spread the liability, of two million clear a year for two years, maybe via a mortgage on your HQ. And it wouldn't be a loan. Collateralised debt obligation. For that at the end of the two years I'd get put up for this place – hang on, I know the form, "considered for recommendation to HM as a potential nominee for etcetera etcetera" – but basically it's queue-jumping. Plus instant access to Her Nibs at Number Ten any time I want it meanwhile. Which wouldn't happen except in emergencies (I'm a very busy man). You needn't fear you've sold the country's heritage, even for a shed load of pieces of silver.' He paused, sniffed his wine, took a swig. 'Nice nose.'

He returned to his main theme. 'I know what you're thinking. "Why's my old client being so generous?" Let's say the current scarcity value's put a premium on your product. Plus I'm a genuine lover of my country. That means backing your people.'

Barnes took his time before answering. To sound eager betrayed the supplicant. 'It has the makings of an astoundingly munificent gesture', he said. 'But you haven't in the past exactly tumbled over yourself to support our chaps. Why now?'

'Change of heart. The last lot went haywire, not just selling off honours, and at well below par, but shouting it from the rooftops like barrow boys with a wilting stock of wet fish. Can't have life's glittering prizes cheapened or they lose their allure. Any little shop girl been in the luxury goods sector five minutes'll tell you that. I'd be restoring the prestige, securing my place in history.'

Barnes stretched out and gripped his glass. 'Sounds... interesting.' One never turned down an offer flat. This offer was dangerous, however. 'It helps hugely if you've done something genuinely philanthropic', he said.

'But I have. You recall my Inclusive Health Foundation, surely?'

Barnes thought of another stumbling block. 'The scale you suggest would give you a bit of a monopoly as donor, wouldn't it?'

'Don't be frightened of words like monopoly. Historically your people have had a monopoly on the patriotic vote. Hasn't always kept you in power.'

Barnes was dogged. 'But it's still restraint of trade. I doubt it'd be appropriate.'

'OK, Markie.' The repeated use of a diminutive struck a chill too. 'But my offer's only good for two years. You can bring in other fairy godmothers after that.'

Barnes thought hard. In around two years time a relatively steady, discreet traffic in gongs could resume. It was more the former PM Lynton's ineptitude in selling honours so crudely that the business had come to public notice than his venality as such. How else was politics to be funded without soaking the taxpayer so as to raise subsidies?

'I'll have to take soundings', he said, 'but in principle your suggestion is not without merit. We'd be free to get coverage elsewhere for outgoings your offer didn't cover?'

'Naturally.'

'I'll see it gets given serious consideration.'

'Good man. You won't regret it. One other thing. A very minor concession. Like the tenner a horse coper hands you back. Token of good faith...'

'Yes?'

'The gym here, keep fit facilities. They're being put out to tender.'

'I believe so. The idea is to move the whole complex out of the immediate Palace of Westminster precincts to make more office space but do our utmost to get the people here, from both Houses, to use the gym complex more. Good personal health's the keynote of the Government's domestic policy. Apart from anything else, the fewer by-elections we need fight from some flabby backbencher dropping dead the better. It's going out and touting for the wretched votes drains our resources so much. And our majority's minuscule, as you know.'

'The gym thing, I'd like to pitch for it.'

'It's nothing to do with me.'

'The Inclusive Health Foundation might help too. You can point me – it – in the right direction, can't you?'

'I dare say.'

'That's my boy.' And Deller actually leant forward, then pinched his cheek. 'Correction. My lord.'

TEN

Angelo and Micky never did get to break in the latest meat consignment. Area Manager told them to get a couple of reliable local lads to do the job. Angelo and Micky tried protesting. Micky by cursing privately to Angelo. Angelo by persuasion to Area Manager over the phone.

Their annoyance was understandable. Hands-on higher education of the cargo in the steamy privacy of a massage parlour, the flesh trade's equivalent of a bonded warehouse, was the only real perk of the job.

In making their case to Area Manager over an open line, Angelo was hampered by having to stick to delicatessen imagery. He pointed out it wasn't everyone knew how to tenderise the meat, process it, well-trimmed but easy on the palate at the same time, lo-fat, good colour, nice cuts (breast, rump, haunch, leg), melted in the mouth.

Area Manager told him to stop arguing and get his and Micky's carcasses up to corporate HQ by tomorrow a.m. Angelo winced at 'carcasses'. It reminded him of that tall dark unfinished business in the refrigeration compartment, the one with an awfully broken neck.

*

Area Manager received them in his office, a hut in the delivery yard of the cannery. Although Angelo and Micky worked for Big Boss, they reported direct to Area Manager. They didn't even know Big Boss's name. The morning air was fresh. A log-burning stove in one corner gave out welcome warmth.

Area Manager sat at his desk. There was another man there. Slim, dark and some way younger than Angelo. He radiated purpose. Toxic, like tritium into the water table from a leaky reactor. He sat in a chair to one side of Area Manager and swung a small vanity case on a loop round his right wrist. It wasn't much bigger than a spongebag. Decorative though.

Now and then the stranger smiled to himself, as if calling to mind an especially pleasurable experience. Not a nice smile. Too concentrated round the mouth. Not sunny enough up in the eyes.

Area Manager got the conversation going. 'You boys have a good trip?'

'Had to get up at five to make it here.'

'I don't mean from frigging Bristol. Your Continental tour.'

'Ange-o went and lost the lighter off the dash board. Rest went OK.'

Angelo scowled at Micky but said nothing.

'Smoking on company premises and in company time's against company policy', said Area Manager, picking his teeth. 'It may even be against health and safety regulations. Must get round to reading 'em some day.' He flicked the toothpick at a waste paper basket. It missed. 'OK, I won't dock your fee over the lighter. But it was still company property, and don't you forget it.' He wagged a finger at them. 'Meanwhile, a new project's come up. Connected with a healthy lifestyle too. Ain't that a coincidence?'

Angelo usually kept quiet in conference. Area Manager had a way of getting him all tongue-tied. He could always take it out on Micky or the meats later. But now he screwed himself up to ask a question. 'I sincerely hope it don't mean no big changes to the diary, Mr Sanders. I promised my youngest I'd take her to Fun World this Saturday.'

'Fun World can wait till she's less young. The Boss is opening a new place. London. Somewhere City gents can go and work out, fit in some nice R'n'R afterwards. He needs staff. Recruited by you two. Under Frankie here.'

Angelo hadn't liked what he'd seen of Frankie even out of the corner of his eye. He was disinclined to look full at him now. He concentrated on the matter in hand. 'Mr Sanders, sourcing personal trainers, that's HR stuff, way over our heads.'

'I said "R'n'R", not the H sort. *Au fond* – that's bottom line in case you didn't notice on your trips through *la belle France* – we're talking techniques to help stressed-out business blokes unwind after a hectic day. Tantric whatsit and associated services. Do I need to spell them out?'

'*Successful* businessmen', said Frankie, speaking for the first time. He drawled his words and examined his finger nails as he spoke, holding the back of his hand away from him. 'Any of the new meats any good?' he said. He didn't even glance in their direction, just eyed his nails.

'They're all top quality', said Angelo, nettled.

'I mean good enough for the West End. Not the ratty oiks wherever you live.'

'Saint frigging Paul's', said Area Manager.

'And their attitude's got to be right', said Frankie. 'We're not talking debt-ridden Bangkok bar girls. More the gracious GFE courtesan spirit.'

Angelo looked at Micky. 'Micky?'

'If it's West End la-di-da…only one might do's Olfat.'

'Olfat! She's the one always puking.'

'Not recently. Honest, Ange-o. It's more she gets car sick long journeys. Good as gold now she got her land legs back. Smashing pins they are too.'

'Olfat?' said Area Manager. 'That name has to go. From now on she's Dee Dee.'

'Yes, Mr Sanders.'

'No, second thoughts Dee Dee's too pole dancer. I've got it, wait…'

'Melusine', said Frankie, examining the nails on his other hand.

'Sounds like a prize cat', said Micky, but well under his breath. Angelo shot a quick frown at him.

'Melusine's good', said Area Manager. 'Pure class.'

'Right, Mr Sanders', said Angelo.

'Talking of which', Micky said, still thinking cat, 'we got a piece of dead goods in the lorry, do for the cannery.'

Christ, of all the moments to bring that up. Angelo could have kicked him.

'Well bloody take it over to the rendering shed like you always do. Usual commission. No, not you Devene. Frost can handle it on his own…' and with huge sarcasm, thinking it was indeed a domestic animal, '…unless it's too heavy for him to lift.'

'This Melusine', said Frankie, looking straight at Angelo. 'She up to it? London, we need class. Tall tail. And darkish…'

Angelo winced, even worse than last time.

'…Blonde comes over as barmaid. Plus fucking Albanians got that side of the supply line sewn up tight for the time being. Bringin' 'em in from all the blondie places, Czech Rep, Hungary, the Baltic, Russia. So dark it's got to be, product diversification being competitive. Wouldn't hurt she's a bit posh. Toff totty slips down a treat with business johns. She don't fit the bill's a waste of time taking her there.'

Micky paused at the door, turned and looked back meaningfully at Angelo. Angelo started coughing. He found he couldn't stop. Micky tried to catch his eye, failed and left the hut.

'What's got into you, Devene?' said Area Manager. 'Thought you said you *lost* the lighter. Sounds like you're on twenty a day.'

'It's nothing, Mr Sanders. Frog in my throat.'

'Well spit it out and pay attention. London you'll be working part the time on a related matter with Frankie here. Word is that mangy old cur did some sniffing around could have dug something up before he got put to sleep. You'll look into it, case he yapped.'

Angelo hadn't the faintest idea what Area Manager was talking about, but he was too worried about the lorry contents to ask questions.

'Where's that moon-faced mate of yours got to?' said Frankie. He looked Angelo full in the eyes again, but not detached, the way he did with his nails. More like the liposuction surgeon had done the time Angelo had tried to lose weight fast, only he'd chickened out the last minute.

'Micky'll really need a hand with this one, Mr Sanders.' Angelo wasn't going to answer Frankie direct. 'A deer we knocked down over Tewkesbury way.'

'What the hell were you doing near Tewkesbury? Bristol to Hereford's west of the Severn.'

'There was this big roadworks, Mr Sanders. Detour, really set us back. And Micky's satnav played up. Then there was this, like I said, this deer. A doe, a solid customer, one the fallow sort. So can I give Micky a hand?'

'Go on, get out. Be back by five past at the latest.'

Angelo left the hut with a casual swagger to show he wasn't intimidated but once out the door he sprinted round the back to where they'd parked the lorry. He needn't have hurried. Micky was having trouble turning in a confined space. Angelo banged on the driver's door. Micky stopped and looked out.

'Don't for the love of Christ unload h… it', said Angelo.

'You sayin' we should'n' hand this one over?'

47

'Are you crazy? Didn't you hear what Fancy Frankie said, how tall and dark's just what they're looking for? And why'd you bring it up the first place?'

'You said Clive'd be OK.'

'Clive, not Area Manager. And I'm not so sure now. We never showed him a piece of goods like this before. I won't risk it.'

'OK. What'll we do with h... it. What'll we do instead?'

'I'll think of something.'

But he was still trying to think of something two hours later. By then they were tooling down the M40 to London to stock Big Boss's new place with top talent. Plus there was this mystery side task. Frankie had gone on ahead in a cream Porsche Cayman S made Angelo jealous, dislike him even more.

Micky drove. Angelo stuck to thinking. He cradled his head in his hands. Their passenger, still in the refrigerated section, was threatening to give him migraine.

*

'What d'you think of this here new bloke we got to work with?' said Micky, breaking a long silence. 'The Frankie bloke.' They passed the Hanger Lane turning off Western Avenue.

Angelo raised his head. 'What's it look like I think?'

'Dunno. S'why I asked. He thinks you hold yourself well.'

'Hold myself well?'

'That's what he said, for someone your size an' age. Only tellin' you what he said. He asked were you married.'

'I should of guessed, that bag he swung.'

'It's not real. He told me.'

'Real what?'

'Snake. Looks it, but it's not. He's fond of animals. Even creepy-crawlies, which he says most people aren't. He'd never have a bag's real snake. He's got whole lots, a collection. Bags, not snakes. Might even leave 'em to the nation, he said. I think he was having me on there.'

'Fake snakes! *"Fond of"*; ble-e-ech!' Angelo made as if to stick a finger down his throat.

'He likes animals. Most animals. None too gone on cats. Give him the creeps, he says. Mostly he's into dogs. He won't have one at home, though. On the road too much, he says. Not fair to the dog.'

'He's got no one to look after it?'

'Can't have, can he? Not that I liked to ask. He seems quite an open bloke once you get to know him.'

'When'd you do that?'

'While you was gettin' paid. Talkin' of which...'

Angelo dug in his pocket. 'Here's your share. Of given it you earlier; didn't want to distract you while you're driving.'

'Ta muchly.'

'Don't count it now, idiot. Keep your eyes on the road. Christ! Look out! You want to kill us?'

'Was her fault. Pulled out in front of me. Did'n' even indicate...So about Frankie?'

'What's he get up to with those animals he's so *"fond of"* is what I want to know.'

'What d'you mean?'

'You are so thick, Michael Frost. Our sweet doggy-loving, snake-hugging Frankie there is a fucking arse bandit. Look at his fag bag.'

'You sure?'

'Stands out a mile.' Angelo cuffed Micky twice round the head. 'Try and drive straight for two consecutive seconds at a time.'

'I am drivin' straight.'

'Straight straight. Not the Frankie up-the-straight-and-narrow kind.'

'You are one big bigot. First you got no time for blacks...'

'Shut up... What you said that time we thinned out the cargo, your nan really a nig-nog?'

'She was from Mandeville, like I said. That's Jamaica. First you got no time for people like her, now it's gays. We got to work with this here Frankie, remember?'

'With him, not under him.'

'Under him too. Don't fool yourself.'

Micky had hit the nail on the head. Angelo slumped back in his seat. 'Yeah, you're right. And on top of that I can't take my youngest to Fun World.'

ELEVEN

'What in hell's Black Rod?' Jeff asked a fellow newsman, thumbing through his briefing notes.

They were covering the State Opening of Parliament. It wasn't much more than a traditional ceremony, bar the bit about the Administration's new slate of laws. But Stevens had figured it'd make a neat hi-here-I-am-in-London piece, the picturesque elements especially.

Traditional England was proving good comfort material again for *Hence*'s readers, comfort with a twist of quaint, like in the 'Sixties. There'd been rumors back home of a 9/11 follow-up. Atrocity stories there got soft-pedalled for the time being.

Black Rod? Golden rod was definitely a plant. Jeff had looked it up. The *Alice in Wonderland* nature of British job titles was breathtaking. Rouge Dragon. Jeff thought of the KKK Grand Dragon back home. Great-aunt Estelle always claimed she'd dated one once. Her SMU senior year, she said, before she married great-uncle Barry. Grand, fine. But rouged?

He'd settled in to Tod's apartment some weeks now. The shower was every bit as unreliable as Stevens had warned. Karola, the Polish cleaning woman, who'd found Tod's body, had told him Mr Snaith 'die peaceful'. She'd used her hands to drive the point home. Mr Snaith OK in life, she'd said, leave no mess when he die, make her no more work as when he live.

Had Mr Snaith seemed worried about anything? Nothings, no, she'd said. Any of his papers still around? No, Karola had said, his paper stuff she'd put in a waste bin or sent to the American States, so his wife can have it.

Jeff seldom saw Karola. Except weekends, when she spent a couple hours each Saturday morning superintending his wardrobe. She was there weekdays too. He relied on her to be, since shortly after moving in he'd found him a kitten. But he couldn't have kept it if Karola hadn't fed it and cleaned its kitty litter tray.

He'd discovered it in a shoe-box, punched with holes to facilitate breathing. Someone had abandoned the box early one morning on his office block front steps. Cheap sons of bitches. The breathing holes did at least suggest the abandoning party had had a conscience. He'd christened the kitten Tucky, after a glittery ditzy cousin on his father's side, older than him and dead now, who he'd been in love with age fourteen. Evenings, he often played with Tucky.

*

Earlier, outside the Houses of Parliament, just as Jeff had been about to make his way in, there'd been a few groups of demonstrators carrying placards. Among them, he'd noticed an unusually well-dressed bevy of women. One of their signs read 'STOP HUMAN TRAFFIC'; the other, catchily alliterative if lewdly, 'PICKET IMPORTED PUSSY'.

They hadn't looked much like your traditional feminists, a rare breed nowadays. Maybe they were some mainstream women's group. Elegant, though. And young for women. On an impulse he'd gone over and introduced himself, flashing his accreditation badge.

'Which of you's your leader?' he'd asked the nearest. Less woman, more girl. She wore a butcher's boy's cap in red leather and a whistle on a ribbon round her neck. She trilled on the whistle. 'Chrissie! Haul your booty over here, girl.' The woman Chrissie slouched over. 'Reporter wants a word with you.' And the red leather girl had turned back to Jeff: 'Hey, handsome, what's your paper?'

Chrissie had looked him up and down. 'Hello there. How can I be of service?'

'You guys some anti-immigration group?'

'Now do we look like guys? Dolls, please. But yeah, I suppose you could say pro-controlled immigration. Controlled, mind, not anti.'

'Why "Controlled"?'

'One thing we're not is racist. Lots of my own regulars are Arabs or Africans. Angie there won't do Asians, but she's got this thing about coriander. Most of us welcome anyone with open arms. Anyone who's not rude, raging drunk or so high he has to be scraped off the ceiling.' She got earnest. It sat oddly on her previously flirty approach. 'We don't see why the hell these East European girls should be shipped in here and start a price war.'

She'd then gone and stood akimbo. Like Andy Capp's Flo, though more lissome. 'In fact it could fucking put us out of business.'

'What business?' Jeff had said, though by then he'd guessed. The fucking business.

'Entertainment.' Chrissie'd grinned. 'OK, since you look a gentleman, escorting. Not street sluts. Escorts. And it is NOT a profession. More a vocation. Not all between-the-sheets fun either. One's got to be good company, keep your end of the conversation up, know how to behave in a restaurant or theatre, act the lady. Later you can go wild, sure, but even then half the time they're telling you their troubles. Business mainly, or how their wives refuse them sex first thing in the morning. We're communicators, basically. A lot of the Russkis and that hardly speak English.'

'This is really great stuff. Look, they'll be closing the doors any minute now. I gotta rush. Can I come do a proper interview with you some time?'

Chrissie'd looked him up and down again. 'Interview or visit?'

'Interview.'

'£300 an hour.'

'I got to level with you. We don't usually pay for interviews less it's a big Hollywood star.'

'Hollywood stars!' And Chrissie's pretty mouth had twisted in a sneer. 'I could tell you things about some of them'd make your hair stand on end. Not just your hair, heh heh... Tell you what, I'll throw in an OWO.'

'OWO?'

She'd raised her eyebrows at his ignorance. 'Oral With Out.'

'I can't accept. Sorry.'

'It's me that's sorry. Officially you're paying for my time and company only. Whatever we get up to in addition is incidental.'

'Can we keep it to that? I mean time and... the other thing. Company.'

'It's your call.'

'I guess it's not like we can quote you by name, give you a credit. See here, I'll have to pass on the OWO thing. But your Hollywood reminiscences are included in the £300, right?'

'An hour. Mine would stretch to the best part of a day.'

'All the better. Say £800 for a morning's worth of top-grade dirt on – what? – four big names minimum?'

'£900 for a three-hour morning, £1,100 for a four-. Can't go lower."

'The dirt, it's the best?'

'Tip-top. The names too. The fee does include a drink and assisted shower plus rub-down.'

'I'll pass on the booze. The rub-down too. How 'bout a round grand for three hours thirty?'

'Hun, you got yourself a deal.'

*

'...Black Rod ...mmm ...a minor official', said the newsman, a British one. 'Heritage isn't really my subject, though I did do a few freelance shifts on the "Sceptred Isle" column in the *Date* some years ago. Talk to Rich Freeman. He edits it.'

Men in robes entered, walking in procession. Behind them came a still more imposing figure, one from the plushest realms of childhood fantasy: a coroneted personage in bottle green velvet jerkin and knee breeches, before whom a flunky paced, head bowed, bearing in his arms a sword upon a cushion. The nobleman sported a neatly trimmed late Tudor-era beard. Jeff thought of the Sir Walter Raleigh in his kids' book about Virginia, the Old Dominion, that he'd pored over as a ten-year old.

'That's Crowthorne, the Lord Great Constable', the British newspaperman whispered to Jeff. His lapel badge said Piers Boadiam. 'It's one of the old ceremonial positions, revived recently. Crowy had some tame antiquaries look up the precedents, and more or less forced the authorities to do the reviving, though the King's being besotted with tradition certainly helped. Apparently when the realm is under threat of "contumely and noxious foes from without", as on a counsel's opinion of the Prevention of Terrorism Act that Crowthorne commissioned it's now accepted as being, the role of "Sovereign's Puissant Champion" vests in the junior hereditary nobleman summoned to the House of Lords. And Crowthorne's it, having got in at a by-election a few months ago, even though he's a hereditary, and pretty old too. I suppose it made sense back in the Middle Ages, the last chap to join in those times being the youngest, fittest fighting man. Today it's plain ridiculous. Can you see Crowthorne bashing a suicide bomber over the bonce with a mace?'

Jeff keyed away industriously.

53

'I know we British look silly, all dressed up', said Piers, peering over his shoulder, 'but so do the parades you go in for back home?'

'That's OK, Piers. Our readers like their England all black-and-white thatch cottages, twin-deck red buses and bike-bound bobbies. There's no mileage in covering your space program.' *Ha, got him there.*

Piers ignored this. 'Tell you one thing's a bit odd', he said. Thoughtfully, as if the notion had only just occurred to him. Jeff felt mild shame at having ribbed him. 'The King's Speech', said Piers. They'd been given a handout listing the principal features. 'The swingeing restrictions on tax haven-based ownership of British media companies they've hinted about the past few weeks aren't mentioned. More and more of this pushing us into getting healthy, yes. Plenty of it. Maybe even tax breaks to encourage joining a health club in the Chancellor's autumn statement. But the absence of any major move against the big off-shore media boys looks a bit like the Government's bottled it. Maybe someone's called in some favours. Ben Lee's got a lot of clout and he's one of Victor Deller's ex-editors. They say he's still close to his old boss...'

Jeff was too busy composing his piece to answer. 'What kind of time does this all take?' he asked Piers presently.

'Till 4 p.m. usually. They organise it perfectly. It won't run on.'

At that moment Big Ben started its majestic chime. Then a sound of shouting. That couldn't be part of the State Opening, could it? The noise was coming from over toward the Thames River side of the building. Piers looked up. He turned to a third reporter, a girl with the name Sammi Psalt on her lapel badge. Jeff had noticed her on the way in. Not bad. But mentally undressing someone in the same line of business struck him as unprofessional.

Physically doing so was another matter. Though he'd been starved of nookie ever since leaving New York, the *Hence* Deputy News Editor there, a redhead with a weakness for dangling participles, had usually attended to his needs. Before that there'd been the Circulation Manager, till she left to join a Satanic cult in New Mexico.

Piers tapped him on the shoulder. 'They've just sighted a dead body in the Thames. A few feet away from the Terrace. They're winching it in now.'

'Wow. Is that usual?'

'No. Least of all during a State Opening.' Piers sat down at his lap top and ladled in a column's worth of clichés. He looked up, pausing, searching for the right bromide. He caught sight of Jeff and said 'This could be the biggest "Corpse Crashes Royal Ritual" story since the votes-for-women activist threw herself under the winning horse on Derby Day in front of the royal box.'

'I must have missed that.'

'You did. It was in 1913.'

TWELVE

The *Date*, pet title in Deller's kennel, supported the government's health policy. It reported developments there soberly:

'...New health facilities for MPs and peers have been agreed with the presiding officers of the Commons and Lords. The package follows tough bargaining involving members of all three leading parties. It aims not just to accommodate MPs and peers when they need a detox, but to get them to look after their bodies before detoxes become necessary...'

The *Era*, David Macnamara's ewe lamb, and much more lucrative, confined the story to five lines in its "Lobby Fodder" parliamentary gossip column.

*

Victor Deller's offer to the Party of major funding eventually proved acceptable. It had taken some digesting from a technical point of view, being an exquisitely complex financial instrument, way in advance even of such razor-sharp City tools as triggered caps or structured collars.

Two things clinched matters. One, Deller's self-restraint in putting off what was virtually an invoice for a peerage, the terms being here more like 750 days than the 30 usual in commercial transactions. Two, the multiple-arms' lengths at which he would provide funds.

They were to be channelled through Albion Sterling Services, an obscure unincorporated association 'thought to be related', as an *Era* article put it, to Deller. The *Era* was no friend of Deller's. So if that was the worst anyone could say, there was little to worry about. It helped that several of the ColLaboratives' legal advisers gave as their opinion that the Elections and Referendums Act of 2000, the instrument supposedly cracking down on dodgy donations, was so badly drafted as to be unenforceable.

The PM put it succinctly in the latest of her Scrabble bouts with Barnes. 'BEGGARS', then in the next round 'CANT BE' and in the third, 'CHUSERS'. It was the nearest she came to admitting knowledge of the arrangement.

The PM and Barnes were at Chequers again, sole occupants of its Smoking Room. The weather had turned late autumnal some weeks ago, a few days before Hallowe'en, and board games al fresco were on hold till spring. This had not stopped the PM's husband going off to spend the day knocking his Titleist Pro VI round Huntercombe.

On the other side of the room a beech-wood fire hissed away, wafting into the room acrid puffs which made the eyes smart. The logs, too young for proper combustion., occasionally emitted a splutter or pop. One *fortissimo* pop made Barnes jump. Outside, the earlier morning's full-bellied low cloud, pierced by a pallid sun around elevenses, had given way to a colder, super-fine drizzle from a sky uniformly grey.

Gary and Jules conducted their security patrol along the Baldwin Terrace immediately under the Smoking Room's windows. The terrace had recently been so christened to commemorate the Chequers Estate's third prime ministerial occupant, thereby shoring up the morale of the ColLaborative Party's elderly sympathisers, a group guilty of poor turnout at the last election.

'You for or against this war she's gone and landed us in?' said Jules. 'Fair perishing for November', he added, rubbing his free gloved hand against the other, which steadied his Heckler & Koch.

'It's the damp gets me.' Gary shivered. Then, 'It's the cost-benefit of war you want to think of. No good taking moral stands all over the place the way the Societists have.'

The Societists formed His Majesty's Opposition.

'So where are you on that then? The cost-benefit whatsit?'

'Higher taxes in the offing. Sure as eggs is eggs.'

'Ouch.'

'Can't fight a war and not get hurt. Well, can you?'

'Suppose not.'

'But on the plus side, it provides the Forces with valuable experience in active combat conditions. Also it prevents the cheese-parers in government making over-deep defence cuts, which'd hamper us in any next war. That's what those Societist peace-mongers can't see.'

'Funny to think of a woman going to war at all.'

'Think so? Aggressive creatures, women. Ever accidentally swipe a mum's toddler with your trolley in a Tesco? Never hear the end of it.'

'I believe you.'

It was now an hour since lunch. Indoors the two Scrabble-players continued trading thoughts. The beech logs gave out a rip-snorter belch and a dense cloud. The PM coughed then exploded. 'Can nothing be done about that appalling fire?' She gestured in the direction of the chimney piece.

'Well we are in the Smoking Room.' It went down badly. The PM stared at Barnes with as stony a set of the eyes as he'd met outside the BM's recent Hittite Exhibition. 'Sorry.'

'Actually', she said, smiling slightly, 'it has been re-designated the No Smoking Room. Not my decision. The Chequers Bequest trustees. They said they could not in all conscience keep the old name, given that our drive for good health, including restrictions on the vile weed, is so central to this Government's vision. Smoking Room has long been a misnomer anyway. Churchill puffed away all over the house.'

Barnes gestured in the direction of the chimney piece. 'Shall I get someone to have a look at it?'

'The fire? Once I could have got our Energy Secretary to handle it. Perhaps I shouldn't have abolished the post after all.'

'Ha ha.'

The PM did not share his mirth. Even her smile was mechanical. 'Tell me about the winning tender to manage the Parliamentary gym and health facilities', she said. 'It was pretty much a walk-over, I gather.'

'Not originally', Barnes said. 'Several people pitched. But when the scale of the DelFitCo plans was revealed, the competitors dropped out.'

'And on just how big a scale were the successful bidders' proposals?'

'The DelFitCo proposals…'

'Del-Fi-i-t-Co-o. Yes.' The PM enunciated the word slowly, as if reluctant to say it.

'The DelFitCo proposals envisaged not just nuts and bolts stuff such as weights and pulleys and cycling machines but a posse of personal trainers. Incredible figures some of them, I must say. Especially the females. *Baywatch* standard. Then there are the swimming pool, sauna room, steam baths, aromatherapy and spa facilities.'

'And – DelFitCo, is it? – could do all that within reasonable cost limits?'

'Apparently. They have their own direct labour force. Construction's handled by one of the group's subsidiaries. DelBuild.'

'Subsidiary? There must be no sweetheart deals in this project. It is a showcase for our good health crusade.'

'The Inclusive Health Foundation gave a grant to push the project through. Arm's length.'

'The think tank people?'

'Sort of. They've done valuable research on how different ethnic groups are prone to different complaints. Afro-Caribbeans and sickle-cell anaemia, for instance. Then they fashioned a model for allocation of healthcare resources in a multicultural society, …future shifts in the national demographic…'

'Specialist stuff.'

'Yes.'

The PM dropped the subject. At the top you had to keep to the broad picture, not get lured down specialist side-turnings.

*

'…And that last five makes me a hundred and sixty-seven', said the PM half an hour later, totting up the score. 'What are you?

'A hundred and fify-four… Getting back to DelFitCo…'

'Good, good', said the PM. 'We'll leave it there then. There's a peace initiative I've got to go and launch. Just where would be telling. But I can say that it's not a million miles away from the Holy Land.'

She got up from the table and touched her hair to check it was in place. She'd abandoned her pony-tail (immature, the image-manipulators deemed it) for a perm.

'Old-fashioned expression, Holy Land', she said. 'Inaccurate too. An unholy mess.'

59

THIRTEEN

Jeff let himself into Tod's apartment. He carried a big plastic bag of groceries. It got in the way of the house keys. His head still echoed with the shouts announcing a corpse in the Thames just off of the Palace of Westminster Terrace. A female one, it had turned out. He'd been trying to think up the best comparison to convey the sense of shock to readers back home. Something impactful to Manhattanites... A parallel with the Boitumelo McCallum case might do.

There were still two weeks before his rent agreement expired. This place wasn't bad. One bedroom with living room comprising a dining area, reasonably tastefully furnished. He put the groceries on a side table and flicked the master switch for the living room table lamps.

Three men stood there. Still. Absolutely still. Like figures frozen in a flash of strobe light.

He'd caught them on a fishing expedition. Drawers had been taken out the bureau and their contents neatly piled on the floor. Not the usual chaos of a break-in. The tidiness was creepy.

But what he really hated was the way they all wore masks. Animal masks. One a fox. It swung a small bag. A second guy looked like some member of the polecat family. Which? The third was one of those dogs with a serious expression. A bloodhound. Or dachshund...

'You're late for Hallowe'en. That was almost two weeks back.' Jeff spoke a lot easier than he felt. He stayed just outside the doorway to the living room. If they rushed him, they'd jostle each other to make it through the narrow gap.

'Forget treat.' It was the fox spoke, his voice indistinct behind the mask. 'Not for you, boy. Just tricks.'

'No multiple-choice questions huh?' Jeff tried to keep it light. He edged ever so slightly backwards.

'Is this the only desk?' said the fox, pointing at it.

'Sure.' They hadn't found what they were looking for then. 'Listen', said Jeff, 'I figure you guys have the wrong apartment.' Nerves made him over-jokey. 'The duchess and her jewels are next floor up.' He stealthily put out his hand behind him to feel for the front door catch. 'Why don't y'all go on home? We'll forget about it.

Me, I'll keep my mouth shut.' He could almost feel the front door catch now. 'I'm a newsman. We don't reveal our sources.'

The dog cocked a leg at him and leapt forward to kick box him in the groin. Jeff jumped sideways and the intruder's foot hit the door. Jeff scooped up a pile of junk mail and flung it at the polecat. He had to get out the front door before they smothered him. The polecat advanced but the couch got in the way. The fox hung back. Why?

Jeff chopped hard at the dog's extended right leg with his free hand and got in a good tough blow. The dog yelped. Jeff fumbled for his keys. He'd automatically locked the front door on coming in the apartment. He couldn't find the keys, stupid fuckers. In concentrating on the keys he trod on Tucky's milk saucer and sent a white wave across the parquet. Tucky bounced out from under the couch and started lapping at it.

The fox pulled a gun.

He held it steady but low, aiming through the doorway arch at Jeff's midriff. The other two animals took up positions well to Jeff's sides, one left the other right, giving the fox a clear aim. Jeff stood still, hands by his side. Should he raise them? Nobody'd said to.

The light in the hallway shone dim. The fox took out a silencer and screwed it on the barrel. Jeff started to sweat. Cold droplets. Clammy.

The fox spoke to his accomplices. 'Leave us, will you, gents? Got some unfinished business with this cocksucker.'

The polecat and dog filed past Jeff. The dog reached into the groceries bag and helped himself to a grape. They stopped behind Jeff and frisked him, keeping him in the fox's line of fire.

Even so they stood way too close, well inside his personal space. They found his keys in his left coat pocket. Why the fuck hadn't he recalled putting them there 'stead of fumbling in his right? The dog opened the front door and closed it gently behind as he and polecat exited, tossing the keys on the floor, well out of Jeff's reach.

'Over here cocksucker.' The crazy thing was, the tone was affable. Some acoustic oddity with the mask? Jeff edged forward, none too keen.

'Down, boy. *Down* I said.' The fox swung the gun up towards Jeff's face and down again. Jeff knelt.

'That's it. Stay-y-y. Good boy.' The gun was pointing straight at his head. Should he try a football tackle? The guy was close enough.

'Steady boy, steady.' The fox eased the tip of the barrel into Jeff's left ear. 'What we're going to try now is an obedience school class.'

Jeff didn't say anything.

'Your cat got your tongue?' The fox eased the barrel very slightly away from Jeff's ear. His voice rose in fury. *'Answer me!'*

'OK.' Jeff's mouth felt as dry as the pulp writers always said it did.

'The old boozer lived here before, what was he called?'

'Boozer? Here? You mean Tod?'

'Tod? That's a fucking fox. You taking the piss?'

'He was named Todmorden. Tod for short. Tod C. Snaith.'

'So it's just a great big coincidence, this Tod? I don't go for coincidences. Say your prayers, cocksucker.'

Jeff lost his cool. 'Coincidences happen, for God's sake. Like I came home when you guys were here.'

'Yeah, maybe. You're with the same American paper he was, this Tod man, right? Did he send any story?'

'What story?'

'Hey, pretty boy, I ask the questions. You answer them.'

Jeff tried to keep his voice steady and neutral without at the same time seeming unhelpful. 'I do not know what story of Tod's you mean. He filed whole heaps.'

'What are his last few?'

'Stuff. Whatever's news. It was before they assigned me here. I never even visited over in England before. Our website has every back number.'

'Nothing about the British vice scene?'

'Vice?'

'Don't play stupid. Commercial sex.'

'Oh, vice. I don't know.'

'Did he file any vice story?'

'Not to my knowledge.'

'Your fucking knowledge! How good's that?'

Jeff was nettled, his professionalism challenged. 'Well I read through Tod's articles before I left. I'd likely recall a piece on British vice. There weren't any.'

'There'd better not be.'

The fox sounded both annoyed and perplexed. Jeff kept schtum.

There was a short silence. Jeff's heart beats slowed slightly. Tucky ran in from the hallway and made a little rush at the fox's shoes, swiping at his laces with one paw. The fox stooped down and with a swing of his bag batted Tucky into the far corner of the room, like an ice hockey forward sinking a puck in the defenders' net. Jeff tried looking round to see how she was but the fox hooked the gun muzzle in his ear again.

The fox straightened up and changed his tone. 'Now what you're going to do is eat meat. Nicely now. Or I'll blow your fucking head off. And then you won't have any left to give.'

Oh God.

'Right?'

'Right.'

'Right what?'

'Right, uh, sir.'

'I'm not your master, you dumb Fido.'

'Right ...uh...'

'"Right, Foxy Gentleman". Say it. "Foxy Gentleman".'

'Right, uh, Foxy...Gentleman.' It sounded sorta cute. Jeff suppressed a giggle.

'Good boy.'

The fox positioned himself. Meanwhile he talked. Informatively. Like a British uncle explaining the rules of cricket to a favourite transatlantic nephew. 'See, I angle the gun so if I fire, I blow the *back* of your noggin off. Splat! Abattoir time all over your wallpaper. That would so wreck the pattern. Osborne & Little by the look of it.'

Jeff didn't answer. He closed his eyes and, yes, thought of home. He hoped to sweet Jesus he wouldn't get his head blown away afterward anyway...

*

The fox said 'You let go before you were told to. Bad boy.'

He'd taken the gun away from Jeff's ear and now aimed it straight at his face.

'No dins for you tonight. Bar what you had just now.' And he turned the gun on Jeff's Tesco bag. Blew it apart. Soundlessly. The silencer made it look like the bag exploded, fermented, a week-old garbage sack in tropic city heat. Tucky poked her head out from under the couch, advanced a pace or two toward the scattered groceries. Then, thinking better of it, she scuttled back under the couch again.

The fox lowered the gun a fraction, not squinting down the sights any more.

'This time I won't put you down, *provided you keep your fucking mouth shut.*'

The fox straightened his clothing. Jeff wanted to die. At least Tucky wasn't hurt.

And then the fox went, scooping up as he did so the flattened bullet where it had bounced off a can of Diet Coke, punctured a box of water softener for the washing machine and split a squash in two before coming to rest, glistening, on the floor by the umbrella stand.

Jeff stumbled to the bath room and spat and spat and spat again till he was all out of saliva. He gargled with Listerine a full ten minutes. He took three sleeping pills. It had to be three, one more than the maximum safe dose, or he'd lie awake till all hours, going over the scene, over and over. Right now he didn't care if he did OD. He wanted to cry himself to sleep, like he'd done out of homesickness his first summer camp. The tears couldn't come.

The pills would kick in full in about quarter of an hour. Meanwhile he stepped in the shower. He wanted to cleanse himself. All over, and soon as possible.

Never before had he so resented the shower's pathetic near-trickle. Stevens was spot on. Third World country, England, couldn't even fix its plumbing. Outdoors, no problem. Outdoors, one big shower.

He lashed out in frustration at the shower rose. His hand caught it a glancing blow which hurt like hell. The rose itself flew off. A small polythene-wrapped packet dropped to the floor. Jeff killed the shower and bent to pick it up, holding off with his free hand Tucky, who'd followed him into the bathroom and now made sideways scooping motions with both paws, a sure sign she was intrigued.

What was in the packet? Jeff tore at it. A filter? Nope, nothing that solid. He tore some more. Spare screws? He got it part-open. Nope to that too. It looked like folded paper inside. His journalistic instincts aroused, Jeff carefully removed the rest of the polythene and unfolded the paper. It was all handwritten notes. Tod's? He sped read down the page.

Well, well, well. Looked like he might have him a story. Maybe even pull off a scoop, and here in dusty old England. He lifted his head, scenting a Greeley. He turned back to the shower head. He tried the tap. A perfect torrent rained down. Next he re-affixed the rose, screwing it on tight. He tried the tap again. He found he could now blend the cold and hot like a coffee maestro an espresso machine.

Great! He'd gotten a perfect needle-sharp shower pressure, with finger-tip-response hot/cold command to boot. England, even its plumbing, wasn't so bad after all. Cradling Tucky in one arm he stumbled off to bed.

FOURTEEN

The ColLaborative Chief Whip, Nicholas Kerr-Tait, prided himself on being every bit as security conscious as the Prime Minister over not putting things in writing. He was a veteran of the whips' office. His whole career had involved the avoidance of textual communications.

It was the children's board game way she went about her business dealings that made him uncomfortable. He found the Scrabble business gimmicky. Worse, it detracted from her dignity as PM.

Ah well, she was a politician, not a political manager like him. There was a world of difference. Politicians in a modern democracy were as much showmen, playing to the gallery, as practitioners of statecraft. Thomas Cromwell, Richelieu, Metternich were Kerr-Tait's heroes. He'd never asked who the PM's were, but common sense suggested a flashier galaxy: Lloyd George, Churchill, even Chazza Lynton.

Ben Lee was less finicky and saw things less complacently. Kerr-Tait's appointment in the first place was a reward by the PM for helping oust her predecessor. If the man couldn't pluck up the courage to broach to the PM the subject that was on their minds, he, Ben Lee, would. Sad the way Nick had been a perfectly competent underling but wasn't up to the top job. That's how it went with a lot of people. Over-promoted. Meanwhile he, Lee, was under-promoted.

Lee chose his moment with care. The monthly security drill obliged anyone who happened to be at Chequers at the time to vacate their places of work and assemble deep underground. The catacomb they were to huddle in was a bomb-proof, biochemical warfare-proof – it was hoped even cat burglar-proof – shelter thirty feet below the old butler's pantry, repository as late as Chamberlain's day of what had been the mansion's sole telephone. With so many terrorist threats in the capital, the security services had pleaded successfully with the PM to spend more working time in the country.

The PM was already seated when Lee arrived in the main subterranean chamber. It took the form of a gallery with bunk beds and storage spaces let into the side walls. Today was a red alert day. One on which personnel simulated active security conditions by walking down the pitiless metal spiral stairs from ground level rather than taking the lift, thus saving the generator expenditure of precious electricity. Lee showed no sign of poor physical condition bar a pseudo-moustache of moisture.

The PM sat in a director's chair, her regular glass of the Midsummer brand of elderflower cordial at her elbow as she worked her way through a ministerial box. Other boxes were stacked to her side. Aides formed a loose barrier between her and junior staff. She too showed little evidence of having braved the stairs. Perhaps her complexion, a good one, had just the slightest extra glow to it.

William Matheson had gone to spend the day knocking his Callaway HX Tour round the Oxfordshire, near Thame.

Lee pushed through the bevy of aides and grabbed then unfolded a spare director's chair, placing it by the table the PM was working at. A CPO quickly intervened, pulling the chair away from him and starting to fold it up.

'That's all right, Gary' the PM said, looking up from her boxes. 'He's with me.' Gary looked grim but desisted. Lee said to him 'You work with Jules Miller, don't you?'

'Yes sir.'

'Thought so. Do give him my regards.'

'That I will, sir.'

The PM said, 'Good morning, Ben. You made it down the stairs in excellent time. More than our Lord Privy Seal's managed to do. Sam's left knee has given way.

Lee said. 'We must assume he'd be a twitching anthrax case by now if this were a real bio-chemical attack.'

'You put it luridly. But yes.'

'Which all goes to show how vital it is to have an entire government, from Cabinet ministers down, in the pink of physical condition.'

'Of course. I've stressed our good health message ever since I took charge.'

You're getting just the least bit boastful, my girl, thought Lee. 'Very ably you've done it too, Prime Minister', he said.

The PM suddenly looked tired. 'Do you think it's really taken hold?' Her voice regressed to dewy-eyed young girl.

Lee launched his set-piece summing up: 'Attendance at the Parliamentary health club complex is at an all time high. Late night sittings are down. You'll recall that we had to reintroduce them as an ad hoc measure under pressure of business—also flexible Parliaments, restoring the power of yourself as PM to dissolve. But even where late sittings have been necessary, the attendance in the Chamber is an all-time post-World War II record, suggesting Members have developed real stamina. I've had the figures checked and there's not a doubt of it. Further, we've had no serious illnesses our side. The Opposition's lost one backbencher to a road accident and another to a skiing fatality. The writs for the by-elections were moved at the end of last week. But you know that…'

*

'…And yet our majority stays tiny', the PM was saying, 'and the Whips' discipline is less easily maintained than ever.'

Lee moved closer. In the artificially lit subterranean setting he resembled some figure of Renaissance intrigue, an Iago about to drop septic insinuations into Othello's ear. 'Kerr-Tait may not have briefed you as to the full story.'

The PM looked up, startled, but when she spoke a few seconds later it was in measured tones. 'Nick? I'd be very, very surprised if he hadn't.'

'Could I fill in what *I* see as, um, the gaps? Then you'll know if he has or not.'

'How do you know what his story is? Oh never mind.' The PM carefully placed her documents inside the ministerial box by her knee. 'Fill away', she said, and snapped the box shut. 'Fill away.'

'Very well. The fact seems to be that the Whips' Office black book listing all the foibles, peccadillos, weaknesses and so on of Party members has not been as assiduously maintained as in the past.'

'I know about the black book. I was in the Whips' Office myself twenty years ago.' The PM's voice turned wistful. 'My first promotion.'

'Of course. You know, then, how vital it is to ensuring a good turn out in a cliff-hanger vote. Without the knowledge of which particular, ah, screw to turn on what vulnerability, let us call it, of which particular MP, we'd fall down on pushing through Government business.'

'I'm well aware of that. The Trafficking Bill's a case in point. In tatters. The Street Offences Acts, Amendment and Consolidation of, another. Withdrawn in its entirety. Our Clean Up Britain campaign risks getting bogged down.'

'The Whips' line is that our small majority is the problem. With respect, Prime Minister, it's more than that. Somehow they aren't managing to amass enough background intelligence about our people. Either your average backbencher has turned over a new leaf...'

'Which defies belief...'

'...Or he's canalising his vices in some new, hitherto unrecorded, way.'

The PM rested her chin in her hand and spoke thoughtfully. 'They don't seem to drink any less. As you know, I've long thought the way alcohol prices are kept artificially low in the bars in both Houses is a national disgrace. But I know better than to try and meddle with it.'

'No indeed, Prime Minister. That would be suicide.'

'Well what *are* the errant back benchers up to?'

'I could make it my business to find out.'

'I can see where this is leading. You want me to task you to a further extension of your little empire, don't you, Ben?'

Lee inwardly grinned, spotting the perfect psychological moment both to come clean, which would help sluice off the reputation he knew he had for deviousness, and move his friendship with the PM up a notch, towards intimacy. Not the sexual kind, perish the thought, but that emotional one in which supreme influence consists. 'Yes, Mary', he said. 'As a matter of fact, I do.'

The PM made no immediate response. Then, 'Tell me, Ben, what would you say if I brought Lyonel Crowthorne into the Government, probably as Lord Privy Seal since Sam's something of a lame duck?'

Stone the crows, thought Lee, but what he said was, 'An exciting choice. Bold too. Would he agree to serve?'

The PM ignored this, continuing instead to explain her motivation. 'He's been closely involved in this combined push by several of the religious groups to replace more of the Monday bank holidays with Friday ones', she said. 'It's not a bad idea in itself. Fridays would go down well with Muslims as it's their special day of the week anyway. And, since it leads up to the Sabbath, the Jewish community would probably quite like it. But the more traditionalist Christians could feel offended. The only current bank holiday at the end of the week is Good Friday. A special case. They won't readily accept any other Friday being granted parity. HM has rather hinted that he sympathises with them, though in most matters of that sort he's pretty ecumenical. I particularly want to keep HM on side just now. We're planning an initiative to do with one of the chief Commonwealth countries and he's useful in swinging the rest of the Commonwealth behind it. So you see we're in something of a fix. If we could get Crowthorne to sign up with our team a lot of the pro-Friday agitation would die down. By great good fortune he's recently dropped hints to the effect that he would not be averse to joining us. A few weeks ago he applied to take our whip.'

'What about that funny old heritage post he's carved out for himself? The Lord Great Constable nonsense. Doesn't it make him seem a lightweight? Promoting him to a proper government job could look like making a beefeater Chief Met Commissioner.'

'He's got great powers of showmanship. Also a very real following among the high-minded element in the country. And that's by no means as obsolete as the London-based media commentators seem to think.'

'Is that a hit at me, Prime Minister?'

'Not in your present role. But to get back to Crowthorne, I'd welcome your views on the pros and cons of having him aboard. If you could keep them to a single side of A4...'

'Will do.'

'As for your new role finding out what's made our back-benchers so... awkward, I'll have Felix draw up a formal minute and get it made official in next week's Party Management Committee meeting. No, not Felix. What am I thinking of? He's a civil servant. One of the advisers, rather... We must have hard information as to our people's voting dispositions which we can act on by next month or our revived Cross-Media Ownership, Restriction of, measure could come unstuck. As an old newspaper man I imagine you'd be the last person to want that.'

Lee straightened his back and spoke with bluff candour. 'Personally speaking, I keep an open mind about such things. But if it's HMG's policy, you can count on my fullest professional support.'

'Thank you. Now be a good fellow and see they call the All Clear a.s.a.p. There's this intervention I mentioned earlier. I'm scheduled to make it any moment now. I can't say more just at present, obviously. But I will hint it's somewhere over a rainbow nation.'

FIFTEEN

Angelo Devene and Micky Frost were waiting on the stairs leading down from Jeff's apartment. Frankie joined them, taking the last steps two at a time and pulling off his fox mask then stuffing it in his pocket.

He scowled. Their passiveness irked him. 'Stop lounging about like you owned the place', he said. 'You'll give the flats a bad name. Especially your mug, Devene, 'd frighten the horses in a knackers' yard. And put your masks away. Kid was right. Hallowe'en's over.'

'You fix him, Frankie?' said Micky on the way out. 'Fix the kid good, eh?'

Frankie didn't answer till they were in the car, then 'I fixed him, yeah. Fixed him so he won't squeal.'

The dime novel tough talk made Angelo want to gag. Especially the way Micky played up to Frankie, like a stage star's stooge.

Micky drove. He found London geography tricky enough even before satnavs mucked his movements up, so went a bit slow. Besides, the speeding fines the CCTV cameras landed you with these days were daylight robbery.

'You put him to sleep then?' said Angelo presently to Frankie. 'Like Mr Sanders said to.'

'He did not. And in London it's me says who gets what, Mister Devene. Including anyone in my squad steps out of line.'

'Well pardon me for asking, Your Maj.'

Frankie twisted round in the front passenger seat and grabbed Angelo's shirt top, pulling his face close to his own. 'Shut it, OK?'

Angelo broke loose. 'Because if you didn't', he said, 'And he starts poking around...'

'He won't. I stopped his mouth good and proper. Kid knows nothing to squeal about anyway. He's an all-American college boy playing hard-nosed foreign reporter. Naïve as they come.'

Angelo knew perfectly well that Frankie had let the kid be, and why. While Micky'd gone on ahead down the stairs he'd hung back, pleading an undone trainer lace. He'd listened at the front door during Frankie's "chat" with the kid, gently levering open the letter box flap to boost volume.

Frankie was gone on the kid. He'd been ready enough to put the older bloke, the kid's predecessor, to sleep, hadn't he? – for that's what Angelo now saw Area Manager must have meant that time back at the meat plant in Hereford when he'd mentioned the old cur.

While frisking the kid earlier, Angelo had also surreptitiously attached with blu stick a little bug, the sort look like ball-point pens, on the underside of the hallway table supporting the land-line phone. If the kid's flat needed visiting in the first place, stood to reason what went on inside it would need checking regular. All Angelo had to do was activate the fake ball-point with a call from his mobile. He wouldn't let Frankie in on what he heard.

Angelo wondered, not for the first time, how close Frankie and Mr Sanders were. And if, supposing they had their differences, he couldn't stir up a nice bit of bad blood between them. Frankie was getting very much on his wick.

'...Meanwhile', Frankie said, 'You two are spear-heading the recruitment drive for Bristol.'

'Bristol?' said Angelo. 'Thought the job Area Manager told us was London.'

'Bristol fuck meat is still our bread and butter. London luxury goods, all lace and ooh la la, are *filet mignon*, chef's special. Now you two are working for me, finished imports for Bristol gone and got cancelled. So we access raw materials inside Britain. Here's 12K for you, Frosticle, and 12 for you, Devene.' He dealt Micky and Angelo the notes, continuing to stress Micky's favoured status by adding the "-icle". 'Frosticle, you go out Heathrow way tomorrow. I'll text you the full address first thing the morning. Devene, ditto. With you it's the Gatwick area. Once you're there, follow the bloke on the spot, no questions. He'll take you to where it's at. Keep your eye on the various goods, decide which is right for us, close the deal, head home with the goods in tow. No socialising with sales staff or other customers.'

'What are the specs then, boss?' Micky had took to brown-nosing like he'd been born to it, Angelo noticed.

'Same as Robbie – Area Manager – said. Brunettes, red heads, the Latina look, all fine. Go easy on blondes. Bad news for now. Stick to Caucasians – that's whiteys to you, Frost. Asians meaning yer Paki are specialist taste's not worth the bother. Asians meaning yer slitty eyes we can get cheaper direct through Korea, Thailand, the Philippines...'

'...Class is not the number one criteria on this occasion', Frankie said. 'Bristol we cater chavs. Always will. Watch your total spend. Overshoot the budget, the difference comes out your personal pockets. Four K a head tops, 'less she's a real joy-stick stiffener. Watch for rings. Albs are worse 'n pikeys. Any suspicous signs, pull out of that round. Early and late lots'll be dogs. Go for the middles.'

Angelo and Micky started counting their notes.

'Sorry it has to be tens and twenties, gents', said Frankie, 'but a whole heap of places don't take fifties. Too many duds.'

'Including a very large sum I was paid to turn a blind eye when I was still on the force', said Angelo, looking up and growing angrier with each second of revisited memory. 'I personally would favour amputating forgers' hands right off. With a snaggle tooth hacksaw, the rustier the better so they catch lockjaw. Those Middle East countries got the right idea.'

'But lawks a mercy, Massa D'vene, what can lil' ol' us do?' said Frankie, winking at Micky, then, reverting to his normal voice: 'This country the bleeding heart brigade's in charge. A slap on the wrist's all they get.'

Too right, thought Angelo. He was beginning to see a way he might shaft Frankie. If there was anything in the kid's flat he'd soon get to know about it, thanks to buggy wuggy. Cook up proof the kid knew something, use it to convince Area Manager Frankie was slacking, get him sacked.

Micky finished his counting first. He folded the bank notes and tucked them away in his jeans hip pocket, gently guiding the car steering wheel with his chin. 'Olfat – sorry, Dee Dee, I mean Melanie – shapin' up nice, Frankie?' he said.

'Melusine. Mel for short. Short is also what she's gone and fell. Pulled only a grand and a half last ten days. She don't score at least three a week by Christmas, ship her back West. Not Bristol. Bournemouth area. The Sandbanks set are into gang bangs big time, pay plenty for exotic talent like her spice 'em up. Plus the town gets a load of stag night business.'

They dropped Frankie by his cream Cayman S. It was too pretty to take on a job. 'Couldn't even use it as a getaway', said Angelo in disgust as he and Micky drove off. Then suddenly, 'Pull over. I want to get a paper. Check my fancy in the 2.45 at Redcar.'

'Get me some toffees will you? Choc-coated.'

73

'That's the third lot you've had in five days. You expecting or what?'

'It's this terrible sweet tooth I get ever since I cut smokes. Worth it though, if it stops you dyin'.'

Micky kept the motor idling. Angelo bought his evening paper and a packet of Rolos. While waiting for the traffic to clear, he glanced down at the paper. A minute later Micky saw him start, drop the sweets and sprint across to their car, barely missed by a petrol tanker. He wrenched open the door.

'You seen the news?'

'No. Your horse win? What about my toffees?'

'Stuff your toffees. They gone and found a dead woman in the Thames.'

'!'

Angelo looked at Micky closely – very closely. His tone when he spoke dripped sarcasm. 'Which bit of the Thames, you ask. Wapping? No. Henley? Give over. No, right smack bang between the Houses of Poxy Parliament and MI Fucking Five.'

'What you starin' at me for? Wasn't me done her in.'

'Is that a threat?'

'Course not. Look, heaps of families dump their dead relates in the River. Cost of a decent Cribb hearse's through the roof now'days. Pakis got to anyway. It's their Hindu religion. I see a piece on it in *National Geographic* down the dentist.'

'Michael. Look hard at me, Michael. Why am I staring at you?'

Micky squirmed. 'Well what?'

'I distinctly recall telling you, get rid of the dark bint dog meat reject on your own seeing I'm too busy, and you ask me where, and I say take a running jump off Vauxhall Bridge, which is where we happen to be crossing to south the River at the time. And I known you long enough to reckon you're that boneheaded you take me literally.'

Micky slumped down behind the steering wheel. 'OK, OK. So I did dump her in the Thames.' He jerked upright. 'I weighed her down good an' heavy. Plenty metal on her, make sure she'd sink. This one they gone and found, it can't be her.'

Angelo exploded. 'So that's where my spanner's gone! I should of guessed. Hunted high and low all last Saturday. I near missed Match of the Day. Thought I might have left it that garage we changed the spare wheel.'

'I'll get you another, I swear. Point is, I shoved it well down her front, tied her shirt thing round, plus I wedged it in her tits; had got all stiff by then, gripped nice 'n tight.'

'And it slipped out, didn't it? As heavy objects will do, specially in choppy water.'

Micky got whiny. 'How was I to know there'd be a big tide and fierce gales the same time?'

'Because it's autumn, that's why.'

A short silence, Micky's way of conceding a point. Then: 'Will they recognise her?'

'No, that's one good thing. She don't even exist. No papers, no nothing.'

'So why the fuss?'

'Cops don't like dead bodies. They got to get out from behind their desks piled with directives on sensitive policing, onto their size 14 feet, do some actual poking around. A dead body smack bang next to Parliament makes for extra red faces, top priority dig. Those MPs won't let loose till the cops come up with someone they can nail it on. And in case you forgot, MPs are our target consumers.'

'So the MPs, specially the ones banging our cuts of meat, might prefer your ex-workmates to forget this one, mightn' they?'

Micky'd made an unexpectedly valid point. Angelo mulled it over. 'I suppose they just might.' And a few seconds later: 'One good thing, Frankie and the other high-ups don't know she ever existed.'

'You might have saved me my toffees.'

'Your bleeding toffees! I'll get you some more the next Pak shop.'

SIXTEEN

Jeff kept schtum over his gun-point intimacy with the Fox. It was too humiliating. And sort of so weird it might even raise a smile with other people.

As for those notes in the shower head, they were so damn cryptic. The way notes often were long after you'd jotted them down. Were they by Tod?

Jeff had next afternoon faxed copies to Beth Snaith over in Dutchess County, NY. They *looked* like Tod's hand, she'd emailed back, but she couldn't say what they meant. Jeff pored over them: names, but crossed through; query marks; arrows pointing from several names to one big word: 'Byr.o'.

The next day he grabbed a strong coffee and rang StrepMag. First he asked for Stevens.

'Hi, Cal. How's Cockneytown? Met with the Queen of England yet?'

'Sir, this one's plain "Princess".'

'How 'bout that! Clean slipped my mind. She dig being demoted?'

'Well, sir, put it this way, how would any of our Presidents' wives feel getting called the *Second* Lady?'

'Nice, Cal. Very nice... Get an interview with the Princess yet, so you can ask her direct?'

'No, sir, they don't do them, the British First Couple. But I emailed you a full description her furbelows and folderols the State Opening. Sir, there's something else. Tod ever file a vice story?'

'Not that I recall. Sounds a bit *noir* for our readers, the out-of-town ones anyhow, and they're a consumer segment we're presently really trying to crack.'

'Nothing like that?'

'Why would he? Experienced newsman like him, 'd've gotten a good feel which stories are fit to print. This a London, England, vice thing? What's in it for us, less government guys involved? Must be thirty years since they did that, couple middle-rank administration appointees caught in the sack with hookers. What made it news our end was both guys were lords. The start of Watergate, but struck me the British did scandal with more class, specially than Tricky Dicky.

New generation power elite in England seem to've lost that old blue-blood red-blooded attitude. Shame, news-wise. Bottom line, nothing doing.'

So Tod had kept any such findings to himself. Jeff asked to be transferred to Gavin Doresett.

'Calhoun. How's the United Kingdom? I hope you're covering more than just London.'

'Not yet. I think I may have a good story right here. My own apartment.'

'Well well.'

'Tod figured he was on to something. Trouble is, he went and died.'

'And that was pure coincidence?'

'Sure looks it. His Polish cleaner swears there was no blood on the sheets. She'd know. It's her washes them.'

'But Tod is supposed to have died of natural causes.'

'Check. And there's no evidence saying any different.'

'Oh dear.' Doresett's voice took on a pitying tone. 'Didn't you do *any* basic criminal investigation in journalism training?'

'Yeah. Some. What are you insinuating?'

'Have you eaten today?'

'Sir, it's mid-afternoon here in London.'

'Yes of course. Silly me. The time difference… Comes of having no one left to ring up in the old country. Alright, when did you have lunch?'

'Look, is this relevant?'

'Do answer me please, Calhoun.'

'OK. Two hours back, two 'n a half maybe. Moussaka. It's the least disappointing of the heat-'n-eat range at Mar…'

'Spare me the food and wine column copy. I don't give a damn *what* you had. Just that it was sufficiently long ago.'

'Well was it?'

'Provided what I tell you doesn't make you sick. Calhoun, when people die, even when they do it in bed, at peace with the world, their muscles relax and they ooze certain liquids. In brief, immaculate sheets are the very last things that should have encased Tod on his exit from this world.'

Jeff said, 'Maybe Karola – she's the cleaner – just bundled them in the washer without looking.'

'Perhaps. But if Tod was found in pristine sheets, it's likely that he died, or was induced to die, elsewhere, then brought home, presumably by the people who assisted at his death elsewhere, if they didn't actually cause it, in order for it to appear that he'd died at home and of natural causes.'

Jeff fell silent.

'Hello?' said Doresett.

Jeff said, 'I found some of Tod's notes. There are arrows, underlinings pointing every which way from, and toward, one word, "Byr.o", like that trade name for ballpoint only with a dot like someone's web site, plus some other maybe names it's hard to make out. Hey listen, why don't I fax you a copy the Xerox too?'

'Too? Who else has seen them?'

'Beth Snaith. It was her authenticated the stuff as Tod's. Notes turned up hid in the shower head. A real find. Plus now I've got a real shower back.'

'Don't show anyone else those notes. This is our story.'

The brazenness amazed Jeff. 'Sir', he said, 'excuse me, *my* story.'

'Calhoun, Tod appointed me his literary executor. Copyright in those notes lies with his estate and the notes themselves are *prima facie* his material estate.'

'What if they're notes for a story? That'd belong to StrepMag Inc.'

'Who's to say? All they've done so far is block a shower head.'

'Oh shit.'

'I understand your anxiety to make a splash in your profession. I'll happily settle for a by-line mention. If I'm associated with a big scoop, I merit a fat bonus. I'm retiring soon. My pension's based on final-year salary.'

SEVENTEEN

Angelo next morning had barely shaved when his phone rang.

'Devene?'

'Good morrow, good sir. Thought you were texting me the address…'

'Drop everything.'

'Gatwick's off?'

'On hold. But I want the money back from last night. Now. Case you blew it on your horse habit.'

This brought Angelo up with a jolt. It had to be Micky had told. Angelo smothered his annoyance. No sense letting Frankie know he'd drawn blood. 'Well OK', he said, all casual. 'What's up?'

'Tell you when we meet. Ten minutes. Usual rendezvous.'

'Shepherd's Bush? In rush hour traffic?'

'Take the tube.'

'The Bush station's closed. It was on the radio. Engineering works.'

'Get off the stop before. And run. Or you can explain to the cops how the babe the *Era* is calling the Millbank Mystery Miss was dead before she hit the water.'

This came as a very nasty shock. Angelo hesitated before answering. 'They definitely know that, do they?' He sounded calm, but as he lifted his free hand to check his chin for any stray bristles he longed to grab a cut-throat and lay about him all over Frankie's chops.

'They just might get to know it if you don't knock yourself into shape so you make daily roll call', said Frankie. 'People work for me clock in punctually.'

Micky's fucking spilled the beans about the dark bint too. Right, my son, you're next, after I done Frankie. You want accidents? I got 'em.

Angelo made it in thirty-two minutes, walking fast from the stop before the Bush, but not breaking into a run. He knew his limits. By the time he found a taxi he'd covered all but the last quarter mile. The rendezvous was only a caff, but Frankie liked it.

Frankie was there already, in his favourite seat by the window. He had a big cup of tea in front of him, weak, no milk, just a slice of lemon. A place like this, they must serve lemon instead of vinegar with the fish and chips for the lunch-time trade, thought Angelo. *Christ, even caffs are getting yuppified these days.*

'You're late', said Frankie.

'Not as late as Micky.'

'He's over there getting a bacon sarnie. So stop putting him down.'

Angelo looked towards the counter. He was, too. 'What's all this about?' he said.

Frankie turned his head and yelled at Micky. 'Frost, if you don't come here this instant…'

Micky walked carefully over towards them. His plate was piled high with a bacon sandwich, baked beans and sausages. 'Best greasy spoon south of the Westway', he said. 'Be a crime not to make the most of it.'

Frankie put his head close to theirs. 'Listen, you two. Dee Dee – fuck it, I'm doing it m'self; Mel – has scarpered.'

'How'd she do that?'

'You've got a bloody nerve asking how. It's you two supposed to be watching her.'

'How can we do that round the clock with you hauling us off to put the frighteners on a kid of a reporter? No notice, no explanation, no nothing.'

'It's called multi-tasking. Now find her.'

'Where'll we start?'

'How about sniffing round the block of flats you stuck her in? Ask the neighbours, the doorman, the newspaper delivery boy.'

'Newspaper?' Micky this morning was very literal-minded. 'Don' think that'll do much good. Mel's not much of a reader. Not English, anyway. I suppose she might of took a Persian paper.' He turned to Angelo. 'It was Persia she come from, wasn't it?'

Frankie lashed out at Micky but the formica table top pressed against his thorax and his fist hit air. For once Angelo sympathised. Micky's stupidity had got chronic. The cholesterol in all those bangers and beans.

'What'd we do with her when we find her?' he said.

'Depends where she's gone and who she's talked to.' Frankie turned to Micky. 'How good's her English?'

Micky swallowed his mouthful too quickly and gasped. 'You might at least let a bloke chew proper.' He took another mouthful.

Frankie grabbed his knife from him and held its blade up under his nose. The point prodded Micky's septum. 'Her English', said Frankie.

Micky parked half a banger in his cheek. He looked like a mumps-stricken chipmunk. 'Basic.' He spoke with his mouth still crammed. 'Knows her lines. "Can I have my present?" to punters. "Ooh you're so big". Hint they're studs, like all the girls are trained to.'

'She understand all she's saying?'

'Doubt it', said Angelo. 'Micky?'

'A bit.'

'Could she make herself clear to whoever she's with now?'

'The cops?'

'One thing we did knock into 'em was how they get sent home if the cops find 'em.'

'Frost?'

'Ange-o's right. She won't go to no cop.'

'What about one of those women's refuge places?' said Angelo suddenly.

'How'd she know where to look? Would you?'

'No. But one of her mates might.'

'Mates? She got mates?'

'Sometimes they get asked to bring along a friend. Lesbo act, or two girls doing the same punter.'

Frankie held up a well manicured palm. 'I've perused the *Kama Sutra* too, thank you. Kindly skip the details till after I sip my Earl Grey, *if* you don't mind.' He raised the cup to his lips and drank. 'She done much muff stuff? Who with?'

'None of our original lot. Mel's the only one was up to London standards.'

'She's not on a trip with some client?'

'If neither of you got the company's cut of the money off her up front makes no difference. You didn't, did you?...' They both shook their heads. '...Then she's still gone and levanted.'

'Pardon?'

'What's that you said?'

'Levanted, Frosticle. A true Brit scarpers. Continentals take what is known as French leave. A duster-head desert doll, like this one, levants.' And Frankie winked at Angelo, trying to get him to join in taking the micky out of Micky. Angelo turned away.

EIGHTEEN

Jeff started seeing Piers Boadiam for the odd drink. Sometimes up Piers's end of town, way out beyond Kensington Gardens. Other times near *Hence*'s rabbit hutch of a bureau, on the Fleet and Chancery intersection. This contained a desk Jeff still hadn't managed to lever open all the drawers of and a part-time British secretary with no ambitions to become full-time. Debbie, from Parson's Green, and likely to stick there.

Piers was hoping to get a job in New York. Jeff needed to know lots of new faces, fast. His contacts book (long-standing sources, pithy quote-merchants, purveyors of technical advice) was pitifully flimsy. And Edgar Godwin's number had been pronounced by a recorded message unobtainable.

Assaying celebs for newsworthiness was trickier than back home. London wasn't just a social, cultural and finance center, like New York. It was the capital, a seat of government. It housed a royal court, an international diplomatic corps and the remains of a homegrown nobility, plus Eurotrash and Eurotreasure. It took in social heavyweights, short-term fame froth, politicians, historic names and the moneyed.

'Who are the hostesses here?' Jeff asked Piers. They sat in the Penthouse Bar of the Beldon, 10 floors up. Piers's choice, the hotel was what passed for a high-rise in England. Good for pick ups, Piers had said.

'Hostesses?' said Piers. 'It's no clip joint, this place.' He was enjoying himself.

'I mean society hostesses. Belgravia, Knightsbridge, Chelsea.'

'Oh… those.' Piers's attention was roaming elsewhere.

'I don't seem to hear of any. Doesn't the In Crowd meet any place beside those Season shindigs, which their dress codes gotten me so discombobulated I can't recall it's an ascot you wear to the Derby or a derby to Ascot…'

'Derby Barbie not Derby Herbie.'

'The hat too, well as the race?'

'We don't call the hat that. I suppose it *is* a bit confusing to a newcomer.' Piers' attention settled on the bar area. 'Hostesses', he said, affecting to think. 'We don't have them any more. London's too cramped.'

Piers stabbed at an ice cube in his Cate Kocktail, a heftily priced brew of vodka, grenadine, crushed paw paw and Roederer Kristal. His attention focussed on the left end of the bar. 'How about asking that knockers foursome to join us?', he said. 'The ones straining the seams of their black satiny dresses. The faces up top'd love to get their lips round a long cool pick-me-up.'

Jeff was less sure. The two girls in question were more the type'd sink their teeth into you, bleed you white. But they were lookers alright.

'Wait', he said, putting out a hand to restrain Piers. 'I got to get this clear. You saying women don't influence politics? Hell, it's only a year since you guys got your second woman prime minister.'

Piers drained his glass and crunched the ice. 'Entertaining has its own rules. You'll see what I mean where I'm taking you a week tomorrow.'

Jeff looked up. 'Where's that?'

'"Thank you, Piers, for sponsoring my social debut".'

' "Social debut"? No shit.'

'I'll take that as thanks. Laura Deller's.'

'Kin to the newspaper guy?'

'Wifey.' Piers had got more than a little drunk. He jabbed at Jeff with a spiral red plastic drinking straw. 'Not that Deller'll be there till later. If then. She gives the parties. Wonderful parties. Everyone goes to them.'

Jeff reverted to their original topic. 'You just said London had no salons.'

'There's more goes on at the Dellers' than hair-dressing. You can't hear yourself think. Some of Laura's talk would make your head spin. American too. You'll have lots in common.'

'Yeah, like I got lots in common with a Maine lobster-catcher, an Angeleno wetback, an Iowa hog farmer, and an Atlantic City dice hustler.'

Piers got up. He went over to the girls. Jeff stayed put, drawing on his own straw. He pushed aside the paw paw pulp.

Piers came back. 'They froze me off. I need a partner. C'm on. You take the tall one. I'll work on her friend.' He grabbed Jeff. As they approached the bar, Jeff saw the tall girl was Chrissie.

'Well hi there', he said.

She looked up. 'Hi.' She hadn't recognised him.

'Chrissie? It is Chrissie, isn't it?'

'It's April tonight. I think. Chrissie in non-working hours. Do I know you?'

'We met the other day. You protested the Parliament House opening.'

'Oh that. I'm not normally passionate about public affairs. You do look familiar. Sorry I didn't recognise you. I'm hopeless at men with clothes on. Look, I can't really talk right now. Outcall.'

'Outcall?'

'Away match. Makes it hard to socialise. But drop round some time. My number's on my website. Londonladies.com.' She glanced at Piers. 'Bring your friend.'

Jeff looked over at Piers and the other girl. 'Speaking of friends, yours seems able to talk right now', he said.

'Mel?' Chrissie looked further over her shoulder. 'It's your friend's doing the talking.' Her voice grew sharp. 'Mel's English isn't good enough to tell him she can't talk back.' Chrissie grabbed Piers by the arm. 'Leave the girl alone, will you? She's taken.'

'By you?' said Piers. He looked dumbfounded.

'She's with me.'

'And you're her chaperone – or what?'

'Just two girls out on the town.'

'Great girls!' Piers looked from Mel to Chrissie and back.

'We're still taken. Sorry, hun.' Chrissie gathered her bag. 'Got your things, Mel?'

Mel nodded. 'We go now?' she said. 'The man say to wait him here.'

'I'll tell Jimmy to page us.' Chrissie turned to Jeff. 'Or can you and your friend leave us be?'

Jeff had sobered up a bit. He said to Piers, 'I think we should.' He dropped his voice. 'Tell you why later.'

Piers looked surprised. Also baffled. It was Jeff took Piers by the shoulder this time. Took him and steered him back to their original table.

'What's going on?' said Piers.

Jeff looked back at the girls. A man he hadn't seen before was standing next to them, bending over them, saying something. The man stood up. He had seen him before. He'd even sat next him. It was the guy he'd met on the plane, Edgar Godwin.

Jeff pushed Piers down in the near chair and moved swiftly over to the bar, turning his back on the girls. He signalled to the bartender.

'Jimmy, right? Two more your Cate drinks, Jimmy. No paw paw pulp.'

Jimmy turned and reached for bottles, fruit, knife, glasses, ice. Jeff pointed at the fruit with his left and waved his right hand, palm downward, signalling No-No. He strained his ears to hear Godwin's words. All he could pick up was 'His Highness' and 'see'. The sibilants hissed like steam from Manhattan manhole covers.

Then a hush hit the room. Godwin came over clear. 'Andy Pandy and Teddy-amo, ladies. Can't keep someone of His Highness's eminence waiting or the prominence of His Highness's protuberance might lose its highness.'

The girls got up and left in the direction of the elevators, followed by Godwin. They walked right past Jeff, all three of them, without a glance in his direction. Must be on their way up to some prayer mat-prostrating pasha's four-thousand-pound-a-day suite to room service him, despite his piety, at a thousand a night, or eighteen hundred the pair.

Jimmy returned with the drinks on a silver tray. 'If you care to resume your seat, sir, I can have these brought over to your table.'

'Oh. OK then.' Jeff turned round to look in case Godwin had come back. He'd hardly join in the fun upstairs, would he? But he'd gone.

Jeff said to Jimmy, 'The guy just left, you know him?'

'I'm sorry, sir, which "guy"?'

'Guy with the two girls. The two lookers.'

'Which girls?'

'Hey, *Jimmy*!' He'd got Jimmy's attention now. 'Watch my thinking-seriously-about-not-tipping-you lips. The fuckin' lookers.'

Jimmy looked down at his tray. 'He, er…, the gentleman comes here from time to time.'

'Guy called Godwin.'

Jimmy looked up. 'Goodwin.'

'Goodwin, not Godwin? That his name?'

85

'Oh yes, sir. I have his card.'

'You got a contact number for him?'

Jimmy shook his head.

Jeff said, in his best ingenuous Dixie, 'I 'preciate y'all might not be auth'rahzed t' give th' matter wahd public'ty, but I's extend'd th' honor 'f an intro-duction to him li'l tahm back. Need to re-'stablish contac' re-e-aal fast.'

'I may have…filed…his business card…somewhere… sir.'

'See, it's this gi-normous deal come up. All a sudden. Unus'ally gen'rous co-mission f'r anyone he'ps close it.'

'It's on business you want to talk to him?' Jimmy put a light but noticeable emphasis on the 'b' word, one he'd now used twice.

Jeff took the hint. Not hard to. 'Business, you bet', he said. 'Fifty get me a glance?'

He slid the note across the silver surface of the bar. Jimmy picked it up, looked expertly round the room for any Inland Revenue auditors, held it briefly to the overhead light, folded it in his weskit pocket and fumbled under the counter.

'This what you're looking for?' he said quietly, putting an open match book in front of Jeff. Aloud he said, referring to Jeff's drink order, 'Shall I charge this, sir, or will you pay for it now?'

'Charge it.'

Jeff jotted down the number. It wasn't scribbled in the flap, the way numbers usually were with books of matches. Instead the book itself served as sheath to a proper business card. On it one Ed Goodwin was described as 'social affairs co-ordinator'. A fax, a land line and a cell phone were listed, also an email address and a web site. Jeff copied them all.

NINETEEN

Jules's mobile jangled. The Bach organ fugue. Jules was a *Phantom of the Opera* fan.

'Jules? Jules Miller?'

'Yes?'

'Ben Lee. We've not met, but you used to pass my people some good tip-offs when I edited the *Date*.'

'Oh?'

'Lighten up, Jules. It's not a crime.'

'Would have been a major breach of discipline. If I ever did. And I'm not saying that.'

'Of course you aren't. And I like your devotion to discipline. Extra important now you've moved up to Counter Terrorism CPO from common or garden rozzer. But that's between you and your superiors. Good friends of mine, some of them. Enough social chitchat. I'm interested in information. Not tip-offs. Solid.'

'Sorry, nothing doing.'

'Sure? Needn't come from you. Don't you know anyone – a colleague, or ex-colleague – could do a bit of digging on my behalf? What am I saying? The nation's behalf.'

'Just what *are* you saying, Sir?'

'No need to "Sir" me.'

'I'd still like to know what you're getting at…Sir.'

'You're cautious. That's good.'

Jules didn't answer immediately. 'A CPO's not much use who isn't', he said eventually. 'His protectee can get killed otherwise.'

'Sergeant Miller, I'm every bit as focussed as you. I need someone to be my eyes and ears. Not a criminal investigation. Not a security one. Just some steady but shrewd observing, find out what certain people are up to. Not invading their privacy. No illegal surveillance. Just the evidence of one's senses. Following which he will prepare me a report, which I will in my turn pass on to some very exalted circles indeed. A souped up version of the kind of tip-offs you used so valuably to supply my paper. Very, very valuably – to the point where your consequent remuneration might intrigue the tax boys.'

A pause. Lee could almost hear the cogs shifting in Jules's brain. Then, in a peevish voice, Jules said, 'I'm knackered with work right now. Near as bad as double shifts, all these security drills. Hey, now I come to think of it, didn't I see you having a word with my oppo Gary the other day? The Chequers monthly red alert thing?'

'Aha, so you know me by sight?'

'Couldn't not, seeing as you're so often in the papers.'

'You keep abreast of current events. Bravo.'

'You're that bloke's so close to Her at Number Ten.'

'Spot on, Miller. Well, how about it? Given my closeness to Her at Number Ten, not just a fee but recognition, solid recognition, will not be slow in winging its way to you.'

A much shorter pause. 'You mean something like a police medal?'

'Why not?'

'An OBE's got more class.'

'Steady, Jules. We mustn't aspire too high. I could probably swing an M.'

'An MBE?'

'Yes. Hardly an MC. That's for gallantry. It's guile I'm after.'

Another short pause. Then, 'I... might know of someone... suitable.'

'How absolutely spiffing.'

'I can't promise anything. Haven't seen him in a while.'

'Then the sooner you renew contact the better, *n'est-ce pas*?'

'Might take me a day or two. We kind of lost touch...There's definitely nothing illegal involved?'

'Nothing at all. Honour bright.'

'Not meaning to sound rude or anything, but how bright is that?'

'Honourable is my middle name.'

'You have to be joking.'

'One of my middle names. I'm officially a Right Honourable, Detective Miller. *The* Right Honourable. Member of His Majesty's Privy Council. Took up the appointment ten days ago. Can't say fairer than that, can I?'

TWENTY

The Deller home, one of those huge 1860s Holland Park structures, resembled a giant's wedding cake, its baker gone to town with white icing sugar. Jeff had come with Piers. A flunky showed them upstairs. They entered a ballroom stretching the depth of the house, the result of knocking two already large spaces into a single cavernous one.

Inside its double doors they were received by a girl in red, Charlotte. Jeff didn't catch her name when spoken but she wore a lapel badge. A tacky commercial touch, he decided. Charlotte held an iPad, scrolling down the screen to con the guest list. Mrs Deller's social secretary, Piers explained. He spoke softly. Jeff welcomed the advance information.

He got knocked off balance by *déjà vu* when, over toward the second fireplace, the third person he caught sight of was Edgar Godwin. Or Ed Goodwin, as the case might be. And he felt downright floored by it when, after pushing through crowds of guests immediately behind Piers then being prodded toward his hostess, he stood face to face with the woman who'd held Diana von Principessa upside down on the airplane.

Jeff seized the initiative. 'Did you enjoy your novel on the flight from New York recently, Mrs Deller?'

'What stupid novel?'

'Believe it or not, our paths crossed before.'

'Yes?' She sounded bored. Piers muttered something. Jeff didn't catch it. He wasn't giving up on Mrs Deller. 'Mid-fall', he said. 'The New York-London run. Trans-Atlantic.'

'Could be. I shop in New York twice a month. What's with the novel?'

'Skip it', he said. She was frowning. She'd been frowning off and on since he first spoke. Clearly young enough, or botoxed enough, not to have to worry about worry lines. He said, 'With all that shopping you maybe don't get too much time for reading.'

She came alive. 'The Citrus sucks. Those Bryn Mawr-ish bag ladies. But I *always* comb the TomeCo Prize short list. Can you claim as much?'

'No. I guess not. I don't get to do so much shopping either.'

She laughed. It had been sticky at first. It was better now. 'And are you on your first visit to this great city of – well, I guess I can say ours. Vic's dad was a Brick Lane barrow boy. Having married the boy's son, I imbibe genuine London antecedents, if only by osmosis.'

'imbibe'? 'antecedents'? 'osmosis'? Oh, yeah, she combed book prize short lists. How glad he was he didn't. 'I'm posted here, Mrs Deller.'

'Who'd you say you were with?'

He explained what his job was, spinning it out. It gave them the chance to look you over.

'I met with your predecessor a couple times', she said. 'Nice man. What's his name again?'

"again"? He hadn't given it out a first time. 'Tod', he said. 'Tod Snaith.'

'He moved on?'

'Sort of.'

'Promotion?' She shivered as she spoke. The shiver made her look vulnerable. Jeff papered over Tod's fate. 'It's more they, uh, felt he was here long enough.'

She tucked her lower right lip under a white, white tooth and looked up at him, Di-style, from beneath black, black lashes.

But now other guests surged around them, breaking over Jeff, Piers and Mrs Deller like waves about a mole. Piers got dislodged as a knot of new arrivals elbowed him aside. More friends surged across the room, pecked Laura, glanced at Jeff, interchanged inanities, passed on.

The Deller daughters, Amethyst and Lapislazuli, nine and seven, made their appearance. They took big hugs from Mother then got led by Nanny round the guests. A slight hush accompanied them, settling on each section of the crowd they worked, the mild impatience of a large but polite gathering temporarily baulked of its champagne fuel.

Am and Lappie shook hands only with the major players. Nanny had a hitman's skill in identifying such targets, *Right On*, *Yoohoo!* and *Chic* her Gideon bibles. The little girls got led away and put to bed. Conviviality broke out again, not sporadic now but *tutti*.

Edgar/Ed Godwin/Goodwin loomed up. 'Well well well. It's my former flying partner. I haven't seen any articles by you on my erstwhile client yet.' He shook Jeff's hand with energy. 'Writer's block?' His palm was damp.

'"Erstwhile"?', said Jeff. Was this another book geek?

'Mark Barnes and I have parted company. Amicably, I stress. The man himself is over there.'

'Where?'

'Talking to the swarthy man with the comb-over. Though it's so subtle you mightn't know it. Ben Lee. The two standing by the big sculpture in pock-marked chrome. If it is chrome.'

'If it is a sculpture.'

'Oho', said Godwin, 'An art critic.' He looked genuinely amused.

Jeff wanted to ask him what his real name was, and what he'd been doing at the Beldon in such questionable company last week. But he couldn't in front of his hostess. Godwin/Goodwin turned his head and ushered forward a clean-shaven man wearing a purple blouson and round his throat a necklace from which metal symbols dangled; jingled too. This man he introduced as Lord Crowthorne.

''Lo, Lon', said Laura Deller, proffering her left cheek to Crowthorne. The right one she withheld. She didn't seem too taken with him. Certainly his chin looked rather weak.

Crowthorne and Godwin/Goodwin turned to Jeff in unison, as if about to launch into a night club act. 'Hi' said Crowthorne. The matey monosyllable was unexpected.

'Hello', said Jeff, a little shyly. He held out his hand. It got gripped as if by a gorilla.

'This is the new *Hence* correspondent', said Godwin/Goodwin.

'*Hence*?' said Crowthorne, retaining Jeff's hand longer than was good form in Jeff's world. '*Hence* means "from here". Where's the "here" your magazine is from?'

Jeff laughed, withdrew his hand, then cut himself short. Was what Crowthorne had said meant to be funny? 'Um, I think we met already', he said, half sure they hadn't but wholly certain he'd seen him before. 'I know your face.' Or most of it, he thought. Not the chin.

'I should very much hope so.' Near pout and half swirl on heel. The body language conveyed touchy self-conceit without being faggy. Jeff wondered how British aristos managed it. No American he knew could have done, even a Patroon Club founder member's descendant.

'Lord Crowthorne is...' said Godwin/Goodwin.

'Yes, yes, Edgar. There's no need to trumpet it to the rooftops. I'm sure this young man knows all about who I am without you needing to brief him.' Crowthorne eyed Jeff, challenging him to prove it.

91

Jeff thought fast. Celebrity manor house owner? Gardening guru? Society anecdotalist? Silver generation style icon? Chat show frequenter? Ex-politician? Penal reformer? There were so many possibilities.

His memory kicked in. The man had worn a beard. Not now. That's why he hadn't immediately recognised him. Jeff said, 'I just loved your green get-up the Parliament opening.'

Crowthorne smiled. Benevolently yet also proprietorially, as if about to pronounce a papal blessing. 'Doublet and hose, to be exact', he said, real vigour in his voice now. 'I owe it to the antiquarian fraternity. It's wonderful how they could look up the records, some of them from Henry VII's time, and discover what the Lord Great Constable wears and how it's always green. There's no other country in the world it would have been possible. God bless England. Allah, Jehovah and Shiva bless it too.'

'Why green?' said Godwin/Goodwin, a bit too promptly. Jeff suspected his job involved feeding his patron with chances to hold forth.

'The most down to earth of reasons', said Crowthorne. 'The unpalatable truth is, the Lord Great Constable's appointed costume was a propaganda ploy, designed to unify England after the Wars of the Roses, and mounted by those *nouve* Tudors. It was to stress the Tudor element that I wore my beard that day.' Now he sounded like a fashionable lecturer on a cultural tour, letting the well-heeled, mildly educated audience in on some behind-the-scenes titbit of national history.

'I still don't see why green', said Godwin/Goodwin. Jeff had been about to ask the same thing.

'Green because it's the common sward from which spring red rose and white rose alike, they, as I'm sure you know, being the badges of the two factions in the Wars of the Roses.'

Jeff said, 'The White Rose guys were the Duke of York's people, a.k.a. Richard III, right? Laurence Olivier in the mainstream movie, Richard Dreyfuss in that camped up scene in *The Goodbye Girl*. I preferred Dreyfuss. A whole heap of pink but much less ham. I rode a White Rose train once, time I did a piece on Howard Castle in Yorkshire.'

Crowthorne's mouth turned up, amused. 'I'm afraid it's Castle Howard.'

Suddenly the whole England thing got too much for Jeff. He boiled over. 'Why do you British get off so much on spelling things different from how they're said?' he yelled. 'And calling manor houses castles when they got no moats or battlements. And other manor houses palaces when there's no royalty in them. And – and sneering at us ex-colony guys who saved your hide in two world wars and one ice cold one just because we fuck up, excuse me screw up, from time to time with your old-world customs? You still hurting over Yorktown or the whuppin' Old Hickory give you at New Orleans? Huh? *Huh?*'

Crowthorne smiled. 'And why do you Americans call one state Kansas and another Arkansaw? Even though they're spelled much the same. Maybe you caught it from us.' He leant forward. 'Huh?'

Laura Deller intervened. 'My home state there's a town called La Jolla, rhymes with lawyer, not with dollar, tho' spelled dollar. Spanish. Only we took it from the Mexicans back in the 1800s.'

Crowthorne laughed. 'I know we're a maddening lot. My own family are among the worst offenders. Our name's spelled Bo-hun but we pronounce it Boon.'

Jeff blinked. Lord Crowthorne, though absurd, was also, like so many other surficially absurd figures in this odd country, oddly intimidating.

A waitress approached. She bore filo *vol-au-vents* on a carved wood platter.

Crowthorne scowled, 'Can't you find something better to put them on than a slice of tree?' Had he addressed his hostess or the waitress? His social status would let him get away with abruptness to either. The waitress was Hispanic. She didn't understand. Crowthorne inspected the platter then turned to Godwin/Goodwin. 'Edgar, kindly tell her not to wave her murdered elm in my face.' Godwin/Goodwin said something to the waitress. Jeff didn't catch it. The waitress nodded, bowed slightly and walked away.

'Gross', said Lord Crowthorne. He fished a slim enamelled box from his coat pocket, prised it open, dabbed an index finger with his tongue, probed the box's contents with his finger and placed a tiny pill on said tongue. Its tip he extended further than Jeff had seen any other human manage since in the pulp comic *Monitor Man* he'd read as a boy. Were saurian tongues some Bohun ancestral oddity, like Habsburg jaws?

'…You know what the Spaniards do to donkeys?' Crowthorne was saying. He'd left trees behind. 'There's a place fifty of them sit on a donkey till it dies. Till it dies. For the fun of it. You see tears in the donkey's eyes before it dies.' His own eyes, brown, had filled with tears.

Jeff found his eyes welling too.

'Mrs D, is there somewhere Lyonel can go and lie down?' said Godwin/Goodwin. 'He's had a busy week.'

Godwin/Goodwin turned to Jeff. 'All the same, he's action as well as talk. A few weeks before Christmas he bought up a thousand Christmas trees. Save them from the woodsman's axe. It cost him over fifty thou. But as he said at the time, it's money well spent if it sustains a renewable resource.'

Crowthorne grimaced through his tears. 'Edgar is a good soul. He puts the best interpretation on the episode. My accountant had been on at me for years to get into forestry as a tax shelter. I for my part saw it as a useful gesture of defiance against the hucksters sullying the festive season with their crassness. Nature has her place in the Creator's scheme of things as well as man his. When I see a felled tree I see red.' He wiped his nose.

Godwin/Goodwin nodded. 'Talking of trees, Christmas is falling off a log when it comes to planting news stories', he said. He was doing his best to jolly things up. 'There's so little else going on. This turned out to be worth four times the cost of promotion in television coverage alone.'

He'd failed to win one of his audience. Laura Deller glared. 'Christmas is the time of year I really love', she said. 'Gifts, soft lights, blazing fires, togetherness. The glow you feel is almost spiritual. Why spoil it?'

Godwin/Goodwin faced her. 'Mrs D, Mrs D, seriously now, how could someone like me spoil something as big and strong as Christmas?' He grasped her hand, trying to soothe, but held it too long.

'For fuck's sake!' said Laura Deller, pulling a tissue from her bag. She wiped both her hands with it. She turned towards Crowthorne. She looked angry. It suited her. 'Is your friend always like this, cheapening what's special with his tacky spin-prone take on things?'

'Why Laura, Edgar's become quite a close associate over the last few months. But to be a good friend demands years. I only met him last summer.' Crowthorne turned to Jeff. 'My great-nephew's bumped into you. He's over in the States trying to scratch a living.' Jeff was puzzled. He couldn't recall meeting any British lord's relative.

'Ours is a cash nexus', Godwin/Goodwin said, looking with sudden contempt at Crowthorne. 'Business. No more.'

'Is he with you or isn't he?' Laura Deller said to Crowthorne.

'If you put it like that…'

'It is extremely kind of you to have had me tonight', Godwin/Goodwin said to Laura. He gabbled his words, as if anxious to get off his chest, before he dried, a speech he'd not learned properly. 'We have met before. You asked me to drop in some time. And tonight, hearing as one does that Mrs Victor Deller was giving one of her celebrated receptions, I felt that that some time had come. All Lyonel here did was let me squire him.'

'I recall you edging your way in at the *Date* reception during the ColLaborative Conference', Laura Deller said. She was still peeved. 'I did *not* say drop in whenever you feel like it. I may have said drop in some time. That means when *I* feel like it. Tonight I don't. Please leave.'

Jeff burned inside with embarrassment. Mrs Deller bristled but was never less than formidable. Lord Crowthorne stood as before, imperturbable. Godwin/Goodwin alone looked shaken. 'There's no need to talk like that.' He spoke very reasonably.

'There's no *need*. I do it because I want to.'

Godwin/Goodwin mumbled something. He drained his glass and walked away, not looking back. At one point he lurched slightly. Laura Deller didn't look in his direction. Jeff did. He saw him buttonholed by the man Lee, who'd walked across the room to do it and stood saying something that looked important. The two of them glanced briefly in Jeff's direction. Then Lee walked away and Godwin fumbled at a side door.

Crowthorne was almost immediately captured by the *Date*'s op ed editor. She'd been waiting for her opportunity like a Taleban tribesman up a side gulley in an Afghan defile. He got towed away to the other side of the room. Jeff and Laura Deller were left by themselves again. The heat and din were overwhelming. Jeff wanted to find out more about Godwin. Goodwin too. Not least which was which.

'When was this party convention thing where you met with the guy Godwin, Mrs Deller? Four, five months back?'

She said nothing but looked at him and nodded. She went on looking at him, doing so almost thoughtfully.

'That's some memory you got there', he said.

'When I couldn't recall the book I read less than a few months ago?' She'd calmed down now, gotten almost humble.

'Yes... well.'

'*Your* memory's so good, to recall the book incident. What was it?'

'The book? Diana von Principessa. *Castle... Castle Dominance*. Never read it myself.'

She laughed. She looked twice as lovely when she laughed. 'You know something? I thought it was erotica. Looked like it. Got stacked with others really are. Turns out it's on chess endings. I'd like to sue those mock-muck-merchants Vere, Bramcusi. There should be a law says publishers can't sell false hopes.'

'All books that sell at all sell false hopes.'

'But there are limits. By the time you unwrap it, open it, wake up to what it really is, it's too late. You're airborne, flying.'

'So you thought it was a shopping and boning novel?' Jeff drew breath. Things were moving fast.

'Why would I want to read about shopping? Just the boning. I like to read about that. Next best thing to watching it. Which in turn is next best to doing some.'

He didn't know what to say. All the studying he'd put in and now he didn't know what to say. He gazed round the room. 'This is a wonderful house.'

'Like to see over it?'

'I'd love that.'

'I'll show it you some time... Give me five minutes. No, we do *not* exit together, idiot. Got to stay some more, build up a smokescreen. Me, I mean. See that door? Not the one Mr whacko Godwin took. I knew if I could get rid of him, His Sanctimoniousness wouldn't linger. One thing that Principessa book does teach, a pawn sacrifice to neutralize a bishop. She really exists, you know, Ms. von Principessa. I googled her. International Grand Master. Grand Mistress? Wow, that's a thought... Listen carefully. The door the far corner. Take it, then the door marked "Daffodil Library". A shrine to dilly Willy M.

Wordsworth that the guy we bought this place from wished on us via a covenant. Can you believe it?'

'Uh, I think so. Where'd you say the place is again?'

'That door. Then third on the right. You can count?'

'Yup. I can read too.'

'Ignore any staff you meet.' Jeff's insolence had not dammed Mrs Deller's flow of words. A good sign. 'The confidentiality clauses they sign when I hire them are extremely tightly drafted', she said, 'by my extremely vigilant lawyers... Third on the right. Rare titles up and down each wall. You can't mistake it. Plus a fabulous ceiling. Gods nailing other god's wives. Vic took it out a Prague palace last year. Not that you'll get to see it that much... less you like it on your back.'

Jeff drew on all his Southern courtesy, then garnished it with Manhattan insouciance. 'I don't think we know each other well enough for that', he said. 'Mish will be fine.'

TWENTYONE

Ring tone. The Indiana Jones theme. Angelo was big into Indie. He didn't recognise the number on the screen, though. It made him cautious. Couldn't be Micky, Frankie, Area Manager or his wife, the four points of his personal compass.

He'd only managed to fit in a single flying visit to his family the whole of the last few weeks. Rats. He had put on weight to compensate. 'Yes?', he said.

'That you, Ange?'

'Who the hell's that?'

'Jules, mate. Jules Miller. Remember me? Three summers ago? We carried out that Battersea Park investigation together. You were still on the force.'

'Oh, yeah. Jules. How're you doing?'

'Can't complain. I've moved on. And up. And you?'

'Moved up? You're no longer with the…?'

'Still basically the old shop. But assigned to special duties. Guarding grandees. Bloody boring, most the time. You do see some funny sights, though. Lips sealed on that, worse luck. Hey, mate, what about we meet for a jar? Talk over old times?'

'Yeah, I'd love to. Thing is, I'm pretty much tied up the moment. Still finding my feet this new job and all. You know how it is.'

'None better. Look, mate, you interested in outside work?'

'What sort of outside work?'

'We can talk when we meet.'

'Giss a clue.'

'Not easy over the phone.'

'Confidential, is it?'

'I'm not at liberty to say. How about the Rose, Thursday lunch time?'

'That place we used to go? Bit near Met HQ.'

'You shy of the law?'

'No. No, of course not. Just a bit awkward if we bump into some old workmates still hard at it when I went and took early retirement.'

'Retirement? Thought you said you had a new job.'

'I do. Pension doesn't stretch far enough.'

'All right then, you choose.'

'Tell you what, I'm working a lot up Shepherd's Bush these days. How about we meet somewhere that neck of the woods? What's this proposal? It is a proposal, isn't it?'

'Tell you when we meet. Thursday still good?'

'Yeah. OK. You know the Bush? Opposite the big roundabout there's a place called the Dog and Duck. Meet you there half eleven. Quiet then.'

Now what was that about? A feeler all right, but from what quarter? Angelo's scenting powers were on the alert today. *Guarding, eh? Well you don't get guarded less you're a snout or a Lord Snooty. 'Grandees' don't mean grasses, so Jules is currently very very well connected. Interesting.*

TWENTYTWO

Twenty minutes after his leaving the party, easily long enough for Jeff to wonder what he'd gotten himself into, Laura Deller entered the Daffodil Library. He'd been there around fifteen himself. The books, all on Wordsworth or by him, looked unreadable, indeed had proved so welded to the wall as to be unpluckable.

They clinched immediately, saying nothing. Presently they rolled onto the wide day bed... disengaged, disrobed swiftly and clinched again. This time they held the clinch.

He wasn't quite through to the home stretch yet, was still in the middle passage where you pound away, stuck into it but at the same time a shade apprehensive about arriving too soon or flagging, especially on a first encounter, when the door opened. A narrow shaft of yellow light struck through from the corridor outside. It captured the two of them, holding them still like photographic models. Jeff kept his back to the door. A silhouette showed there.

'Oops. Sorry. Wrong room. That you, Mrs D.? If so, thanks a million and goodbye. If not, pass on the message to the real Mrs Daffodil, will you? Grand party.'

The intruder shut the door. They heard his footsteps retreat down the passage. Jeff was beyond immediate resuscitation. He unplugged and said 'Goddammit. You know who that sounded like?'

'Yes. Mister Creepo. The one I told to get lost.'

'Godwin?'

'The one dripped sweat all over my hand.'

'He's called Godwin. Or Goodwin. You called him Godwin.'

'I only called him what Lon Crowthorne did. He'd know who his own aide is.'

'You said you met him at a convention.'

'Conference.'

'The ColLaborative Conference, you said.'

'That's him. That's the one.'

'God. I mean Jesus Christ.'

'Did he recognise us?'

'He said your name just now.'

'Said it, but like he wasn't sure.'

'He said it.'

'It *is* my house. I do what I want my own bedroom.'

'This a bedroom? Doesn't look lived in.'

'They're all my bedrooms if I go to bed in them. This is my house fuck it.'

'Yes. Yes of course.'

'And you? Did he recognise you?'

'Don't know. I had my back to him.'

'You know him, right?'

'We met once. An airplane. He never saw my naked back.'

'Don't be funny. And get *off* of me. You're heavy.'

'I'm not. Not trying to be funny.' Jeff crossed to the door, turned the key then returned to the day bed. He sat on it. 'I'm trying to assess possibilities', he said.

'Your back does not look like the back of the Chairman of DelFitCo, CEO of DelPLC Holdings and major holder of other Footsie 350 stocks. It's half the width. And lots less hairy.'

She sat up too, swung her legs over the edge. The two of them leaned forward, hands on knees, side by side. They might have been a couple of old friends on a park bench, discussing life.

'I love it how you flipped when that asshole Lyonel-de Crusader-descendant-Crowsnest put you down about Howard Castle.'

'It kinda bugs you…'

'The way the British can still be snotty?' She stretched her arms, lovely arms.

'I'm dying for a cigarette', he said. 'It's weird, haven't smoked since junior high.'

'You can't smoke. It'll set off the alarm… I'd kill for one myself.'

'What are we going to do?'

'Will you please be quiet? I'm trying to think.'

'I better go.' He pulled on his socks. His tie had disappeared. He felt under the day bed.

'Don't go. We only just met.'

'I don't mean… I want to see you again.'

'So stay.' She ruffled his hair.

'How'd you get away from your own party?'

'Easy. I tell the house steward and Charlotte – my PA, pretty girl in the red Fern Field – tell Charlotte I have to take a call. They spread the word, case a guest wants to speak with me meantime. Then they turn off the lights.'

'And guests leave in the dark?'

'I have the side doors to our private apartments pre-sealed off. The exit's the default route. There are overhead lo-wattage bulbs. Dim, but they work.'

'Don't guests think it odd?'

'Brides, grooms leave the reception early. What's so different?'

Jeff inwardly sighed. 'Tell me', he said, 'what's that man just now do? Who is he?'

'You're the reporter. Investigate.'

'I hoped you'd know.'

'You've no idea what it's like, being a media mogul's wife. The rivalry, the enmities, the jealousy. And the security. All the fucking time. Even during fucking.' She sighed. Audibly.

They lay back. Presently she said, 'What's this?', toying with it.

'Confederate silver dollar.'

'The South will rise again, huh?' Then, by a natural mental jump, 'Want to give it another whirl?'

'Sure.'

They gave it another whirl.

'Beautiful' she said presently.

He said nothing.

She held him at arm's length. 'Cat got your tongue?'

He froze. The fox had said the same thing.

'Hey, loosen up' she said. 'You fuck good.'

He said nothing.

'You know,' she said, 'you're quiet for a reporter. I like it like that. Pretty too. Pretty period.'

'Wha-?'

'Straight pretty. You're not bi, are you? Some guys your looks can be.' He blushed, thinking of his enforced gobble on the fox. The room was too dim for her to see the blush. 'No', he said.

'Listen, you want to stay for dinner or something? I'm having maybe thirty of those guys back there go on down the dining room. The crème de la crème. I wish. Come too if you want.'

'That'd be nice. I won't be in the way?'

'Don't be dumb. It's a fork supper. Look, I got to go right now.' She was on her feet already, touching a comb to her hair. 'Make yourself at home. Shower's through there. Or you could take a dip. Pool's in the basement. There's shorts the top drawer the bureau.'

'This must be a huge house.'

'It's OK. Handy. Vic wanted something closer to the Parliament complex. I nearly died I saw those miniature Lord North Street homes. No real yard, no room for a gym even. Grade I listed so tight you can't remodel your own ass. Out here the kids can go play in the Park, catch some sun. There's so little of it this awful island you got to soak up what you can when. Least a melanoma's low risk. Look, I really got to go…' She leant over him and kissed him on the nose. 'I won't be able to talk with you a whole lot at dinner. People watching and stuff.' Jeff pulled his pants on. She'd dressed already. She took a ball point and a business card from her bag, scribbled on the card and pulled down his pants.

'What are you doing? I'm freezing.'

'There.' She scooped up his nuts and tucked the card well down between his upper thighs, releasing the nuts. 'Call me some time. Not the print number. That's Vic's and my's voicemail. The one in ink.'

The corner of the card pricked his nuts. He was always pricking himself on some guy's business card. He assured her he wanted to see her again.

'Me too.' She looked into his face. 'What'd you say your name was?'

'Jeff.'

'Not that. I got that. The whole thing.'

'Jefferson P. Calhoun. My by-line's in *Hence* magazine. "Letter from London".'

'We take *Thither*. Let me think… It could look suspect I switch periodicals over night.'

'For God sake. I'm not trying to sell you a subscription.'

'I'll tell Charlotte add it to next month's paper order.' She was at the door now. She turned. 'Thursday?'

'Thursday I got two press conferences to cover. Friday?'

'I have this business trip to Avon County, down the M4 Freeway.'

'The following Monday?'

'Perfect. Monday's child is fair of face.'

TWENTYTHREE

It was Tucky found the fake pen, batting with her right front paw at the underside of the hallway table. Jeff was paying her only half his attention. The other half he'd devoted to an article he was composing on a campaign in England to repeal the hunting ban. Repeal was surprisingly popular, not least with townies whose kittens had fallen prey to urban foxes. Till he read that he'd begun to get over his own experience as fox's prey. The instant he took it in he feared for Tucky.

The clatter of pen hitting floor made him look up. Tucky had turned tail and charged him, pulling up short while still a foot away and baring her tiny teeth. It looked a snarl, but he hoped was love.

Stopping by to scratch her tum, he walked over to the table, lifted off the phone set and examined the table's underside. Scraps of Blu-Tack stuck to the wood. He picked up the pen, stared at it hard, fiddled with it. Back to his laptop, find out what the pen was.

Five minutes googling established that it was a standard model bug. No prizes for guessing who'd placed it. Clearly the fox and his woodland buddies. But if they wanted to hide their surveillance, why'd they emerged from their dens?

When in doubt ring Doresett.

'Calhoun? Good afternoon...Yes...yes...I see...yes. Surveillance is not my subject. People very much are. Especially Tod, whose death seems to have precipitated all this.' A pause while Doresett marshalled his thoughts. He continued: 'Assumption One: Tod killed unlawfully... fox mask and associates visit, to intimidate you... you find Tod notes... you not intimidated...intend investigate Tod's death further... – Editorial Interpolation: good for you – you find listening device...Assumption: the fox lot installed it...You agree so far?'

'Yes.'

'Question: why don't the fox lot kill you too? Sorry to sound callous. It's an obvious point.'

Jeff was caught here. He hadn't mentioned what the fox had done to him. He wasn't going to now. 'Guess they figured two deaths the same apartment in two months'd look too damn suspicious.'

'Fair enough. Another aspect. The fox asking you whether Tod filed vice stories. Does he work for some prostitution ring?'

'I don't know. Vice is hot here in England. There've been a couple bills cracking down on it. They failed to pass, though. It's connected with immigration. Upmarket hooker I came across was protesting foreign competitors. She knows this weird guy I met the airplane coming over could be a general fixer to high-ups. Hey, this bug. Could I reverse it, kind of? Listen to what they're saying?'

'If I were you, I'd either neutralise it and if you're lucky wait till someone breaks in to try and re-activate it, when you catch them red-handed, or don't neutralise it and send false information to the eavesdroppers.'

Jeff stuck the pen right back where it had been originally.

'I hope it's not relaying this conversation?', Doresett said.

'No. I'm calling from the bathroom', Jeff said, bending a fact. From what he'd read on-line, the ballpoint had to be activated from elsewhere. 'With the power shower running full to drown out our conversation...', he said, bending another fact.

'...Ah, the shower', said Doresett. 'Useful for more than keeping clean. Well, write it all up and submit it. Throw newshound Stevens a juicy reportage steak. Not his usual New York strip sirloin. London broil.'

Later Jeff wondered why he'd risked the eavesdroppers hearing he'd discovered their bug. Maybe it was because now he wanted a showdown. He'd gotten tired of being treated like a sex object, first forced into servicing a dominant male then spied on like a co-ed by gonad-heavy frat boys inserting a mini-camcorder in the women's locker room.

TWENTYFOUR

Jules at the Dog and Duck had struck Angelo as noticeably warier than in the old days. Angelo had spotted him sidling into the public bar, darting glances in every direction – in case a suicide bomber dropped by to denounce beer-drinking, thought Angelo – and lit the blue touch paper on himself to ram his point home.

'Jules! Over here. It's the Saloon these days.'

Jules had plonked himself down. 'You're looking well', he'd said, meaning, as often with the phrase, more its opposite. 'Put on a bit since I saw you last.' He'd playfully swiped at Angelo's tum.

Angelo had ignored this, something he was obliged to do a lot these days. 'What'll it be?' he'd said.

'Whatever you're having.'

'Lo-cal tom juice? Really?'

'You? Wave bye-bye to bitter? Never.' Jules had spoken with conviction.

'Don't know as I might not. This poncy shirt-lifter been put over my head is always needling me about my weight.'

The joshing done, the beer bought, Angelo had looked hard at Jules. 'What's this deal?'

Jules had knocked back a hefty swig, wiped his mouth and kept his hand up close to said mouth. When he'd next spoken it was softly, if hissing. 'I need someone can suss out what a bunch of MPs are up to.'

Angelo said, 'Are you bonkers? That's over 500 people.'

'Not the lot. Selected cross sample.'

'Selected how?'

'How they vote. Or won't. More won't. Bloke set me onto this is scared Number Ten could lose the whip hand.'

'Why should MPs vote Number Ten's way? It's us sent them there.'

'This here protecting makes you see things different. Your typical MP has his freebies. Least he can do is think the way his bosses tell him. You game to look into why they gone and broke loose?'

'Could do. Need to ponder it.'

'Angelo, mate. You were never put on this earth to "ponder". Executive, that's where the rewards are truly at.'

'Rewards. Glad you brought that up. How much?'

'See, my management team think cash has got slightly iffy at this present point in time.' Jules had paused. 'How does a gong sound?'

'Hollow.'

'Is that your last word?'

'I could go on. Brassy. Tinny. Warns you dinner's up in seaside guest houses.'

'Don't be so literal.'

'You mean some kind of award then. Well bugger that. Can I eat one? Can my kids wear one?'

'Hold on. You got your pension. And this new job you told me about, you must be coining it. Wouldn't you like respect as well? Walk tall in your local community?'

Angelo had softened. Verna and the kids would love it. 'What have you got in mind? And who's offering it? Not you.'

'No, not me. This bloke is. The... personage asked me to look out for a suitable...other personage. Meaning you. He is...well connected.'

'And?'

'He has friends in high places. Friends who only have to snap their fingers for an award to drop into your lap.'

'I thought there were controls these days, following the hoo-ha when Chaz Lynton was in charge, stop that sort of fiddle?'

'Only the top stuff. Like lord. Now don't take it personal, but you don't quite make the lord grade.'

'No. I see that.'

'Lower down it's a free-for-all. Has to be. Too many people involved. It'd take years to screen 'em. If the powers that be say Joe Bloggs gets an MBE, he will. Provided he hasn't collected a criminal record. Which you haven't.'

'No.'

Angelo must have sounded a bit doubtful. 'Sure?' Jules had said.

'No. Though speaking of that, what happens if you do? Later, say? Theoretically of course. Do they take your letters off you when you're banged up, like they do shoelaces case you top yourself?'

'Search me.'

'Now a get out of jail free ticket, that I would definitely go for.'

Jules had looked down at his glass before speaking. 'Has a bad boy done something he shouldn't?'

'Course not.' Angelo had pulled on his mental throttle to accelerate out of trouble. 'It's just when I play Monopoly with my youngest, that's the one card me and her really fight over.'

'Because', Jules had said, 'if I thought you even half had, I wouldn't have come here.'

'Bollocks to that.' A pause. Angelo had moved to head it off. 'Other half?'

Angelo fetched the drinks, full pints. 'Other half' was a misnomer. 'Still', he'd said, 'A get out of jail free card would help. I'm curious, is all. Grooming grasses never come my way much when I was on the force.'

'You were chiefly Big Ears Branch. Listening. That's how you'll find out why those MPs aren't being good boys. It's all boys, by the way.'

'Say I get caught?'

'Speaking wholly theoretically, you'd be looked after.'

'So there *are* get out of jail free cards?'

'Don't fence, mate. Do you want the job or don't you? I'm not here for the hops.'

Angelo had taken the plunge. 'You're here for a yes vote. OK then. The ayes have it.'

'Good. Report in not less than two weeks to this name.' And Jules had given Angelo a business card. 'He's not the one in charge, more project manager.'

The card had read "Edgar Godwin". Angelo had said 'I don't bring it up again with you?'

'From now on you don't even know me', Jules had said. And then, fostering a spark of friendship in case Devene was ever useful again, 'Tell you what, I'll turn up at the Palace the day you get your gong. Press my nose to the railings, watch you hold it up to the crowd in your topper and tails.'

TWENTYFIVE

Subsequent meetings with Laura took place in St John's Wood. Jeff had found a compact little love nest there.

'Why do you live in a has-been neighborhood?' said Laura, hoisting her earrings from her lobes. It was her fifth visit. 'No shops. Or none you'd want to shop at.'

He agreed. It was the softer option, given her fiery nature. He hadn't let on how their nest was not his true home. With her even a love lair might seem too like a sleazy motel room. He'd done what he could. Put a photo of the two of them over the mantel.

Jeff had good reasons for not meeting Laura at his main apartment. Tucky. He loved the little critter. But Laura, in whose wonderful eyes he thought he could detect flecks of green, might resent her personally. In truth, he was trying to run two females simultaneously. One might skitter around on four legs, weigh a pound and have tiny little tin tack teeth. The other stood, sashayed and even swayed (when on a dance floor) on two gorgeous gams, carried around ninety and packed a mean bite to the shoulder (when climaxing), as his right humeral tissue could testify. They were both members of the double X chromosome club, a notoriously tricky sodality.

The fifth grapple was over. Jeff and Laura lay facing each other, companions in satisfaction, their breathing slightly heavier than usual.

'Why'd you turn me down that time our eyes met on the airplane?' he said. Already he looked back on their very first glimpse of each other with fond memory.

'Down?'

'It looked that way. You went back to your book. *That* book. Diana von Something. But you weren't reading it. You held it upside down.'

'It didn't soar. Plus, I felt punk.'

'I'm sorry', Jeff said. He put his arms round her. She hid her face against his chest.

'None of it's the real reason.' His chest muffled her words. 'I thought you were the most beautiful thing I'd ever seen', she said. 'Ever, ever.' He kissed her. 'What I didn't like', she said, 'was your friend.'

'My friend? You mean Godwin? But didn't you say you'd met him the ColLaborative Conference?'

'Darling, we agree he's bad news.'

Only much later did he realise she'd ducked his question.

'Anyhow', she said, 'I couldn't do anything about you then.' She twisted the corner of a sheet round her fingers. 'See, I got caught once doing something about…about that kind of thing.'

He tensed himself for an unpleasant revelation.

'Corniest spot on earth', she said. Then, almost musingly, 'Or would be if it were on earth.'

'I don't get you.'

'Like an earth closet but not on earth. Airplane rest room.'

'Oh.' Yes indeedy. So banal a spot for two airplane passengers to meet then mate that it had become a joke.

'Don't go all white like that', she said. 'I've had…been with…quite a few guys.'

'It wasn't that… Well yes, it is that. But, hell, Laure, there's the risk.' He said 'Laure', conveying tenderness, instead of 'Laura', burying '-ra' in the Creole speech he'd grown up with.

'Mostly it was in my first marriage.'

'But you're on your second now…'

'Third. Mind, I'm utterly loyal to Vic.'

'Utterly?'

'I might have gone once, twice with other people…' She was speaking in a whisper now, '…but he always knew. Does that add up to approve?'

How in hell would I know, thought Jeff. The things people told you about their marriages. He'd come across other instances when interviewing people for *Hence* TJs.

'I never met your husband', he said.

'Vic. You know, I'd love to bring you two together.'

'That would be interesting. But a good idea it's not.'

'We don't have sex much any more', she said. 'Vic and me.'

'Much?'

'Not as such. He…he likes to watch. He hears a lot too. Gets to find out the damnedest things.'

'For example?'

'The other day he told me some government guy let drop how Mary Matheson discusses really important issues using plastic letters from a kids' game to create words you can read, then break up. She won't mention them out loud. Thinks it's a security lapse if she uses her voice or puts things on paper.'

'Wow. Even Nixon never got that paranoid.'

'Vic said he sees her point. You can phrase your message clearer that way.'

'Can I use that? About Mary Matheson?'

'Why not? It's well known she has this yen for Scrabble.'

'And you heard it from Victor? Not that I'd mention that.'

'Vic looks, listens, lets other people talk themselves dry, then wades in for the kill. Trouble is, he's come to use the same technique in the bedroom. Look on a lot, not touch. Or not much.'

'Look on while you and…who?'

She nibbled his chin a little, stroked his hair again. She went on: 'That time in the rest room, I was put on film. Video-ed. It's worse than caught live.'

'I can imagine.' Jeff cursed himself for such a weak response.

'Can you? *Can* you?' Pause. 'Five days after the flight, a DVD arrived. All safely done up. One of those bubble wraps. Vic'd left for work. Thank God. I couldn't have hid how I felt.'

'I thought you said this was during your first marriage?'

'My first husband was called Vic.'

Jeff said, 'The first guy you married was Peter Swayle.'

'Peter V. Swayle. Who I always called by his second name. Which in full was Vickery. For which Vic is short.'

'Ah.' Jeff made this as neutral as he could.

As for Laura, if you went by her tone of voice she'd stayed calm. But it became clear she was furious when she began to struggle into her street clothes. 'Don't bother to see me out', she said. 'And don't bother calling me a cab. I can pick one up the corner.'

The mandatory pacification program that ensued took him a full half hour. After he'd cajoled her back into bed he went over to the kitchenette to fix coffee. Coffee, the stronger and more aromatic the better, calmed her down where it made other people nervy.

He mentally shook himself to clear his head and addressed the contradictions in Laura's account of herself. Why had she muddled him over which marriage she'd committed which adultery in, especially since it bore on when she'd got videoed; whether or not, or

111

how well, if at all, she knew Edgar/Ed Godwin/Goodwin; and how many men she'd gone with and when?

'What happened?' he said, pouring her cup three-quarters full, already expert as to how she liked it. 'The video', he said.

'I sat down and watched myself. Full face. Know something? I wasn't bad. I could earn good money in porno flicks. I really came across the way I felt. Even turned myself on a little. The camcorder only caught the guy's back.'

'And his back, like my back that first time your place, was a lot thinner than your then husband's?'

She giggled.

'Thicker then?'

She giggled again. He marvelled at what she did and didn't take in bad part. 'About the same', she said at last, 'only black.'

'Jesus.'

'You Southerners never let up on the nigra, do you?'

'I didn't mean… Only…'

'Forget it. The question was, who'd shot it, the video? And was he after me or…the other party?'

'What happened next?'

'I'm still waiting to see.'

'It happened *recently*?'

'Just before I met you. I haven't been with a single guy since. Not one. I swear.'

'What's the name of the guy you were with?'

'Pass.' A pause. 'Do something for me', she said.

'OK. What?'

'You wouldn't ask what if you really loved me.'

'How'll I know if you won't tell me?'

'Don't bully.'

'I said OK before I asked what it was you want that I do. That's a blank check.'

'I didn't cash it yet. I will now. Investigate this video thing.'

'You mean, who shot the video?'

'It would be a start.' Another pause. 'How's your investigation into Godwin?'

'I can't make him out. Whoever he is. He doesn't answer any numbers or emails, so why hand them out? And why call yourself by so many names when they're all so alike? You put up a fake ID, you make it as unlike your real one as you can, right? Not a variant so close people get muddled.'

'Maybe he wants people to get muddled.'

'But that draws attention to his fake IDs. What's the point?'

'Can it. Come here.'

He came here.

*

They'd said their goodbyes and he'd just leant forward to open the front door for her when she said 'Want to buy some magazines?'

'What?'

'Glamour titles. *Chic* and *YooHoo!*. Vic's ready to sell. I heard him mention it.'

'Gosh. Why?'

'Raise cash, I guess. The *Date* needs a lot put into it. Or for some new investment. He has other commitments too. Would your people be interested?'

'My *Hence* people?'

'Who else?'

'It's Arlene calls the shots. The publisher. She could be. I heard she thinks we're too concentrated on the East Coast. But the English market'd likely be something totally else. She'd need guidance.'

'Why not yours?'

'I'm a writer. I love journalism.'

'No need to dump it. But move up to the business side. At least pitch for an advisor's role over any new acquisition. Ask Arlene. It's Arlene Strepsky, isn't it?' He nodded. 'Yeah, I know her. Not well, just met with a few times. I could maybe get you a commission on any deal. Finder's fee.'

'I could use it. This place here's...costly.'

'They don't give you an apartment as part of your job?'

'Sure they do', said Jeff hurriedly. His renting the love nest had nearly been rumbled. 'I meant London's so costly.'

'You arbitrage a sale to Arlene and you can afford to have me round to some place is in-now, not has-been.' She smiled at him. 'How's that for a deal?'

TWENTYSIX

The next day Jeff stayed home the whole morning. There was Godwin/Goodwin to get hold of, Chrissie to fix a meeting with, Tod's notes to have another stab at deciphering.

Easier said than done, the whole damn lot. The latest numbers he'd got for Godwin/Goodwin turned out as unobtainable as the earlier ones. The website was unknown. He suspected he'd get a bounce back on the email too. Chrissie's number had a recording saying callers were to leave a message. The original of Tod's notes had long ago disintegrated. Jeff's A4 copy had disappeared.

Disappeared? He searched everywhere, even pulling out his grips and other baggage from on top of the closet. Nothing. Karola must have put them some place. She was due at 11.30. He spent 9 to 10 turning the apartment upside down, 10 to 10.30 putting things back in their places and 10.30 onward in an armchair waiting for Karola to arrive.

Tucky was keen to play but Jeff was not. Very not. He kept thrusting her away. At just past 11 the door bell rang. Karola was decidedly early. Jeff put Tucky in her tray and the tray in the bathroom. He opened the front door. A man he'd not seen before stood there.

'Morning', said the man. He stood just the least bit awkwardly, as if nursing a foot injury. 'Andy. Andy Dean. You must be the new tenant. I'm the handyman for this block. It's mostly sorting out rubbish issues. The Council's new rules on what goes in which colour bag. Enough blather. I heard from Mrs Wyczowski about your shower. Sorry about that. It was last summer, the drought. Mr Snaith was keen to observe the water restrictions so he asked me to slow the flow. I rigged up a makeshift filter kind of thing in the tap head. I heard from Mrs Wyczowski how you were upset the shower didn't flow properly.'

'Thanks. I fixed it, as it happens.'

'You sure? I could take a look.'

Jeff's cell phone gave a muffled ring. 'Don't bother', said Jeff distractedly, turning his head. 'And please don't go in the bathroom. Tucky's there.' As if to confirm this the rattle of toiletry items was audible through the bathroom door. What had she patted? Dental floss? A nail brush? It sounded so deliberate you'd swear it was a human. 'Keep your cotton-pickin' paws off of my Davidoff, you hear?' he shouted toward the bathroom door. His cell phone rang a third time. Where'd he left it?

'I'll be on my way then. Cheers', the man Andy said. Jeff turned in the direction of the ring tone. The front door shut behind him as he did so. The caller was Doresett, picking up Jeff's earlier message asking about Laura Deller. She for one had slipped through the net. Jeff had found nothing about her on-line.

'Name rings a bell', said Doresett. 'You mean Victor Deller's current wife? I think I can…' His voice got faint. He came back on the line. 'Born Laura Gloria DeFalbe. God, some parents have no ear. Let me see… Family from the Golden State. Old Frisco Earthquake Era money.'

'What did she do before marrying Deller?'

'She was seen around at one time with David Macnamara, the *Era* Group chairman. Rumour is he never got over her leaving him. He's so anti-American you could just about believe it was personal pique.'

'So Victor Deller not only made money, he married it?'

'Third time lucky. You know the saying? Your first wife you marry for sex. Your second to raise a family. Not till your third do you get to marry for love. Here money, Deller's tough, cold heart's desire.'

TWENTYSEVEN

Angelo had known the bug in the American reporter kid's flat couldn't last for ever. What he hadn't wanted was for someone to find the thing stuck under a table. Also, the bug only transmitted the kid's side of the conversation. Irrelevant, most of it. And boring? But Angelo'd been a listener on the force long enough to know you always struck gold eventually.

Which was how he'd heard the kid mention a sheet of paper with stuff on it to do with the bloke had lived there before, the one Frankie'd bopped. Had this been what Frankie was looking for the night of their break-in? If so, once Angelo'd passed it to Area Manager, Frankie's stock would drop.

One good use of the bug was to indicate where the kid kept the bit of paper. From the crackle with which the kid had folded it at the end of one of his early confabs, and the slither of a drawer being closed afterwards, Angelo had reckoned it was in the table the phone sat on.

He was chuffed by how completely the Andy Dean maintenance man act had worked. The first time, he'd called just as the foreign char was sitting over her mid-morning coffee. It had been child's play to swipe the sheet of paper from the phone table drawer. Angelo had gone into the hall ostensibly on his way to check the living room for damp after a complaint from the flat below about water leaks. The char had stayed sipping in the kitchen.

Then there was the time he'd overheard the char tell the young master in advance how she was planning a spring clean. Result? He'd been able to remove the bug just now, well before she got started.

Next Frankie. Angelo sat up straight in his car, which he'd parked across the street from the kid's flat when listening in, and called Area Manager.

'That you, Mr Sanders?'

'You know my voice, Devene. What is it? DEFRA Inspector's due any minute. Which reminds me. Clive says you never handed over that roe deer last time you were here…'

'She turned out maggoty, Mr Sanders. Too far gone for processing.'

'If DEFRA gets heavy we'll have to put a hold on fancy meats anyway. They can close us down for a tiny thing like deer. Country's a bloody police state...Why are you ringing?'

'I wondered if you got any news of Melusine.'

'Melusine? Who the hell... Oh yeah, the new, er, slaughterhouse operative. Why should I?'

Good. Frankie's tried a cover up. 'Didn't Mister Francis...

'Who?'

'Beg pardon. Force of habit. It's how he likes Micky and me to call him.'

'More fool you.'

'He *is* the boss.' *Stir, stir.*

'No. I am.'

Angelo got boy-scout earnest. 'The very point I try and mention when he leans on us to say "Mister Francis". He ain't 'avin' it.'

Area Manager clicked his tongue with vexation. Nothing more, but celestial music to Angelo. 'What's this about Melusine?', said Area Manager.

'Didn't Mister..., did'n' Frankie tell you, then?'

'Tell me what?'

'How she's gone missing.'

'Missing?'

'It struck me as one of the staff people the health club place might have got some info. Frankie don't like us mixing with them, me and Micky, which is why I come straight to you.'

'Start from the top. When did she go missing?'

'Not sure. Frankie only told us this morning.'

'He there? Put me onto him.'

'He only give us the barest run down. I respect need-to-know confidentiality as much as the next bloke, but it'd help if we were told basic stuff. Oh well.' Angelo sighed loudly, adding 'When I left him he was still on his breakfast. Earl Grey with a slice of lemon.' *That's 'specially good. Stress his late start, and how his taste in tea makes him too superior for dirty work.*

'You and Frost keep looking', said Area Manager. 'I'll ring him right away.'

Oh no you won't, thought Angelo, but all he said was 'Best of luck there, Mr Sanders. I try him several times myself. He don' answer.

He's often like that, I regret to say. Don' make things any easier. There's one more thing, Mr Sanders.'

'Yes? Make it snappy. I can see the DEFRA man's car coming up the hill.'

'I found a bit of paper at the flat of that geezer you said we should look into in case he talked, that time we was with you.'

Area Manager's voice dropped in pitch. 'Yes? You mean Tod Snaith?'

'The one you called a mangy cur.'

'I may have expressed myself in such terms.'

'Frankie missed it. I found it when I went back. The bit of paper. Wasn't easy swipin' it. The new kid, the one's replaced Snaith, had some piece of fluff there, in the bath room. If she'd come out when I was in the hall foldin' it up I'd've been in deep manure.'

'What paper? DEFRA's here now. He's parking his car.'

'It don' make much sense. Not to me. It might to you. Or the Big Boss. I don't recall you ever tell us his name.'

There was just the shortest of pauses before Area Manager answered. Then, 'Fax it me. And post the original. Registered mail. *Now.*' The connexion went dead.

Angelo folded his mobile. What with the DEFRA visit, Area Manager wasn't likely to get in touch with Frankie just yet. And even when he tried there'd be a further delay. Back at the Shepherd's Bush caff, while Frankie was in the gents and Micky was getting himself a round of toast, Angelo'd surreptitiously keyed *#06# on Frankie's mobile. It'd given Angelo the IEMI number, which half an hour before calling Area Manager he'd phoned Frankie's service provider and notified them of, claiming Frankie's mobile had been stolen. They'd promised to blacklist it. When Area Manager phoned Frankie and couldn't get through he'd think Frankie was slack about keeping in touch.

Next Frankie himself. This was a lot trickier, seeing as how Frankie didn't like him much. Better go through Micky. 'Micky? That you?'

'Ange-o. Where are you? Missing you, man. Can't we hunt as a pair, like we always done?'

'Micky, I can't get through to Frankie. Tell him when I find Mel I'm going straight to Mr Sanders with her.'

'*When*? You know where she is?'

'Might do.'

'You could cut me in. You'll need help handlin' her anyway.'

'Not yet. Tracking her down calls for a bit of the subtle. Later, maybe, when we need to rub it in how she's been a bad girl. Meanwhile you be sure and tell Frankie I'm going with her to Mr Sanders.'

'He ain't gonna like that.'

'Mr Sanders don't like it how Frankie's gone and let one of our star turns slip through his fingers.'

'Star turn? But she wasn't.'

'Oh no? Area Manager don't think so. He's got the idea Frankie's creaming off some of Mel's takings for himself.'

Micky said, 'He'll go spare, Area Manager will.'

'That's Frankie's lookout.'

Now all he had to do was find Mel. Exactly what Frankie'd told him to do anyway.

TWENTYEIGHT

Jeff realised he'd left Tucky in the bathroom ever since the handyman had called. God, must be like half an hour. He hoped the little thing wouldn't have got lonesome. She was a sociable creature. He opened the bathroom door with apprehension.

Tucky had gone to sleep. She lay curled up in a crescent, her head flat on the floor, purring carefree. He stepped out into the hall. The table with the land line phone had not been pushed back properly against the wall. He lifted it to put it straight. The ball point pen had gone. The handyman! Could he also be one of the two masks had frisked him the night the fox had...? He'd even stood awkwardly. Why? Because he had a limp. One he, Jeff, had saddled him with when he'd chopped at his leg.

Damn, though, the man had half an hour start. Not a hope of following him. Jeff drifted back into the living room, stared hopelessly out of the window, wondered what to do. The street sure was quiet this time of day. He looked down at a Subaru parked opposite. A man got out and went into the newsagent ten yards down the street, behind the letter box. A few minutes later he came out, clutching a newspaper. Jeff was slightly long-sighted and in any case recognised most British dailies by their design, type face and size – broadsheet or tabloid. This wasn't any title he knew. But from the horse and ring-topped winning post that took up most of the front page it had to be a racing paper.

The man stopped and held it open, studying it, then folded it small and studied it some more, jotting down notes on the page with a pen. Jeff's mind began to wander. Finally the man thrust the paper in his coat pocket and stood up straight, yawning and stretching his arms skyward. It was the handyman, Andy. Jeff raced down stairs.

By the time Jeff got to the street the guy'd disappeared. No chance of even noting his licence plate. Jeff knew his heisting the pen meant he withdrew the surveillance too. How'd he gained access to the apartment block to start with?

Jeff turned to what 'Byr.o' meant. It was the only word on the original bit of paper hadn't been crossed out. He'd tried anagrams of Byr.o. He'd tried substituting numbers for the letters of the alphabet (2 25 18.15). At first this had looked promising: 18.15 could mean a quarter past six in the evening. Was the capital 'B' there to indicate 200 rather than 2, giving 225? He'd always hated rebuses, spelling bees and all that other mental torture they practised on kids…

TWENTYNINE

Angelo reckoned Jules's proposition had legs. Upon those legs he started building dreams. Do a deal with the cops? Maybe even get reinstated? He'd have to pin the dark bint death on Micky. Had Micky left any personal identifying marks on her? What were they these days? DNA, did it wash away? Mel had seen him kill the dark bint too. Now she'd got away. Mel had to go too, then.

His Indie Jones ring tone started up. It was Area Manager.

'Devene? Sanders. I still can't get Frankie. Tell him to ring me.'

'But Mr Sanders, I can't get him eith…'

'Go round there.'

'I don't know his address. Part of all that need-to-know hush-hush busin…'

'Got a pen? Get writing.'

Angelo took down details of a top floor flat in a Swiss Cottage conversion. He might have known there'd be a cottage involved. All he said was, 'Be round there in a flash. But he may be ou…'

'Hang around till he turns up. Where's that document we talked about?'

'In the mai…'

'Registered?'

'Of course. I got the counterfoi…'

'Don't bother. Provided that document arrives.' Area Manager rang off.

Angelo resumed his murderous dreams. They became domestic. Reinstated. Could see the wife and kids regularly. Solid pension, plus whatever bribes he could collect on the side.

By now he was seated and sipping a mocha latte in front of an internet café monitor screen. *Hence* back numbers had proved useless. Precious little sport. No racing at all. Angelo thought to look for Mel other ways. He abandoned www.hencearchives.com/ and keyed in 'Mel', 'escort', 'London'. Some independents came up. Mels abounded. The fifteenth looked a lot like her, bar the hair style and colour.

Looking closer he saw it wasn't his Mel after all. This girl had a mole on her throat. Only three other Mels to go. He called them up.

No. She must have changed her name. Only she wasn't Mel in the first place, was she? What had she been? Olfat. Christ, how could one forget? Well she wasn't going to advertise as Olfat.

Os...he thought of Olivia. Had a nice ring to it. He wished he'd chosen that for Mandy. Hello, here she was. He nearly choked when he saw Mel's trade name: Mandy. He wanted to ring Verna then and there, make her go straight round and get their team vicar to rechristen Mandy something less obscene.

He pressed on with 'Mandy''s website. Questions, questions. He decided he was 18 or over, over if it was years, bit under if it was stones, and that, yes, he did want to Enter. Even fucking fucking involved form-filling nowadays.

At last he was through to Mel's virtual personality. He read through a banal welcome message; a false age; bogus eye colour ('sparkling, come-to-bed green' ones; must have bought herself coloured contact lenses); a claim to appreciate the finer things in life, including the company of affluent and sophisticated business gentlemen; her pledge of a warm and friendly welcome; her vaunted intelligence and sophistication, making her an ideal companion for dinner dates, parties, receptions, the theatre.

He couldn't be bothered with her rates since he wasn't going to pay her. He noted her number carefully, however. As he clicked his way back through the various websites to the primary Google list he alighted on 'Male escorts'. That gave him an idea. He knew someone whose cup of tea a male escort might very well be. An Earl Grey cup with a slice of lemon in it.

THIRTY

Only last week Jeff would have rather relished a visit to Chrissie. Conversely, now he'd started properly seeing someone again he felt slightly embarrassed looking Chrissie up at all. His professional duties took precedence, however. She answered after a dozen rings. He tried to set a time that afternoon.

'Today's right out', she said. 'As for tomorrow, it's our second busiest day of the week.'

He was intrigued enough to ask what top busiest was. The journo in him. 'Fridays. That's why it's called Friday, after some German love goddess. Noon on we're up to our eyes, literally.'

'Our? That girl Mel living with ya then?' He spoke jauntily. Escorts induced a boulevardier outlook.

'Come round tomorrow, see for yourself', said Chrissie. 'Can't squeeze you in till tea time. Still, what's tea without crumpet? Seriously, traffic through here's murder Sundays. They've been with their wives or girlfriends all day Saturday. But even if they did manage a hump then it was (a) vanilla and (b) squeezed into any time left after washing the car and a round of golf. By next morning they've worked up such an itch for a decent bit of kink they're like a rutting ram on rhino horn.'

He and Chrissie eventually settled on six pm, a two-hour stint minimum at £500 for revelations rating 8 out of a possible 10 on the *National Enquirer* scale of salaciousness about at least two stars on $5 mill a flick or up.

'Sweetie, you haggle like a pro', said Chrissie, half rueful, half admiring. *'Dosvidanya.'* From her accepting a half K instead of the full one they'd agreed their first meeting, Jeff guessed imports had indeed forced down prices.

Chrissie ran her body shop out of a second-floor mansion block apartment off of Gloucester Road. Escort etiquette demanded she defer telling him the exact address till he'd called her from the local subway station.

She hid behind the front door when opening it. She wore a fur-trimmed bra and tight French knickers, both the non-fur bits in black lace, also outrageously high heels. Nothing else. 'In case you change your mind about the fun stuff', she said in answer to his look.

'No chance', he said, thinking hard of Laura but not sounding as unswayable as he ought.

'Then I'll slip into something less slinky.' She peeled off in front of him. He gazed round the apartment, chiefly to avert his eyes. 'Place is bigger than it looks', he said.

'I bought at a good time. Been doing this ever since uni. Put me through an MBA. And you know what that costs in tuition fees.'

'I don't. It as fierce as back home?'

'Twenty to twenty-four, even for a Brit like me.'

'Bucks or quid?'

'Quid. As much as eighty for a foreigner.'

'Like Mel?'

'Mel's hardly the MBA type, poor lamb.'

'But she's in the same business as you, right?'

'The blunt end.'

'I thought you were a team?'

'Temporary arrangement. Five years from now I'll either have moved up to management or on. Got my own restaurant. Maybe even a chic little boutique hotel. Mel's more the type to wind up round the back of M-way service stations bent over a car bonnet getting her tank pumped full by long-distance lorry drivers for the price of a hot meal.' Chrissie shuddered. 'Look, we're supposed to be discussing stars. Kev's into water sports. Did you know that?'

'Kev?'

'Kevin Lincoln. Not Kevin Hoover.'

The mega hunk in the $850m-grossing Robo Babe IV, *Jeez*. 'I didn't know he even liked girls.'

'He does if they're flat-chested and dress as Brit prep school boys. Shorts, blazers, caps, satchels. Not schoolgirls. They're a special taste too, but more mainstream. Mind, he'd never go for the real thing. Under-age is out where our clean-living Kev's concerned.'

'Well, well, well.' Jeff jotted down the details. Not that he could more than hint. He didn't do Hollywood gossip much, anyway.

'Who else d'you want to know about?', said Chrissie. 'Closer to home any good?'

'Guess London's home for now. '

'I meant New York. I have to be careful about London. My line of business you do better to keep your mouth shut.' She winked. 'Other than a BBJ.'

Jeff looked up from his notepad. 'Boeing Business Jet? Big Beat Jackpot?'

'Acronyms really aren't your thing, are they? I should have remembered, from when we met. Birthday Blow Job. Don't they give them where you're from?'

'All the days of the year.'

'Atta boy. See, I can speak Yank.' Chrissie, who'd slipped into something casual, took hold of him by his tie and tried to loosen it. 'Eighty for a quickie?' she said, opening her eyes extra wide.

He prised her off, half laughing. 'It's your Brit clients I'm most interested in.'

'I shouldn't. Really I shouldn't. It's discretion we're selling almost as much as sex. Sometimes more, where the guys don't have sex are concerned.'

'You get many of those?'

Chrissie crossed her legs, cupped her chin in her hands. She looked very fetching. 'I tell you, there was this one really weird dude Mel and I put on a show for a few nights ago. OK voice, no chin. Surreal costume. Imperial purple shirt, plain front, buttonless, like a C of E bish wears. Or the costume one of those Russian dancers kicks his heels up in. Necklace with all kinds of charms on it. He got himself all het up as to how we were whores. Well Whores'Я'Us, right? So there's Mel and me slurping away till our tongues are raw and Mr Puritan Preacher punter man waving his arms and denouncing us and telling us we'll fry in hell and do you know he goes and passes out. Stroke? Syncope? Funny thing is, I felt dirty. Sullied. Not because he'd had it off with us, but because he hadn't, then fell off his trolley. Sudden upset of human dignity stuff. Haven't felt that way since my first year in business, when if I ate snatch at all it was thru gritted teeth.' Her eyes took on a faraway look. 'Those days there was one client who liked it chained to a St Andrew's Cross…'

Jeff looked down at the floor. Chrissie turned, grasped that he was uncomfortable and said 'You're from the Bible Belt, aren't you? I suppose crosses are still sacred in those parts. Sorry.'

'My great-aunt Estelle's time they burnt them. Klan guys did. It's more…'

126

'...Well anyway, a St Andrew's is a standard subbie accessory. Not that I'm religious. Not since my convent days anyhow...'

'You Catholic?'

'Not strict. I don't even do strict in business. Some girls like to. Get their own back.'

'Uh huh?...' Jeff still felt uncomfortable. He tried steering the conversation back onto wholesome ground. 'Was this the night I ran across you guys at the Beldon? You and Mel?'

'Could have been.' She thought a moment. 'Yes, of course it was. And you were with that nice-looking boy.'

'While you were with someone calls himself Edgar Godwin.'

'Edwin Godber.'

'Excuse me?'

'Edwin Godber.'

'Not Edgar Godwin? Or maybe you mean Ed Goodwin?'

'No I don't. I saw him write his name when he booked us in at the reception desk.'

'But he wasn't your client, was he?'

'Of course not. Just the facilitator. I'd never met him before that evening.'

'"Facilitator" 's good. I definitely like "facilitator".'

'Fuck off.' It was said friendly fashion on the whole. 'I hate "pimp". You think zits.'

'So do lots of people. S'why the marketing pros gave it a good weaselling, polished it into something slips down smoother with the consumer. It's not hookers and whores any more, it's escorts and "girl friend experiences"; "facilitators" and "agencies".'

'You don't have to tell me about marketing. I'm an MBA, remember?'

'I should write a piece about it.'

'Someone already has. It was in *Product Position Weekly* a few months ago.'

'You subscribe?'

'I'm not a complete bimbo, you know. I can, and do, read in my spare time. Not just trash. I like to keep my MBA in shape by following trends in marketing.'

'Sorry. Guess I was a tad insensitive.'

'That's OK. Now what else did you want to ask me?'

'That night. The client was upstairs in a room, out of sight?'

127

'Of course. Happens all the time a four-, five-star hotel like the Beldon.' Chrissie got up, crossed the room and adjusted the cattleyas in a vase, about $500-worth by Jeff's reckoning. The gift of a high-roller regular?

'Roll on more six- and seven-star hotels', she said. 'Us escies can up our rates.'

'But I overheard him, EG let's call him, say something like you and Mel mustn't keep His Highness waiting.'

'His Holiness, not Highness.'

The penny didn't just drop. It plummeted. 'Shiy-y-yat. Purple blouse. Bangles and dangles of more faiths 'n you can shake a stick at. Upper-class accent. It's Lord Lyonel Crowthorne, isn't it?'

'Is it? I wouldn't know. Is that a real lord? Most punters use fake names. Not just the lords, ladies too. OK, there was this duke used to pay by personal cheque drawn on Coutts, but he was the exception. Also before my time. Worse luck. I might have ended up Her Graceful mistress of three castles and a Mayfair mansion. You'd be amazed how many escies do pick up a title. Beats boutique hotels, however niche. Every now and then I look at a glossy in the hairdresser's, spot a photo of Lady Muck – and muck's the word, believe me – flashing her entry badge in the Ascot Enclosure and I think, hey, wait a sec, you were that multiple squirter Ayesha kept the Greenbach, Angel, Lettiss trading floor chief's stag night going for five solid hours without a break, time I was a skimpy assistant gang banger-ette learning the ropes.'

'And how'd you meet Mel?'

'On a job. Threesomes, foursomes and moresomes the punter could call up anyone anywhere, Flavia from Belgravia, Elsie from Chelsea, Lily from Piccadilly, or he gets 'em supplied blind by his facilitator. Some guys like hiring a pig in a poke. So Mel could've caught someone's eye somewhere or got sent along on spec or called up to fill a last-minute gap. Point is, Mel and me, we got chatting afterwards. She told me how she'd been brought over here to work in the hotel industry then got conned and I said well, hun, you *are* working in the hotel industry, this here where we just performed's not just standard prestigious, it gets rated in Mr and Mrs Smith and I hope you realise how big time bijou that is, but she said no, not that side of hotels, and I said, well, hun, you don't make much as a cleaner with no English, and if you haven't got a work permit you don't get promoted, so I wouldn't whinge about it, and she said no she'd got kind of used to it but there were these thugs breathing down her neck all the time and preventing her doing any sight-seeing or contacting her cousin up in Brum and taking most of her earnings off her, so I said if they let you go on an outcall they've got a bit careless, and you should think of going indie rather than stick with an agency anyway, and I know a guy can get you your own website so you don't just pull in a decent whack but get to keep it, at least more of it than you do with your present people, so the long and short of it was she came and holed up with me.'

'Where's Mel now? She a long-term house guest here?'

'Hardly. But ordinary paying guest house-guest for the time being, sure. Till she gets fixed up on her own. I've got this spare room not earning its keep. Truth is, it's too small to earn much of one. Use it to store my protest placards mostly. That's a scream, isn't it? Only a few months back I'm barracking MPs all I can to keep out the likes of Mel and now I'm putting her up. Muggins me. Luckily she can just about squeeze in there. Provided she leaves her tits in the corridor, heh heh.'

'She there now? Can't be. I'd've heard her moving around.'

'She's on an out call. Since…what's the time?'

'Twenty of seven.'

'That's odd. She's been gone since late this morning. Can't be an all-nighter at that hour. Wouldn't be out of town either. Most days our grade escies don't travel beyond the 0207 area.'

'The inner city phone zone?'

Chrissie nodded. 'The eights and even more, the M25 and further out, that's cheap slag territory. Some of them are so desperate for custom they go bareback. Next stop's an AIDS clinic.'

'Don't guys ever book an escort for as much as four hours then?'

'Of course, but not much on Sundays. End of the working week's different.'

'Call her. If you're worried, call her.'

'I don't want to interrupt her mid-session. Unprofessional.'

'Won't she've switched her cell phone to message reception mode?'

'Mel's not used to mobiles. Still, I think I'll give it a try.'

Chrissie dug out her mobile from where she kept it safe from punters' probing fingers under a dominatrix's peaked leather cap enhanced with a *SchutzStaffel* double lightning badge to lend

129

authority, cued Mel's number and waited, biting her lip. Jeff noticed how different was Chrissie's and Laura's use of the same facial contortion. But then Chrissie was doing concerned, not invitation.

'Nothing', she said. They looked at each other. Both with worry now, not flirtily any more.

He said, 'Don't you guys leave each other a contact address, case the punter's a…?' He couldn't finish.

'Psycho? Normally, yes. Basic escie vigilance. Trouble is, Mel's new to it all. Before she came here I imagine she just lay back and took whatever her facilitators shovelled at her. They're low on initiative where she comes from.'

'Just where is that?'

'Who cares *just* where? Roughly where's easy. Middle East. One of those countries they treat women like thoroughbred race horses, mate them to someone they've never met just to cement a business deal, sweat them in material covers up their natural appearance just to stop a rival appreciating their pure filly lines, retire them when their breeding days are over.'

Her ferocity of tone surprised him. 'You mean Arabs?'

'I'll rim some raghead in work hours if he pays extra. Doesn't mean I have to brown nose him in leisure ones. That's downright obsequious. I'll be fucked – pardon my French – if I do obsequious except in a master/slave fantasy role, and at a premium price.'

THIRTYONE

In selecting the male hooker most likely to distract Frankie, Angelo reckoned the more he resembled the American kid news reporter the better. God knows that look had got Frankie creaming his jeans right enough. It'd even stopped him using his gun. Not his pistol, though. Har har.

The gun was what worried Angelo. He'd never carried one full-time himself. You didn't need to with bints. Any of 'em dug her toes in, a slap round the chops usually broke up the log jam. Angelo had stopped worrying about spoiled goods now he'd left the flesh industry's road haulage sector and was moving up to a management buy-out.

Frankie's gun... Even now Angelo couldn't bring himself to achieve strategic arms parity by toting one as well. When on the force he'd twice applied to become an AFO. He'd done a few sessions at private shooting ranges too but had hated the noise. And his hands had bloody shook too much to hold the thing steady.

Face it, listening in was more his, Angelo's, thing. It involved sound but not din. And if a show of mega strength was ever truly necessary...well, for what else had God in his pearly-gated precision tool room invented the industrial-size spanner?

Angelo's decision to use a queer whore might be spot on tactically but it didn't make the task of clicking through on-line male escort portfolios any pleasanter. Their cocky, knowing poses grated. Then there was the whiteness of their bloody teeth. Not to mention the cared-for quality of their effing hair, of which they had so much they could afford to cut it short, or even shave it off.

There was the perfection of their six-pack torsos. Angelo'd been into six-packs in his time. But nowadays the contents had begun to spill down towards his crotch and were pushing his belly out.

He finally settled on a saucy little number with the obvious alias of Pierre. Looked as fake Frog as a counterfeit Cartier on a Caledonian Market street trader's stall. Should suit Frankie to a tee, though. Angelo booked Pierre by email for an outcall to Frankie's at ten o'clock next Sunday morning, adding plenty of detail about the kind of role-playing turned the client on.

Next Angelo rang Micky. The tricky bit would be to prevent Micky meeting him at Frankie's. Could he just say meet him? Not tell him the place was Frankie's at all? Had Micky ever been to Frankie's? Only time would tell. And you can't wallop a quick answer from time, whatever size spanner you use.

In the end he fixed it for Micky to meet him at 'a' Swiss Cottage address round about one pm the day of rest, Sunday roast time. He let Micky think he'd have caught up with Mel by then. Well he would have almost, seeing as he was going to get her round there himself, only a bit later.

He fetched the unmarked lorry up from where they'd stored it down across the river and took it to the next road from Frankie's, parking it there overnight. His plan depended on Frankie's keeping his Porsche right outside his flat. So the weekend would be best, when the surrounding yuppies zipped off to their weekend second homes.

Next he tested the door bells for numbers 1 and 2 in Frankie's house. Nothing. So Frankie, when he eventually got home after his Saturday shopping, would be the building's sole occupant.

It was to lure Frankie out onto the street then back inside his flat again with a guy he'd never met that Angelo had booked Pierre for Sunday morning. A good, innocent time of the week. Lulled even a degenerate smear of filth like Frankie into being off his guard. Angelo took up his post watching Frankie's main entrance from Saturday afternoon on.

To relieve the boredom and siphon off some of the tension Angelo started in on his finger nails after just thirty minutes. He gnawed silently and spat out the strips like pips from a satsuma. About seven there drew up the cream swirl of steel Angelo had coveted from his first meeting with Frankie. Two men got out. Slim, both of them. Frankie was one. They went in the front door, laughing and indulging in sexually charged horse play.

Angelo sat in his stolen Subaru gobsmacked. Christ! What if Frankie'd picked up some nifty little piece for the night already? Angelo hadn't thought of that. Did Frankie do all-nighters, even weekenders? Or was he a quick poke bloke, in and out like a dip stick testing the oil level in a car, wipe the rod clean and throw the rag away? Meaning the new 'friend' would be leaving good and soon. Angelo started in on what was left of his nails.

By nine-thirty he'd got seriously worried. There seemed no way round his problem. Just then a pizza delivery scooter drew up. While its rider turned his machine round, Angelo got out of the Subaru, hope renewed. He darted round the back of a bulky 4x4 so's to stand at the flats' main entry when the delivery boy approached it, as if he'd been waiting there twenty minutes. A quick renewed punch on the door bells to numbers 1 and 2 established that the occupants were still away. That left Frankie at the top the only possible candidate for a home delivery of wop nosh.

Angelo stepped casually out of the shadow into the delivery boy's path.

'Grub's up. Great', he said, rubbing his hands.

'Name of Evans?'

Angelo ignored this. He hated telling direct lies. 'Thanks, son', he said. 'I thought you'd never get here. I could eat a horse.'

'One extra spicy pepperoni. One diavolo. As ordered.'

'Straight from Hell's kitchen, the wife always says.' Angelo winked at the delivery boy, invoking male solidarity. He got no response, bar: 'The party booked the order chose the plastic option.' Sounded like a coded plea for a tip.

Angelo gave the boy three pounds in cash, waved goodbye to him as he sped off then glanced at the slip. So Frankie was Frankie Evans, was he? Funny how little one knew of the people one wasted.

He resisted the urge to bite a chunk out of the pepperoni, for now he came to think of it he was famished. He took the pizzas across to the car, where he cast around for something nasty enough to souse them with to induce Frankie to get rid of his guest fast. Nothing. He recalled a biggish Indian corner shop in the next street, back near where he'd parked the lorry. He drove there at the double.

They had Duphalac, a tasteless, odourless laxative in liquid form he'd come across a few months back when his youngest had got a stoppage after a raw pastry blow-out. Rush back to his old parking space opposite Frankie's. A quick but liberal sprinkle of the pizzas with Duphalac. Then the laying of them, popped back snug inside their boxes, on Frankie's front door step, complete with credit card slip. A ring of Frankie's bell, a muffled announcement through the intercom that a traffic warden was about to write out a ticket for his scooter so sorry he'd have to rush, then a dash back to the Subaru.

A minute or two later Frankie opened the door, looked up and down the street, shrugged his shoulders and scooped up the pizzas. Angelo strongly doubted a man of Frankie's stamp would ring the pizza place to ensure the delivery boy got his tip. Luckily pizzas needed eating hot. Frankie'd get stuck into his without delay.

Angelo settled down in the Subaru's driving seat to wait. His nails had nothing left worth gnawing. He fiddled around with a few radio stations, read his A-Z, tried playing games with the streets in it. Like how he'd get from Maida Vale to Docklands if he could only drive straight or turn left, but not right.

About 10 a black cab drew up outside Frankie's. Empty. Good. Must have been summoned there from within. Presently the main door of the house opened and Frankie's young man appeared, clutching his trouser tops. Angelo silently mouthed a prayer of thanks, a malefactor's Te Deum. He gave it another hour then, having in the late night quietness distinctly heard a lavatory in Frankie's house flush not once, not twice, but three times, strolled contentedly round to the lorry in the next street. He stretched out in the back of it, relishing his fleece-lined sleeping bag bought on exes and the generous space to stretch his limbs in.

THIRTYTWO

The Pantheon lies just off Pall Mall, near where stood the Prince Regent's Carlton House, tragically long demolished. Some of the latter's more opulent features are said to have been used in the Pantheon's construction. The Panth, as its fonder members call it, draws the cream of upper-class 40s+ groovers of both sexes. Its strength has been to recognise that even toffs no longer object to spending leisure time with members of the opposite sex. Also that toffs of both sexes like to boogie just as much as do their social inferiors, even if they look a lot sillier doing so. Reciprocal visiting rights have been negotiated with several clubs overseas, including the Patroon in New York.

Victor Deller had belonged to the Pantheon for fifteen years. When he originally asked Lord and Lady Barnes to lunch there, it was on the understanding that Mrs Deller would be of the company as well. He received his guests with Charlotte Elver at his side instead.

'Laura had to fly to New York at the last minute', he said. 'Charlotte here agreed to stand in.'

'We met at Laura's party some weeks ago', said Barbara Barnes, holding her hand out. 'You were wearing that lovely dress. You remember the pretty girl in the red Fern Field, don't you, darling?' She'd turned to her husband.

Barnes nodded, but perfunctorily. He looked tired.

He needed to know when Deller's down payment on a peerage would be forthcoming. The Confessor Street HQ's lease had fallen in and the first quarter's rent as a sitting tenant was due any minute. Yet the Party kitty was parched to the point of drought. His recent calls to Deller had been turned to leg and swept over the boundary. Barnes had been consoled with the pledge of a face-to-face meeting in the very near future. This Pantheon get-together must be it.

He took the initiative. While the others were investigating the menu, a huge A3 document, he looked about him and repeated loudly the words his host had once used in the House of Lords: 'Nice place. Wouldn't mind joining myself.'

Deller's memory, a good one for incidents of that sort, was instantly jogged. He grinned over towards Barnes and mouthed the words 'Choose. Eat. Digest. Later we'll talk.' He moved his lips exaggeratedly, like a mime artiste.

The last teaspoonful of *crème brûlée* with a hint of clementine had just slid down when Deller said to Charlotte, 'I suggest we have coffee upstairs in the gallery. Why don't you show Barb round? Also take her to where she can powder her nose. But she mustn't miss the Boldini of Tum Tum in the Card Room. I'll meet you in the gallery in two ticks.' Turning to Barbara Barnes, he said, 'The gallery is twenty feet up and gives the most spectacular view of the atrium, especially its marble floor. We'll join you in a few minutes. Meanwhile, can you let me have a couple of words with Mark here?'

The women moved off. Deller walked round the table and took the chair next to Barnes. 'A *digestivo*?'

'No thanks.'

'Sure? The Club Drambuie is excellent.'

'I need to keep a clear head. Our figures demand it.'

Body shape or finances? 'Your figures...' Deller repeated the word slowly, as if swirling a rare vintage round his mouth.

'Thin figures, Victor. Starveling.' Barnes suppressed a belch. The crème brûlée had been delicious, but a course too far.

The ambiguity disposed of, Deller put his cards on the table. 'The cutback in ad spend aross the entire economy has not made things easy', he said. 'I'm looking to off-load some of my titles. And remember, we never set a specific timetable for any contribution by me to your funds.'

'Nor a specific timetable for ennoblement of you by us. That's one title you intend to acquire still?'

'Neatly put.' Deller reached inside his jacket for the slim pocket note pad. 'The *Date* needs a new leader-writer. Interested?'

'I'm flattered. But I'm also serious, Victor. We must have that help soon or the agreement is off.'

'Very well. But selling a periodical, even a candyfloss society one, is more than a day's work. It's not like clearing your barrow of wet fish.'

Barnes recalled Deller's love of wet-fish allusions from before. 'Could you manage some sort of declaration of intent?' he said. 'It might help get us a more sympathetic hearing from the ground landlords.'

'Remind me, who are they?'

136

'The de Bohun Estate.'

'De Bohun. Isn't that Lon Crowthorne's family?'

'Precisely. His ancestors have owned the freeholds of all that bit of Westminster since Henry VIII took it from the monks.'

'And are the Bohun people easy to deal with?'

'Not bad. In fact quite civilised. But unlike the monks, they aren't much disposed to charity. A brightly lit tree in Abbey Square each December to gladden the hearts of Christmas shoppers is about it.'

'Well what do you want from me?'

'Something we could show the de Bohun Estate people. A Personal Guarantee, for instance.'

Deller shook his head, conveying amused tolerance of Barnes's financial naivety. 'PGs are the shortest route to poverty I know', he said. 'Worse than drink, drugs or a gambling habit. Or rather, a PG *is* an exercise in gambling. At the longest odds, against the house, with its built-in advantage, and no control by the placer of the wager as regards timing.'

'By all means come up with an alternative.' Barnes wasn't giving in. 'But you must move fast, Victor. This Government could well not be in power much longer. Apart from anything else, its majority's proved much too small for comfort and the Opposition is very hostile to Mary's war. You mentioned timing. That cuts both ways.' Barnes looked around them. His fingers itched to use Scrabble tiles, but pre-formed spoken words would have to do. He dressed them up in euphemism till their own mothers wouldn't have known them. 'Your... hire purchase agreement needs to be both honoured now and concluded within more like a year to be on the safe side. I admit that's rather sooner than the two years we spoke of the first time we discussed this. But the political situation has changed. If the agreement is not concluded, the... commodity you've got your eye on could well get withdrawn from the market. It's in short enough supply already.'

Deller switched direction. 'We aren't supposed to talk business in the Club. Bad form.' He leant forward, as if cajoling. 'Are you sure you won't have a little something?'

'Positive, thank you.'

'Not even to keep me company?'

Barnes shook his head. 'What have you got in mind?' he said, humouring his host.

137

'Something we can sip at in leisurely fashion. I want to sketch you out a little stratagem.'

'We can do that just as well over coffee. Which by the way, shouldn't we be taking with the ladies?'

Deller smiled at his guest's pushing for an adjournment. He correctly put it down to jumpiness. All he said was 'Very well.'

At the top of the stairs leading to the balconied gallery, he pointed out the beauties of the hall to Barnes.

'The ground floor looks like an elaborate carpet from up here', said Barnes, peering over the balcony to the pattern below.

'Pure Travertine marble', said Deller. 'Imported from Italy at vast expense when Ormskirk was producing material just as good at a third the price. Victorian sentimentality over Italy.'

They sat down. Oblivious to club rules, Barnes reverted to business. 'Surely coffee can wait, Victor. Do let's try and clear things up before Barb and your secretary get back.'

'This is a huge building. Charlotte knows how to spin out a tour of it for as much as an hour if need be.' Deller called a waiter and ordered coffees. 'And could you get a message to Miss Elver?' he said. 'She'll most probably be in the Card Room. A pretty young blonde in a nut brown dress, gold watch on her wrist, pearls round her throat. Tell her "half".'

' "Half"?' said Barnes.

' "Half"?' said the waiter.

' "Half". Half an hour. She'll know what I mean.'

'So what's your stratagem?' said Barnes once the waiter had gone.

Deller leant forward. 'Pressure on Lyonel Crowthorne', he said, pushing on his knees with his hands. 'Pressure which he will then transmit to the people who run his urban property holdings, they in their turn easing the pressure on you.'

'I thought you only knew him superficially.'

'I do. My wife knows him much better. And my *Date* knows him best of all. It can't publish any details, though, given he's a regular contributor.'

'What details?'

'Wait and see. But I'll tell you this much. Mary Matheson's belief that he'll attract the do-gooder vote could prove ill-judged.'

'How can I "Wait and see" if you won't publish any details?'

'One of my more formidable freelance journalists might have to develop a conscience about the public's right to know, combine it with a longing to see your ColLabs keep their HQ and warn Crowthorne he'll pass some murky facts about his private life to a rival newspaper if he doesn't get more generous with his ColLab tenants, which he'd be wise to do anyway now he's joined a ColLab government. Let's think. Seeing as his lordship's so keen on religion I think one of the Sabbath organs. The *Triumph on Sunday* or the *Sunday Era*, perhaps.'

'But they're mere rags.'

'Rags are just the thing to handle a stinking mess with.'

THIRTYTHREE

Angelo spent an hour squirming around on the hard floor of the lorry trying to find a position that didn't ache. Then he gave it up. Stuff the fleece-lined sleeping bag. He was off to the nearest hotel, cheap or otherwise. With Frankie trotting backwards and forwards to the crapper all night long, the invigilation job he'd set himself was unnecessary.

By ten next morning he was on site again. He'd driven the lorry to Frankie's street and parked it opposite Frankie's in place of the Subaru, which could now be dumped. Bathed, shaved, after-shaved, deodorant-ed, Angelo repeatedly flexed his right arm, soon to be the spanner-wielding one.

About ten Pierre turned up, chewing on some gum and with a personal player earpiece stuck each side of his head. Angelo beckoned him over to the lorry. He asked him if he remembered the role he'd been hired to play. Pierre detached his personal stereo, asked Angelo to repeat the question and on taking it in assured him he had.

'Good', said Angelo. 'Now, sonny boy, spit out the gum and stow all those wires you got round your neck.'

'Hey man, no need to get heavy.'

'For what I'm paying you I'll get as heavy as I like.'

'Yeah, paying me. Where is it?'

Angelo paid him. 'Go and loiter by that Porsche', he said. 'And mind you look sexy. Think model at the Motor Show. Remember, when my friend comes down, be sure you give him plenty of…'

'Yeah, I know. Cruise him.' Pierre sounded bored.

'Correct… If that means what I think.'

'And you? Mind if I ask where you come into all this?'

Angelo realised that Pierre had his doubts as to whether he, Angelo, was an A1-at-Lloyd's deviant. He worked more pink into his act. 'I may have forgot to tell you when I first got in touch, but me and my *friend*' – Angelo leered horribly as he stressed the word – 'like to play at Cops and Cottagers. You go upstairs with him but leave the front door unlocked. I burst in, all dolled up in my police uniform, while the two of you are hard at it. I then threaten to haul you down the station for questioning unless... and that's when you invite me to join in.'

Pierre swallowed a yawn. 'Brill scenario.'

'Which reminds me. You brought those toys we talked about?'

'Here.' Pierre patted a bag he was carrying.

'Including the ball gag? Particularly into ball gags, my "friend" and me.'

'Yeah? Good on you.' Pierre's eyelids drooped.

'Well what are you waiting for?' said Angelo. 'Get on with it.'

'How are you going to get him down here on the street, your friend?' Pierre seemed to have woken up. 'It's Sunday morning.'

'You'll see. Now give it five minutes then press his doorbell and tell him his Sunday papers have arrived. Number three, top button. He's up already. He opened his living room window just before you got here.'

Angelo had already rigged the sound system in the lorry, angling the speakers with a directional laser so they aimed straight at Frankie's floor. He'd made sure by thoroughly professional equipment-sourcing then siting that the bulk of the noise he was about to unleash would be heard by Frankie only. One didn't want all the neighbours out on the street too.

Pierre strolled over to the front door, pressed the bell, then went and stood by the Porsche, as instructed. He looked at its roof and gestured over towards Angelo to express his shock. Good. The brilliant red-dyed brand of ketchup Angelo had much earlier squeezed all over the Porsche roof was showing up nice and gory. He gave Pierre a thumbs-up.

Angelo switched on his sound effects. To the flat-dweller in Number 3 the heart-rending sound of a vehicle prang, the first great sickening crash of metal, shattering ping of glass fragments cascading everywhere, secondary shock as the rear of the car swung round and ricocheted off something solid like a concrete bollard – the works, in short – was beamed right up and into his living room.

Pierre, standing right underneath, was barely affected by the noise. Good. It showed Angelo he'd aimed his sound bomb right. As for Frankie, if any prestige marque car-owner could withstand the urge to race downstairs and check it wasn't his darling been hit, he'd need the cold-blooded insouciance of a white van man.

Frankie proved normal on that one. Following a brief twitch back of the curtains of the principal window of number three and a peek out towards the Porsche's roof, the street-level front door opened. Frankie came out. Angelo watched him strut smartly over towards where Pierre stood. They started talking, Frankie pointing angrily to the Porsche roof, Pierre making what looked like soothing gestures. Presently Frankie calmed down a bit.

Soon after, it was clear the two men were hitting it off. Then Frankie went inside again – Angelo got a bit worried at this point in case Frankie had dropped his concern about the Porsche – but no, it was all right, here he was again with a bucket and cloth. Pierre helped Frankie wash the goo off. After that Frankie and Pierre went inside the house.

Angelo grabbed his mask, not an animal's but a human face this time, plus a novelty policeman's helmet, the sort selling in tourist trash shops. He also took his spanner and a face towel. Tooled up, he got after them like a ferret down a bunny burrow.

THIRTYFOUR

In his frustration, Jeff strode up and down Chrissie's flat. 'Doesn't Mel make a note of her hot dates anywhere?' he said. 'Time? Place? Day of the week? How to get there? She must need to keep records some place so she can check up on them.'

'She'd use her mobile', said Chrissie. 'And even if we could access it, she wouldn't've texted the stuff in English.'

'What's she use if not English?'

'One of those Middle East languages. I said Arab just now but to be honest I'm not sure. Where's that place they had the ayatollah?'

'She from Iran?'

'She might have said something like that once.'

'It's Persian they speak there. Also Azeri and Kurdish.'

'That's a great help.'

'Let's at least look in her room.'

They looked. 'It's not exactly the Belshazzar Suite at the Beldon', said Chrissie, shame-faced as a Home Counties hostess. Mel's outfits were hung not in a cupboard but on a mobile clothes shop frame designed to take coat hangers. Skimpy polythene covers enclosed each garment.

'She have any writing tools?' said Jeff.

'Try that bedside cabinet.'

'Oh yeah, I see.' The drawers were set flush with the wood surround. Jeff pulled them out, curling his fingers round each side. Chrissie looked over his shoulder. 'Nothing', she said, her tone dull with disappointment.

It wasn't quite nothing. Some tissues; two packets of condoms; a fruit-flavoured vaginal lubricant; a novelty key ring with a lucky rabbit's foot attached but no keys; a Beldon room service bill for a jeroboam of Pol Roger; a Greenbach, Angel, Lettiss giveaway pen. Jeff grabbed at the room service bill. 'It's got some marks on the back', he said.

'You sure? There's no writing.'

'She could have rested another bit of paper on top. Weight of the pen tip made the marks.' Jeff held it obliquely up to the light. 'Aha. An address.'

143

'Can you make it out?'

'Some.'

'It could be anyone's.'

'It could. But it's all we got.'

They worked on it together, collaborative as palaeographers deciphering a tomb inscription. Which in a way was what this might be.

'Flat three, 36 V-something something Road, then a zip.'

'Post code.'

'Post code then. How many numbers your post codes got?'

'It's not just numbers. There are letters as well. Give it to me.' Chrissie held it up to the light, squinting. 'NW something, I think.'

'The Road looks almost like Private Road. Then there's the V. Could that signify "Very Private Road"? Is that possible downtown London? NW means North West, doesn't it? Would the North West side be downtown?'

'Not quite. But calling a road "very private" is plain silly. Like a kid writing his address "The World, The Universe".'

'Could that be a 3?' Jeff pointed.

'NW3? Hampstead.'

'Is that far?'

'Up beyond Regent's Park. We still don't know the address for sure.'

'Only one way to find out...' Jeff pulled out his mobile. Twenty rings and it got picked up. '...Gav, Mr Doresett sir, is that you?'

'Who else would it be? I was just starting brekker. Now my soft boiled egg'll go hard.' Doresett sounded grumpy. He mellowed. 'I liked your story about the British Prime Minister communicating via Scrabble tiles', he said. 'But it's not as ground-breaking as you state. When the American Embassy in Moscow was found in the early 1980s to be so heavily bugged there was no alternative to rebuilding from scratch, the staff meanwhile talked to each other using word-forming toys from a children's spelling game.'

'Trust you to know that.'

'And trust the other fact-checkers here not to.'

'They should get you to head up that department.'

'They should. You might mention it to Stevens. Anyway, you didn't muck up my boiled egg to discuss Scrabble. What do you want?'

Jeff explained about a very private road in Hampstead.

'Not "very"', said Doresett, witheringly, before Jeff had even finished. 'Nor "private". Virgil Prout Road, I imagine. Part of the Greyfriars urban property portfolio. Writing out a Virgil Georgic was the standard Greyfriars punishment and Prout the Greyfriars Fifth Form Master, a name Frank Richards purloined from *Stalky & Co.*, while Kipling borrowed it from the Bach editor.'

'Tell him to get on with it', whispered Chrissie in Jeff's free ear. It tickled. Jeff stuck a finger there and scratched. 'Mr Doresett, not meaning to be impolite, but is this going anywhere?'

'It depends why you want to know the address. But don't mind me. I'll have to put a new egg on anyway.'

Jeff explained why he and his friend wanted to know the address, leaving out the complex bits.

'In case you haven't got a London street map', said Doresett, who clearly had, 'it's over near the Central School of Speech & Drama.'

Jeff repeated this to Chrissie, who was taking it down. '...Drama', she repeated, then turned to Jeff. 'It's drama time all right. Let's go.'

Jeff turned towards her. 'What if Mel's in big trouble? It could be scary. Don't come, please.'

'We'll take a big stick to hit 'em with', said Chrissie. 'Two big sticks.'

'Where'd we get us some big sticks on a Sunday?'

'Mel's room. My protest placard holders. Demos are all very well. This calls for direct action.'

THIRTYFIVE

Angelo tiptoed up the last flight of stairs. He went slowly to give the happy couple plenty of time to get stuck into each other. He sidled along the corridor outside Frankie's front door, back to the wall, spanner down his trouser leg and gripping it by its end.

Pierre had left the front door of Frankie's flat a tiny bit ajar, as instructed. His performance out by the Porsche had struck Angelo as pretty good. He'd certainly got them both a toe-hold in Frankie's home. Angelo pushed the front door three-quarters open, using one swift movement to kill any creak.

He could hear murmurings from a room to the right. The bedroom, presumably. Angelo recalled what his old instructor had always stressed when training the lads on the force in stakeouts: 'The intruder will nine times out of ten be on unfamiliar territory. He can't be sure which room has the safe in it, which drawer of the sideboard holds the silver, which box in the housewife's dressing table contains the jewels. He is the explorer, you the trap-springer, familiar with the terrain – *if* you've reconnoitred the site. The disadvantage is all to him, the advantage all to you.'

Angelo pulled out the spanner, wrapped it in the towel to avoid breaking anyone's skin when he hit them, wished for plenty of luck and stepped through the bedroom door.

Frankie had his back to him, about to carry out some unspeakable act on Pierre, who lay on the bed. Both were naked, Pierre aroused. Probably Frankie too, though Angelo couldn't see from where he stood. He would have liked to shut his eyes on that sort of thing. But it would've meant being blind to whatever else went on. He brought down the gift-wrapped spanner really hard on Frankie's right arm, his shooting one, knowing it'd glance off to the right. He swept the spanner back to the left in a forearm drive that took out Frankie behind the right knee.

Angelo reckoned that as a right-hander, Frankie would have to have kept his gun to the right of the bed. Angelo's two blows were aimed at pushing him over to its left. Frankie moved to get up and would have turned to close with his attacker. Angelo didn't give him the chance. Being heavier but less agile, his best hope was to smother the younger man. He threw himself on Frankie, yelling so's to confuse him.

When Angelo'd first appeared in the doorway Pierre had squealed with delight. 'Go for him, tiger.' Though in a mercenary's mouth, it sounded sincere. When Angelo hit Frankie the second, devastating blow, Pierre began to twig the BDSM act was for real. He recoiled up towards the bed head, bending his legs back under him like a horror flick starlet trapped by the Beast from the Basement. With a final heave of all his weight Angelo threw Frankie onto the bed, engulfing Pierre. He poured a succession of blows onto the two of them.

Pierre's neck got broken early on. His body now lay mostly on the floor, pushed over the end of the bed, which had come away from the wall on smooth-running castors. His head lolled like a chicken plucked and ready for the pot. His calves and feet alone remained on the bed.

Frankie was tougher. Or luckier. He got off with a smashed up right arm and held his left wrist at an awkward angle. Limply, it occurred to Angelo. *How very fitting.* Angelo trussed Frankie in his own sweaty, semen-bespattered sheets, readjusted his, Angelo's, mask and helmet, which had got dislodged in the mêlée, and stared at Frankie, resting his hands on his hips.

Eventually he gave tongue. 'Good morning, sir', he said. He dropped into the officialese used in the popular mind by members of the force: 'I was hoping you could assist me with my enquiries. Instead you've gone and placed yourself in a most awkward situation, sir. Resisting arrest. Sad error of judgement, that.'

'What the bloody fucking hell are you talking about?' Frankie began to get his bearings. 'Devene?' he said, focussing his eyes awkwardly. 'Angelo? Is that you?'

'Plod to you, sir, if you please. Police Constable Plod.'

'Devene, you cunt. Stop playing games.' Frankie tried to make himself more comfortable. 'Fuck! My arm.'

'Indeed, sir, your arm. It appears to have sustained a modicum of contusion, if not fracture. However, I would not advise sexual congress with your arm, either at this or any other juncture.'

'Stop fucking with me, Devene. I know it's you.'

'Do you?' Angelo spoke with his day-to-day voice now. 'Good. I'll drop the disguise then.'

He took off the mask and fitted it on Pierre's dead face, pushing it crooked so the eyes got hidden. He didn't like dead eyes open. At the same time he didn't fancy using his fingers to close these ones. You never knew where eyes like Pierre's had been. He turned back to Frankie, still wearing his tourist helmet.

'You know, Mr Francis, you've still got a lot to learn about us blokes in blue. I've a notion you don't rate us very high. Well I'm going to give you a lesson in police brutality. See if I can make you change your tune. Though as a fucking degenerate queer, you probably couldn't whistle any kind of tune to start with.' He thrust the ball part of the gag into Frankie's mouth and fitted the straps round the back of his head.

THIRTYSIX

The ministerial black two-litre Jaguar XJ had completed most of its journey from Chequers to Downing Street by now, gobbling hydrocarbons as it went. Green transport, the subject of many a government scolding to the masses, took second place to prestige, speed and the security that speed bought. The traffic had not been too bad, even around Hanger Lane. Or not for politicians. The motor-cycle police outriders holding up their gauntleted hands at lights, and whistling at civilians as if they were sheepdog trial participants, created jams for the people, not their overlords.

The Prime Minister was too engrossed in her conversation with Ben Lee to notice the road conditions.

'This *Sunday Era* exposé of Lionel Crowthorne', she said. 'Is it all true?'

'I'm very much afraid so, Prime Minister.'

'He's got to go, then.'

'It'll devastate him. He's a sensitive man underneath all that religious flummery.'

'There are no two ways about it.'

'He's suing them for invasion of privacy.'

'Much good that'll do us.' The Prime Minister closed her eyes and for several seconds massaged the lids with her fingertips. 'Drat the man', she said. 'Only a month after I welcomed him into the Party, gave him a job even. Why can't you keep your trews fastened better?'

'Me, Prime Minister?'

'You plural. Men.'

A short silence. 'He didn't of course actually undo his trews.'

'That's a quibble, Ben. And you know it.'

'Well, technically he hasn't done anything wrong.'

'He wouldn't have done anything wrong even if he had undone his trews. Not technically. That's not the point. In politics it's perception, perception, perception. Like location in house-selling. You of all people should know that. It was your wretched *Date* and its sanctimonious editorials helped bring down the last government.'

Lee glanced out of the window. They were travelling through Hyde Park by now. A snarl-up on the bridge ahead looked like being

149

impassable, even to the posse of police attendants. The Jaguar, its passengers' bodily safety paramount, turned aside onto a leafy pathway normally forbidden to all but Environment Department vans. A big cat it might almost have been, loping through the forest.

'Useful thing, terrorism', said Lee, musingly.

The Prime Minister opened her eyes. 'How so?'. Her voice was sharp.

'I was only thinking that without the security threat we would never have set foot in this stretch of woodland. It's rather lovely, what with the leaves just budding.'

'That's enough, Ben. Never, *never* belittle the terrorist threat.'

Lee, abashed, fell silent.

'Who exactly was it exposed him anyway?' said the PM presently, abandoning her rigid posture and relaxing her torso against the seat back. The gesture exposed her throat.

Rather a good one, thought Lee. 'Crowthorne?' he said. 'It was a classic stitch up. A *Sneerer* reporter masquerading as a call girl. '

'*Sneerer*?'

'Sorry. The *Sunday Era*, known to us media folk as the *Sneerer*. The nub of the story's in my press digest.' He meant the summary of breaking news he provided the PM with each morning.

'And Crowthorne was actually idiot enough to fall for this stitch up?'

'It seems so.'

'But that miserable rag has done this sort of thing so often! There was the pseudo-oligarch's wife they tricked Princess Miranda's boyfriend with only last year – those indiscreet remarks about the rest of the royal family.'

'People's memories are short, I'm afraid', said Lee.

'But Lyonel's an educated man. Doesn't he recall them pulling a trick like that before? And anyway, that clandestine reporter has made such a career of it I'd have thought her cover was well and truly exposed by now.'

'They used their Religious Affairs correspondent this time, Prime Minister. Good-looking girl, but a total unknown. Evidently she was more than Crowthorne could resist. You know his passion for inter-faith debate.'

'God damn and blast him to hell!'

THIRTYSEVEN

Angelo said to Frankie, 'Nod your head for "Yes", shake it for "No". Got it?'

Frankie stared at him. He said nothing.

Angelo brought the spanner hard down on Frankie's right wrist, his sole good one. Frankie arched his back and tried to scream. All that emerged was a smothered squeal.

Angelo said again, 'A nod for "Yes". A shake for "No". Why won't you learn?'

Frankie shrugged one shoulder only, his left.

This interested Angelo. 'You mean you don't know?'

This time Frankie shook his head.

Angelo said 'Why not both shoulders?' A thought struck him. 'I got it. Your smashed right arm makes it too painful. Am I right?'

Frankie nodded his head. There was sweat on his face. The forehead and upper lip mostly.

Angelo thwacked his spanner against his left palm, his favourite warming-up gesture. 'Do you know what a spanner is for?' he said.

Frankie nodded.

'Then tell me.'

Frankie raised his eyebrows.

'Blink your right eye for each letter of a word', said Angelo. 'Unless you're left-handed. You're not left-handed, are you?' His voice was light, friendly, almost reassuring, like a concerned teacher taking trouble with a backward pupil.

Frankie shook his head.

'The number of blinks gives the letter you want', said Angelo. 'So one blink for A, two for B, twenty-six for Z', he said. 'You'll find you duck words with late letters in them: even ones you need often, like R, S, T. But no other short cuts. Because, each time you make a spelling mistake, I whop you with this here spanner.'

Frankie's eyes might have widened a touch. It was hard to tell.

'You blink your left eye to mean full stops and so on', said Angelo. 'One blink means a comma, two a full stop, three a semi-colon, four a colon. You might need five for an exclamation mark, but I wouldn't recommend it. Too much trouble. Got it?'

Frankie nodded.

'Good. Now once again, what's a spanner for?'

Frankie thought a bit then started blinking. He'd have looked comic but for the sweat.

'Maybe it's pain sweat', said Angelo, thinking out loud. 'I do hope so', he said.

Frankie stopped blinking, tried to shake his head. His hair where he parted it was matted, a small cake of blood showing. Nothing too gory.

Angelo said 'I'm afraid I lost you. It might have been your lack of punkuashun. Incy wincy commas got as much right to be treated proper as big words. I hate poor punkuashun. And there's a lot of it around these days. Especially with oiks who went to state schools. Are you an oik, Mr Francis?'

Frankie hesitated, then slowly nodded.

'Are you?' said Angelo. '*Are* you?'

Frankie nodded again, more vigorously this time.

'First time we met, you inferred I was an oik', said Angelo. 'Do you remember?'

Frankie shook his head.

'You said the girls we took so much trouble to bring over from Mouldy Over and points east were only fit for ratty oiks in Bristol', said Angelo. 'Inferring I was one.'

Frankie writhed his legs as if trying for a more comfortable position.

Angelo raised his spanner arm well above the shoulder and hit Frankie very hard on his left knee. Any crack or crunch, of bone or cartilage giving way, got smothered in Frankie's whimper. His face twisted in agony and a tear or two welled up in his eyes.

Angelo said, 'Once again – and please go vewy vewy careful with the commas and stops – what is a spanner for?'

Frankie started blinking. There was often a pause of a couple of seconds or more between each one. Clearly he had to think hard to calculate the right number. Slowly, very slowly, his answer emerged: 'I don't know.'

Angelo hadn't given him the blink code for an apostrophe. Frankie indicated it by spelling it out.

'You don't know?' Angelo sounded appalled, though appreciative of Frankie's attention to detail. 'What? After at least ten years educashun, even if it is state? Mr Francis, you're a hard case in need of some remedial classroom attention.' He leaned forwards, almost brushing Frankie's cheek and spoke softly in Frankie's left ear. He might have been caressing it he was so gentle. 'A spanner is what us rough grease monkey types, or ratty oiks to you ponces in fancy cream sports cars, tighten up limp wrists with. Wrists as have got loose as their owner's morals. Loose through too much swinging of fag bags.'

Frankie's head drooped. Tears, more plentiful now, trickled down his cheeks like raindrops on a window pane.

THIRTYEIGHT

Jeff drove alone. He'd told Chrissie he was NOT taking her and that was final. She'd pleaded, then gotten argumentative, then relapsed into pleading again. At least she hadn't sulked. He liked her for that.

He parked cautiously in Virgil Prout Road, approached the apartment building cautiously, climbed its stairs cautiously, crept cautiously along the corridor to the apartment. When he saw the front door was slightly open he held back, debating with himself what to do. A trap? Naw. Too obvious.

The building was very quiet. Jeff pushed on the door, still cautiously. It opened rather stiffly.

He was inside now. He knew there was someone else there. He couldn't say how. He just knew by the feel of the place. He gripped Chrissie's stick. It was more a pole really. The wood felt warm, comforting. He used one end to prod full open an internal door that was slightly ajar, the first one on the right. Prod it as if infected.

His instinct had been good. There were two people inside. He could see them from the doorway. He drew closer. Both lay quite still. So still he all but jumped. His instinct had been less than good. They were too still to be unconscious. His mouth felt dry, but not with thirst. He entered. The one full on the bed looked a post-car wreck version of the Foxy Gentleman, wrists mashed like a fox's paws caught in a trap. He didn't know the other one.

'Hey there…' A whisper came from his left. Jeff whirled round. Micky lay on the floor. 'Why, it's the kid', Micky said.

Jeff didn't know it was Micky.

Micky said 'For the love of God, get me some water.' He'd been shot. With Frankie's gun. Jeff didn't know that either. He got a glass of water from a kitchen, the third room he tried. Tension made his fingers clumsy. He returned to the bedroom and held the glass to Micky's mouth.

'Pour slow', said Micky. 'So it don't spill… Thanks.' He closed his eyes. Jeff wondered if he should feel the guy's pulse. He felt the guy's pulse. He'd forgotten how many beats to a minute were usual. But this guy hadn't enough. It didn't take Rex Morgan to know that.

Micky opened his eyes. The water had revived him. 'You don't know me, but I know you', he said.

'So who are you?' said Jeff.

'Micky Frost.'

'I'm no wiser.'

'You're the bloke lives in the flat we searched…' Micky stopped and retched. Nothing came up. Jeff gave him some more water. Micky sipped it slowly. 'Sorry I said "kid"', he said. 'You're no kid. More a *mensch*.'

Jeff hadn't lived in New York without picking up Yiddish. Only a smattering, but he knew *mensch*. 'You Jewish?' he said.

'A bit.' Micky grinned. He looked terrible. 'Not the bit you see. The bit you see's a mix. Of all sorts. Liquorice All Sorts. Black, white, pink…' Micky stopped again. He retched again.

His mind must be wandering, thought Jeff. 'You were one of the guys in masks that night at my apartment' he said, 'right?'

'Guilty as charged.' Micky had got some of his old spirit back.

'The dog?'

'Dog?'

'The masks. One was a dog.'

'Ferret.' Micky lowered his head to his chest. Jeff hoped he was relaxing, but Micky didn't raise his head again. He looked like he might drop off altogether. And not to sleep. Jeff knew he had to get to basics fast. No time to circle the subject before plunging in.

'How'd Tod die?' he said. There was no answer. Jeff said 'Guy in my apartment used to live there.' He nudged Micky. 'Before I moved in. He died. It was you guys did it, no?'

Micky took his time. 'Not me', he said at last. It was clear he found speaking difficult. 'Frankie', he said. His breathing came in gasps now. 'He told me that one time… Frankie told me things he kept from Ange-o…'

'Who's Ange-o?'

Micky ignored this. 'He just died, your friend…', he said. He picked up some strength. 'Tod, was that his name? Weak heart or something… Frankie made to rough him up… Made, not did… The pace must of…'. He retched again, but now he'd started talking he wouldn't stop. 'Must of got too hot. Bloke collapsed. He'd passed on, not out. Frankie didn't know that then. Frankie said when he found it was the real thing he put him to bed in the flat. Make it look like he'd died at home. It wasn't Frankie's fault. Wasn't anyone's.' He retched yet again. This time he brought up blood. 'Wasn't Frankie shot me neither.'

'That is Frankie, isn't it?' Jeff gestured toward the Fox on the bed. 'That guy over there?'

'Where? I don't see too well. Can I have some more water?'

Jeff gave him some more water. 'What did Frankie want with Tod?' he said.

Micky was finding it hard to swallow. 'Don't know', he said. 'Mr Sanders reckoned he'd got nosey... But he said that later... After your friend died.'

Jeff couldn't make the last bit out. 'Sanders?' he said. 'Who's he?'

'Sanders?... Area Manager to you... Me too. It was Ange-o got to call him by his real name.'

'Who's Ange-o?'

'Angell-o', said Micky, stressing the '-ell'. He was very pale by now and paused between groups of words. 'I called him Ange-o for fun... Was how he drove... Like that racing driver once... Argie... Best of all time, they say... We were in the lorry...a year or two ago...ten bints in the back...and the Croat speed cops got onto us... Ange-o lost 'em... On mountain roads too... Ange-o was my partner... Mate partner...like when he was on the...force...in a patrol car... We were good mates...though he does lose his rag...easy. Slagged off my nan once... Well, sort of... She's not black... Jewish... I wasn't telling him that, though... Just wanted him to...say sorry to the shvartzers... He was a real partner most days... Not the new kind,...sex and that... He'd hate that.'

'Is that him?' Jeff pointed to Pierre.

'I still don't see well', said Micky. There was a pause. 'I'm dying, aren't I?'

'You'll be fine.' What else could you say?

'Silly to ask', said Micky. 'I know I am... OK, I got a low IQ. But I was loyal. I'd've done anything for Ange-o. I loved him...Not Frankie's sort of love. Real love... I'd've kept my mouth shut. Why'd he take me out?'

And Micky died.

Jeff looked round for something to cover him with. He didn't like to take a sheet from the bed. They'd been used to truss the guy that this guy next him who'd just died – Micky? Micky Frost – hadn't said was Frankie. It must be Frankie, though. That front guy of the two on the bed. Jeff took a closer look. It was certainly the Foxy Gentleman, but caught and savaged as if by hounds, his hen-house heisting days over. Jeff felt glad. Freer of his burdensome memories too.

Jeff went out the bedroom door, found a bathroom. It was the door between the kitchen and the bedroom. First he washed his face and hands. Thoroughly. Cold water for his face, hot for his hands. Then he rootled around, in search of something he could shroud the bodies with. He found a box containing clean bed-linen. No sheets. Just duvet covers. They'd have to do. He emerged from the bathroom, his hands so full, the pile of bed linen so high, he couldn't see in front of him.

He near as dammit cannoned into Godwin.

THIRTYNINE

The 8th Earl of Crowthorne was indeed devastated by his dismissal from government. Not just wounded; lacerated. The hurt inflicted on his *amour propre* festered, turned septic, proved fatal. His funeral took place in the former chapel, rechristened ten years back the Faith Dialogue Hall, of the World Interdenominational Foundation's British headquarters. These occupy a vast and hideous Surrey mansion, commissioned from G E Street in the 1860s by a prosperous button-manufacturer. Crowthorne, as one of the WIF's Honorary Presidents, had elected in his will to be buried there.

Ben Lee, representing His Majesty's Government, and Mark Barnes, on behalf of the House of Lords, were among the pall-bearers. The others (besides an antiquarian and a herald) included the crooner Sir Pip Porter, whose ecumenicism consisted of being all things to all age groups, and dress-designer Dame Fern Field, whose green pro-Gaia faith was so pantheist as to invest even atoms with divine afflatus. Lee and Barnes bore the rear corners of the coffin. Sir Pip and Dame Fern held the front corners. It gave them better exposure to the TV cameras.

As Barnes discovered, pall-bearing required concentration. While pacing solemnly up what had once been a nave, his face set staring ahead, he had only just avoided tripping on the protruding edge of a commemorative brass plaque set in one of the decorative floor tiles.

Now the service was over. For Barnes, unused to interfaith eclecticism, it had been bewildering: a smidgen of Tridentine requiem; a sprinkling of Cranmerian vocables out of the Book of Common Prayer; some paragraphs from Series 3 of the Alternative Service Book; a hymn to the Earth very loosely inspired by Mahler's *Lied von der Erde*; a gobbet of Kaddish garnished with bars from Bernstein's Third; the requisite four takhirs; sound bite-size chunks of the *Aruda Purana*.

He and Lee stood out of doors. They were in the governing council's sector of the Foundation's burial ground. The weather was sunny but breezy, also rather cool.

'How'd it all strike you?' said Lee out of the side of his mouth to Barnes, of the ceremony. Shared physical labour in an act of public solemnity had brought them closer, shrouding their mutual antipathy.

'Confusing', said Barnes. 'But overall rather elegiac.' He too spoke softly.

'It was a bit off the way we had to take second place in a coffin-carrying procession to two old showbiz war-horses.'

A rogue gust of wind disturbed Lee's comb-over. While wrestling with it, he said 'What did you think of the old Crow's obituary?'

'Which? The *Date*'s or the *Era*'s?'

'The *Era*'s. The *Date* was so bland.'

'A bit debunking. Even for these irreverent times. Informative, though. I hadn't realised the de Bohun surname was a 19th-century affectation.'

'Was it? I missed that.'

'Apparently the family's name was 'Boone'. They "medievalised" it in the 1840s. They'd been Middlesex market gardeners. London's spread made them rich. A Boone got into Parliament. Pitt the Younger bunged him an Irish barony for supporting the 1801 Union...'

'Well I'll be damned.'

The coffin appeared round a corner, borne by undertakers now, creeping slowly like a mutant beetle whose hard-shelled thorax surmounts twelve spindly legs.

'What chiefly interested me in those obits was, were they were going to mention how Crowthorne died', said Lee.

'There's a rumour he'd had a first heart attack some weeks earlier. While visiting a call-girl.'

'I've heard that too. But apparently what really finished him off was an op to have his chin enhanced. The general anaesthetic.'

'What a rock to founder on. A weak chin.'

Lee had a new thought. 'How'd he get to be an earl?'

'His great-great-grandfather sat in Gladstone's Cabinet. Rewarded for supporting Home Rule. Ireland again.'

'You could say Crowy was following in the Grand Old Man's footsteps. Consorting with tarts.'

'You saw the *Sneerer* exposé then? Disgracefully slanted. Lyonel was a preening pain in the arse, but a fundamentally honest one.'

'Did the exposure really kill him? Simply because he got shown up as a sexually obsessed crusader for decency? The *Era* didn't even hint.'

'He was over-obsessed. Underneath the skin, Puritans can be very priapic.'

The coffin edged ever nearer. Barnes turned his gaze in the direction of the grave, as yet unoccupied. Not yawning. Just slackly open, like an adenoidal moron's mouth.

'Is there an heir?' said Lee.

'Not to the title. He mentioned a great-nephew once. Dead sister's side of the family. Boy went to America. Hasn't been heard of in years.'

'Disappeared?'

'Gone to the bad.'

A woman in a thick veil standing in front of them turned her head. They couldn't see her expression but the gauze across her face conveyed severe reproof. The two men fell silent. Singing could be heard from far away, borne on the breeze. Sweet voices, in *a capella* counterpoint.

FORTY

'Godwin!' said Jeff. 'Jeez-uss, you gave me a fright.'

'Hello, Jefferson. Clean duvets, eh? What are you up to?'

Godwin leant across the passage, supporting himself with his outer arm against the opposite wall and blocking Jeff's way.

Jeff remembered this guy was Mel's 'facilitator'.

'One of your girls looked like she was in danger', he said, dumping maximum blame on Godwin so's to get the upper hand. 'I came here to see if I could help.'

'I reject the expression "one of my girls", which the girl in question is not.' Godwin shook off Jeff's blame like a wet dog water. 'But if you mean Olfert Ahmadi, otherwise Mel, she's safe. She was asked up here on business – a business with which I have no financial involvement. She found her way across London, caught sight outside in the street here of a certain lorry she's all too familiar with and in something of a panic rang me.'

'Why you?'

'As the only reliable male authority figure she knows, I imagine. Does that sound boastful? I said to come to my flat. She's there now. I came on here to look around. What's going on anyway?'

'There are three dead guys in the bedroom.'

'Three!'

'Yeah', said Jeff. 'One of them only got to be dead a few minutes back. The other two were DOA. My A, not theirs.'

'So you took out clean duvets to cover them with, eh? Better put them back. Have you rung 999? You mustn't touch the bodies.'

'I touched one already.'

'The police won't like that.'

'Tough.'

'Have you rung 999?'

'The guy I touched, I gave him a drink of water. Before he died. OK?'

'Better not say that to the police. You have alerted them? They hate clever talk.'

'I talk how I want. Till the cops turn up. Could be I'll talk how I want then too.'

They entered the bedroom. 'What a very squalid mess', said Godwin.

The scolding note riled Jeff. 'Who in hell are you anyway?'

'We've met twice. I've given you my card.'

'I've seen another card with your name on. Only it's not the same name. And even when it is the same name, name is all it is. Anyone can use a name. Any name. So who in hell are you? Come on. Give, before I really call the cops. We don't have much time.'

Godwin sat down on the edge of the bed. 'I do spread a few aliases around, I admit.' He shifted backwards. He came up against Frankie's feet. 'Look here', he said. 'Can we sit somewhere else? There must be a living room.'

In the living room Godwin took the only sofa. There were two armchairs. Jeff chose the one by the window, exposing Godwin's face to the light so's to be able to read whatever was written there. Calling the cops could wait. Actually it couldn't. But he sensed he was about to crack the Godwin enigma. Cops would have to take a back seat.

'Well, Jeffers', said Godwin, as if they were old school friends. 'You've stumbled on quite a find. The scoop of your career.'

'Yeah, maybe. All the more reason I want to know who in hell you are.'

'You do go on about that. I'm me. What about you? Mel's self-appointed white knight. That's odd casting. Let's get back to the bods. Whose are they?'

'The little guy on the left as you go in the door said he was called Micky Frost. Said he once burglarized my apartment. There were three of them, all in masks. One the other guys in there definitely did. I...' He still didn't want to talk about his run-in with Frankie, of whose identity he was now almost certain. 'I'd know him, that other dead guy, any place. I think he was called Frankie. But the third guy in my apartment that night is not the third guy in the bedroom.'

'What did the people in your flat want?'

'I found it myself later. One of them took it off of me like maybe a week after. I know it wasn't the third guy in there.' Jeff nodded toward the bedroom. 'Guy came to my place, heisted it from under my nose. Said he was some janitor. But there's no such person. It was a fake ID – like yours. He may be the same guy as Ange-o or Angelo, the guy Micky said shot him.'

162

'I think I see.' Godwin spoke slowly, confused by Jeff's numerous 'guys'.

'Any those names mean a thing to you?' said Jeff.

Godwin consulted his watch. 'They police are taking their time. When did you ring 999?', he said.

Jeff said, 'Talking of cops, Micky said something makes me think Angelo was one once.'

Godwin opened his collar, blew down his shirt front. The room was indeed hot.

'You *should* know...', said Jeff. He'd discarded the overawed feeling of his first months in England, with its snotty lords and weird customs and nutty language and tricksy pronunciations and way too much history. He felt a surge of confidence.

He said, 'From something else Micky said, I figure Angelo drove a truck brought hookers here from Europe. You, Mister Godwin-Goodwin-Godber-Goddam-Whatever, had to know that, or you wouldn't have mentioned "a certain lorry Mel is all too familiar with" blah blah.'

'That's your guess work.' Godwin went to the window, looked out. 'Even the lorry's gone.'

'Sit, sir. Sit.' Godwin sat. Jeff experienced a power surge. Being top dog felt good. He said, 'You know, Mister, your role in "facilitating" Lord Crowthorne's meeting with Mel and the other escort that night in the Beldon never made the *Sunday Era* the way his did. Maybe it should.'

Godwin said, 'OK, OK. Enough of the ethics lecture. I know of an Angelo. I've never met him. Angelo Devene. He's supposed to hand me a report. You'd hardly get a criminal to prepare one. You might very well get an ex-policeman to. I don't know the details. I'm just a post-box.'

'Who's got the key?'

'I beg your pardon?'

'The key of the post-box you personate. Who's checking out the mail?'

'I don't know.'

Jeff had on sitting down dragged forward the other armchair and swung his feet up. Now with one foot he pushed the armchair away. Its back castors caught on the corner of a low coffee table and it fell over, barely missing Godwin's toes. Godwin flinched. Jeff got up. The press exposure threat had unlocked Godwin's tongue earlier. One more hard push and he'd extract the truth. 'So who has the key to the mail-box, Ed?' He righted the chair then stood over Godwin. 'Or do you want to get roasted in the *Sunday Era*? Roasted, Ed. Till you're cooked as a Thanksgiving turkey.'

Godwin looked tired. Old too. 'Ben Lee', he said.

FORTYONE

Barbara Barnes had begun to get used to her new name. Her immediate problem was who to invite to a function.

'Mark. Can you hear me, Mark? Mark! Are you there?'

A groan emerged through the barely open study door. Inside it was book-balancing time. But for Barnes the weight of debt hanging over Party HQ rendered the necessary equilibrium impossible. Short of levitation.

'Mark, please address the issue.' Barbara stood just outside, in the corridor, peering through the door. Her husband's sanctum wasn't exactly inviolate, but while outside it she felt more in control.

'Issue?' said Barnes, half turning in his chair. 'What issue?'

'We owe Victor Deller a return for his lunch last month at the Pantheon. Dinner, I want to make it dinner. The problem is, do we invite him and Laura or him and Charlotte Elver?'

'Laura of course.'

'There's no of course about it.'

Barnes kept his place in the accounts by wedging a pen at the requisite page. He moved over to the door, flung it wide open, spoke firmly and to the point: 'Charlotte that day was no more than a secretary standing in for her boss's wife...'

'Unless he's bonking her.'

'Even if he is, it's nothing to do with us. Laura's his wife. If you have one half of a married couple to dinner you have the other.'

'I don't want to seem slow in recognising a new set-up. It's clear Charlotte Elver is more than a secretary. Secretaries don't flaunt Fern Fields. Why, she could end up the fourth Mrs Deller.'

Barnes had started back to his desk. He was obliged to turn round. 'Wait till she does.'

'You're being obtuse.'

'I'm being a rock of common sense.'

'Etiquette isn't about common sense. It's about pecking order, recognising signals, sending messages. Something's up with the Dellers. I can tell.' Barbara Barnes fiddled with her bracelet, a sure sign of frustration. 'I literally don't know where to turn', she said.

'I've tried the Court Circular people. I've emailed the agony aunt who does that "Social Minefield" column in the *Scrutineer*.'

'In my opinion you must invite Victor and Laura.' And Barnes, closing the door behind him with a nice blend of the gentle and firm, returned to the task of balancing his books. It bore an uncomfortable resemblance to building castles in the air.

FORTYTWO

Jeff had no immediate riposte to Godwin's revelation about Lee. But after thinking it over he said, 'And what does Ben Lee need to know about a slate of upcoming laws he can't find out by asking his boss, Mary Matheson?'

'I told you, all I do is tend his post-box. His in-tray.'

'And why hire a guy like Angelo?' Jeff was thinking out loud by now. 'A hoodlum, bugged my apartment, my phone, my whole way of life...' Before he'd finished speaking he knew why. Because Angelo was a bugging whiz.

Jeff said to Godwin, 'Let's get back to you. Or yous, multiple. Why so many yous?'

Godwin shrugged. 'I need to be findable but not centre stage. My memory's now rotten. So I choose user-names similar to my real one. Same principle as on-line passwords. Edgar, so Edwin, Edward, Ed, Eddie; Godwin, so Goodwin, Godber, Goodman. If one doesn't work when accessing a site, the next may.'

'Why findable but not center-stage?'

'I broker information. I do it under different guises so clients hostile to other clients needn't feel I have divided loyalties.'

'You mean you're a private investigator?'

'No, no, no.' Godwin rolled his eyes ceiling-wards. 'Information-gathering isn't like that. Information's a commodity, the hottest.'

'So you're more a PR person?'

'N-o-o.' Godwin uttered a small howl. 'You're way off beam. *Much* more specialised, and dealing in much harder, more solid info.'

'So what's an info broker do?' Jeff turned towards the window and resumed the armchair. He put his feet on the coffee table this time.

'What a commodity broker does. Only with data. "Stories" to you journalists, more accurately their raw material. With hustlers on the fringe of the profession, such as spin doctors – quacks more like – you're looking at leads, rumours, gossip, scandal, innuendo, dirt. But for us mainstream professionals it involves sourcing the story's kernel, refining it for the market and placing it with a purchaser. Journalists mostly. You retail our products to the public.'

'So I'm no more than a store clerk?' said Jeff. 'Thought you said first time we met how you admired the Fourth Estate.'

Godwin bobbed his head in recognition of Jeff's point. 'You've got a good memory – much better than mine – but in one case you were as much a retailer as a sweet shop sales assistant. That story you wrote in your mag about Mary Matheson using Scrabble tiles to discuss sensitive material... I'm pretty sure you were set up.'

'Horseshit. The source was impeccable.'

'Your immediate source may have been. What if it was info at second hand? Who was your source?'

'Come on, Mister Godwin. We don't reveal our sources.'

'It doesn't matter. The point is, it could have been deliberately fed to your source, with a view to its being passed on to you.'

'Why feed it to anyone?'

'To make sure it gets back to Washington, using you and your mag as conduit.'

'Why wouldn't a British paper do?'

'Because it'd risk getting filtered through to Washington via press digests, losing its impact, if it got picked up at all. Washington meaning not just your country's political nerve centre but your President. It had to be somewhere President Washington would come across it in person. She reads your mag and trusts its statements.'

'It's so weird how Washington can mean Ms. President or the federal capital', said Jeff, musing.

'Don't you want to know why someone especially wanted it to get back to Wilmur Washington? Master Calhoun, Master Calhoun, where's your nose for a story?'

That stung. 'Well', said Jeff. 'Why?

'To let Washington know HMG has tumbled to something Washington didn't know HMG knew.'

'What's that?'

'The Americans eavesdropping on HMG via satellite.'

Jeff sat up straight and put his feet on the floor. 'We do?' He stared at Godwin.

'You'll say why not use diplomatic channels to tell your President', said Godwin, ignoring Jeff's question. 'Because the satellite snooping against an ally is clandestine, hence a deniable op. Now there's an added dimension to the story. Think it over. Then, if you want to go further, we can discuss my brokerage fee.'

FORTYTHREE

Lady Barnes respected her husband, both for his attainments and judgement. But she was only a human, and a female one at that. She compromised over her dinner party conundrum. The night it took place Barnes discovered that both Charlotte Elver and Laura Deller had been invited. A Mr Mecklenburger from the American Embassy was to be the foil for Charlotte.

There was no archaic nonsense *chez* Barnes involving sexual apartheid at the port stage, women trooping out of the dining room as if to exercise first choice of lifeboats on a stricken ship, men staying behind to discuss weighty matters while sinking gently, fathoms deep, in fortified wine. For one thing, the Barneses didn't keep port. But it did come about that towards the end of the evening Deller and Barnes ended up together in Barnes's study, two males, each with a glass of something heady. Meanwhile Barbara and Charlotte chatted in the drawing room over coffee. Laura accompanied Mr Mecklenburger round the garden, paying especial attention to the rose bed. It was a balmy night.

'What's that ex…, excuse me, that *extraordinarily* sumptuous display?' said Deller, mellow with liquor but still able to express astonishment. Barnes's study ran along one whole side of the house. In a corner of the room, flanked by a pair of huge globes, one terrestrial, the other celestial, stood a variant of the tailor's dummy. From the truncated neck downwards it was draped in a free-hanging cloak-length garment, ermine-befurred about the shoulders, crimson silk velvet from the upper arm to near ankle level. A rod pointing upwards from the neck ended in a wooden hatter's block. On it sat a coronet.

'Ah. My ceremonial secret', said Barnes. 'Those are my peer's robes.'

'Keep them at home do you?'

'No probing, please, or I'll feel obliged to change the subject.' Barnes was wholly at ease with Deller by now. He unbent slightly. 'I hope I can still trust you to keep things under your hat.'

'Has any titbit of information you've let drop in my presence ever seen the light of day?' Deller sounded belligerent.

'Well, the item about the PM and her Scrabble tiles seems to have got out somehow.'

'That wasn't me. If it had been, it would have surfaced in one of my publications. Someone else blabbed. You must see that.'

'Yes, I do on the whole.'

Deller moved towards the robes. He seemed fascinated by them. 'That outfit', he said, 'do you keep it at home all the time?'

Barnes didn't answer him directly. 'I hope you'll respect another confidence', he said. 'The fact is, I'm on a committee to prepare for the next coronation. While His Majesty is in excellent health, he's not a young man. There's no sense in getting caught unprepared. With so many more peers around these days even than in 2018, and most of them elderly, we're looking at ways to cut down on some of the ceremonial come the big day in Westminster Abbey, save precious time. I thought I'd try on my costume – robes – while I was about it.'

Deller ran his hand over the dummy. He felt the cloth. 'It's very heavy', he said.

'It is. With the coronet as well it may be too much for the more doddery chaps. To say nothing of the old duck peeresses. We're looking at light-weight synthetic alloys for the next generation headgear. Don't for God's sake breathe a word of that either.'

'Of course not.' Deller ran his hand over the metal of the dummy's coronet. 'I suppose I couldn't try it on?' he said. The voice was shy but eager, like a small boy begging a spin on his elder brother's mountain bike.

'Hmm. It might not fit.' Barnes was temporising. 'What size head are you?'

'No idea. I don't ever wear hats. Or coronets. Or not yet.' Deller turned back in the direction of the dummy. 'Go on. Just for a second.'

'Oh all right.'

Both men put their drinks down. Barnes lifted the coronet off the hatter's block. He handled it with great care, fingers lightly gripping the circlet as a fiddler the neck of his Amati.

'I'll kneel', said Deller. And before Barnes could expostulate he knelt.

'That's not necessary', said Barnes, embarrassed. 'It isn't so very heavy when you're holding it.' He held it forward nonetheless. As he was about to place it on the other man's head, Deller looked up, took the coronet from Barnes's hands and donned it without assistance.

'It's a bit tight', he said. He remained kneeling. 'I must be a size or so more than you.'

'Careful', said Barnes. The anxiety pushed his voice higher than usual. 'It'll cost a mint of money to stick any of those balls back on.' He was trying to recall who Deller's gesture reminded him of. Then it came to him: Napoleon, wresting the crown from the Pope at his coronation as Emperor in 1804.

'You're still keen then?' he said. He didn't need to say about what.

'Keen as ever.' Deller got up from the floor. He pulled a chair over and sat down. He still wore the coronet.

'Crowthorne's death made absolutely no difference to our rent demand, you know', said Barnes, also seating himself. He took up his drink. 'The de Bohun Estate trustees say they're obliged to get the best terms they can whatever the other circumstances.'

'Including the last member of the family dropping dead? Who are their trust's beneficiaries now Crowthorne's gone?' The coronet had slipped slightly over towards Deller's right eye. He took it off and placed it on Barnes's desk. A dent remained briefly across one corner of his forehead.

'His interfaith foundation perhaps', said Barnes. 'It doesn't matter. Party HQ still needs the money.'

'I've found a purchaser for *Chic* and *Yoohoo!* We're signing this week. If you can hold on till then I'll see you home and dry.'

Barnes did some calculations in his head. 'I can defer things to the end of the month. No longer.' He got up, picked the coronet off the table and replaced it on the hatter's block. The nap of the velvet of the cap of maintenance had got slightly ruffled. He smoothed it with one finger, gentle as a lover caressing his mistress's neck. 'Soon you might have one of these of your own', he said.

'But in a larger size, eh?' Deller smirked. 'I don't awfully care for those ball things', he said, pointing at the coronet. 'Isn't there something I've read somewhere about strawberry leaves? I like strawberries. Even without cream.'

'Those are for dukes. We may be desperate but we can't dish out strawberry-leaf coronets. The honours system would collapse.'

171

FORTYFOUR

Jeff had been jolted by Godwin's latest revelation. To give himself time to think it over, he reverted to Godwin's calling. 'I know another guy that his specialty is information. Gavin Doresett. British guy in our New York office.' The setting sun shone straight into the living room window, drenching it rosy, as if filtered through blood.

'Oh yes', said Godwin. 'I heard he'd ended up on some American mag or other. It was yours, was it?'

Jeff was taken aback. 'You know Gav?'

'Obviously. Though he's no broker. I bet he helps with fact-checking. He does, doesn't he?'

Jeff nodded.

Godwin shook his head in apparent sorrow. 'That neurotic anxiety to avoid howlers. The bane of American journalism. Anyway, Doresett is no broker. I dig out hard stuff in the real world. Some of the time on commission. Some of the time as a speculation. Stuff journalists wouldn't have time to try for, or their bosses these days spend the cash to fund direct.'

'But you know him?'

'Doresett? We used to work together.'

'Where?'

'NIRI.'

'What's that?'

'National Information Research Institute.'

'Never heard of it.'

'I should hope not. Anyway, "Neary" doesn't exist now. It got closed down years ago. Once the Cold War was over it became obsolete.'

'From which I deduce it was some spook outfit.'

'Well we certainly didn't advertise our existence. But we weren't spooks. More backroom boys, though with good friends in shadowy places.' Godwin crossed his legs and leant back on the sofa. 'My word but it was drudgery before computers came along. On the other hand, you learned to use your memory. It's a skill that rather atrophies once a PC does the searches.'

'Well bards reciting all of Homer got made redundant once writing came in. Boo hoo.'

Godwin raised his eyebrows. 'You had a classical education?'

'Not really. A module I studied at college was dead white European males.'

'That's as well. Because you've now got three of them on your hands, haven't you? In a flat that's not even yours.'

On his hands? Jeff didn't own any corpses.

'And when are the police coming?' said Godwin. 'I thought you said you'd rung them?'

It came to Jeff that his situation looked bad. Still, Godwin's was hardly squeaky clean. He felt he still hadn't got everything out of him. 'I told you why I came up here', he said.

'And I told you why I did.' Godwin leant forward, suggesting frankness. 'Very well, let's pool our information. Then we really must report the crimes properly. Here's my side of the story so far. As I told you before, I have a number of clients on my books, including Victor Deller and until recently Lyonel Crowthorne. Normally I wouldn't even reveal a client's name, but for once the situation demands it. You must know all about Deller even if you haven't met him. And I introduced you to Crowthorne myself. We may not have seen eye to eye about everything, but I can tell you this. He was the victim of a massive injustice. Not just the exposure itself but what he was supposedly getting up to. In his admittedly rather sanctimonious way he was trying to start a refuge for trafficked women.'

'You didn't pimp for him that time at the Beldon?'

'No I bloody well did not. He didn't summon those girls to have sex with him but to offer to arrange honourable retirement from their squalid trade, especially the foreign one, Melons, or whatever she's called. I won't deny he may have let his enthusiasm run away with him.'

Jeff recalled Chrissie's account of Crowthorne's seizure. 'Enthusiasm?' he said. 'He passed out.'

Godwin wrinkled his nose in distaste 'It's called getting too involved with your subject', he said. 'So what if the old boy's heart had got a bit wonky? You wait till you're in your late seventies, see how well you cope.' He became formal once more. 'Unfortunately his genuine concern led to that appalling *Sunday Era* exposure.'

Godwin tapped his right index finger against his left, ticking off an item on his list. 'Let's turn to Deller. And this is not for public consumption. What should especially interest you about Victor Deller is that he's asked me to keep an eye on what his wife gets up to. I don't know how many times you've been to bed with her, but I think you should stop. In your own interests. She's a highly dangerous woman.'

Jeff was much more jolted than before. 'How so?' He tried to keep his voice steady.

'For one thing, she's a compulsive liar…'

'Not so much a liar she twisted the Scrabble story, which you say is genuine and she got fed. Who by? Wouldn't she get it from her husband? He's close to guys in the Administration here.'

'If he got it from someone, it was third-hand by the time it reached you. Info like that could only have come initially from someone close to the Prime Minister. One of a handful of people. It wasn't Deller cooked it up, even if it was him who fed it to his missis.'

'Laura Deller told me her husband told her the Scrabble thing, which he got from some Administration high-up.'

'If she said that about Deller she's lying, Calhoun. She's lying. I know she is. I was nearby when Deller and Barnes discussed it. I overheard them. Deller's not just a newspaper proprietor he's a former mandarin. He'd never breach the rules…'

'Unless he's a crook.'

'…Even if he did – even if he was – he'd make sure his own newspaper ran it first. Not one of the titles in his stable ever did.' Godwin paused. 'Or is she banging Barnes, got it direct from him?' Godwin spoke to himself, speculating out loud.

Jeff felt a sharp pang. 'You don't know that.'

Godwin turned to Jeff. 'Knowing Laura Deller, I imagine she's told you all kinds of cock and bull stories about her love life, yes?'

By now Jeff was sucked too far in for an outright denial to convince. 'She might have.' Even to himself it sounded grudging.

'Look, I know you've been with her on at least one occasion', said Godwin. 'The night of that big party at the Dellers' house. You forget I'd spent a whole flight across the Atlantic in the next seat to you, that time we first met. When you turned over to go to sleep the gigolo jewellery thing round your neck rode up above your shirt collar. It was visible from the bedroom door many weeks later when you got your leg over with Mrs D.'

'The Dellers have their own kind of marriage', said Godwin. 'Not to everyone's taste, but durable. Journalists who get too involved with the people they do stories on – their careers can suffer. A bit like Lyonel Crowthorne.'

Jeff fought back. 'And you tailed Laura Deller in the airplane just so you could keep tabs on her? You weren't in New York on Lord Barnes's behalf. It was to spy on your client Deller's wife, like a sleazy small-time private dick. Which is what you are, for all your fancy talk about brokering information. No wonder she went for you at that party. She must've known by then how you'd spied on her for her husband.'

Before Godwin could answer Chrissie appeared in the doorway. 'Pipe down you two', she said. 'Sunday's a day of rest. I could hear you shouting at each other from the far end of the landing outside this flat. You'd left the front door open. Where's the Francis Evans whose name's on the door?'

'Chrissie! I told you not to...'

'You most certainly did. But I'm fed up having to take things lying down.' She waved to Godwin. 'Hi, Ed. Where's the bathroom?'

'Hello April. Second on the left.'

'Oh yeah', said Jeff. 'You two know each other already.' Chrissie exited.

Godwin turned to Jeff. 'The situation's getting too complicated for a bear of limited brain like me', he said, taking up a pen from the coffee table. 'I need to make some notes.' He took out a pocket diary and tried writing. 'Damn', he said. He shook the pen, then tried scribbling hard with it on the page, jerking it back and forth like a child doodling. 'First my Blackberry's on the blink now this'. He put the pen down. Jeff stared at it in horror.

Chrissie re-entered the room. 'Has anyone rung the police? You've got at least three dead bodies in this flat. Maybe more. I haven't looked in every room.' She went out again.

'Good God', said Godwin. 'She's right. Where's the phone?'

'How should I know? It's not my apartment', said Jeff. In his agitation over the pen he was brusque. 'Use your cell phone.'

'And get treated as a prime suspect? Are you mad? Besides, it's not working.'

'Can I see that pen?'

Godwin got up to look for a land line. 'Here, catch.' He tossed the pen at Jeff.

Chrissie came back in. 'One of them's still alive.'

'No!', said Godwin. 'Which one?'

'Feller with his forearms pulped. Says it's his flat. Francis Evans, I presume.'

Jeff had been examining the pen. He waved vigorously at the other two, put his fingers to his lips to enjoin silence, stuffed the pen well under a fat cushion and looked up. 'We've been bugged' he said softly. 'We should assume every word we've said since entering this apartment has been overheard by the guy planted this listening device.' He pointed in the direction of the pen.

Godwin and Chrissie stared at him.

'Well I've got nothing to hide', said Chrissie, louder than Jeff but less than normal volume. 'I've only just got here.'

'And I was second on the scene', said Godwin, also less than normal volume, but not much less. 'Which is when I found him'. He said this to Chrissie, but pointed to Jeff.

Jeff turned on Godwin. 'What about Mel?' he said. 'You blurted out her whereabouts.'

'I only said she'd come over to my place.'

'Who knows your address? Your clients? Which of them wants Mel so dead Mel went and holed up with you soon as she spotted a truck outside? Think, Mister Godwin.'

'Act too', said Chrissie. 'We need to get over there. Fast. Wherever "there" is.'

Godwin had aged five years in five minutes. 'I live down in Dulwich', he said. 'Other side of London.' This time he spoke truly low.

There was a groan from the bedroom. The three of them near jostled each other getting through its door. Frankie had propped himself on his good elbow. 'Just get that bastard and I'll die happy', he said. He too had aged.

'Who?' said Chrissie.

'Who? That cunt Devene, that's who. Angelo Devene. Five eleven. Paunch. Rest of him thick set but still muscular. Short grey hair. Ears with big lobes. Good features. Vile temper.' Frankie twisted round. His face was paper pale with agony. 'He's got my gun.'

'We'll never catch him', said Chrissie.

'Yes we will', said Jeff. 'If he listened in to what we said he'd have to be nearby.'

'Take the Cayman', said Frankie. 'Cream job right outside these flats. Keys are in my pocket.' He tried to reach for them but couldn't move his hands. His face gurned in pain.

His navy chinos were folded neatly over the back of a cream-upholstered bergère. Chrissie felt inside them. 'Here they are.'

Jeff turned to Chrissie. 'You stay here. Call the cops. Paramedics too. Try and make this guy comfortable. Ed and I'll take the car.' He turned to Godwin. 'Come on, Ed. Time's a wastin'.'

FORTYFIVE

When whoever it was had broken through the front door and started up the stairs, Angelo had darted out of Frankie's flat and hidden behind a big house plant on the landing. The intruder had turned out to be the American kid reporter. More proof Frankie had misread things right from the start.

Angelo had then got into the lorry, moving it out of sight of the flat lest the kid start monitoring the street. He wasn't too worried. What with Frankie's, Micky's and Pierre's bodies to handle, there'd be plenty to keep the kid occupied.

Parking spots hadn't been as plentiful as earlier in the day. It had taken Angelo a good half hour to find a suitable berth. The lorry needed to be reasonably near the building where the flat was if he was going to listen in to what went on there. In the end he'd had to bribe a young Asian man in the street parallel to Frankie's to surrender a space so he could site the lorry within transmitting distance. One corner of Frankie's building had been just visible across the strips of garden behind the houses. It was enough.

On overhearing Mel's new whereabouts, Angelo prepared to hit Godwin's place. He had the man's address card already. Jules to thank for that. Angelo took as transport not the lorry but a minicab. He took with him the spanner and the rest of the bondage toys. Also Frankie's gun.

He used his time as passenger to review the situation. Micky and Frankie out. Mel still to eliminate. Area Manager to neutralise. There'd be no proof of his doing in Frankie, Micky and Pierre. Even if an investigation marked him as a suspect, there was always the stink he could threaten over being asked to spy on MPs. Then there was the bit of paper he'd swiped from the kid. It had to have value or Area Manager wouldn't have been keen to acquire it.

He took out the photocopy he'd made of the original. It made no more sense than when he'd last looked at it, two days before, when on an impulse, his mind harking back to the MPs business, he'd rung Jules for help with deciphering the contents.

'Ange? I *told* you not to contact me again.'

'I need your help. Who's Byro?'

'No idea. As it happens, it don't matter so much you ringing me now. I'm on secondment.'

Angelo was intrigued. 'What secondment?'

'Not sure it'll last long enough to be even a temp thing. Boss is so near he won't pay me my wages on time. I'm off if he doesn't come up with the dibs by the end of the week. I only took it on to afford those higher taxes the flamin' MPs gone and lumbered us with.'

'You must be mad to work for him.'

'What makes it worse is, he's a millionaire.'

'So's anyone owns his own house if it's London.'

'A squillionaire then.' Jules had been stung into saying more than he ought: 'Proper loaded, anyway.

'Loaded? Owns two London houses, does he?'

'Two? He's one of the biggest media blokes in the country.'

Angelo had pounced. 'Oh?' he'd said. 'Who?'

'No one you've heard of.'

Angelo had risen to the challenge. 'That *Era* bloke owns a string of nags', he'd said. 'Including a Derby winner, June Maroon two years ago at 45-1. It'll come to me in a minute... David Macnamara.'

'Him?' Jules had got lured into more boasting. 'Much bigger. Same line of business though.'

'Who?'

'Well, Victor Deller if you must know.'

'Never heard of him.'

'He only owns the bloody *Date*.'

'Never look at it. I tell a lie. I did once. Tipped nothing but also-rans. In Gold Cup week too.'

'But you must have *heard* of him?'

'No. Who is he? Would he be your boss over this research project you asked me to do?'

'No way. He's media, not government.'

'I wonder if there's all that much difference.'

'You're thinking of those diaries that ex-*Triumph* editor wrote when he got sacked. How he leant on Chazza Lynton to pull out of Seleukistan. You don't want to believe everything you read in books.'

'Or the papers?'

'That's different. They're news. Lose credibility if they make things up. History's more dodgy. The clever clogs as write it can't

179

even see eye to eye over what causes revolutions, let alone modern stuff like high prices.'

Angelo had wrenched the conversation back onto its tracks: 'This job of yours with the man Deller...'

'Bit of moonlighting really. A stint as his driver. Regular wage don't go far. That's why it pisses me off when he drags his heels over my pay packet.'

'You weren't put there to spy on him by any chance?'

'Come off it. Would I say if I was? Not that I am.'

Angelo hadn't believed him. From which he'd concluded Deller would be worth investigating. 'What if you do?' he'd said, putting Jules on the spot. 'Spy on him. For me. My research. Which you know all about since it was you got me involved in the first place.'

'What's Vic Deller got to do with your research?'

'Never you mind.'

Had Jules been fencing or had he really not known whatever Deller's involvement was? Perhaps Deller had no involvement. Still, in for a penny in for a pound. Angelo had reckoned he might as well go ahead with his plan. 'I could have found a lead to your Dell-boy over the MPs thing for all you know', he'd said to Jules. 'Just keep your eyes and ears open. You're his driver. Bring the car round. Say you're doing it for its service. I'll bug it up. Not only might you hear some useful info you can pass on to your real boss, or you to me then me to him... It's your choice. Not only that, but you could maybe sell some extra meaty bits to the *Sunday Era* or somewhere. Bonus, sort of. He dumps on you re wages. You dump on him as payback. More money in it for you too.'

Jules took this in quickly for once. 'He dumped on me, yeah. It's not right. Exploit an employee's loyalty...make him wait for his wages... OK, Ange, done.'

FORTYSIX

The mood in the Dellers' car as they started home from the Barnes dinner party turned swiftly volatile. Deller had detected a foreign body attached to the back of his wife's coat when helping her on with it before they'd climbed in.

'How was the garden under the soft moonlight?' he said, putting two and two together as they swept up Constitution Hill.

'Meaning "was it a nice screw you had with Mecklenburger in the rose bed?"', she said. She looked away from him, out of the window, into the night. 'God it's close for May.'

'Why not take your coat off?'

'Comfort blanket.'

As she leant forward now to search for an atomiser in her handbag Deller felt her coat again, and extracted a rose thorn. He switched on the rear compartment light, held up the thorn and looked at it.

'Mermaid', he said. He leant sideways and pressed the button to cut off the intercom connecting them with the chauffeur. The horse had pretty well bolted from the stable already, but he could at least nip any further indiscretions in the bud. 'Or perhaps New Dawn', he said, still examining the rose thorn. 'One of those prickly varieties.'

'It didn't stop us admiring them. Luscious scent.' She looked round at her husband. He still held the thorn. 'I must have brushed up against a spiky bit', she said.

'Or two', said Deller, leaning over and twisting another thorn from his wife's coat.

'Actually', she said, turning to face him fully, 'it was Si used it.' She meant the coat. 'As a rug.' She toyed with her hem. 'Chivalrous. Risked his skin. He lay on his back. I rode him cowgirl.'

'They're long, the thorns', said Deller. His fingers clenched slightly as he held the thorns, but his voice stayed steady. 'Pierced the cloth. Mecklenburger's back's going to be more than a little scratched.'

'So American foreign policy stumbles on while he spends a few days in bed. Face down.'

She turned further and looked out of the other window. A flotilla of three stretch limos was edging into Knightsbridge from the top of

Wilton Place. Some pop princess and her court leaving the Berkeley. Or Staines tanning shop slappers on a hen night up the West End.

'You fix your deal with Barnes?' she said, still looking out of the window.

'He'll accept a further delay.'

'Till you pull off the StrepMag sale?'

'Yes.' Deller opened his own window an inch, flicked the thorns through the gap then powered it shut. 'Thanks for letting them know I was up for it', he said. 'Even if it was via young Calhoun.'

'Least I could do for my darling hub.' And oddly enough, despite her flings elsewhere, she meant it.

They'd forked right along Kensington Gore by the time Deller next spoke. 'Time to close that one down, don't you think?'

Their marriage might by now be short on physical intimacy. Mentally they were so attuned she knew what he meant.

'Jeff?' she said. 'Why's it time?'

Deller had reached the limits of his courtesy. 'Think you can still pump more pleasure out of him before he tumbles to your call-girl business?'

'Don't be coarse. It's a dating agency.'

'Your friend Jeff is a journalist. If he finds out about your "dating agency", the entire media will. I can see the headline: "Press Lord Wife's Vice Ring".'

'You're not a lord yet.'

'And you don't get to be a lady till I'm a real lord. If then', he added under his breath.

'Meanwhile I have to settle for Mrs?'

'Some bright sub might come up with "Media Baron's Wife a Madam?". Till then, yes.'

A brief silence. 'Thing is, I feel real good when I'm with him.'

They were held up by a temporary traffic light. Road works. It stayed red for ages.

'You do know he's got some piece of fluff somewhere?'

'Oh? Who says so?'

'A man. He reports to me. She's called Tucky.'

'Spiteful tittle tattle.' The light at last turned green. They moved forwards. 'I'll see him one more time anyway', she said.

'When?'

'Tomorrow. Maybe say goodbye. If you got proof of the fluff.'

'I'd drop you off tomorrow but I've got to go down to the plant. Sort out some management issues.'

'Management?'

'Middle management, not shop floor. You don't have to come.'

'Too right. The shop floor's here in London.'

'And Bristol. Don't forget Bristol.'

'Blue-collar.'

'Sandbanks too.'

'Semi-white-collar there. Can't you get some junior executive to handle backwaters?'

'Not this time. One of the middle managers isn't answering calls. Playing hard to get, perhaps.'

'You really think so?'

'No. His silence, it's...disquieting', said Deller, frowning. 'And you?' he said. 'You'll stay in town and really might say goodbye?'

'Maybe it is the right moment', she said. 'Security angle... And if he's really two-timing me... But you better fucking show me proof.'

'Of course he's two-timing you. He's a journalist, I keep telling you. They're like stud farm stallions: cover anything that smells promising.'

FORTYSEVEN

Jeff drove the Cayman. Godwin sat behind, in the foetal position that only sporty cars dare impose on their rear passengers.

'You comfortable back there?' said Jeff, swerving to avoid a rash cyclist and jabbing the horn. It blasted out First Call, the introductory fanfare at American race tracks. 'Jesus!' he said.

'I'm not comfy', said Godwin. 'But I do feel safer.'

'Shame on you, Ed. I got me a licence age fifteen. Drove my mom's pick-up to high school every day of each semester my sophomore year thru graduation.'

'Just remember to keep to the left.'

They'd stopped at a pedestrian crossing. An elderly gentlewoman shuffled across the black and white rectangles, a retreating queen in a game of blind chess.

'Left, left, left.' Jeff banged his head on the steering wheel.

They picked up speed again.

'…And second right after the church… Christ', said Godwin, 'do you have to corner like that?… You were saying?'

'Laura: "highly dangerous woman", sez you back at the Virgie Prout place. How?'

'The way she behaved to me at that party. It was the act of a malicious hysteric.'

Jeff wasn't unsympathetic. He'd seen that side of her too. He defended her all the same. 'Doesn't make her dangerous.'

'I scent danger off her, is all.'

'C'mon Ed. There has to be something more solid than your nose to go by.'

'She sleeps around. Classic security risk.'

More an *avant garde* one, Jeff thought, recalling aspects of Laura's bedroom technique. Not something to be shared with Godwin.

'Who gave her that item about Mary Matheson using Scrabble tiles?' said Godwin, speaking mostly to himself. 'I keep coming back to Barnes. Barnes? Not the type, I'd have thought. And would he have known anyway? That puzzles me.' He addressed Jeff direct. 'Did she ever talk to you about her other boyfriends?'

184

'Whoa. For her to do that would be kissing and telling. All the worse when the guy the gal's telling is a guy she's kissing.'

'Anything. Anything at all.'

'I can't beat a confession out of her. You think back home we're a bunch of boll weevil-accented Teamster goons with a scab? Some us try to play the gentleman.'

'All right then, Robert E. Lee…'

'Hell, Lee.' Jeff near totalled the car the brainstorm struck him was such a thunderclap. 'You just said it. The dark guy talked to you the night of the Deller shindig… Dark.'

'Ben Lee. So what if he's dark? They say he's got a touch of Romany.'

'Dark, Ed. Dark. A dark guy would have a dark back. A black back even. If he'd been burning up in the sun. As he might if he'd been returning here from some place he'd been on vacation. Picked up with Mrs Deller in an airplane restroom.'

'I don't quite follow you.'

'No reason why you should, Ed. But a lot of jigsaw pieces just fell into place.'

He wondered if there'd ever really been a video of Laura and Lee. Who cared? 'It's Lee fed her the Scrabble thing', he said with conviction. 'Now let's focus on this Angelo Devene character. I owe him one for burglarizing my pad, a second for grabbing my archive, a third for putting one over on my maid and a knockout for putting another one over on me – on my own doorstep, too.'

'Remember he has a gun.'

'Stolen. He won't know how to use it too well or he'd have him one all his own.'

'I hope you're right.'

'It's my day for being right, Ed.'

'If you don't stop calling me Ed, I'll call you Cal.'

'Go ahead. My boss does.'

When they reached the turning to Godwin's home road Jeff stopped the car and turned round to look at Godwin. 'Come here, Ed', he said, patting the leather upholstery beside him. 'To make plans I need you up front as co-pilot.'

It was almost dark by now. Godwin managed to open the passenger door, wriggle out of the car then re-enter, lowering himself clumsily onto the front seat. 'You have to be bloody fit to get in and out of one of these things', he said.

'It's a sport car, Ed', said Jeff. 'Takes an athlete to use one. OK, now assume this guy Angelo's inside, how do we break into your apartment without us getting shot to death?'

'I've been thinking about that. There's a french window. Lucky it's a garden flat.'

'OK. You go to the front door. Distract Devene's attention. I'll take the back yard route.'

'And when I knock on my own front door he just let's me in, does he?'

Jeff looked out the car window, tackling the problem his own way. 'It's Sunday evening...', he said. He had an idea. 'Hey, whyncha be the minister...?'

'Minister for what?'

'Preacher. Reverend Smith, Jones, Whoever. You say you're him, dropped by to get you, the real you, to attend your neighborhood church.'

'Oh, you mean the Vicar. I've only met ours socially.'

'Devene won't know that.'

'He'd suspect. In Britain men of God don't tout for bums on pews. And people here don't go to church much anyway.'

'Damn. Well, be some neighbor asks you round to watch TV. Anything.'

'OK. A canvasser maybe... I know, a Jehovah's Witness.'

'Fine. You go in front. I'll sneak round the back way.'

'It's me'll draw Devene's fire.'

'It's your place, Ed. Mel's your house guest.'

Godwin sighed. 'The obligations of a host...' he said. 'All right then.'

FORTYEIGHT

The Dellers' car was level with the Albert Hall by now. The Albert Memorial loomed on the right. Fresh gilded, it shone more than ever in the spotlights trained upon it, piercing the warm dark sky like some gargantuan monstrance housing the relics of the saintly Prince Consort.

'Want to do it now?' said Laura Deller, stretching her legs.

'What, here? In the car?'

'Why not?'

'Don't be a tease. Besides, I've had a bit to drink.'

'Your drink intake's been neither here nor there for months', she said. 'Press the tit to draw the curtain first. You won't know it, being self-made, but sex in front of the hired help saps their will to serve.'

He reached across to press the button but couldn't quite make it.

She stabbed at the intercom switch. The car turned sideways as she did so and her finger hit it a glancing blow. She stabbed again. 'Driver', she said.

'Yes, Milady?'

'Please draw the curtain.'

'Yes Milady.'

She stabbed at the intercom again to turn it off and turned to her husband. Deller struggled with his zip.

She gestured towards the curtain: 'The new man. Where'd you get him?'

'He's called Jules. Ben Lee rang me to find him a job.'

'He fell down on the last one?'

'Got a bit stale, Ben said. Needs to recharge his batteries.'

'If Ben Lee's persuaded you to take him on it's for more than stale batteries. Keep tabs on us is my guess.'

'How would you know?'

'I said, just a guess.'

But it was too late. She'd given the game away. Deller's mind, notwithstanding his drink, was quick.

'Bloody hell!', he said, spitting out the words like hot bits of potato. 'It's me should have guessed. That Scrabble story the

187

American mag ran, *Hence*. You passed it on, having got it from Lee. You're humping him too, aren't you?'

She didn't answer at first. Then, 'You can do that zipper up. I lost interest.' She leant over and pulled it up for him.

Deller made no effort to resist. 'You really are a tease', he said.

'When we get home I'll call up one of the girls, see if she can't turn you on the way I used to.'

'Not tonight.'

'You haven't seen half what's in my stable.' She fiddled with her mobile, clicking on the portraits. She paused on the fifth. 'Mel. Now there's a babe'd make Mother Theresa's mouth water.'

Deller's interest flickered. 'Which one's Mel?'

'The Persian kitty-cat.'

Deller lowered his window two thirds. 'It is close', he said. 'You're right.'

He dabbed at his face with the red handkerchief from his breast pocket. 'I feel stuffed to the gills after that dinner…', he said, poking it back in.

'Look on peachy Mel as a late night snack. You could at least show appreciation. The things I do to crank up that pathetic sex drive of yours. Most wives wouldn't go to nearly so much trouble.'

'No, I suppose not.' By now Deller sounded weary. 'It's good of you.'

'I'll call her up then, OK?'

'All right.'

'Tell her come round to our place in, like, the next hour? We'll throw this party in the Daffodil Library. The sexy ceiling might prime your pump.'

'Oh God.'

'Gods. Scads of gods.' She text messaged Mel, then continued, '£300 for sixty minute's worth, OK? I'd comp you, but it's gone midnight. Even house regulars got to pay full rates then.'

'Do you have to bring that up?'

'I'm not in this business for my health. But I am for yours. It's sick, how you take your low sex drive lying down.'

Five minutes later and they drew up outside the gate. The driver kept the car motor idling as he held the back door open, first for Mrs Deller to alight then her husband.

'Can I have a word with you, Milady?' he said to Laura.

'I'm not Milady.' She smiled. 'But shoot anyway.' She called to Deller, 'Go on up, Vic. I'll join you in a while. I dropped my atomizer in the car.' Then, to Jules, 'Well?'

'It's last week's wages. They're a bit overdue. I don't like to bother Mister Deller. Could you…?'

'Speak with him? Sure. How much? So I know what I'm talking about.'

'Two thousand all told. There are deductions…'

'A two then three Os. Even a math flunk like me should be able to handle that. OK, Jules.' She looked searchingly at him. 'Jules What? Mister D didn't say your other name.'

'Miller, Ma'am.'

'OK, listen up, Jules Miller. My husband's got a very, very, very big business deal coming to a head the next few days. It's taking up his time, his concentration, 24/7. I'll see you get paid the instant it eventuates. You OK for a day or two?'

'I can get by. Thank you, Mrs Deller.'

'Sure you don't need five hundred, Jules, tide you over?'

She searched in her handbag.

'I'm fine now I know you're helping, thanks.'

She snapped the bag shut. 'Great. Good night, Jules.' She had betted successfully that making the interim payment offer a second time would cement his acquiescence. She turned away and walked up the path. 'Shit' she said to herself and kicked at a stray stone.

She joined her husband in the Daffodil Library. 'I hope you really dig Mel's act tonight' she said. 'It could be a farewell performance.'

'You closing down the business?'

'Not while there's a chance a girl of mine turns you on. I mean it when I say I do this for you. But if your deal goes sour… And word's got out. Now the hired help wants to foreclose.'

189

FORTYNINE

'It's all very well HM putting in for an American Learjet or a Gulfstream as his Royal Flight aircraft', said the PM, a touch pettishly, nursing an unusually strong elderflower cordial. 'He doesn't have to worry so much about buying British. For us in government it's crucial.'

'I suppose you can shop around more if you're King of lots of other countries', said Lee. 'Which he is, after all.'

'But America isn't one of them. Or not for two centuries. Yet where else does one buy an executive aircraft these days?'

'At least it wasn't under your premiership that this country lost its commercial aircraft manufacturing base.' That mollified the PM. Lee had known it would.

They were aboard the sole Avro RJX-85 to survive the post-9/11 cancelling in 2001 of its production run. Apart from American engines, a model sufficiently British to make it the patriot's natural choice of civil air transport. Its thirst for fuel was easily slaked as well – a comfort to green-leaning media commentators.

The Avro had been lent the PM by Sir Pip Porter. He had rescued it from degrading retirement as exhibit in an aviation museum, simultaneously snapping up a lifetime's supply of spare parts. Ordinarily he used it on his world tours.

They were off to Aberdeen to attend the decommissioning of a 1970s oil rig. A negative event in itself, though not unconnected with shoring up the ColLaborative Party's rocky position in Scotland. Which is why Lee had proposed to tack on the opening of a new nuclear power station as follow-up. By coupling it to the closure of a carbon fuel source, he'd convinced the PM, the public would get the message that atoms were the sole option.

One especially useful modification Sir Pip had made to his Avro was a soundproof composition chamber, used by the great man to work on his songs while jetting to gigs the far side of the globe. The PM and Lee had sequestered themselves there for a private talk while the rest of the prime ministerial suite stuck to their ordinary business in the principal passenger section. The PM's husband had announced his intention of slipping away once they landed and knocking his new

Bridgestone B330 round the Balnagask links. The high winds of Scotland's East Coast made his choice the only sound one, he'd said, to anyone minded to listen.

The PM downed the rest of her elderflower cordial in a single gulp. 'Refreshing', she said. 'Healthy too. You should give it a try, Ben.'

'I'm happy with my fizzy water, thank you.'

'To business, then. First, I have been informed that the Americans have stopped their satellite surveillance.'

'Why, Prime Minister... Mary... That's marvellous.'

The PM beamed. 'Good, isn't it? You handled the communications side of the business very deftly. Congratulations.'

'Thank you, Prime Minister.'

'Second, Party finances. Sitrep please.'

Lee saw he couldn't postpone the bad news. And there was no one else he could delegate its reporting to. His ascendancy as the PM's innermost adviser by now was too total. 'I'm afraid Victor Deller's beginning to look like a busted flush', he said. 'My source there reports staff wages are more than a week overdue.'

'But couldn't that be a typical rich man's penny-pinching?' The PM was calm, as yet.

'He's selling a couple of his magazines too.'

'All media magnates offload some of their titles from time to time, surely?'

'There's more to it than that, I regret to say.' Lee took a big breath. 'Much more.' There. He'd broached the subject. 'He and his wife are behind that breakdown of discipline business affecting some of our people in Parliament', he said. 'My source at the Dellers' overheard it all. They accidentally left the car intercom on, he says. It isn't just our side they've suborned. Opposition chaps are involved too, though naturally that's of less immediate concern.'

'Deller *and* his wife? What's she got to do with it? I thought he and Mark had arranged party funding between only the two of them.' The PM was but mildly concerned as yet.

Lee bent forwards and whispered in his boss's ear. It took some time. He opened his lips extra wide to maximise clarity. In doing so he at one point nearly caught his mouth on her earring. A stylised Scottish thistle, it and its twin had been presented to her by the ColLaborative Executive Committee north of the Border.

191

When he had finished the PM sat for a while staring ahead of her. 'I see', she said. There was a pause. The engine note changed slightly. They were losing height. 'The lengths men will go to for a few seconds of pleasurable friction...', she said, echoing Eleanor Roosevelt. Lee said nothing. 'This is the end for him', she said.

'Financially?'

'Financially too. I was thinking more of his reputation. But you are right. Financially.'

Gravely perturbed, she drifted from the main point. 'What will happen to the *Date*, I wonder.' She reverted to Deller. 'What a waste of all that drive and talent and sparkle and... well, I suppose vigour.'

She turned to Lee. 'Could you ask them to get me another drink? A whisky.' And she added, as if to excuse her intemperance, 'We are visiting Scotland. No ice.'

Presently she said 'Why on earth did he do it?'

'Well, he wanted a peerage, didn't he?'

'But to mire yourself in scandal to that extent?'

'He's not exactly the first.'

The PM said, 'A mere life barony, God help us. It's not even as if the Lords have much power.'

'I suppose it's the kudos attracts people.'

'Kudos without power is all icing and no cake.'

'Deller has a preternaturally sweet tooth.' Lee regretted this the moment he'd said it. Too epigrammatic.

'And Deller's wife?' said the PM, after a pause. 'How much was she simply swept up in his ambition?'

Lee looked hard at his shoes. He said nothing.

'Have you not met her?' said the PM.

'A bit.'

'Well? Is she a Lady Macbeth?'

'I'm not really qualified to judge.'

'We'll be landing soon. On Scottish soil. Lady Macbeth or Patient Grizelda? Active egger-on of her husband or passive plaything to his hubris? Answer me, Ben.'

'I really can't say.'

'Can't you, Ben?'

'Er, no.'

The PM stared out of the window, though there was nothing to see but thick cloud. She turned back her head. 'Ben, Ben', she said. 'Do you recall when you first joined my team? You were subject to Developed Vetting. It's not the leisurely checks by a retired policeman that it used to, tracking down musty skeletons in your teenage toy cupboard. Trivial stuff like revolutionary flirtations at university. I've known about your liaison with Mrs Deller ever since it started. To the very night.'

'I...see.'

'Till now it was your own affair. Literally. And hers of course. Now it's one of state. Do you understand me?'

'Yes, Prime Minister.'

'So which of the Dellers has the upper hand in that marriage?'

'...I suppose I'd say her if forced to choose. But I don't really know him any more.'

'"any more"?'

'I used to work for him, as you are aware. Since I left I've rather lost touch...'

'You dare talk of losing touch? Your hands have been all over his wife.'

'Mary... Prime Minister!' Lee had never before been a victim of his current boss's repartee. He suddenly saw what it was like to lead the Opposition and get lashed by the PM's Indira Gandhi Growl.

'You've got to cut loose from her if you want to stay with me', the PM said. 'It may be too late already. Indeed it may be too late for me if I get dragged into this...'

The red light over the door leading to the rest of the plane started to flash. A soothing baritone issued from the public address system: 'a slight degree of turbulence' decreed a return to seats and fastened seatbelts '...unlikely event of an emergency landing... passengers please review the safety measures card in the seat pocket in front of them...'

The PM and Lee looked at each other, but said nothing. Lee resumed his seat. The PM buckled her belt.

193

FIFTY

While Godwin prepared to mount the frontal assault, Jeff crept down a path Godwin had indicated. It led to an abandoned railroad track, now a leafy grassed walk where locals exercised their dogs. This ran along the back of the row of houses in one of which Godwin's apartment was situated.

Jeff's moxie count was way down. He recalled what that gun of Frankie's had done to his groceries bag. He switched his cell phone off. A single hemidemisemiquaver of ring tone could give his presence away. Staying in touch wasn't worth death.

They'd arranged that Jeff would wait ten minutes then advance across the open space. Butterflies invaded his digestive tract, like turkey vultures swooping on a stranded wagon train.

He counted the last few seconds on the long thin hand of his Haurex Challenger, a gift from Laura. When there were still two to go he couldn't take it any longer. He swallowed and moved off across the lawn.

The drapes were drawn shut behind the patio door. When he got near he heard voices from within. A woman's and at least one man's. Angelo Devene? Was that bass rumble his voice? How had Andy the handyman sounded? He tried to remember.

The drapes got drawn apart. Light blazed out into the dusk. Jeff flinched. A man's voice boomed out. 'Calhoun! Come on in.' It was Godwin. He pushed what he called his french window open. 'Meet Mel', he said.

Jeff entered.

'Mel, Cal', said Godwin. 'Cal, Mel'.

For want of any better salutation Jeff shook Mel by the hand. 'Are you guys alone?'

'We seem to be so far', said Godwin. 'You must have outpaced him. Not surprising, the way you drove.'

'Who "him", please?' Mel looked towards Godwin, but gestured towards Jeff.

'Good point, Mel', said Jeff. 'We think it's Angelo Devene. One of the two guys drove you here from Europe. The big one.'

'Big one he kill Hafize. Hit her with bar. Hit her more. She fall dead.'

Godwin looked at Jeff. 'So that's why Devene had to silence Mel here.'

'His partner Micky Frost too', said Jeff. 'Another witness. Used to be his co-driver on trips. The small dead guy over by the door in the bedroom.'

Godwin nodded. He was about to speak when they heard a loud roar and the First Call horn of the Cayman. Jeff dived for the front door of the flat, yanked it open just enough to squeeze through and crawled into the hallway. He felt no shame in going on all fours. Devene could have the apartment and its occupants in his gun sights. A minute later he returned, walking upright. 'God dammit', he said. 'He took it, the car. Must have hotwired the motor.'

'Is he leaving us alone then?'

'I guess so.'

'We should still find Mel somewhere else to stay. It isn't safe here.'

'Why can't she go back to Chrissie's place?'

'You mean April's?'

Jeff nodded. 'But she can't anyhow. I'm being dumb', he said. 'She could have let lotsa johns know where she lives', he said. 'Including Devene.' He couldn't ask Mel point blank if she did in-calls at Chrissie's, even supposing she knew the term.

'That's out, then', said Godwin.

'I know a place. St John's Wood.' Jeff turned to the girl. She was too dark, but not too bad. 'Sorry, Mel', he said, 'it's more or less back where you just came from.'

Mel shrugged. 'I go where you tell me. Is my life now. Escorter.'

'Where is this place?' said Godwin.

'Place I rent. Not my main apartment. It's good and…discreet.'

Godwin raised his eyebrows. To Jeff they spelled out 'love nest' as sure as if he'd used Scrabble tiles.

'Yes, Ed', he said. 'It's where I met you-know-who. Well, you said I should give her up.'

'Come on, Melchizedek', said Godwin, turning to Mel. 'Have you got a coat?' Mel fetched her coat. Jeff helped her on with it. '*Mamnoon*', she said.

'Excuse me?'

195

'It's Farsi for "Thanks".'

'You're welcome, Mel. And thanks, Ed, for translating. Hey Ed, while you're at it, what's Farsi for "in-calls"?'

FIFTYONE

Angelo had pinched the Cayman in defiance of Frankie and the kid. A spur of the moment thing. Once he drove off from Mel's Dulwich hideout, he saw what a foolish choice it was. The car stuck out a mile, one vehicular sore thumb. The main reason Frankie'd acquired it probably. Showcase himself. Pull boys.

The Cayman would get so hot it sizzled if Frankie's next of kin reported it stolen. Would they, though? Did they exist? Least it could move.

He pulled into a bus stop bay to give the matter some thought, swerving with such suddenness that the car behind, a meek little Metro, gave a half-hearted honk. Angelo let retaliatory rip with the Cayman's First Call then killed the horn in mid bar. He started to sweat. Be crazy to get done for breach of the peace.

Three victims down. Mel deferred. That left Area Manager over Hereford way. A hundred and fifty miles? Give the Cay bird her head and zip down there in a couple of hours, late at night, beat out of Area Manager the identity of Big Boss. Be a pleasure roughing Area Manager up after all the years he'd lorded it over yours truly and Micky. Poor old Micky. But he'd got gabby.

Angelo glanced at the Cay's petrol gauge. Quarter full. How much did these babies burn a mile? No good asking Frankie. That was one bloke whose driving days were over. Angelo chuckled, and rummaged in the glove compartment for the owner's manual.

FIFTYTWO

Unlike most people, Jeff didn't mind Mondays. A day of business. Vibrant. For a newcomer to England the two time-off days, Saturday and Sunday, tended to drag.

This Monday was different. It turned too vibrant, too early. At 7.30 Laura rang.

'How about three?' she said.

'Three this afternoon?' He wasn't properly awake.

'When else? I'm around then for a couple hours. My Pilates instructor called off. Says it's 'flu. Grippe. I can't shake this idea he's HIV Pos. Only he did it twice before, and you start to wonder…'

'This whole week's real hard. My boss is over from New York.'

'But you don't sign till Thursday.'

He'd forgotten it was her husband they were buying from.

'Look, if it's that you're bushed…', she said.

'It's not that. Bernie – my editor, plus Arlene and her attorney, Leo Horne – get in tonight. I should see them to their hotel.'

'Where's that?'

'Beige's. Mayfair.'

There was a slight pause the other end. 'I hear you got another female tucked away in another apartment.' You could feel the air crackle as the icy front swept in.

Jeff nearly fell out of bed. 'Who in hell said that?' She'd sounded so friendly till now.

'Is it true?'

'Of course it's not true.' He did some petaflop thinking: 'another female' must mean Mel. But he'd only offered her the spare apartment last night. It was a stopgap sleepover anyhow. She'd be gone someplace else today. Who'd told Laura? Had to be Angelo Devene. What was his connection with Laura?

'…I want to hear it's not true from you in person', she said. 'Face to face. I want to see your lips say it. And there are other things I want your lips to do. So be there. Bare. Three.' She rang off.

Though shaken, he fell asleep again. Ten minutes later the land line rang. It dragged him from an erotic encounter with Chrissie. The caller was Bernie.

'Cal? How are things in London? Listen, our flight's delayed. We might not be with you till late *late* tonight. Contact the Transatlantic desk in London for ETA updates. Meantime Arlene says to let you know your despatches are a knock-out. Keep 'em coming. And now a lord's gotten caught up in a vice story, England's the Big Juicy again. Near as good as when Princess Di was alive.'

'Thanks. I might have an even more major story evolving from it.'

'Terrific. I... Hold on. Arlene wants to speak with you...' The sound of a phone changing hands, then:

'Jefferson P. Calhoun. How are you doing, young sir?'

'Fine Ms. Strepsky. Fine.'

'I am so pleased you could fix our hotel. Though I'm sort of leery about Beige's for business. Do you know it was my Clyde's favorite place? But it's not appropriate for meeting with a big player like Mr Deller. Too, his wife's Californian. West Coast they don't get Beige's conservative retro look north of San Diego. So this trip we're bringing Gavin Doresett. He has visiting privileges some very exclusive swank club just off of Pallmall Street – Avenue? – where he says there's this private lounge, the Prince Regent Rooms. Book it for Thursday evening, will you? Use his name. Me, Bernie, Leo Horne, Gavin, who's hosting as he's the club member. You of course. You found yourself a girl friend there yet? Some haughty earl's debutante daughter? Be glad to have her along.'

'Not really, Ms. Strepsky.' This wasn't the time to come clean about his love life.

'Chase stories leaves you too pooped to date?'

'Well, you know how it is...'

'Let me give you some advice. Don't get so wedded to the job you end a monk. I like my senior editors mature but spoken for. Married men or women, with children. If they go gay, which of course I'm completely relaxed toward, then a live-in partner and Maine Coon they can go all Norman Rockwell over.'

'I got a cat, coincidentally...' Doesn't make me gay, he thought but decided not to say so. Arlene might be a closet fag hag. '...Tho' I'm only an associate editor.'

'You made senior editor half an hour ago. Bernie didn't tell you?'

'Thanks... I don't know what to say.' Jeff felt hugely grateful. 'Thank you. I feel very very honored.'

'…Getting back to the Dellers, she's a social heavy hitter – I came across her times back home – but an IQ featherweight. She placed a regular order for *Hence* months back, before this acquisition even looked like it'd eventuate. Methinks someone likes to play at intellectual, pass herself of as Vassar alumna from the neck up. Meantime Vic Deller's got some woman paralegal he wants she tag along with him, sneak preview the magazine sale agreement small print. And I guess you could ask the girl you have at the bureau. That'll be nine not ten. I don't go big on odd numbers but it balances out the genders some.'

Jeff scribbled notes till his fingers ached. He'd barely put the phone down when it rang again. Sometimes this happened as a post-conversational burp, like the phone had wolfed a rich meal too quickly. He ignored the first two rings. At the third he unhooked.

'Jefferson? This is Debbie. Are you in soon?'

Worrying about his office time-keeping was not like Debbie. 'Mr Stevens and the other top execs are flying in tonight', he said. 'I had to liaise with them on hotel bookings, dinner arrangements.'

'You could have asked me. I'd have been glad to help.'

'Nice of you, Debbie. But it needs the personal touch. Any problem your end? I'll be in by eleven latest.'

'I managed to get that desk drawer open. You know, the one stuck so?'

'Oh yeah.' Trust Debbie to get off on something so tangential to filing stories. 'Look, I'm sort of in a rush…Can it wait till I get in?'

'I thought you should know there's a memory stick there.' He could almost hear Debbie's lower lip jut in a pout.

'Oh?' he said.

'There's a note with it. Shall I read it to you? Won't take a jiff.'

'OK.' He was getting more interested. 'This in Tod's handwriting?'

'How would I know?' Debbie half-barked the words, her way of conveying chagrin. 'It's not as if he sent me any letters. Even birthday cards he plonked on my desk like office memos, and rubber date-stamped with his initials not signed. You'd think they were valentines, anonymous. The note doesn't say much. Here it is: "shower head note refers". Four words.'

'*E pluribus unum*'s only three.'

'Sorry?'

'"From many, one". United States motto. It's not length that counts, Debbie. It's pregnancy.'

There was a pause the other end. He was up to here with phone pauses today.

'Are you sexually harassing me, Mr Calhoun?'

Was Debbie truly offended? Maybe she'd gotten so used to Tod's hands-off approach she read every friendly gesture as a pass. Or was she fishing for a quick cash settlement? 'Not that kind of pregnancy', he said.

'There are lots then?'

'Look in Webster's, Debster. I'll be there in twenty minutes.'

He dressed at frantic speed, tearing off a button on his shirt, mis-knotting his tie, pulling his socks hardly a toe-width above the ankle bone so that bare leg flesh peeped from between his pants hems and loafers.

He now knew what the cryptic legend 'Byr.o' on Tod's wad of paper meant: 'Bureau'. Not only the article of office furniture but the *Hence* office it was located in. He of all people, a fellow American, should have known that. He'd been a jackass.

He was on his way out the apartment when the land line phone rang, the fourth call in an hour. He wanted to ignore it, but if you're a newsman any call might mean a big story or a TV station offering you a break into visual media. He turned back.

It was Chrissie. 'Jeff? The police talked to me about the dead bodies yesterday. They want to talk to you too. I'm only warning you.'

'God, I forgot all about that.'

'You left the scene of a crime without reporting it. That's serious.'

'It was to go save someone else from getting hit.'

'That's what I told them. You'll have to prove it.'

'I can do that.'

'They… they may suspect what I do. I pushed my MBA for all it was worth, said I was a marketing consultant. But this is a murder investigation. It could dig deep. They asked about Mel, how I know her, how she came to be flat-sharing with me. I said she's just a lodger, temporary kind of thing, tide me over a bum period financially. But she's got no MBA she can hide behind. And her English is none too good. If they find her she could spill whole lots, including how she earns her keep.'

'Maybe it's time you switched jobs. Put that MBA to good use in the real world. Come on, Chrissie, join the real world.' She made a moaning sound, distress not sexual ecstasy. He lowered the jokiness a notch. 'I'd tell you to roll your sleeves up', he said, 'get your hands dirty, only…'

Chrissie did then giggle, but not for long. She started to stammer. 'I c-can't say I had much fun with them. C-could we, um, meet up after they talk to you…?'

'Yeah. Why not?'

'Compare notes?'

'Co-ordinate our stories to the cops, you mean?'

'Well it'd be too late by then, wouldn't it? And anyway, we've got nothing to hide over how we know each other. I'm one of your sources, nothing more. In fact you haven't even paid me for all my Hollywood revelations.'

'God, I forgot all about that too. I'm very sorry. Yeah, we must meet up. I'll settle the tab then.'

'Please don't think I'm dunning you. It'd be more…well, as I said, compare notes…'

Her diffidence melted him. 'Can I buy you dinner?' he said. He didn't know it, but he'd been moving that way for some time.

She answered quickly. 'That'd be lovely. Eight? My place?'

'Eight. Your place. But only to meet up before going out. There a good restaurant in your neighborhood? Unless you're hot to eat in…'

'I'm easy, really. But I'd like a restaurant more. There are millions near me.'

'You choose one. Not Italo-American. I can get that back home. Any other cuisine. Not Korean.'

She stammered some more. 'Th-this isn't a professional date, you understand? I…'

He cut her off mid-sentence. 'I know', he said. 'It's amateur night. Amateur meant lover once.' He took a deep breath, then the plunge. 'We could make it mean that again.'

There was a long silence. This one he didn't mind. It went on for half-ever before she spoke. 'Amateur night it is.' She sounded like a little girl affirming her belief in Santa. Strong creed, soft voice.

'Gotta go', he said. 'Listen, I like you. I mean *really* like you.' He put down the phone before she could answer. He felt absurdly happy. As he left the apartment he gave a little skip.

*

The office. He strode in, poised for business. The memory stick lay on his desk, fruitful as a grenade with the pin pulled. It weighed down the note Debbie had mentioned. Debbie herself sat at her desk. Her nail file, lip gloss and Garfield mug of Kenco, skim milky and Splenda-sweetened, she had pushed to one side. From time to time she sneaked a glance at him, watching to see what he'd make of the memory stick contents.

'You looked at this Debbie?'

'Not a single peek. Cross my heart.'

'You got no idea what's in it?'

'No. I said, didn't I? Oh by the way…'

'Yuh?' Jeff had plugged the memory stick in by now and was waiting for the file to open.

'…I'm leaving. This friend's asked me to help out in her dress shop…'

By now the file was open. Jeff scrolled down the pages to get a quick overview. He lingered on the odd lurid detail as and when it caught his eye. The names were mostly familiar. Victor Deller, Angelo Devene, Micky Frost. Laura Deller. Fuck. He'd feared Laura's involvement ever since her phone call earlier, when she'd let slip she'd heard – not about Mel but about Tucky, he now saw – hence must be in the loop on Angelo Devene's one-man wire service. It still came as a shock, still hurt, though less now than had it been a week back.

Some names he'd never head of. A guy, Robbie Sanders. Another, Clive Lane. Their activities included people-trafficking, prostitution, illicit meat products-processing and distributing, also criminal conspiracy. A news story gold mine, with some of the top names in England as nuggets. Jeff metaphorically licked his lips and settled down to a concentrated read.

'…Will two weeks do, Jefferson?' Debbie's finishing school delivery distracted Jeff in mid-paragraph.

'Two weeks what, Debbie?'

'Notice. My contract says a month, but…'

'Probably. I'm sure we can work something out.' He looked at her. The Garfield on her coffee mug had his teeth bared in rage, not his trademark wicked grin. Time he did the concerned, managerial thing. 'I'm sorry you didn't enjoy working here', he said.

'Journalism's not what I thought', she said. 'Where's the fun sitting over a desk and straining your back to get a stuck drawer open? I feel my "highly motivated passion for unfolding events" – which *is* what Mr Snaith advertised for – has been taken advantage of.'

'You're wrong there, Debbie. Your services to news-gathering will not go unremembered. Opening a stuck drawer was your finest moment. Tutankhamen's Tomb all over.'

FIFTYTHREE

Angelo made it to Hereford in two hours forty minutes. He'd got the feel of the Cay by now. Handled nicely? Exquisitely. Hugged the road? Lambada-ed with the tarmac, her embrace of it got so *intime*. Centrifuge scale g-force on cornering? Felt like he was Apollo moon-shotting each time he accelerated out of a curve. Second-guessed his direction needs the instant his finger tips grazed the steering wheel. A touch on the brakes and she stopped sooner than yesterday. Bucket seat snug as if custom tailored. Comfier leather didn't line a de Sade devotee's most de luxe dungeon.

He got into the Meadow-Sourced Meat Products complex using his swipe card. The light was on in Area Manager's hut. Angelo entered without knocking. He carried his sex toys bag, but left Frankie's gun in the Cay boot. His spanner he held concealed down a trouser leg. He'd got good at that.

Area Manager was bent over the log-burning stove stuffing it with papers, a tooth pick in his mouth. Wurzel-shire was cooler than London but not enough to warrant a fire at night. Looked like Area Manager was cooking something. The books probably.

Area Manager turned round. 'Devene! What are you doing here?' He kept the toothpick in his mouth.

'I still can't get hold of Mr Francis. I told you he'd gone AWOL.'

'Yeah Frankie. Where the hell is he is the question. I knew things had gone wrong when I didn't hear from him. We're in enough trouble as it is. DEFRA's gone and got heavy over our slaughtering practices.'

'Mister Sanders?', said Angelo, all nice and deferential. No point in dissing him before he took him out, or he'd lose surprise. 'I been sort of meaning to ask', he said. 'Who's the boss?'

'I am, idiot.'

'The Big Boss.'

'Never you mind. Now fetch me something to get this stove going properly. Cut across to the rendering shed. I know for a fact we've got a few tins of oil there.'

Area Manager kept poking papers into the mouth of the stove. He had his back to Angelo now and squatted to push a big sheaf right to the back, balancing on his soles. Angelo stepped forward, unsheathed his spanner from his trouser leg and swiped the feet from under him. Angelo's forearm drive was true as ever. Area Manager fell to the floor.

Angelo pressed immediately down on Area Manager's back, caught up a pair of cuffs from inside the sex toy bag and snapped Area Manager's wrists behind him. The cuffs were trimmed with pink leopardette but the steel beneath was butch strong. It took five seconds. Area Manager breathed hard but put up no real resistance. Angelo followed up with some ankle fetters. These were the normal kind. Chain links. Gunmetal colour. Ratchets bit the flesh. Nothing freaky.

Area Manager hadn't struggled once. Winded maybe. 'You'll take money off other blokes want to get fit but can't be arsed yourself', said Angelo. 'Bad mistake.' Area Manager didn't answer. Maybe he was concussed. His manacled wrists, liver spotted backs of hands above fur trimming round the narrow bits, looked meaty-cum-dinky, like a rare mutton chop with a paper pom pom tucked on the end of its rib bone.

Angelo scratched his head. He stood, then with his foot prodded Area Manager in the small of the back. 'The Big Boss', he said. 'Name.'

'Get stuffed, Devene.'

This gave Angelo an idea. He grabbed Area Manager, hauled his head forwards and thrust it in the stove. It wasn't hot enough yet to do more than singe him. But he could find breathing tricky. 'The Big Boss', Angelo said.

Area Manager coughed madly. He wouldn't stop. A 60-Gitane Brune-a-day hack, sounded like. No wonder he'd fussed over the loss of the TransitCo lorry's cigarette lighter. Now he breathed noisier than ever, great gasping lung-fulls. Like his life depended on it, thought Angelo, smiling at the understatement. Soon Area Manager lost heart, started wheezing. Presently he stopped. Angelo inserted the spanner handle delicately round the side of his head and rattled the inside of the stove. Clouds of smoke emerged. He coughed. Area Manager didn't. Area Manager's body sagged by now.

Angelo knew the inside of the rendering shed reasonably well. He took Area Manager's set of keys off him and wandered over, whistling in harmony with the swelling dawn chorus. The sixth key he tried opened the door. He was hoping for ideas on how to get rid of Area

Manager's body. He'd had enough of lugging corpses round Europe. Besides, his sweet little Cay hadn't the storage space of an Aldi trolley.

He saw a meat hook hanging from a rail. Wood handle, metal curve ending in a vicious point. He grabbed it and went back to the hut. It took him a long time to drag Area Manager over to the shed. He'd had to tie his heels together first, throw off the fetters, insert the hook between the strands of rope then tug. He wouldn't even have had any rope if he hadn't brought the sex toys bag along. I won't ever knock kinky goings-on again, he thought.

He attached Area Manager's tied heels to a notch on a pulley, then pressed the button that hauled it up till the carcass swung free head down. He'd better slit Area Manager's throat before he dismembered him. Get rid of all the blood, like he'd seen Clive do with pigs and cattle and ponies, a few times dogs and once a pet llama. This bit he dreaded. *I'm not cut out for a life of violence. Don't like guns. Nor too gone on blood. Or not in gallons. Reminds me, better ditch Frankie's gun.*

The lights of a car turned in at the gate, transforming the inside wall of the rendering shed into a bright but blank cinema screen. It made the rest of the interior seem as dark as if dawn was still to come. Angelo wheeled round at the first flash, instantly killed the overhead light, then stood motionless. An expensive-sounding saloon door slammed shut. Footsteps. A silhouette in the door frame.

'Anyone there?' A posh voice, but with hints of street. 'I'll count to three', it said. 'Then I lob in one round of CS gas. Another, if need be. Next I shoot whoever staggers out. And you will stagger, believe me. That, or choke to death inside. Shoot you's going to look legal. Owner of private agri-business premises catches armed thief breaking and entering, struggles with him, owner's 12-bore goes off accidentally, thief killed. If you're not armed already I can always put a clean gun in your hand afterwards. Your dead hand by then. Juries in these parts are full of country people still livid over that Norfolk farmer, Blake, jailed unjustly for taking down a burglar. They'd never convict me.'

Angelo believed him. He came forward.

'Hands up, please', said Posh Voice.

Angelo put his hands up.

'Be so good as to throw down that implement you're holding.'

Angelo threw down the meat hook.

'Right. Let's have a look at you.' The voice flashed a powerful torch in Angelo's face. 'You must be Angelo Devene. I've heard about you. Never met. How'dye do?'

'Who are you?' Angelo did his best to shade his eyes from the harsh beam of light.

'You don't recognise me?'

The voice shone the torch on the ground. Angelo took a good look. Dawn was better now. Enough to make out faces. The CS gas canister too. He'd never seen the man before. 'Recognise you? No', he said.

'I'm your employer.' The owner of the voice held out his hand. His left hand. His right hand held the torch. In the crook of his right arm he supported a shot gun, broken open now, as a dangerous firearm should be. He'd put the CS gas in his pocket. He spoke again: 'I said, "How do you do?". Where are your manners?'

*

Deller had disdained sleep after Mel performed. Once Mel had left and his wife gone to bed he'd taken the Arnage and swung down to Herefordshire, several hours earlier than he'd first intended. He'd driven himself. The last of the wine fumes from the evening before had soon blown away. To be on the safe side he'd downed a fistful of Pro-Plus.

Now he sat in the Meadow-Sources Meat Products manager's hut, perched on the desk, swinging his heels, chatting to Devene, companionable as a factory floor work-mate.

'...So it was you recorded Jefferson Calhoun's phone conversations? Good man. Sanders told me the gist of them.'

'I labelled them all. Mini CDs. Rough list of contents, but it tells you what comes where. Had to. I didn't feel Evans was pulling his weight.'

'Good man.' Deller went to the filing cabinet and rummaged. 'These them?' he said presently, holding up some mini CDs in a polythene food bag.

'Looks like it.'

Deller took out the CDs and riffled through them. He pocketed one and skimmed the rest in the direction of the stove. Two entered its mouth. Most missed.

'You've got a lot of clearing up to do', he said. He didn't mean just the CDs. 'Move against Jefferson Calhoun first', he said. He noticed Angelo's blank look and added, 'You see why, don't you? He's much more dangerous than the Iranian girl. Better informed, for one thing. Better at imparting it for another.'

'And her?'

'If you catch Calhoun, he'll lead you to her. But make sure you get him to tell you her exact whereabouts before you dispose of him.' Deller looked sideways at Angelo. 'I'm sure you can have fun doing that. Now what's been going on here?' Deller looked at the stove, *mille feuilles* of charred papers spilling from its mouth. 'Where's Robbie Sanders?'

'No idea. Scarpered, maybe. Like Evans done. First sign of trouble and people like that are off.'

'Evans, yes. He's another mystery. Sanders, though…that stove's still warm.' Deller leant forwards, stared at the floor near the stove. 'Hullo, 'ullo, 'ullo', he said. The echo of PC Plod gave Angelo hope. He takes after me, he thought.

'A toothpick', said Deller, picking it up. 'Sanders's favourite chew. If he did leave here, it could have been on an involuntary basis.' He turned to Angelo. 'What's your opinion?'

'I only got here half an hour before you did', said Angelo, lying fluently. Deller's courtesy unnerved him nonetheless. 'He wasn't here when I arrived', said Angelo.

'Then there are the company records', said Deller. 'He hasn't burned them all. Must have "scarpered" in something of a hurry.'

Angelo felt even less comfortable. He did stolid, overdid it, sounding Stepin Fetchit: 'Don' know nothin' 'bout no papers.'

Deller looked carefully at Angelo. 'Where's Lane?'

'Clive? Haven't seen him either.' Angelo had no trouble saying this. Was the plain truth.

'Nor Frost?' Angelo returned Deller's gaze steadily and shook his head but said nothing.

'If I calculate right', said Deller, 'of at least five people work for me, four have disappeared or not turned up to work.' Deller kept looking at Angelo, who didn't answer, then said, 'Well, Devene, I won't trouble your head with any more questions. Looks like you're promoted to commanding officer as the only survivor on the field of battle. Congratulations.' He held out his hand again, the right one this time. Angelo slowly took it.

'Have something to wet your whistle', said Deller, withdrawing his hand and taking out of his pocket the canister of CS. He tugged at its release ring.

Angelo jumped back. 'Hey, what the hell are you do-...?'

'Relax. It's only a thermos. Coffee. Sorry I've got nothing stronger to toast your promotion.'

'I wouldn't anyway, thanks. It's a bit early in the morning.'

'Good man. Sober muscle is muscle you can trust.' Deller swigged some coffee before offering Angelo any. 'Re the CO matter', he said, as Angelo drank, 'you hold acting rank. Pending satisfactory probation.'

Angelo took the canister from his lips. 'Can I ask how long would that be?'

'Of course. Though the probations I set are more performance-led. You deliver on two or three tasks and your promotion gets ratified instantly. OK?'

'Yes. What tasks, though?'

'What you ought to be asking is how long they'll take to execute. I don't mean they're not urgent.'

'No. I see that.'

'Good. After eliminating Calhoun and the Iranian girl, you will make sure my missing operatives either stay missing as disposable waste subject to landfill – you get my drift?...'

Angelo nodded. 'You mean bury them?' he said.

Deller nodded too, then said '...And they needn't be dead first if it's a remote enough landfill site... *Or* make sure they report for duty. It's up to you. They'd be under you from now on if they did come back in. Could you stamp your authority on men you took orders from only yesterday?'

'Definitely.'

'Of course we may never have to find out.' Deller looked at Angelo harder than ever. Angelo dropped his eyes this time. 'Well, get cracking', said Deller. 'You've got transport?'

'Yes, sir. She's parked behind the shed.'

'She safe?'

'Hun engineering. Handles a treat.'

'Not road-worthiness, you bloody fool. Secure. Not stolen, is she?'

210

'Not very.'

'She is, then. Don't play games with me, Devene. Ditch her. At least fifty miles away. Pick something up in Bristol.' Deller went over and rummaged in Area Manager's filing cabinet, in the folder under 'Transport, personnel use of'. Low-priority incineration status. 'Here's a standard agreement we have with a used car dealer in St Paul's. Get him to lease you something nippy but unobtrusive.' He tossed Angelo a wad of notes. 'There's some cash. Account to me for every penny of expenditure, with receipts, countersigned by the payee, and each payee's ID and contact details too.'

Deller looked out of the window at the morning light, full now. 'What sort of day's it going to be?' he said.

The question surprised Angelo. 'Not sure', he said. 'Warm again? I didn't watch the forecast.'

'Warm, yes. But will it be warm enough? Do you know what I think we're in need of? A storm.' Deller's tone had altered, becoming almost ruminative. He sounded like a gentleman farmer who kept a diary of his observations.

'A storm?'

'Clear the air.'

'Does it need clearing?'

'Electrical storm. Lightning. Jewish.'

'I'm sorry, sir. I don't quite get you.'

'Torch this place, Devene. Don't look so stunned. Change of plan. Torch, d'you hear? The lot. Hut. Rendering shed. Abattoir. Cannery. Lane's office. Do it discreetly, though. I need to raise money on the business. Insurance payout's surefire. There's a financial storm brewing too. Europe-wide. Liquidity's the best umbrella.'

'Torch?' Angelo bounced back. 'Let's not forget destroy the evidence.'

Deller walked over and patted Angelo's cheek. 'I can see you get up pretty early in the morning. Smart fellow. Two goals for the price of one. Well, what are you waiting for? There are plenty of cans of oil in the rendering shed. Spread it carefully, so it covers everything, but thin, so it all burns.' He looked round the hut. 'Sanders seems to have made off with the office matches. And since smoking on company premises is illegal there'll be no pocket lighters here. What's your car?'

'Er, a Porsche, sir.'

Deller smiled. 'So you like life in the fast line? Temperamental creatures, those young man's models. You'll still have to ditch her. But once this is all over I'll buy you a new car, whatever make you want. Meanwhile a Porsche cigarette lighter's as good as any other. You can start a nice fire with one, can't you?'

'That I can sir.'

'Good.' Deller was at the door now. 'Give me ten minutes to get over the brow of the hill before you pour the oil.' He turned back and beamed amiably at Angelo. 'Mind you souse Sanders liberally. A body doesn't burn as easily as a document. Oh, and cut his teeth out first. You'll find buzz saws in the rendering shed. Dissolve the teeth in acid. Off site. Dental records have put more people like you away than a hundred Sherlock Holmeses ever could.'

Angelo had started the instant he'd heard the name "Sanders".

It hadn't escaped Deller. 'Yes, Devene', he said. 'I saw him. My eyes are good. And my torch is even better. You lie to me ever again...EVER, you're dead.'

'Very well, sir.' Angelo swallowed. 'One more thing...'

'Yes? Make it snappy.'

'I still don't know your name.'

'No, you don't. You're still acting rank, remember? Make substantive CO and you'll be briefed on all sorts of things, my birth certificate included. Now get blitzing.'

'Pardon?'

'Get a move on with the bloody blitz! Not the Luftwaffe bombing us Londoners. The word also means lightning. Capiche?'

*

On arriving back in Holland Park Deller placed the CD on his wife's pillow. She was still asleep.

FIFTYFOUR

Jeff took in the time with a start. Ten after one. Debbie had left. Not just the bureau but seemingly her job. He'd been so absorbed in Tod's memory stick he hadn't taken in her clearing her desk. Her coffee accessories had gone. Also her Dilbert strip cartoons, scissored from the *Date*'s 'Kidz' supplement. The bureau looked more grown-up. But also more austere.

He shivered, shrugged and grabbed the phone. 'Mel?'

'Olfert now.'

'Olfert. All right.' What was it with these women who sold sex? Picky over work aliases as film stars with stage names. 'Jeff here', he said. 'Jeff Calhoun. Ed Godwin's friend, came with him last night and rescued you from the bad guy, Devene, over at Godwin's place.'

'Yes, sir. What you like? You come here, tell me your like, I do it.'

'Well see, Mel, it's more I need to use the apartment. You got some place else you can go?'

'Not Mel now. Olfert. Is how I was born. My cousin at Birm-, how? Birm'n'm, he await me. Await me months. You know him?'

'Can't say I do. Where is he in Birmingham?'

'Omeed. Every one know him. Drive best taxi in the town. Find way round Bulbul Ring, top spots. He say he could get to them with eyes poke out, like law court do you my country.'

Jeff shuddered. 'We'll call him, get him to meet you off of the train. Can you be ready to leave by...' He looked at his Challenger. '...Twenty of three?'

'When I go to Birm'n'm be with Omeed I stop try to please, live how I like. But now you save me, I please one more time. So OK.'

*

The session with Laura went less smoothly. He found her on the street entrance to his love nest when he returned from putting Mel in a cab at the taxi rank in the high street. Anticipating a stormy opening scene, he nonetheless said a polite hello. She answered as to an old friend.

'Come on up', he said as they climbed the stairs. 'I know you don't want to get seen by the neighbors.'

'You worried they'll ask who this other floozy is you got tucked up?' The higher they climbed the darker her mood.

'Laura, I have no other woman in my life.' By now they were inside the apartment.

'But you have another place, right?'

'Yes, where I live when I'm not with you. But it's so well known it's almost open house.' And that was no more than accurate, given the fox's break-in. 'I got this place here so we could be private together', he said.

'Together', she said, like an echo in a canyon. She looked hard at him. 'Who's Tucky?'

He was so relieved he laughed.

'You duplicitous rat. Who's Tucky?'

'A dead cousin.' "Kittycat" would give the wrong message.

'Well she must have died real quick and been kissing kin, 'cause I got a tape of you making smoochy noises at her. Sweet as molasses, they sound. You never made molasses noises to me. I don't cut it as candy? Not dead enough? Not close enough a relate?'

'You're not the same species, for Christ sake. The live Tucky's a pet kitten. Named for my cousin.'

'So you're balling cats now?'

She moved to the mantel and took up the photo of the two of them. She tore it in half, down the middle. She put the half with Jeff on it in her purse. The half with her on she handed to Jeff. 'For your grand-kids' family album', she said. Before he could put it away she snatched it back and traded it for her photo of him.

He took the Challenger off his wrist. 'Here' he said, holding it out. She waved it away. He glanced at the new photo of an old him, put it in his coat pocket. He stood up. 'Want something?' he said. 'Coffee?'

She shook her head. She moved to the door, as if about to go.

Jeff said, 'I know about your call-girl ring, Laura. It's most all there in Tod's notes. And what isn't, I can fill the gaps.'

She stopped, then stepped back into the room.

For the first time since they'd met he held the initiative.

'Well?', he said.

She flushed palest pink, the tops of her cheeks, where the bones lay, those good bones had first won him. She said, lips tight, 'I'm a home-maker. My kids. Fixing parties. Victor's the businessman.'

'Like hell he is. Tod put who does what in detail. You're boss of the paid-sex outfit. Up there with the other Fortune 100 women CEOs.'

'We're not listed, you fool.' Her voice hissed on the '-isted'.

'Bet your yield's up with theirs. High as a street ho's skirt hem.'

'It was Vic's idea.' She added, 'I was put in to run things.' She looked pleadingly at him. 'Please believe me. I take back "fool". '

She was at his feet now, hands round his thighs. 'Don't let them lock me up. What's your darkest desire?'

He recoiled.

She was standing again now. 'Don't lock me up.'

He felt revulsion, less at what she offered than her hinting what her girls must do to stay in business. Did Chrissie ever go that far? Thinking of Chrissie hardened him.

'There's not much else to say, is there?', he said. 'Tod was someone I worked with. I have to make sure the dirt he died to dig up sees the light of day. I can't re-bury it.'

She looked at him, without expression now, then turned on her heel.

'See you Thursday', she said.

He was astounded. 'You'll *be* there?'

'I told you. It's Victor runs his businesses. No one else. I'm still his wife. Help out when he needs me. I'll go along, hold his hand.'

'You hold his hand, you'll get caught in the cuffs they clap on him.'

She laughed. The bitterness was audible.

FIFTYFIVE

Barnes, Kerr-Tait and Lee met at Barnes's house, though summoned by Lee. 'Not at Confessor Street', Kerr-Tait had said, when the question of locale had arisen. 'And certainly not the House. A private residence might just escape media attention.'

Kerr-Tait and Lee arrived within ten minutes of each other. They trooped upstairs to the study. The peer's robes and dummy had been removed. But the room had always been cramped. Barnes trundled the globes into a wall cupboard.

Lee opened. 'Deller's about to rat on his obligations', he said. Following the rapprochement between him and Barnes at Crowthorne's funeral, he had been fully briefed by Barnes as to the negotiations with Deller.

'How do you know?' said Kerr-Tait.

'Private sources', said Lee. 'But reliable.'

Kerr-Tait nodded. The Whips' office ran almost entirely on private sources.

Barnes fidgeted. 'If that is indeed so', he said, 'the Party faces financial meltdown.'

'Financial?' said Kerr-Tait. 'That's manageable. Banks'll always lend to the party in power. Not least the ones we've bailed out. What's more worrying is Parliamentary meltdown. The PCP almost certainly won't pass next week's Foreign Media Ownership Bill.'

'Then we could lose power', said Barnes. 'Will your banks lend then?'

'I'd better tell Mary', said Lee.

'That's my job', said Kerr-Tait.

'Tell her yourself, then.' And face the flak, Lee thought.

'Gentlemen!' Barnes rapped the table. 'As host I am *ex officio* chairman.' He turned to Lee. 'Ben, *will* she resign if the Bill fails?'

'Might do.'

Barnes turned to Kerr-Tait. 'Nick, the Media Bill is a major legislative item, isn't it?'

Kerr-Tait nodded.

'Making the vote on it in effect a confidence vote.' Barnes turned back to Lee. '"Might" resign, Ben? You can't be more certain?'

'Dissolve, if I know her', said Kerr-Tait.

But do you know her?, thought Lee. He said, 'A dissolution might be tricky so soon after the last election.'

Kerr-Tait said, 'Tell that to the press. They're already speculating she may call another.'

Lee said, 'If some senior figure on our side could carry on as PM without dissolving, her position would become untenable.'

'What are our chances of winning an election called tomorrow?' said Barnes.

'Evens', said Kerr-Tait.

'Odds on', said Lee, simultaneously.

'Come, Ben. It's not as good as that', said Kerr-Tait.

'William Hill think so', said Lee.

'How do you know?' said Barnes. 'No dissolution has been announced.'

'I had someone ring them for a quote.'

'Joe Coral don't think so', said Kerr-Tait. 'Their website. They didn't need ringing.'

'Paddy Power leans to the Coral view', said Barnes, apologetic. 'I only know because Barb has an account there.'

Kerr-Tait laughed. 'It seems we all looked into it.'

'*I* don't gamble', said Barnes, annoyed.

'You have at times', said Lee. He glanced towards Kerr-Tait, who discreetly shook his head. 'With Deller', added Lee quickly. Both men had heard rumours of Barnes's insider trading.

Barnes said, 'It's more I didn't know what his finances were like at the time.'

'Dark horse, eh?'

'Deller's no dark horse. Quite the opposite', said Kerr-Tait. 'A former favourite who's now gone and scratched.'

'I'm out of my depth in this turf talk', said Barnes. 'Can we discuss matters in down-to-earth terms? Just what *is* the situation?'

Lee summed things up. In doing so he began a gradual take over of the chairman's role. '...It is now known that Deller, abetted by his wife, has suborned a number of MPs into withholding support for various government measures.'

'How?' said Kerr-Tait. His 'How?' dripped scepticism.

'I'll come to that in a minute. His motive was money. The failure of those measures to pass into law has benefited him enormously in a financial point of view…'

'How?' said Barnes. On his lips the word suggested innocent curiosity.

'Directly by letting him sell off some of his media empire to an overseas buyer before the deal would have had to be OK-ed by the regulatory people at OfMed. If it had been subject to that sort of scrutiny when we intended – what Nick was referring to just now when he mentioned the Foreign Media Ownership Bill – Deller would have had to wait a year or more to complete the sale, perhaps have seen it abort altogether.'

Kerr-Tait said, 'And how has Deller benefited other than directly?'

'Indirectly, by putting him in a position to make millions in share-dealing since he knew such-and-such a measure would never reach the statute book. Meaning he could go short or pick up stock at rock bottom prices.'

'Have you got proof?' said Kerr-Tait. 'It's tantamount to insider trading…'

Well duh, thought Lee. He'd never rated Kerr-Tait very high.

'…But I thought you said he was probably reneging on his commitments to us?' said Barnes. 'If he is, surely it's because he hasn't got the money, not because he's changed his mind, and on some whim? In any case you say he's made millions.'

'Was in a position to', said Lee. 'Not necessarily did. He could have taken the wrong punts, especially given this sudden financial storm. Who knows exactly why he's pulling out? He's ratting. Isn't that enough?'

'No.' Barnes was sticking to his guns. 'It may be a temporary blip in his cash flow. It may be more serious. With all this stock market turmoil, it's anyone's guess.'

'I do think he's in trouble, yes. Money trouble. Bigger fish even than him have gone under the last few weeks. Corporate giants. Here, in the States, on the Continent. Look at the roll call: Greenbach, Angel, Lettiss; InterContConGlom; Van der Beurse NV; Bruch Gesellschaft.'

'How did he and his wife nobble the MPs?' said Kerr-Tait.

'The oldest way in the world…'

'Bribery? Come off it…'

'Bribery, yes. But with honey, not cash.'

'Honey?'

'Honey traps. Old as time. Older. Jehovah fixed the Fall using Eve. The Dellers targeted every vulnerable MP they could. If you accept politics is showbusiness for ugly people, that amounts to a hell of a lot.' Lee had let acute cynicism show. There was a shocked silence.

'My God', said Barnes. 'The Parliamentary health complex. I thought some of the personal trainers looked too good to be true.'

'Some of the female ones were genuine. The male ones all were. Deller seems to have drawn the line at running rent boys. Too unreliable, perhaps...'

'Too few secretly homosexual MPs any more to make it worthwhile', said Kerr-Tait. His tone made it clear he knew what he was talking about – to within a single percentage point of the 646 Members. 'As to the mainstream, I've never heard of anything so ridiculous in my life', he said. 'You can't nobble an entire party with a few loose women.'

'They didn't need to. Our majority's so tiny it only took a dozen MPs subject to undue pressure to sway things either way. Often fewer.'

'Backbenchers can be an awkward lot, I agree. And some of the mavericks recently have invoked their human right to individual conscience as justifying indiscipline over votes. Which doesn't make my job any easier, I can tell you. But they don't sell their votes.' Kerr-Tait corrected himself: 'Or not for something as fleeting as sex. Peerages, knighthoods, government posts...well, that's what we became MPs for, isn't it? The plusher seats on the EU gravy train...works with chaps who've reached their career ceiling. Some'll come to heel for as little as a quango chair. But only the dregs.' He shook his head, saddened by how cheaply MPs priced their souls.

'I imagine they were persuaded, or convinced themselves, that it didn't matter so much with lesser bills', said Lee. 'Blackmail threats are both persuasive and convincing or they're not blackmail. It's only this big one has brought matters to a head.'

Barnes said, 'One of the House of Lords barmen warned me about Deller. I wish I'd listened.'

'Who?' said Kerr-Tait. 'Not old Dickie?

'Yes.'

'That's rich from Dickie.'

'Why?'

'Dickie's been supplying their noble lordships with girls for years.'

'Pimping?'

'Of course.'

Barnes put his head in his hands. Only briefly. He raised his head. 'Then Deller must have come along and Dickie reckoned he couldn't compete', he said. 'A corner shop swamped by a supermarket chain.'

'Feasible', said Kerr-Tait. 'But I shall want convincing.'

Barnes recalled a detail. 'He spat at the mention of Deller's name before Deller started up the health complex', he said. The allusion meant nothing to the other two. 'So he distrusted Deller before Deller drove him out of business.'

Kerr-Tait leant across and patted Barnes's hand. 'Does it much matter?' He spoke with real sympathy.

Lee's mobile rang. 'Excuse me', he said. Kerr-Tait said something to Barnes. Lee waved a hand at him signalling to him to be quiet. He put his other hand over the mobile's mouthpiece. 'It's him', he said.

'Deller?' Barnes mouthed the name.

Lee nodded. 'Hello, Victor... We were just talking about you... Meet? Where? ...Where in the Park? And which park? ...Hyde Park, the Queen's Temple. OK.' He snapped the mobile shut. 'Which queen?' he said to Barnes and Kerr-Tait.

'What are you talking about, Ben?' said Barnes.

'Deller wants to meet. He said the Queen's Temple in Hyde Park. I don't know where that is. Or what. He doesn't mean the Temple off Fleet Street, does he?'

'Kensington Gardens, not Hyde Park', said Kerr-Tait. 'My nanny took me there as a child. That 18th-century summer house structure. Have you got a map of the Park anywhere, Mark?'

'Somewhere.' Barnes rose.

'I'll show you exactly', said Kerr-Tait to Lee. 'But why's Deller going in for Smiley encounters, hole-and-corner stuff in out-of-the-way spots across London? Did he say?'

'No. His exact words were "You'll find out in good time".'

'Should we come with you?'

Barnes re-entered the room. He carried an A to Z. 'Here', he said.

'No', said Lee to Kerr-Tait's question. 'He particularly asked to see me alone.'

'When?'

'Now.'

Barnes looked at his watch. 'You couldn't get there in less than 20 minutes.'

'More if the traffic's bad.'

'Bicycle?'

'Have you got one?' said Lee.

'Barb has. If you don't mind a lady's model.'

'Can I take your A to Z?'

Barnes gave it him. 'There's a crash helmet too if you want.'

'They mess my hair up. I'll risk it without.' Lee had taken to gel to hold down his comb-over. He didn't tell the other two that.

'Ring us as soon as you get anything out of him.'

Lee left the room.

Barnes turned to Kerr-Tait. 'Would you like something while we wait? Tea? Coffee? A proper drink?'

Kerr-Tait shook his head. They sat at the table for a few minutes. Neither said a word.

'You don't have any playing cards, do you?' said Kerr-Tait. He spoke almost diffidently. 'At tense moments I find patience a comfort.'

Barnes now shook his head. 'There's Scrabble.'

'I'll give it a try. What is it?'

'A word game. The PM loves it.'

'Oh that. Yes, I know all about it. Sorry, my mind was elsewhere. I think perhaps I won't.' Kerr-Tait drummed his fingers. Barnes recognised the rhythm. The William Tell Overture.

They sat many more minutes, but less than an hour. It seemed an age before Barnes's mobile rang. In pressing its keys he became all thumbs. 'Ben?'

'Mark! Is Nick still there with you?'

'Yes. When can you be back here?'

'I can't. I fell off the bike. Cut my knee open. I must get a tetanus jab right away. I'm going straight to A&E. I did at least see Deller. Can I return your wife's bike another time?'

'Of course. But can't you even tell us what happened?'

'If you don't mind a quick summary.'

'I'll just set my mobile up with the mike thing. Then we can both hear.'

Barnes fiddled with the amplifier unit.

221

Lee's voice came over, hollower than usual but clear. 'Prepare yourselves for a shock.'

Barnes's heart jumped. 'What kind of shock?'

'Can you both of you hear me?'

'Yes.'

'Yes.'

'Deller didn't just target backbenchers. He caught much bigger game in his honey-smeared heffalump trap.' Something – the tumble from his bike? – had cleansed Lee's language of Whitehall-ese.

Kerr-Tait leaned forward, as if Lee was in the room. 'Who? No one in the Cabinet, I'm sure of that. Nor among the junior ministers. Their voting records are impeccable. Who, then?'

'William.'

'William who?'

'William Matheson. Mary's husband. The Prime Ministerial consort. The First fucking Gentleman, as the press put it. Less the f-bit.'

'Oh God.'

'But look here. He's…well, he's just an old golf buffer.'

'That's not how Deller tells it. Billy Boy was aiming his balls at a round of holes all right. Trouble is, they weren't golf balls. And the holes weren't on greens.'

FIFTYSIX

Stevens came by the *Hence* bureau Tuesday at precisely five of 11. He'd told Jeff 11. 'London's always a fun trip as well as business', he said, walking cheerfully through the door. His mouth turned down. 'For some', he added, shutting the door behind him.

'For who?' said Jeff. To pick up on casually dropped phrases was good apple-polishing.

'Arlene's buying up Bond Street, depleting that greenback reserve of hers. Leo Horne's looking up some old law school buddy made it into investment banking, got sent over here and works in the City financial district. Gav's relaxing at this club we're all meeting up Thursday. Probably hit its cellar and humidor already. Me, I get to go to the office.'

Jeff knew he wasn't really bitching. He asked Stevens how he felt after his flight.

'Bushed. But at least clear-headed. Like I part-*ayed* all night, only with Mormons. On past form jet lag won't hit till near three London time. I'll grab me some sleep then.' He looked round the room. 'Where's the British girl Tod hired? You let her go?'

'She quit. Yesterday.'

'You can run this place meantime? Tod always said it needs an associate as well as a full-time newsman out chasing stories most the day.'

'I want to speak with you about Tod.'

Jeff told Stevens the nub of what he'd learnt yesterday from the memory stick.

As Stevens listened he got more and more gleeful. 'And we're the only guys know all this? That's fantastic. Cal, you write it up, we'll definitely run you for a Greeley. Greeley, heck. Two-bit award. Make that a Pulitzer.'

'It was Tod did most the spade work. It's his story.'

'Only he's dead and you aren't. No one's going to put him in the Magazine Writers' Hall of Fame now he's passed on.' Stevens eyed Jeff. 'You they might.'

'Tod should get credit. And some kind of salute to his widow, Beth. Maybe even a fee. Gavin Doresett would endorse that.'

223

'What in hell's Gav got to do with it?'

'He's Tod's literary executor.'

Stevens wrenched Debbie's old chair from where it stood in front of her desk, swung it in front of Jeff's and sat astride it, the back toward Jeff, as if poised for a Dodge City shoot-out.

'Get one thing straight, Cal. The personage edits *Hence* is W. Berndorf Stevens.' He poked his chest with his thumb. 'Not you. Not Doresett. And no way is it the late Todmorden C. Snaith, who was on full salary, generous benefits too, till the day he died and never wrote a word of anything literary. Gav and his executor-ship don't come into it. What Tod wrote was something called journalism, which pays for you, me, this office, our corporate trip First Class to England, Arlene's shopping, Gav's club. And by the way, Tod's widow inherits his pension. She can't claim payroll privileges as well. That clear?'

'Excuse me, sir, but Tod did nine tenths of the investigating on this story so far…'

'"So far"? It isn't finished yet. There could be a lot more tenths to go. And *you*…' He tipped the chair forward, pointed at Jeff's chest with a forefinger, failed to connect, rocked back, '…are gonna be the reporter supplies them.' Stevens fumbled in his pockets. 'Gimme a pen, will you?', he said. 'So when I lunge I really connect with your chest.'

'All I want is that Tod's input wins recognition.'

'OK.' Stevens gave way on the minor point. 'We'll bill him as associate writer. But when a story this size breaks, our readers want to know all about the guy broke it. A live guy. One they can see on TV, hear speak at lunch clubs, touch at meet-the-press soirées. And fête. Fête? Turn into a nationwide celeb. Not some yesterday hack his address is Hart Island Cemetery. Jesus, Calhoun, I'm offering immortality – till you retire your 65th birthday. Don't deep-six the gift in a back alley dumpster.'

*

However fierce the argument with Stevens, Jeff felt cosy inside. His date with Chrissie last night had been bliss, none more than when they'd left their coffees barely sipped, skittered back to her apartment across South Kensington's greasy wet paving stones, dodging the rain drops, and dived beneath her duvet.

'You can't think how nice a change it is to bed a feller with no rubber pulled over his wossit', Chrissie had said.

Jeff had been too engaged elsewhere to answer.

'You don't mind my past?' she'd said. He'd stopped nuzzling her long enough to murmur a no. She said, 'Bet you've sometimes had sex for business reasons.'

'Now and then I couldn't get out of it', he'd said, thinking of the fox. He felt less furtive there than formerly. He might even tell Chrissie one day.

'We all do it sooner or later', Chrissie had said. 'And since for me it *was* business you needn't get jealous.'

He'd hoped she wasn't going to be one of those women couldn't dam their flow of words during sex. She wasn't. Had turned out she could keep her larynx idling in neutral, if not her mouth shut. But then her mouth had done more than talk.

*

Stevens got up, turned the chair round and sat on it properly, his back against its back, his body opposite Jeff's across Jeff's desk.

'Now let's talk magazines.' Stevens took reading matter from his attaché case. 'We just bought these two British titles, *Chic* and *YooHoo!* ' He flung copies on the desk. 'You looked at either?'

Jeff picked them up. 'Sure. Before I left New York I gutted six months' back issues in 10 hours like they were college grind study assignments. Looked at the current number once or twice since coming over here. They're both of them fun reads, but strictly brain cell-lite.'

'How about you do me a report? What they need to turn 'em round, hone 'em, make 'em leaner, cooler, youther-oriented, grab more of what for some years'll be very shrinking ad space buys.'

Jeff was about to say "of course" when it struck him that this was not in Stevens's job remit. Unless he'd been made StrepMag Editor-in-Chief. Jeff's own promotion to Senior Editor was being gazetted in the next issue of *Hence*. He'd seen the proofs. There was no accompanying mention of anything for Stevens.

'This been OK-ed with Arlene?' he said.

Stevens didn't answer directly. He stood up and looked out the window, but speaking clearly. 'Till now Arlene's been her own Chief

Visionary Officer Vice-President', he said, 'planning for the future, as well as Life President. That was fine with one magazine title. Three titles, both sides the Atlantic, cranks things up some. Who's going to run the two British acquisitions? And how? In tandem or apart? With us, the mother magazine? Are we mother? *Hence* might sink to ugly sister.'

Jeff said, 'Arlene hasn't thought out *at all* what she wants to do with her two new titles?'

'She was offered them out the blue. At a good price. She was in the mood. Following a modicum of due diligence she snapped them up. A *modicum* – as StrepMag majority shareholder, she can do what she likes. But if she isn't steered right, these two new properties could drag us all down. Seen it happen with magazines before, even when the fish gets swallowed is a small one. Can turn out a piranha, eat its way thru the big one's gut, kill it dead. Here there are two maybe piranhas to one gut. Double risk of a downside.'

'I'm a writer not a business analyst.'

'You know the scene over here. You know the magazines.' Stevens looked over at the glossy wodges of laminated paper in Jeff's hands, their backs to him, their front covers obscured. 'What are their goddam names again? Already it slipped my mind.'

'Why'd she buy them?', said Jeff.

'Why's she sucking dry Bond Street? Got spend-itis. It won't last. And when it's over she'll develop a bad bellyache, less you map me out a strategy for what is now a triple-title high-end periodical portfolio...'

Stevens didn't wait for his answer. 'I always favored your assignment to London', he said. 'I had to push it through against Arlene. She feared you might be too young for the job. Too...uh, winsome as well.'

'Winsome? Meaning I'd get laid a lot?'

Stevens looked uncomfortable. 'Well I guess she could have had that in mind. She never spelled it out exactly. But...'

'Well I didn't. Not by lots of people. Lots of times by one person, yes.'

'You're unmarried. No reason you can't play the field...' Stevens faded mid-sentence, looked hard at Jeff. He'd detected reticence. 'Unless...you telling me you made it with someone is a news story...?'

Jeff came completely clean. 'I had an affair with Laura Deller.'

Stevens pursed his lips. 'I knew there was something... This the bad guy's wife you told me about?'

'More than wife. Co-conspirator. Maybe controlling spirit. I can't decide myself yet.'

'This is not gonna play well with our burgeoning homespun readership "off of the sophisto seaboard", in Arlene's words. This broad of yours is an all-American wife.'

'So's Morticia Addams. Who Laura Deller could out-evil with her eyes closed.'

'Morticia Addams also happens to be a mom', said Stevens. 'Your Laura got kids?'

Jeff faltered. 'She does have two daughters, yes.'

'Age?'

'I don't know. Ten? Eight?'

'The very worst to try and discredit in a media counteroffensive. They look just darling?'

'I saw them once. Glimpsed.'

'Anyhow, they can be fixed to. Make-up, wardrobe – smart packaging'll work wonders. Little tykes tug on the heartstrings every which way – long as they're not some Amy Carter know-it-all trying to stampede the thermonuclear warfare debate.' Stevens paused, remembering. 'And you know what? If Saint Jimmy had had her hair crimped in Little Orphan Annie curls, fitted her with contact lenses stead of those crappy glasses and put her up on TV he might have won the 1980 weapons argument against Reagan.'

Jeff ducked his head to hide a smile. 'The kids aside', he said, 'it's over between us, Laura Deller and me.'

'But you can't write up the whole business and leave out her leading role.' Stevens got up and flailed his arms in frustration. 'It's such a honey of a story, Goddammit. You got way too close to it, Cal. Then there's the question who started the romance. It could look like home-maker with two cute little girls got seduced by suave cosmopolitan compatriot exploits her disorientation after she left the good old US of A. Your Laura has only to do one TV interview with her kids either side of her, get one of them to say something sappy like "Please, Mister *Hence* reporter, let us have our Mommy back" and you, worse *us*, are history. Too, you're no choir boy. You sweet-talked some of my staff into the sack when you worked out of the StrepMag Building, didn't you?'

'I don't have to answer a question incriminates me.'

'That says "yes" like you tattooed it on your forehead. I covered crimes of passion once, back when I started in this business, Cal. Guy takes the Fifth Amendment, nine times in ten he broke the Sixth Commandment.'

Jeff flipped. 'For Crissake, *Steve*. Quit calling me Cal.'

Stevens looked at him astonished. 'You don't like "Cal"?'

'Do you like to be called "Steve"?'

'You make me sound some crusty old fart. It's more good manners. I would not address Arlene as "Strep" even if it didn't sound like she was some virus. You just don't monkey with a family name, OK?'

'But you monkeyed with mine. Mine and a Vice-President's of the United States.'

'John C. Calhoun?' Stevens spoke thoughtfully. 'Haven't had him come up since high school history club. You want to fight any kind of Civil War era duel, my name is also that of a noted Reconstructionist, Tad Stevens.'

'Fuck Reconstruction. Stop reconstructing who I am.'

Stevens softened, yet without standing down. Jeff began to see why he was editor. 'OK, Jefferson', said Stevens. 'It'll sound weird calling you "Jefferson". I liked "Cal" better.' He took the magazines from the desk where Jeff had left them and inserted them one by one in his attaché case. He looked up. 'You kin to Calhoun?'

'You kin to Thaddeus Stevens?'

'Nope. My dad was born Stefanidis.'

'Me and Congressman Cal, yes.'

Stevens snapped the attaché case shut. 'Yeah?', he said. 'How?'

'Cousin or something.'

Stevens punched Jeff playfully on the shoulder. 'I'm gonna buy you lunch, Jeff, cement your re-naming. There some place good round here? What's this London Broil Gav Doresett said was a local version of New York Strip Sirloin?'

'You really don't need to expose yourself to London Broil, sir. Any more than you should risk your duodenum on Cabinet Pudding, Windsor Soup or Jellied Eels. In England they went out with fogs,

Eliza Doolittle flower girls and public beheadings. I know a gastro pub we could try.'

FIFTYSEVEN

On leaving the tarmac paths, Lee had got off Barb Barnes's bike and pushed it the last hundred yards towards the Queen's Temple. The going had been heavier across grass, which was long and far too moist. His shoes had got soaked. He'd propped the bike against the bulbous southern end of the Temple and gone round the front. There were three entrances, all open to the elements. He'd poked his head in the centre one. Nothing. He'd gone round to the right-hand one and advanced into the building.

A blow had struck him in the face, a true knuckle sandwich with plenty of bone and beef filling. He'd reeled back.

'That's for fucking my wife behind my back', Deller had said. He'd stepped out from inside the building and wrapped a handkerchief round his fist. Evidently he'd stood behind one of the Temple's internal arches. 'When it was me got you your first big career step too', he'd said. 'God, I detest ingratitude.'

'I only did her once or twice.' Lee had been shocked into pseudo-frankness; "once" was a gross underestimate; even "twice" was an inadequate body count. He'd held a hand to his right eye. There'd been swelling already.

Deller had come forward and pulled Lee's hand away from his face. He'd grinned. 'You're due a beaut of a shiner', he'd said. 'Lean forward and I'll hit the other eye. Give your face some symmetry.'

'No thanks.' Was Deller serious? To avoid a second blow Lee had made light of the first: 'I'd rather look a bruiser than a panda.'

Deller had tightened the handkerchief round his fist, pulling at it with his teeth. Then he'd let go. 'Once your face is front page you'll be famous as either.' He'd spoken distinctly now his mouth was unencumbered. 'What you say is true, though. One black eye could be a domestic accident. Just. Two means you couldn't not have been in a fight – and lost.'

Deller had walked to the north end of the Temple and peered round it. 'No one', he'd said, then turned his head back towards Lee. 'Be a good chap and see there's no one your end either.'

Lee had begun to wonder if Deller wasn't deranged. He didn't know him that well any more, but…The pain round his right eye had intensified. 'I'm not up to seeing much right now', he'd said. He'd squinted round the southern side. 'There's no one very near.'

Deller had unwrapped the handkerchief on his fist and licked the sore place. Lee had taken advantage of this amateur first aid to get in ahead. 'Listen, Victor', he'd said. 'I know all about your corrupting the Commons.'

Deller had rewrapped his fist. 'Do you indeed?' he'd said, knotting the hanky. 'How?'

'I've got my own inside source. You may be a press mogul. I'm an ex-investigative reporter.' He'd gone into greater detail, but hadn't mentioned Jules or Angelo.

Deller had smiled. 'You seem not to know about Mary Matheson's husband', he'd said, 'to name but one of a galaxy of the Great and Good. Not Good. Not Good at all.' He in turn had gone into detail, mentioning names, lots of them, all big, not all MPs either. He'd described the setting up and running of the project, making the huge, sordid operation sound like a straightforward business venture, with undoubtedly a risk element – as which business venture didn't have? – but costed, monitored, site-managed and project-overviewed, paying attention to budgetary constraints, optimised allocation and prioritised strategising, with sideways nods at such modern techniques as Capability Maturity Model Integration.

Lee's mind had reeled. It had been like sitting through an INSEAD seminar in rapid French – never his best language – while poring over *Who's Who* and battling a hangover, so that the illustrious personalities had both danced on the page and stoked the throbbing pain behind his eye. He'd ignored Deller's management science and fastened on the two aspects that interested him. 'Your offer of money to the Party was just a smokescreen, then?'

'Not initially, no. But on getting the London call-girl business up and running we realised we could buy an entire legislature. That was Laura; bright gal. Cheaper, yet much bigger, than a political party. Besides, the party in question is only one of several. Three including the DeLiberatories but four, five, six if you count those Celtic Fringe nationalist nitwits as well. Not that I take them seriously, but all the more reason to go for the entire House. Besides, your ColLabs won't be in power for ever. Maybe not even next month.' Deller had smirked. 'Thanks to me and my missus.'

'And the peerage? Didn't you ever really want one?'

'Are you mad? Tatty bit of nonsense. Look at the shower they make lords of these days. It might be different if they still distributed dukedoms. Or even earls, though that creeping Jesus Crowthorne didn't do their standing any favours.'

Lee hadn't expected this. He'd put a naïve question: 'You honestly think you're duke material?'

'Why not? I've controlled about a dozen MPs' votes for the last few months. Those 18th-century borough-monger behemoths like Newcastle didn't do any better.'

Another thought had struck Lee. 'Just how rich are you?' he'd said, putting another naïve question.

'One never knows from day to day. My darling *Date* has always got rosy prospects around the corner.' Deller's face had crumpled. 'Bugger her. She hasn't turned it yet.' He'd gone on to describe his initiatives in detail, as if pleading with a bank for extra credit. 'I've tried everything. The "Kidz" supplement. Didn't attract enough pre-teen ABs. "Hot Date", an upbeat lonely hearts page. Got overrun by pervs. A bingo game with the numbers called by astrologers; we christened it "Date with Destiny". Fell foul of OfDice, the Gaming Commission as was, and attracted some blistering comments on the letters page by among others a leading futurologist. We couldn't not run it as he's head of an Oxbridge college. Regular photos of fluffy animals on page 5. Our general technician and scientist readership evaporated; vivisectionists abound in the white-coat world – bloody mouse-murderers. We might have picked up compensatory C2s if we'd splashed racks on page 3, but there are some things I won't stoop to. So I sold off my glossies. That'll shore the *Date* up for another twelve months.'

Lee had sat down on the grass, oblivious of the damp. 'I'm gobsmacked.' This Deller was another Northcliffe, drunk on printer's ink. What was it about newspaper-owning sent people mad? Or was it that overgrown children were preternaturally attracted to the business? Hearst, McCormick, Beaverbrook, Maxwell...; the list stretched back decades.

'What you have to do is decide how to handle William Matheson's bit of naughtiness', Deller had said. He'd got businesslike again. It had focussed Lee's attention. He'd reverted to behaving as if Deller had remained a figure of high seriousness throughout.

'God knows how Mary will react when I tell her', he'd said.

'Don't, then. Look, here's what you do.' Deller had sat down on the grass next to Lee and put an avuncular hand, his good one, on Lee's shoulder. To any passer-by they would have seemed a mentor with acolyte, as in Millais' 'Boyhood of Raleigh'.

'There's only one security risk left in my team', Deller had said. 'A murderous thug called Devene.'

Lee had raised his head. Jules Miller had mentioned Devene.

Deller had removed his hand from Lee's shoulder and struck the turf with it. 'Worse', he'd said, 'a bare-faced liar. To me, his boss.' He'd continued, 'On your side there's an American correspondent for his half-baked New York gossip-cum-heritage mag. It's through him that Scrabble story about Mary Matheson got out. It was you told Laura, wasn't it?'

Deller had bunched his other fist. The knotted handkerchief had lent it extra menace. Lee had quickly nodded. It had come to him that he'd better find an excuse to work from home for the next fortnight, or the black eye adorning the PM's chief adviser would be the subject of awkward public comment. Could he say he'd fallen off his bike, banged his eye on the handle bars?

Deller had continued: '…Then she told the young American, though she said it came from me. Oh, and there's a wog whore fell out with Laura's management cadre…'

Lee had begun a wince, only his eye hurt too much. 'You know', he'd said, 'Laura's role in all this would be the hardest to keep quiet.'

'Balls. Her client list, if published – and it bloody well will be if I or her face a police investigation – would undermine just about every pillar of the Constitution: armed services, C of E, judiciary, even one or two royals. Don't worry there, Benjamin, my son, my son. There's going to be so much kept quiet you could hear a pin drop. Just as well. Your own involvement bears none too close a look.'

Lee had not been able to think of a good response. 'No?', he'd said. It had sounded lame.

'Which is why I overlooked your and Laura's little frolic. Sorry about the black eye. Turn this way.' Lee had flinched slightly but had done so. 'Hmm', Deller had said. 'It's going to make a lovely front page. Good thing we invested in multi-pixel colour printing.' He'd taken out a mobile phone and before Lee could turn away had snapped him full on. 'Couldn't do it justice in monochrome', Deller had said, looking at his mobile and clicking it again to save the pic.

Lee had blenched. 'Must you…?'

'Oh all right. The *Date* spikes your eye as part of the deal.'

'Which is…?'

'My Devene thug erases the American and the Iranian girl. He's onto it right now. You get Devene taken out immediately afterwards. I won't ask how, but you can do it. Mistake him for an Al Qaeda-ista perhaps, unleash those trigger-happy Counter Terrorism boys I know you keep in good touch with. The threat to national security has its useful side…'

Lee had started. He'd said much the same thing himself not long ago.

'…Upshot: Mary Matheson's premiership is saved, and your position with it. Her marriage too', Deller had said. 'Laura and I quietly withdraw our unique breed of hands-on personal fitness trainers from the parliamentary health and keep-fit complex, plus a phased winding down of my investment there. OfMed stays reined in from queering my magazine sale. What else?' Deller had scratched the tip of his ear. 'Have I missed anything?'

'Where does that leave your other business interests?'

'We'll get by.' There had been nothing mad about Deller now. And precious little suggesting money troubles. Deller had said, 'Got some provincial enterprises wash their faces nicely. If you could arrange it so that more of the central and local government sit. vac. ads were switched to the *Date* away from the *Era* group I wouldn't say no…'

'It all amounts to a pretty tall order.'

'You can swing it, Mister Lee. Tell you what, as an incentive bonus I'll let you have it off with my wife again. Only this time I watch.'

FIFTYEIGHT

Jeff arrived at the Pantheon early. He wanted time to unwind before Arlene's celebratory dinner. She and Deller were to have signed their magazine deal mid-afternoon.

Earlier he'd taken advantage of Arlene's liking for a table of balanced sexes to call her up and ask if he could bring this girl he knew, meaning Chrissie.

'So you took my advice', Arlene had said, speaking from Beige's Dr Johnson Suite, 'and junked the monk habit. About time. You did it darn quick, I will say. Wish Bernie and my other execs put through directives like that. This girl you know, she British?'

'Yes.'

'Pretty?'

'Stunning as a taser.'

'Blue-blood?'

'If she is some earl's daughter she didn't tell me yet.' He'd only ever heard her called Chrissie. Who were her folks? 'No handle in front of her name that I know of', he'd said. 'But she can write the letters MBA after it.'

Arlene's intake of breath had sounded like a scornful sniff. 'We're lousy with business talent as it is', she'd said. 'In the plus column, she'd boost the attendees to four girls, four guys. Leo dropped out with some bug he says he picked up at lunch. Over-ate, more likely.' She'd hmmed a second or two. 'Eight's an auspicious figure in Chinese numerology', she'd said. 'OK then.'

*

Jeff had come to the Pantheon Club alone. Chrissie was meeting him there later. He was shown to the Strangers' Room. It was intimated to him that he'd have to stay there till they'd located Doresett, technically his host for the evening. He sat down by the window and picked up the *Evening Era*.

It wasn't a paper he knew well, but you couldn't miss its front page splash: 'Wilmur backs Mary' with sub-heading 'US meddling in

UK poll claim' and some scathing comments from well-known anti-American public figures in Britain. Intrigued, Jeff read further.

Following the Opposition's imminent parliamentary lack of confidence motion over the Government's Middle East war, some bright hack had cornered Brewster Cotesworth IV on his private line at Winfield House and secured a devastating quote. The hack had asked His Excellency if it was OK by the US for Britons who worked for UK-based American companies to vote ColLaborative in any coming general election, given that Prime Minister Matheson had joined war as an ally of President Wilmur Washington's.

Cotesworth, caught off guard, confused specifically by the unfamiliar term 'general' election and more broadly by the convoluted way the question was phrased, alone in his residence's master bedroom, with not even his wife to give advice, and bereft of spokesmen to do his thinking for him, had said it was fine by him. His mouth sealed his mission's doom.

The *Evening Era* had unearthed photos of both Mary Matheson and Wilmur Washington, each with eyes wide and lips parted, positioning them such that they seemed to gaze at each other in mutual rapture, like a gym slip junior miss and her crush the school lacrosse captain in an Angela Brazil story.

Inside items included a high-minded editorial scoring American interference in its oldest ally's internal politics and on the op-ed page an essay on the Thelma-Louise pattern of self-destruction in women-only relationships, with lacerating observations contributed by a self-hating feminist intellectual and worked artfully into the text by the writer. The by-line bore the name Sammi Psalt, the journalist Jeff had seen with Piers at the State Opening. The bitch.

Annoyed, Jeff flipped through the other pages. He noticed a tiny corner in the City section reporting a government U-turn on tax breaks for artists using UK-registered recording studios. Sir Pip Porter was thought to be a major beneficiary, it said.

You bet he was. His Avro was fitted with one. Jeff recalled that Sir Pip had lent the PM his Avro recently. He'd covered the Aberdeen trip for *Hence* and particularly remembered that detail. The *Evening Era* didn't mention it.

Jeff turned to the gossip page. He got absorbed in an item speculating as to what had caused 'Government guru' Ben Lee to take up cycling, the man having been spotted pedalling furiously across

Hyde Park towards Kensington Gardens the previous Monday when he was famous for most days using a ministerial limo even to cross the street. Jeff didn't notice Godwin till the latter tapped him on the shoulder.

'*Guten abend, Herr Oberarzt*' said Godwin.

'Excuse me?'

'Weren't you promoted senior editor yesterday?'

'Well yes.'

'*Oberarzt* is senior editor.'

'How'd you hear?'

'I rang my old friend Gavin Doresett in New York, at your office there. They said he was on a business trip abroad. I asked about you and they told me you were being promoted. Congratulations.' Godwin's right upper lip lifted in distaste. 'They then tried to sell me a year's subscription.'

Jeff changed the subject. 'See this?' he said, pointing to the Cotesworth story.

'Yes. It was in the lunchtime edition too. David Macnamara never misses a chance to clobber the Americans. Hilarious.'

'Hilarious?'

'For us British. Though you've only yourselves to blame. Reward a novice with an embassy for bankrolling a politician and diplomatic cock-ups are inevitable. If your Wilmur Washington had bunged Cotesworth some harmless bauble – a Cabinet post, say…' Godwin looked sly, 'and sent a professional to London, she could have avoided all this. As it is, Mzzzzz. President is broadcasting a "clarification" in about ten minutes. In other words a retraction.' Godwin looked at his watch. 'Come and watch it in the telly room.'

'You *are* a member here? Because I'm not.'

'Got elected the year after I came down from Trinity. Come on. The best seats get taken if you don't look sharp.'

Jeff followed Godwin across the atrium and up some wide stairs. They snaked round into some shabby corridors. Inside the Television Room Channel 8 and a Half's Early Evening News was showing. The anchor duo (earnest, caring and comely young woman yoked to facetious older man), sat on a stylised studio bench and batted one-liners back and forth between film clips.

'Are they going to do a running commentary on the President even as she speaks?' said Jeff. He'd never watched 8 and a Half.

'Terrible, aren't they?' said Godwin. 'No, they'll show a clip of Wilmur Washington's address *then* pick snide holes in it.'

Godwin was wrong there. The mix of reportage and comment was endemic. 'And now to Washington', the male anchor said, 'where earlier today President Washington – namesake of the man who overthrew George III's colonial rule two centuries back…'. You could almost hear the tee hee, '…announced a clarification on the London crisis involving the American ambassador…'

As the picture switched to Washington DC Jeff felt a surge of patriotic pride. He whispered to Godwin. 'She looks good, Dubya Dubya, doesn't she?'

'Not bad. Of course, she's lost weight since her inauguration. Though like a lot of black women, she carried her excess poundage with a certain oomph.'

'Know why they say she slimmed?'

'No.' Godwin sounded intrigued. 'Health? Presentability? Why?'

'So there's less of her for a racist assassin to aim at from inside of his School Book Depository. Sick but scarily to the point. Secret Service guy told me. Why she usually wears black too. Harder target.'

A chorus of Ssssh-es silenced them.

FIFTYNINE

Angelo had disobeyed Big Boss. He doted on the Cay far too much to abandon her and had driven her home to show to Verna and the kids. But he'd taken precautions. Changed the number plates for a start, choosing the gem of his collection, WA 5TE, an in-joke hint of what he intended doing to Mel and the kid. He'd also got her re-sprayed fire-engine red. His eldest, Mandy's, favourite colour.

He'd only spoken to Big Boss once since they'd parted at the meat plant. It was to take BB's call letting him, Angelo, know the American reporter, the Kid, would be at a dinner party at the Pantheon Club off Pall Mall on the following Thursday night.

Angelo hadn't set out immediately for London after taking Big Boss's call. Instead he whisked the family round Fun World, cramming the three kids into the tiny back seat of the Cay like…like illegal immigrants in a Meadow-Sourced Meat Products lorry, it occurred to him. But after an hour at Fun World, a feeling that he ought to get cracking began to gather steam. He pressed into Verna's hand half the notes BB had given him to use on exes, kissed her and the girls goodbye and raced up to London in the Cay. He now lay in wait along the street from the Pantheon till Pretty Boy emerged. Then zap time.

Hanging on to the Cay had emboldened him. He ignored Big Boss's other instructions too, both to screw out of the kid before wasting him the Persian girl Mel's whereabouts, then to waste her too. There just wasn't time for such refinements.

SIXTY

When Jeff entered the Prince Regent Rooms at a quarter of eight it was with Chrissie in tow. Not quite on his arm. 'Not here', Chrissie had said on their way up the stairs, gently tugging her hand away as he'd tried to thread it through his bent elbow. 'Not now either.'

Had she said that because she might encounter ex-clients? Or worse, current ones?

Jeff repressed the thought as unworthy. But like all repressions it had a habit of blundering about in far reaches of the mind. Take her away from London and its bad habits, he thought. Why not back to New York? He'd have to get Bernie to agree to his returning there. Unless he left *Hence*. Get a job with another magazine? Not easy in this recession. Shit.

The first person he and Chrissie met on entering the Suite's antechamber was Arlene. Either the opulent surroundings or her leap from single magazine-owner to triple-title media mogul-ette had led her to act *grande dame*. Doresett, their nominal host, was nowhere to be seen.

'Chrissie?', said Arlene, on being introduced. 'That sounds so pretty! Chrissie what, though? I do need both names for the place card. Jefferson, would you kindly fetch that blank one from the top of the table?'

Jeff scurried to do her bidding, so never heard what Chrissie's surname was. He returned with the blank card and stood in front of Arlene.

Chrissie was to her right. Laura Deller glided up on her left.

'Jefferson Calhoun', said Arlene, introducing him, 'our new star. When I was a girl, being a good writer included penning an elegant hand.' She looked straight at Jeff. 'Could you enscroll your friend Chrissie's full name on that card? In best copperplate?'

Jeff took the fountain pen she offered, slowly unscrewed the cap, then hesitated.

'Why Mr Calhoun, you surely know your date's full name?', said Laura, oozing poison. 'I mean, it's not like you picked her up in the street.' She smiled, eyes icy. 'Is it?'

Jeff longed for something to silence her. A massive cerebral haemorrhage, say.

Chrissie came to the rescue. 'I expect he's not quite sure about the spelling...' She looked round the company, bright as if malice and social pitfalls didn't exist. 'I'm Miss Bere-Poole. Double-barrelled. Only it's spelled B-R-E-A-K-S-P-E-A-R hyphen P-O-L-E. Our quaint British ways, heh, heh...'

'My dear young lady', said Arlene, pure Mrs Astor at Newport, 'a "Breakspear-Pole" need not apologise.'

'You are so lucky your family didn't go settle in America', said Laura to Chrissie. 'Think how those ignorant Ellis Island clip-board clerks would've mangled the name.'

Chrissie started on a polite response but Laura cut her off, pressing the attack. 'Haven't I seen you someplace before?' she said.

'Not socially', said Chrissie, speaking clearly. 'I'm positive about that.'

Jeff panicked. What if Laura came back with a vicious put-down? He should have briefed Chrissie about Laura beforehand.

'...You may have made use of my professional services', Chrissie was saying. 'You or your husband.' She lowered her eyelashes. 'Or you *and* your husband.'

Laura stepped back, like she'd all but trod on a rattler. For a second her face flashed horror. 'Maybe', she said and turned towards the window. 'Where is Vic anyhow?' She crossed over to the other side of the room and almost collided with Doresett, who emerged from a side door conferring with a white-coated waiter.

'My, that was a quick getaway', said Arlene, following Laura with her eyes. She turned to Chrissie. 'What exactly is it you do, dear?'

'Marketing strategies mostly. Freelance.'

'How very high-powered. Too high-powered for Mrs Deller, evidently.'

Arlene turned to Jeff, grasping his hand. 'Jefferson, I meant to tell you, but it slipped my mind. Joe Bramcusi's joining us for dinner. Si Mecklenburger might look in too, but only for coffee. I was going to ask you to drop out, make room for Joe, grab a steak someplace instead – charge it to me, of course – but that was before I met your lovely date here. Not just a pretty face; smart as a whip. I insist you two stay. Luckily nine's an even more auspicious Chinese number than eight.'

SIXTYONE

The PM sat alone. As regards humans. Animal companionship she did have. Her new acquisition, Harold, a boisterous Westie, lay curled up on the floor next to her desk. He represented the last attempt to arrest a slide in her poll ratings that had started two months back and speeded up with rumours of Lord Barnes's involvement in insider dealing, attaining Cresta Run velocity with the Opposition's tabling of its no confidence motion.

Harold was more than a pawn. She had become genuinely attached to him. They were at Chequers, in the No Smoking Room. From time to time she fondled Harold's ears.

The PM nursed her trademark elderflower cordial and turned towards the desk to con a draft speech Felix had presented for her approval twenty minutes earlier. She soon lost the thread of his argument. Sign of a bad speech. (She refused to consider whether her powers of concentration might be under par.) Ben Lee would have put together something more cogent. Lee... She missed Lee, officially on sick leave due to concussion after falling off his bike. In reality, she suspected, up to something less mentionable.

His irreverence irritated. His knowingness embarrassed. Why, then, did she miss him? Not his speech-writing, hand-crafted to her specifications though it was. She supposed it was his devotion, at bottom. And his independent non-minister status. Above all, he was a media virtuoso.

Dismally she passed to the revelation of what her husband had been up to. Felix's tendency to word play in his speech-writing – the passage on terrorism, for instance: 'we shall show no fear, yet fear no show of strength...' – began still more to shape her vocabulary. William... She gave her rich, Bar-honed lexicon its full rein: bunking up with floozies not foozling his way into bunkers; sinking his putz, not putts; scoring chicks, not eagles...

What a lot of golf terms had sexually charged secondary meanings. How right she was to have loathed the game all these years. From golf widow to...divot divorcee?... No. She couldn't break up with William, simply could not. As a proper politician one had to be ready to realign one's thinking to cope with any new set of circumstances.

242

She abandoned her husband and his grubby hobby, cast her mind over her Cabinet. By no means all of them qualified for membership. Or even in one or two cases for membership of the Mother of Parliaments. Any Parliament, come to that. Even joke ones like the Duma. (Her russophobia lingered long after the Cold War had burnt itself out.)

She put down her glass of elderflower cordial and stretched out her hand to ring for a whisky, then withdrew it. In whisky lurked ruin. Mother's ruin: gin; Premier's ruin: whisky. Her mind – not wandered, she insisted to her inner conscience – took a detour...

...Premier, a good brand name for a whisky... Branding, part of business no less than of politics... The business world, that stultifying but lucrative afterlife where ex-politicians supplemented their pensions and bathed in consultancy fees or directors' emoluments their wounded pride, cicatrices inflicted on the ego by their ejection from office... The afterlife. Did it exist? For statesmen (statespersons? She shuddered at the gender-neutral neologism) there was the authorised biography, collaborated on with some ambitious academic or sympathetic practitioner of higher journalism. If one was big enough, a few hostile pen-portrait books might appear as well – hatchet jobs to tickle the masses by the sort of crowd-pleaser who scribbled barbed witticisms for the *Era*.

Then long years being wheeled out at party conferences; watching one's successors muck things up while gagged by protocol from saying so; attending sycophantic young whippersnappers' book launches; trudging the lecture circuit (vicious circles, stale with hot air), the munificently rewarded delivery of bromides to businessmen; the odd television interview; hints of one's decline making it into the staider kind of gossip column.

Eventually the last few weeks; the final departure from terminal illness; the *Date* obituary; the *Heliograph* ditto, but more anecdotal, less self-consciously part of a journal of record; the quiet interment (no state funeral, please God not); an entry in the next supplement to the *Dictionary of National Biography*; a mention in some encyclopaedia articles – and one faded from memory till no more than a tie-breaking answer to a question on 'University Challenge'.

A knock on the door. Harold sprang to his paws and gave way to a frenzy of barking. The RAF attendant entered and said, 'The gentlemen from London here to see you, Prime Minister.'

243

Mary Matheson put down her cordial.

Nicholas Kerr-Tait. Sam Knighton. Two other party high-ups, but to lend weight of numbers, not for any intrinsic avoirdupois.

'Good evening, Mary', said Kerr-Tait. 'I imagine you know what this is about.'

'The mute with the bowstring?'

'Mary, please. This isn't the Topkapi Palace.'

'And when it was', said Knighton, speaking confusedly but with discernible relish, 'the odalisques got tied in sacks then dropped in the Bosphorus.' His demotion at Mary Matheson's hands some months back still festered. 'Dropped, not strangled', he emphasised.

To the PM it became clear that Knighton's dislike of her was built on pure misogyny. She had supposed it due to her having replaced him with Crowthorne.

'You won't deny', she said, 'that you're here to tell me to…'.

'Retire.' Kerr-Tait interrupted her. 'For the good of the party – and incidentally the country.'

His cutting her short said more about her loss of authority than could any Janissaries' uprising.

'I was going to say "step down"', she said, in her characteristic musing tone.

'May I suggest for the official statement something like "spend more time with your husband"?' said Sam Knighton.

'You may not.' The PM showing her sharp side.

Kerr-Tait at least showed contrition. 'I didn't mean to rub salt in the wound.'

News of William's extra-marital activities must have leaked days ago, as well as of the errant MPs' lack of party discipline and Mark's sharp share-dealing. I should have kept all mention of everything to the Scrabble board. So thought the PM.

'What if I fight?' she said aloud. 'Or resign and call a leadership contest?'

'We've looked into that', said Kerr-Tait. 'The numbers in your favour just don't stack up, I'm afraid. That's why we've come to see you.'

'You're very sure of your numbers.'

'It's my job to be.'

'Your job…yes. For a change.' When Mary Matheson gave way to fury it erupted late but scorching. 'Our backbenchers were all over those Deller-procured prostitutes. Yet you dare imply you were on top of your job then?'

She'd landed a direct hit on Kerr-Tait's self-confidence. 'It's all water under the bridge, Mary', he said. The cliché showed he was rattled.

'No good crying over spilt milk', said Sam Knighton, lumbering with a cavalry squadron of time-worn proverbs to Kerr-Tait's aid. 'Tears won't put it back in the bottle', he said. Harold sniffed appreciatively at Knighton's right trouser hem.

'It's cartons nowadays, you fool. And I'm not crying.' But the corners of her eyes were moist. Harold made energetic love to Knighton's right leg.

'Please, Mary. This isn't exactly a pleasant duty for any of us.' Kerr-Tait ignored the attempted rape of his colleague's nether man.

'Mark Barnes has already resigned', said Knighton, looking not at her but over her head. Harold started on his left trouser hem, first the sniff, then the priapic lunge.

'How do you know?'

'He's sent in his resignation to Ben Lee, who's technically his boss. No doubt a copy is on its way to you.'

'Thank you. I shall confer with Ben.'

'Any delay will only make matters worse, you know', said Kerr-Tait.

'You'll have my decision within the hour.'

After they withdrew she rang Lee.

'Don't do anything irretrievable', he said. 'There's just a chance I...'

'Too late, Ben. The rats have drawn blood. And they're too many for me.'

'How do you know? Did Nick say? 'How do you know he's telling the truth?'

'He'd never lie about numbers. He's good at numbers, you see. Not so much feelings, or the way people's minds work. But counting heads – yes.'

'Look...please. Give me a couple of hours.'

'It's too late. Goodbye, Ben. Goodbye from Chequers, that is. I'll see you in London once you're up and about.' If Ben Lee had been around the party revolt – fanned, if not organised, she was now certain, by Kerr-Tait working with Sam Knighton – might perhaps have been averted; 'perhaps'? Better than that: probably.

'...Oh by the way', she said, 'did they deliver my get-well-soon card?'

'Yes', said Lee. 'Much appreciated. I...'

'The shop didn't have a concussion one. Felix hoped a 'flu one would do. He scribbled "diplomatic" before the word "'flu", just to, well, let you know we know you haven't really got 'flu.' Agitation had made her clumsier of speech than usual.

'I'm not suffering from concussion either', said Lee.

'You might as well have been. Some sort of blow to the head anyway.' She found she could tell him after all. 'If I'd had the benefit of your brains from the start', she said, 'I'd still be in power.'

SIXTYTWO

Jeff found himself seated opposite Joe Bramcusi, who looked preternaturally slim for someone of 40. Smooth-skinned about the face too. Bramcusi drew Jeff's full attention by rejecting the set menu and asking the waiter if they had any house specialty.

The waiter paused a moment, looking nonplussed. 'There's lamb cutlets Pantheon, sir.'

'Give.'

'Sir?'

'Lamb cutlets I understand. Pantheon I don't.'

'Lamb cutlets smothered in breadcrumbs with an anchovy-and-egg sauce binding.'

'Sounds just great. Fix me a Pantheon, will you? With a cress order on the side, no dressing. And lose the lamb.' Bramcusi looked across at Jeff. 'I don't have much yen for meat.'

He seemed alert. Jeff recalled what they said about him: slept three hours a night, ran his operation so hands-on he was everywhere at once, like the Holy Ghost. He'd introduced vertical integration to Vere, Bramcusi, combining a talent agency, book publisher, movie and DVD production outfit, also a publicity machine, all directed by one restless intelligence, his.

'You *are* Jefferson P. Calhoun?' Bramcusi said. Each name card faced its owner, not, fatously, a *vis-à-vis*.

'Yes.'

'Gather you're sitting on quite a story.'

'How'd you hear that?'

'Arlene. Bernie filled in on some details', said Bramcusi. 'Nothing so solid he gave away the plot. British-oriented, this story?'

'Mostly. There's an American involved.' Two, Jeff thought, not for the first time. I'm the second, dammit.

'You didn't run it yet?'

'The story? It only came to our notice this week.'

'It was that hot, you'd get it in this week's issue.' Bramcusi had a quick mind alright.

'There are a few points need clearing up', said Jeff.

'That so? Cops involved?'

How'd he know? 'Yes.' Jeff had been interviewed by two of them that afternoon. They'd been polite but thorough. They'd be back in touch soon, they'd said. It might be best if he didn't leave the country. He treasured the 'might be best'. They were chiefly interested in the Francis Evans he'd found in 'a state of acute physical distress', as they'd put it. The cops had also asked Jeff about the two dead guys and taken a statement. He'd gotten a feeling they didn't mind about either of them much…

'…Much?' said Bramcusi, breaking in on his train of thought.

'Cops much involved?' Jeff shook his head. 'Not yet.'

'The size, this story of yours…' Bramcusi closed his eyes, as if at a séance. 'Big', he said, opening them. 'No, wait.' Bramcusi closed his eyes again. 'Huge', he said, opening them again.

'Uh…yes.'

A waiter brought in a plate with a neat hillock of brownish scrapings on it. For Bramcusi. The rest of the party got a small lox mousse each, shaped ring-wise like a bagel.

Arlene asked Laura Deller where her husband was. Laura said he'd specially requested that they start without him. Arlene shrugged, frowned and picked up her fork. Bramcusi pushed the brownish mess around his plate, then looked over at Jeff. 'The story, it has book potential?'

'Uh… I guess.'

'Give time for the cop investigative dust to settle. Meantime you write the book, which if it's complex it'll take a month or two minimum anyhow. I don't rule out a movie maybe two, three years down the line. It's your story? You research it? Or you maybe got involved?'

'Uh…both.'

'But that's good. Sell you, the author-participant, as much as the book. Photograph well?'

'Excuse me?'

Bramcusi sighed. 'Do you come across all purty through a lens?'

'I don't know.'

'TV experience?'

'Not really.'

'We'll screen test you.' Bramcusi took out a card and scribbled some words on it then flipped it across the table. 'Go see this man tomorrow. He's not bad for a Brit pap. Shoots a mean movie sequence too. You don't wear a stripe shirt, OK? Or a hound-tooth check coat. HD's caused mayhem in menswear. He can rush me some footage, stills too, by late-afternoon.' He leant back, looking at Jeff clinically. 'I'd say you'll do fine on screen, but it's nice to know for sure.'

'Uh…thanks.'

Bramcusi nodded his head in Chrissie's direction. 'That your date?'

'Yes.'

'Good-looking girl. She done any modeling?'

Not modeling modeling. The euphemism kind, yes. Jeff didn't say that. 'I don't think so', he said.

'Two of you an item?'

'For now.'

'Stick with her long enough to promote the book. Golden couples have synergy. Worth more than twice one golden boy, even if he is an author. Get you both on the *Late Show* even, which as you know is damn hard you're not a buddy of the anchor.'

'That'd be great, if we're still together.'

'You better be.' Bramcusi stuck a forkful of brown dust in his mouth. 'Hey, this is goo-ood', he said.

Deller entered the room. He looked harassed. He leant down and said something to Laura then went and sat between her and Chrissie, at one end of the table. It wasn't the proper seating arrangement but when Arlene expostulated he shrugged. He placed a mobile by his outer knife. He ignored the mousse for a roll, which he bit into and chewed moodily.

Jeff looked over at Deller, conning him for signs of guilt. He darted an occasional glance up toward Laura, who had sinned so much she had outgrown guilt. She looked good tonight, he had to admit. Not as fresh as Chrissie, but very carefully turned out, precision-finished.

Deller's phone vibrated. It made his cutlery clink as if in a railway dining car. He picked it up. 'What, already? Which?' He leant across to Charlotte Elver, who was between Gavin Doresett and Joe Bramcusi: 'Charlotte, please go and look at the news agency flimsies in the hall. No wait, I'll do it myself.' He got to his feet. 'Sorry about this, Arlene. But I do still have other interests…'

One of the waiters approached him. 'Excuse me, sir. Activated mobile telephones are not permitted in the club house.' Deller began to expostulate then stopped and left the room.

Arlene looked put out. She turned to Stevens, who she'd placed on her right. 'Vic Deller's behaved inexcusably', she said. 'I'm too upset to say the few words I'd planned. Be a good Eagle Scout and make my speech for me, Bernie. Time it for after dessert.' She passed him a sheaf of cue cards.

'…Leave adjustments to your StrepMag contract to me', Bramcusi was saying to Jeff. 'Probably get you a sabbatical. Should be a six-figure deal minimum, less 10 percent to us and around twenty to StrepMag. I'd like to say mid-six-figure, meaning five hundred thou and up, but I don't hype hope. Movie rights etcetera would be on top. Them we take twenty per. That OK with you?'

'You bet.' Jeff said it without thinking. Only later did he work out how small a slice he'd be left with. Best be a big cake, then.

Deller returned. He sat down and drank off his glass of pre-dinner Bollinger Grande Année 1990, hitherto untouched, then followed it with the glass of the 2000 René Muré Vorbourg Grand Cru Gewurztraminer they had been poured to sluice the mousse with, then the glass of Clos Rougeard Saumur-Champigny Le Bourg 2003 paired with the main course. He called to the waiter. 'Refill my glasses, please.'

'Which one, sir?'

'All three.'

…Jeff interrupted Bramcusi in mid-flow. 'There's something I got to check out.' He rose from his chair and said to Bramcusi in a whisper as he passed behind him, 'The story's not a wrap yet.'

Deller's behaviour had not been greatly noticed. Laura, who sat on his right, knew him too well. Chrissie, on his left, knew him not at all. Charlotte Elver's job entailed ignoring things quite as often as noticing them.

Jeff went down to the hall. News agency 'flimsies', as Deller termed them, were print-outs the wire service machines spewed all day. Jeff zipped through a dozen sheets, then another dozen. North Korea rattling its nuclear sabre… Trouble in Beit Hanoun, on Israel's western flank… Ah, here was something. Pres. Washington's disclaimer of any intention to meddle in the upcoming British election had issued too late to head off a mob invading Regent's Park then investing Winfield House, potentially the biggest anti-American demonstration since Vietnam. But why should Deller want to read about that?

Tod's memory stick had never covered the Dellers' prostitution racket in detail. So when Jeff came across a mention of the Bristol police raiding a kebab takeaway in the St Paul's district and arresting two men on suspicion of people trafficking, he thought little of it. Then, just as he was about to start in on the sheaf of earlier news stories below, one vaguely familiar name caught his attention. Clive Lane. Lane, 46, was being questioned by the Mercia Police in connexion with suspected arson affecting agri-industrial premises belonging to Meadow-Sourced Meta [*sic*] Products just outside Hereford.

Jeff couldn't recall whether Meadow-Sourced Meat Products had figured in Tod's notes. And was Lane the other name of the Clive guy mentioned in them? But this had to be the cause of Deller's perturbation. He turned, about to walk across the atrium then up the stairs and back into the Prince Regent Suite. Godwin came strolling in his direction, in close conversation with another man.

'Hello, Jeff', said Godwin, looking up. 'Have you met Sir Michael Farrer?'

Jeff shook hands. 'Pleased to know you...' he began. But there was a shout from the other side of the atrium. Godwin looked across it then up above him, yelled 'Christ!' and backed away precipitately. Farrer let go of Jeff's hand, so that Jeff fell back too. Farrer, slow to react otherwise, got hit by a falling body, Deller's, legs and arms flailing. Farrer was knocked to the ground, his head cracking smartly against the marble. He lay stone still.

Deller groaned and twitched his body but didn't get up. The Pantheon head porter came foreward.

'Please, ladies and gentlemen, stand back. No sir,' – an officious young man had stooped and was trying to make Deller comfortable; no one dared look very closely at Farrer – 'he must on no account be moved... Risk of internal injuries made worse. You there, Peter...' to a younger under-porter, 'fetch blankets.'

Jeff happened to notice Deller's mobile, which had jumped from the breast pocket of his suit and leapt clear when Deller hit the ground. A matt black object, it had slid across the splendidly patterned marble floor, coming to rest on a dark patch where it blended in, like camouflage. Jeff strolled over and scooped it up. He darted into the gentlemen's cloakroom, just off the atrium down a couple of steps. He locked himself in a cubicle and scrolled down the call register till he found the last number to dial Deller. He pressed Call. It got answered almost immediately.

'Victor? You saw the news item? Listen, it's not the end. My man has got AD lined up for this evening. Victor? Are you there?' When no one answered, the voice signed off, aborting the call.

Jeff reflected. He could keep calling the number. But that wouldn't tell him whose it was, even supposing the other party answered. He didn't know the voice. Who was AD? Supposing he scrolled down all Deller's stored numbers? To his surprise there were none. In frustration he went through the entire menu. Presently he came to photos. There was one only. A man with a black eye. Jeff looked closer. He knew the man. No, not knew, but he had seen him. Where? When?

Recently. Very recently. Today. Then he had it. The *Evening Era* gossip column, two hours ago. He sped back to the Strangers' Room. Its sole copy of the *Evening Era* lay on a table in front of an elderly gentleman. The oldest member? Jeff coughed. Nothing. Jeff didn't know if he could grab the paper or whether its position meant it was reserved. He tapped the man on the knee. 'Excuse me, sir. Can I glance at your *Evening Era*? It's real urgent. Guy riding hell for leather at Kensington Park…'

'Racing results, eh?' The elderly gentleman beamed, hearing Kempton Park. 'Help yourself.'

Jeff grabbed the paper. He leafed through it till he hit gossip. The picture of Ben Lee was none too good a likeness. It didn't have to be. The hair gave things away, streaming from one side of his head as he pedalled away. Jeff flung down the paper and turned to go.

'You, sir.' The elderly gentleman called after him. Jeff stopped dead. 'Your fancy win?'

'By a mane.'

SIXTYTHREE

It took several minutes for news of Deller's plunge from the Pantheon's balcony to reach Arlene's guests. The head porter broke the story, crossing the dining chamber carpet with heavy, majestic tread and whispering in Laura Deller's ear. She stood up, threw down her napkin and rushed from the Rooms. Arlene stared after her. Charlotte Elver got up, asked Arlene for permission to depart and followed Laura without waiting for a reply.

The head porter took up a position in the centre of the carpet and gave those who remained a short account of what had happened. He played down the sensational aspect, making the incident sound no worse than the mis-alignment of a fish knife on a doily. He urged his listeners to stay calm, apologised for intruding and exited.

Arlene looked silently straight in front of her, like a ship's figurehead, though less serene. Stevens patted her hand. It was as far as he dared go. You didn't bear hug Arlene, or high-five the Pope. 'It's a done deal', he said, meaning StrepMag's acquisitions.

'I know', she said, shaking her head. 'I know. It's also a great deal. Only I was never before so dis-respected at my own dining table. Maybe when Clyde passed on I should have sold out after all.'

'Arlene, the President reads us. Albany reads us. Soon Bucking-ham Palace will read us and the chief minister on Downing Street that His Royal Highness in Bucking-ham Palace put there to run England will read us. All because of you.'

Arlene sniffed. Nasal drip now, not disdain. She grimaced. Then smiled. 'You're right. I guess an upside that hi-profile makes the pain hurt less.'

Jeff came out into the main atrium.

'There he is', said Peter the under-porter, pointing at Jeff. 'The gentleman standing with the other gentleman when the incident took place.'

The head porter came forward. 'Are you hurt, sir?'

'I guess not. I don't feel hurt.'

'That could be shock. May I suggest you sit down, sir?'

Jeff sat.

'Are you ready to make a statement, sir?'

A man Jeff had never seen before came over and held out his hand. 'Russell. Club Secretary.'

Jeff didn't want to shake hands. His own were already shaking.

'Hi, Russ', he said, hiding them.

The man cleared his throat in a very British way. '*Bernard* Russell', he said. 'How do you feel?'

Jeff turned frank. 'Tell the truth, kinda weird. Is Deller dead?'

'Not that we can tell.'

'The other guy? The guy he hit?'

The head porter and Russell looked at each other. The head porter nodded at Russell.

'Sir Michael Farrer is gravely ill', said Russell. '…If you could just tell us what happened…'

Jeff told them.

'…Deller had been drinking up there in the Prince's Rooms', he finished. 'Maybe affected his balance. So what's his crashing twenty feet mean? Slipped? Jumped? Pushed? Accident, suicide bid, attempted murder victim?'

'Speculation at this point would be inappropriate', said Russell.

Laura came up to their group, pushed Russell and the head porter aside. 'You're useless', she shouted at Jeff. 'You couldn't even break his fall. Just stood there and let someone else cushion it.' She thrust a finger in Jeff's direction, its nail a vivid mulberry. She glared at the two other men. 'If my Vic's lamed for life, you're witnesses that I hold this man personally responsible.' Then she walked away. Her neat rump swayed more provocatively than usual.

*

An hour later and Jeff was ready to go home. News of Mary Matheson's resignation following her no confidence motion defeat had flashed round the world within that last hour. It drowned out the incident at the Pantheon everywhere but at the Pantheon.

Jeff had said what he had to, first to Russell then the paramedics then some cops and finally Arlene and Stevens. Chrissie had no hang-ups about taking his arm this time.

'I meant to ask', he said on their way out to the street, 'how'd you manage to see off Laura Deller so quick? That eyeball-to-eyeball showdown before we ate?' His hands had stopped shaking.

'She hired Mel a couple of times to spice up married life with her old man. Mel told me all about it. A hint that I knew made Dragon Lady back off. She doesn't scare me.'

'You're in a small minority.'

'Nasty thing. She stands to get about five years for procuring. It's seldom more, worse luck.'

'They have to find her guilty first. The Dellers can buy a heap of law know-how meantime.'

'Can they? Apparently he's in a coma. Mel told me they kept sniping at each other about their finances in between gropes at her bits.'

'Sniping?' The word had caught Jeff's attention. 'What kind of sniping?'

'Oh, his newspaper loses money. She spends it. They owe everywhere. Servants unpaid. Tradesmen ditto. The usual.'

'I thought she was loaded.'

'Maybe her money was tied up with Greenbach, Angel, Lettiss. Maybe InterContConGlom. Maybe other credit crunch victims. Or she could have invested with that Ponzi scheme scammer, Forrest Forbes-Knox.'

'What about her vice ring? Can't she cash in on that?'

'Come on.' Chrissie looked at him with fond disrespect. 'The escie sector's small-cap. OK, you do well as a sole trader, though money laundering regulations make it a nightmare to bank takings. It's never going to be a Footsie 100 stock. Least of all with the competition I was protesting against the day we first met.' She switched from finance to justice. 'What if Mel testifies?'

'What can she say?', said Jeff. 'The Dellers hired her personally? It's the link between Angelo Devene and Deller needs proving. I'm not sure even Tod's dossier did that. What are Tod's notes worth in a court of law anyhow?'

Godwin joined them. 'Farrer's dead', he said.

'Jesus', said Jeff.

'Christ', said Chrissie, then: 'Who was he?'

'My bread and butter for the next six months', said Godwin. 'I'd just got him to start talking about some scheme of the Government's to ratchet the Seleukistan war up a notch. Deller stopped that by falling on him. A one-man D-Notice.'

'D-Notice?', said Jeff.

'Gagging order. On sensitive matters. Renamed DA-Notice of late. Much used to save Establishment face over security cock-ups.'

'Did Deller fall or did he jump?'

'Clambered over the balcony and let himself drop from what I could see. Broke Farrer's neck instantly. I'd been grooming the man for ages, blast it.'

'You don't think Deller knew the Farrer guy might do a Deep Throat with you and figured jumping on him was the only way to stop awkward stuff getting out?'

'He couldn't have known. Besides, why would he care? I saw his wife pitching into you across the hall. What did she say?'

'Accused me of negligence over her husband's injuries. I guess she loves him after all.'

Godwin nodded. It would have been easy for him to say 'I told you so', thought Jeff. He felt grateful for the man's tact.

Chrissie squeezed Jeff's arm. 'You come on home', she said. 'A nice hot cocoa's what you need.'

'Mind if I walk you to your taxi?' said Godwin.

Chrissie turned to Godwin. 'OK, but he is pretty whacked', she said of Jeff. 'I should get him to bed. By the way, I've decided to retire.' She cocked her head to one side. It was a gesture she did well. She addressed both men: 'Well, swap callings, really. I've always fancied nursing. One of my sexiest get-ups is my black stockings, stripey tunic and white cap with red cross on it. Jeff'll make the perfect patient.'

Godwin smiled. 'This won't take long. Calhoun? You still up for that story about you know what?'

Jeff struggled to remember it. 'The snooping thing?' he said.

'That's the one. Word is Mecklenburger's about to be *PNG*-ed. Expelled the country.'

'It's what they do to diplomats are spies', said Jeff to Chrissie. 'Which hence is sort of what Mecklenburger has to be. Am I right, Ed?'

'Yes. They can't have done it with a Yank before, though. Apparently Mecklenburger tampered with Mary Matheson's sun hat out at Chequers. Fitted a minuscule variant of the Minox LX to the brim, read what she and her closest cronies told each other in their Scrabble games.'

'How d'you hear about all this?'

Godwin didn't answer. That instant, Jeff knew he had Secret Intelligence Service connections. Godwin had feared press exposure too much. Even his aliases were more confusing than if they'd been more dissimilar.

Jeff said to Godwin, 'The night I met Laura, Ben Lee came across the room and spoke with you some. Your Chequers source, I deduce.'

'No comment.'

'What'd he say?'

'He asked who you were. He'd been Laura's number one boy friend till you turned up. He reckoned you were next on her list. The way she started looking at you.'

'Hey', said Chrissie. 'Show some respect for this 'ere current squeeze and junk the palaeo-history lesson.' She turned to Jeff. 'I'd already guessed about you and Dragon Lady. The way she breathed fire...'

Godwin said to Jeff. 'It was Lee told me about Mecklenburger. Don't quote me. I assume Mecklenburger or some other agent was spying on Lynton long before Mary Matheson took over. You'll recall Lynton left office under a cloud. How'd that cloud swell to such dangerous proportions? I'll tell you. Drip feed to people like me, by people like Mecklenburger or their arm's-length media-suppliers, of stuff damaging to Lynton.'

They were on the pavement by now. Jeff stood on the outer edge. He was about to step into the road when Chrissie pulled him back to kiss him. Godwin did step out. A squat fast red car hit him low, flipped him over, slowed then accelerated. Its horn blared First Call. The driver slowed again and did a V-sign from the driver's window.

'Hit-and-run hog!' screamed Chrissie, jumping in the air with rage.

'Hit man, not hit-and-run', said Jeff. 'He slowed. Why? Check he'd got the right guy, that's why. He didn't. Get the right guy. He wanted me. How's Ed?'

From the gutter: 'I'll live.'

They looked towards the red car. It had stopped fifty yards away. A head craned out the passenger's side and snarled at them. Angelo, leaning across from the driving seat. Then he accelerated. Very fast. A rubbish lorry turned out of Carlton House Square, the sort with a big mechanical crusher up back. The main street's one way there. Angelo hadn't expected any oncoming traffic. Fair enough. But he'd overlooked the possibility of a lateral obstacle. The red Cay ran

257

straight into the side of the rubbish lorry. Its top got sliced off. The chassis slid under the lorry, caught fire and exploded, Angelo with it. A man in a hi-vis vest jumped from the rubbish lorry cab and ran off.

Godwin sat up in the gutter. Jeff moved out behind him and held his right arm up, fascist style, to warn off oncoming traffic. Chrissie leant over Godwin, who blinked his eyes. 'Sister April? Is that you?'

Chrissie tittered. 'How are you, Edwin?'

'Bloody. But only a bit bowed.' He had a nasty black-red gash on his chin. His trousers were ripped. More blood flowed from his left leg. 'The bin man driving the lorry pulled into the car's path deliberately', he said.

'Who?'

'Chap killed the driver of the red car. He ran off. That denotes deliberate.'

'Did you see the car driver's face?' said Jeff. 'Andy, my apartment block handyman.'

The blaze died down. A fire engine came jangling up the street from the direction of Trafalgar Square. Another appeared, down towards St James's Palace. They cordoned off that part of the street.

'How are you, Ed?' said Jeff. 'Think you can make it back to the sidewalk?'

'I'm going back in that club to have a gigantic drink', said Godwin, half rising, then sinking back.

Gavin Doresett came out onto the Pantheon's steps, talking to Stevens. He saw Godwin. 'Edgar Godwin! Well I'll be damned. Is that really you?'

'It is. Help me up, will you?'

Doresett helped Godwin up. Stevens had walked away, waving goodbye. He wanted to try and dispel jet lag with early bed, he'd called out. He looked exhausted.

'Are you OK, Edgar?', said Doresett. 'I must say, you seem in good shape despite all the years since we last met. The blood apart.'

'Get the porter to fit me up with some spare trousers, will you? They keep extra ties for guests who turn up open-collared. They must have kecks too, in case a member gets debagged.'

Doresett looked worried. 'Are you sure you're all right? Head not hurt? Let's see… Who's the Prime Minister?'

'Sir Samuel Knighton. Frightful shit. Ousted Mary Matheson earlier this evening. Caretaker appointment, thank God. You wanted me to say Winston Churchill, didn't you?'

Doresett laughed. 'No. But I'd have accepted Mary Matheson.' He glanced across the street. A man with a blue hard hat pulled low over his face was walking on the opposite pavement in the direction of the Haymarket. It must have blocked his view because he collided with a parking meter and the hard hat fell off. It was the rubbish lorry driver.

Doresett stopped laughing. 'Hello', he said. 'I know that man.'

Jeff came forward. 'It's the guy jumped from the garbage truck. Who is he?'

'I'm trying to think. He used to slip us stuff on the *Date* diary. Ben Lee found him useful. He's some kind of policeman. I met him a few times, standing in for Ben. It didn't do for the editor to meet sensitive sources direct.... Name? Um, one of the occupational sort. Butcher, Baker, Cook...'

'Candlestick-maker?' said Chrissie. She'd kept close to Jeff and again slipped her arm through his.

'Chuck it with the nursery rhymes, April', said Godwin. He'd scrambled to his feet. His face had stopped bleeding. His shin still oozed.

'No, no', said Doresett. 'She's on the right track. A trade that's obsolete.'

'Franklin? Reeve? Pardoner?' said Godwin.

'Aren't those all characters in the *The Canterbury Tales*?', said Doresett, thinking out loud. 'My God. Miller! That's it. Julian? Jude? Jules Miller. Thank you, Edgar.'

SIXTYFOUR

Guin's lunch clientele – now mostly electronic publishers – has held up. It's emptier nights, though. The maître d's job is maintaining the exclusive façade while doubling surreptitiously as a business-getter. It was a good place for Jeff to take Chrissie their first full evening after arriving from London. Select, yet tranquil. Chrissie'd been to New York before, but on business. Hotel visits. A private orgy or two. An all-night outcall to a threesome at an arbitrageur's faux manor in the Hamptons. Once a gala reception, where her MBA'd helped her impersonate a glass ceiling-busting finance superwoman, even if her looks and an indefinable allure had suggested more a broker's 'buy' call in go-go stocks.

*

Jeff and Chrissie were still on their pre-dinner margaritas. Presently Chrissie rose to go and freshen up her face. Jeff loved the way she walked. He followed her with his eyes as she turned a corner and disappeared.

The barman placed a saucer before him. It held a twenty and a ten. 'Your change, sir.'

'Change? I didn't settle the bar tab yet.'

'It's not a bar tab, sir. Gentleman over there says to tell you it's redemption on a loan.' The barman pointed toward a dark corner. A young man in a tuxedo lifted his champagne glass in a quiet salute. He was sitting with three much older banker types. The last of the pre-recession clientele. They looked sleek, prosperous. Him too. He wore a weskit in yellow tartan under his tux coat. Jeff didn't know him.

'Is this some mistake?', he asked the barman.

'The gentleman said you might think so. He says it's the twenty you gave him the night he asked for spare change. Plus interest at five percent over LIBOR.'

'LIBOR?'

'London Inter-Bank Offer Rate. He said to say he's British. How he's fallen on his feet. And he apologises for his great-uncle snubbing you over Howard Castle. I didn't get that. But he made me repeat it till I'm word-perfect.'

Jeff looked again. The gentleman in question stuffed his fists in his eyes as if about to cry, ground them in his eye sockets the way a kid does, then took them away and grinned. It was the failed mugger, now a success at parting people from their money on a large scale.

'Well I'll be...' said Jeff. Lord Crowthorne's great-nephew.

Where'd Chrissie gotten to? Jeff turned to look. The maître d' brought a couple of menus. Jeff took his and turned it over. Its blank side. He'd start his book while waiting. 'Guinevere's name tells you the era it opened. Camelot.'

THE END